RAVE REVIEWS FOR *USA TODAY* BESTSELLING AUTHOR JOY NASH!

IMMORTALS: THE CROSSING

"I read this book in one sitting because it is just too good to put down. Don't miss out on one of the best paranormal romances of the year!"

—Romance Junkies

"Nash's latest hero is a charming rogue with a compassionate heart, while her heroine is a desperate mother willing to sacrifice everything to save her son . . . Mac Lir is a hero to die for."

—*RT Book Reviews*

IMMORTALS: THE AWAKENING

"Nash takes readers on a fast journey, keeping the action going from beginning to end. Cutting-edge drama, creative characters and a plot that moves like fire all create a great read. The Immortals series just keeps getting better and it may be hard to top this fantastic addition."

—Paranormal Romance Writers

"This book is fantasy romance done right and done well."

—All About Romance

DEEP MAGIC

"*Deep Magic* is filled with the imagery and magic of Druids during the Roman Era . . . Strong, lyrical writing with well-drawn settings and characters bring the story alive. Suspense and twists [illegible] nse ending makes this [illegible] enchanting tale."

[illegible]iews Today

"Nash follows *The Grail King* with a love story that completely envelops the reader in a magical world. Skilled at merging reality with Druid legend, she illuminates a dark age with fiery passions, political complexities, and an enchanting story."

—*RT Book Reviews*

THE GRAIL KING

"Not since Mary Stewart's Merlin trilogy has the magic of Avalon flowed as lyrically off the pages. Nash captures the myths of the Druids in a fresh, exciting approach delivering a tale that grabs hold of your heart and reaches deep into your soul bringing forth joy . . ."

—*RT Book Reviews*, Top Pick, 4 1/2 stars

"*The Grail King* turned out to be a rare jewel of a book, which grabbed my attention from the beginning and kept me enthralled until the very end . . . Wonderful, complex characters, an exciting, adventurous plot, and a great romance . . . Do yourself a favor and read *The Grail King*."

—Once Upon a Romance Review

CELTIC FIRE

"Joy Nash has created a lush world for senses of all kinds . . . This is a wonderfully fast-paced read full of romance, love and fantasy that will continue to burn in the hearts of readers after the last page is turned."

—Fresh Fiction

"Joy Nash is definitely one to be watched. She has great world-building skills, and her own personal magic with the pen is guaranteed to make hers a very strong name on the market in the not too distant future."

—Love Romances

A DARK BOND

His eyes were light, she thought. Blue, maybe? It was too dark to tell for sure. Starlight dusted his profile. His cheekbones slanted sharply, and his bold nose and strong jaw matched in angularity. It was a supremely masculine face, unexpectedly softened by lush eyelashes and the supple fullness of his lips. A dark, restless energy clung to him.

"I think I'd better go," Maddie said.

"No." His tone was one of quiet command. Inescapable. "No, I think not. Not quite yet."

Then he was standing close. His hands, warm and large, cupped the back of her skull. His mouth was barely an inch from hers. He inhaled her startled breath and gave her a slow, wicked smile. Then he took her lips in an aching kiss.

Other books by Joy Nash:

SILVER SILENCE
A LITTLE LIGHT MAGIC
IMMORTALS: THE RECKONING (Anthology)
IMMORTALS: THE CROSSING
IMMORTALS: THE AWAKENING
DEEP MAGIC
THE GRAIL KING
CELTIC FIRE

The Unforgiven

Joy Nash

Dorchester Publishing

DORCHESTER PUBLISHING

Published by

Dorchester Publishing Co., Inc.
200 Madison Avenue
New York, NY 10016

Trade ISBN: 978-1-4285-1122-4
E-book ISBN: 978-1-4285-1189-7

First Dorchester Publishing, Co., Inc. edition: August 2011

Printed in the United States of America.

Dedication

To my biggest fans and cheerleaders:

To J—for all the groceries bought, dinners cooked, and chauffeur-dad miles driven

To J2—for your beauty, brains, and creativity, and for your intellectual curiosity about absolutely everything (well, except sports)

To K—for all the discussions on moral philosophy and religion, for your cheerful good nature, and for being at all times a peacemaker

To C—for your awesome scientific mind and your love of story, and for the book of your own that will be on the shelf someday, if only you can resist the time-sucking dark side of video gaming

To M—for the Metallica

And lastly, to the unknown woman who stopped by one of my book signings a few years ago. We chatted about Druidry and other esotery, and on your way out of the bookstore, you handed me a book about the Nephilim, saying, "I think you'll like this." You were right. Thank you!

When men began to multiply on the earth and daughters were born to them, the sons of Heaven saw how beautiful the daughters of Man were, and so they took for their wives as many of them as they chose . . . At that time the Nephilim appeared on earth.

—*Genesis 6:1-2,4*

What I've felt, what I've known
Turn the pages, turn to stone
Behind the door,
Should I open it for you?

What I've felt, what I've known
Sick and tired, I stand alone
Could you be there,
'Cause I'm the one who waits for you?

Or are you unforgiven, too?

—*Metallica, "The Unforgiven II"*

Chapter One

London, East End, Present Day

The last thing Artur Camulus wanted to see in his flat was a goddamned candy-ass archangel. But there it was, lounging on the sofa, white wing-tip loafers propped on the coffee table. Watching the telly. Drinking whiskey.

Artur's telly. Artur's whiskey.

A miniature ax man began chopping away at the inside of Artur's skull, right between the eyes.

"Bloody hell. Isn't anything sacred anymore? Get out, you sodding celestial prat."

Gabriel's hair was, as always, perfect. His pale eyes consumed the screen. A spotty adolescent boy took the stage of *Britain's Got Talent*, and Artur's blood began a slow boil.

"Blast it all to Oblivion."

The angel patted the air. "Pipe down, will you? I want to see this. There's no Simon Cowell where I come from."

"No wonder they call it Heaven."

"Shush!"

Artur killed the switch. Cowell's big white teeth disappeared.

"Hey! I was watching that!"

"Right. And now you're not. You've got a lot of nerve, Gabe, coming here."

Ivory wings unfurled as the archangel drew to his full height. "Temper, temper. Come now, Artur. I know those two lovely . . . ahem . . . *ladies* . . . currently relaxing in your bed have taxed your endurance, but didn't your mother tell you? We must mind our manners, even under duress."

"I'll give you duress, you nancy poof. Get out, before I rip your wings off."

"Is that demon humor? Rather unamusing, I must say. But then, I suppose one can't expect comedy from a Nephilim."

Artur stiffened. He knew what he was; he didn't need a bloody git of an angel rubbing his face in it. As if he'd asked to be born. He hadn't. But he could hardly escape the truth of what he was: five thousand years ago, his ancestor Samyaza, a fallen angel, had copulated with a human woman. That forbidden union, and others like it, had produced a race of unnatural, soulless creatures. Gabriel and his archangel brothers had named Artur's kind Nephilim. But Artur would see himself in Oblivion before he answered to any such slur. He called himself by the name given to his celestial ancestors before their fall: Watcher.

For half a pence, he'd kick Gabriel's pearly white arse into the street. Unfortunately, he couldn't. Heaven's messenger enjoyed unique immunity in the human world. Artur's magic, powerful as it was, wasn't worth shit against him.

And didn't the dickless bastard know it.

"Really," Gabe huffed, picking lint off his sleeve, "it would serve you right if I did leave."

"Serve me right, then. Please."

Gabriel frowned and tugged at his vest. The garment was white, like everything else about him. Suit, shirt, tie, socks, shoes. Hell, even his skin and hair were sickly shades of parchment.

Artur took a deep breath and pinched the bridge of his nose. "Enough bullshit, Gabe. Why are you here?"

"I've come from Glastonbury."

Glastonbury? Glastonbury was Clan Samyaza's territory, home to five of the clan's Druid adepts. On occasion, it was even home to Artur himself. Needless to say, archangels were not frequent visitors.

"Why?" he asked.

"I was summoned, of course. By one of yours."

Artur snorted. "Unlikely."

"But true. And not surprising, really, given last night's dustup. Such a tragedy."

A twinge of real unease pinched Artur's throat. "Dustup? What dustup?"

Gabriel examined his fingernails. "You really have no idea, do you? But of course not. The great Artur Camulus, guardian and chieftain of Clan Samyaza, has, of late, put himself completely beyond reach of his responsibilities. Inaccessible by phone, text, or e-mail."

Likely true, Artur thought. He'd been drunk as a boiled owl these past three days. His cell was certainly dead. He couldn't remember the last time he'd checked e-mail.

"Modern technology." Gabriel sighed. "*So* overrated. I much prefer celestial messaging, don't you? Old-fashioned, perhaps, but foolproof. Of course," he added with a self-deprecating chuckle, "I am biased."

"Brax would never summon you." Artur's half brother would never stoop so low. "None of my people would." At least, Artur was certain neither Morgana nor Niall would. As for the others . . .

Cade Leucetius, the most recent addition to Clan Samyaza, was something of a loose cannon, but as much as Artur loathed the rough Welshman, he couldn't imagine him summoning an angel. Leucetius's instinctive Watcher distrust of blessed creatures rivaled Artur's own.

But then there was Cybele. One never knew what Cybele might do.

"I don't know why your people mistrust me," Gabriel complained. "So unfair! What have I ever done to Clan

Samyaza? It's a case of shoot-the-messenger syndrome, I tell you. And how many times have I had to deal with *that* petty human prejudice over the last few millennia?" He shook his pale head. "Thank heaven Cybele is—"

"Do not," Artur hissed, "utter that name in my presence."

Gabriel's pale eyes lit. "Ah! A sore spot! Still angry, I suppose, that she threw you over for Cade."

Red rage exploded. With a snarl, Artur lunged. A heartbeat, a white blur of movement, and . . . *pain*, splitting the back of his skull. He opened his eyes to find himself laid out on the floor, blinking up at one very smug angel.

"You know, you really should do something about all that excess testosterone." Gabriel dusted his palms. "Again and again, it leads to unpleasantness."

Artur lurched to his feet and stalked into the kitchen. A whiskey bottle, nearly empty, stood on the counter. "Blast it," he muttered. "That was new."

"And excellent, I don't mind telling you."

He gulped down the dregs and tossed the empty. The alcohol burned an angry path down his throat. "Why even bother? You can't get drunk."

"Ah, but I can irritate you."

Artur grunted.

Gabe huffed. "You know, most people rejoice when angels visit."

"I'm not most people. As you so kindly pointed out, I'm Nephilim. Half angel, half human. A product of sin and depravity. A cursed atrocity. An archdemon. Dung under your immaculate slippers."

The angel sniffed. "Your unfortunate ancestry is no excuse for incivility."

Artur shut his eyes. "All right. I give up. Just tell me: how in the name of Oblivion do I get rid of you?"

"Hmmm. Let me think." A long finger tapped bloodless lips.

"Ah, yes! I've got it. Shut your gob and receive my message. That should do the trick."

"Fine. Talk. Then leave."

"Now that's more like it!" Adjusting his vest, Gabe raised one hand. "Hail, Artur, full of—" He broke off with a chuckle. "Well. Perhaps it's best I don't go *there*, eh?"

"Just get on with it."

"As you wish. Hail, Artur Camulus. I come to you with a message from Cybele Andraste."

Artur gritted his teeth.

"Demon annihilators have hit Clan Samyaza. Twelve dead, four wounded. Come quickly."

"*Bloody fucking hell!*"

Gabriel exhaled. "That's all."

Artur was already out the door.

Chapter Two

London, England

Father Jonas Walker was too beautiful to be a man of God. Graced with the musculature of an athlete and the face of a movie star, the priest shone like an angel. His handsome face all but leaped off the computer screen. His lips moved with perfect grace:

"Demon Annihilators Mutual Network is an international nonprofit organization dedicated to the eradication of demonkind. I'm Reverend Jonas Walker, international director of DAMN, and this is a public service announcement. Have you, or anyone you know, experienced demonic activity? Been the victim of hellfiend influence? Suffered an attack by a possessed human?

Walker leaned closer.

"Or have you perhaps encountered the greatest evil—the hybrid atrocity known as a Nephilim? Half human, half spawn of Hell, Nephilim possess all the cunning and skill of human and demon alike. Begotten in sin, steeped in evil, these archdemon overlords live to prey on the weakness of mankind."

The priest straightened.

"My brothers, my sisters, if you encounter any damned being, be it common hellfiend or Nephilim archdemon, know that prompt reporting saves lives—and, more importantly—souls. Call or text your sighting to DAMN's New York City headquarters at 01-212-555-7734. That's 01-212-555-7734. Do not falter. Do not delay. Your life—and your salvation*—depend on YOU."*

Walker lifted a fist, revealing the letters D-A-M-N in red ink on the backs of his fingers.

"Death to the Nephilim! Hellfire to hellfiends! Annihilation to demonkind! Thank you, and God bless."

The computer video feed froze on the red flames of the DAMN logo. For several long seconds, silence dripped like blood.

Cade Leucetius jumped to his feet, sending his chair clattering to the floor. He paced the room, his fury a living, writhing presence inside his chest. "I say death to them. The whole lot. Every last sodding DAMNer. Beginning"—he pointed at the screen—"with that one."

Brax Cocidus shook his head. The bandage on his right temple, stark white beneath his nut brown hair, was stained where the blood had seeped through. "Walker didn't conceive the attack on the Glastonbury compound. The man's being used, Cade, by—"

"To Oblivion with that. I—"

"Cease."

Artur Camulus raised a hand. The room fell silent. Garbed in unrelieved black, Clan Samyaza's chieftain cut an impressive figure. The absence of color accentuated the paleness of his skin. His long black hair, tinged with gray at the temples, was gathered in a severe ponytail, exposing the harsh angles of his face. His eyes, set deep under black brows, resembled nothing so much as glittering chips of black ice.

Artur, guardian and protector. Well, as far as Cade was concerned, the man had done precious little guarding or protecting in the past year. He itched to smash the bastard's face.

Of course, he didn't dare.

Artur held a roll of parchment. Ornate script the color of

dirty rust flowed over the gilded paper. The ink carried the metallic scent of blood.

"At dawn today, this scroll appeared at my door. Clan Azazel claims full responsibility for the attack on our people. The missive states that Vaclav Dusek himself created the weapons Jonas Walker's DAMNers used to murder our kin."

"But . . . Dusek is a Watcher. A Nephilim." Cybele Andraste, standing by the window, held herself stiffly, nursing a cracked rib. She looked up from the glass. "Walker is a menace, but the man doesn't strike me as a hypocrite."

Brax brought up a photo on his laptop screen, an image of Vaclav Dusek shaking hands with none other than Father Jonas Walker. "This photo was taken yesterday. In front of DAMN's international headquarters in New York City. Dusek has accepted an appointment as DAMN's European director."

"So we have no reason to doubt the truth of Dusek's claim," Artur said. "That the weapons used in the Glastonbury attack, primed with Watcher magic, were supplied by Dusek."

"Clan Samyaza magic," Cade muttered. "Not Clan Azazel magic."

"Indeed," said Artur. "The wardings against Clan Azazel magic were in place. We never thought to ward against our own power."

A mistake that had cost them dearly. A mistake that Cade would rather have gone to Oblivion than make. And yet here he was, alive. While so many others—his own infant son included—were not.

Gareth, the only Watcher dormant to have survived the massacre, sported a raw gash on his left cheek and a burned leg. His already fair skin was even paler than usual, his freckles and ginger hair providing an almost garish contrast. He spoke now, for the first time, gritting his teeth against the pain. "A Watcher—a *Nephilim*—leading a demon-annihilation organization? That's insane. It's only a matter of time before someone at DAMN figures out what Dusek is."

Cybele glanced at him. "Maybe someone already knows."

"Maybe," Brax allowed. "But it's a good bet it's not Walker himself. Cybele is right. The man is a sincerely pious Roman Catholic priest. He'd slit his own throat before he knowingly made a deal with a Nephilim."

"Well, someone at DAMN isn't too holy to deal with the damned," muttered Cade.

"Consider," Artur said, "that for millennia Azazel's descendants have sought to destroy our kin. Now, with Samyaza magic in his arsenal and an army of zealot demon annihilators to wield it, Dusek is closer to the goal than his ancestors have ever been." He released the parchment. The paper fluttered to the floor to lie like a deadly snake in their midst. No one moved to take it.

"So you understand," Artur continued, "Jonas Walker is only a distraction."

Cybele, lips compressed, returned her gaze to the oily shine of London rain on the window glass. Her curling blonde hair, usually her most striking feature, hung in a limp rope down her back. A slight stiffening of her spine and the black pepper scent of grief told Cade how close she was to breaking down. As he was. But his anguish took a more active form: anger.

He rounded on Artur. "Distraction?" He slapped his fist into his open palm. The motion caused the gash on his left shoulder to burn. Magical wounds didn't heal as cleanly as those inflicted by human weapons. Especially when one's own clan magic caused the injury.

"A dozen dead bodies," he spat. "Two adepts, three human concubines, seven dormant children. I hope you're not suggesting, Artur, that we allow their murderers to live."

The first bomb had detonated in the children's wing, before

the clan adepts even realized the wards had failed. Six DAMN annihilators, heavily armed, had breached the compound's protections. The clan had sprung into immediate action; not one DAMNner had made it out alive. The police had shown up shortly after the battle ended, summoned by a suspicious neighbor. Cybele, despite her injury, had woven a glamour of normalcy, and the officers had quickly departed, leaving the survivors to dispose of the bodies of both kin and enemy.

The stink of burned flesh lingered in Cade's nostrils even now, days later. Clan Samyaza's future, in ashes. Cade's own son, dead. The infant's human mother had abandoned the boy on Cade's doorsteps just days before.

Cade had not been pleased to see the infant; he had not yet even given the baby a name. He barely remembered its mother; he'd slept with her only to dull the pain of Cybele's rejection. But Watcher children were few, and every one represented the survival of the race. There had been no question that the baby would be raised in the clan. But now the promise of the child's life was lost to Oblivion. Cade would never forgive himself for that. Never.

Brax had lost two sons and both their human mothers. Artur had lost a son, a child of ten, also born of a human mother. Three other boys, Niall's sons, had died. Morgana had been the mother of one of Niall's lads. She and Niall's human concubine had died trying to save their children.

The strain of loss clearly showed in Brax's eyes, but Artur's countenance showed no trace of grief. Cade could not even catch a scent of emotion, however faint. He wondered if the bastard ever felt anything.

Artur's Druid powers were, of course, vast. His right to Clan Samyaza's chieftaincy was unchallenged. If Artur had been present the night of the DAMN attack, he very well might have succeeded in saving what Cade and the others had lost. Instead, Artur had arrived at dawn, as the blood from the slaughter dried on the walls. And only then because Cybele had sent the archangel Gabriel to fetch him. As far as Cade was concerned, Artur should have stayed in bleeding London.

"Twelve lives under your protection," Cade hissed through gritted teeth. "Your own sons, your nephews, murdered in their beds. Swatted like flies. While the great Artur Camulus fucked his London whores."

A muscle twitched in Artur's jaw. A dark flash in his eyes was the only hint that Cade might be close to crossing a line.

"Sit, Leucetius."

Cade's fists flexed. "And if I don't?"

Brax, eyes flaring crimson, slapped his palms on the table on either side of the computer, half rising from his chair. "Stop this. We've all suffered losses. Fighting among ourselves is not going to help anything."

Artur ignored his brother. "A challenge, Leucetius?" His eyes hardened into obsidian. The odor of barely suppressed violence reached Cade's nostrils; his pulse spiked.

"Come on, then." Artur's voice was deadly soft. "Do it."

Suicide, to take on Artur. Every Watcher in the room knew it. The ancient words of challenge, once uttered, would seal Cade's doom. Artur was far stronger than any of them—stronger even than all the other Watchers in the room at once. Cade did not doubt that Artur could—and would—tear him to pieces. But not before Cade inflicted some damage of his own. He shifted onto the balls of his feet, preparing—

A touch on his arm dragged him back to sanity. He jerked his head around. He hadn't even noticed Cybele moving from the window. Their eyes tangled, and for a moment he was lost in the clear, sad gray of her irises. His heart clenched, and he cursed himself for still wanting her, when she had never wanted anyone but Artur.

"Cade. Stop this. Please. It isn't helping."

She was right, of course. Giving Artur the pleasure of

killing him was no solution. A shudder passed through him; he nodded once.

Artur's gaze fell on Cybele. "Take your hand off him."

Cybele's green eyes flashed. Her hand did not move. Her Texas accent dripped contempt into each syllable of her reply.

"Do us all a favor, Mr. Master and Commander. Choke on that arrogance. There are six of us left. *Six.* That's assuming . . ." Her voice faltered, then steadied. "That's assuming Lucas is alive." Cybele's brother had been out of touch with the clan for months, and Cade knew she'd been anxious about his silence even before the massacre.

"You want to take more of us out, Artur? Great. Crawl on over to Vaclav Dusek and offer your services as assassin."

Artur's expression didn't change as he absorbed the tirade. When it was done, he simply raised one eyebrow and turned his back.

Cybele's throat worked. Cade smelled a rush of sour heat. He wasn't fooled. Cybele wasn't so much angry as she was hurt. She craved Artur's fire, not his frost. She loved the bastard. Only the devil in hell knew why. Cade certainly didn't understand.

He removed Cybele's hand from his arm. She was right about one thing. Clan Samyaza couldn't afford to fight among themselves. Hatred among the clans was one aspect of the curse delivered to the original Watcher angels after their fall from grace, and their half-human children had inherited it. Every Nephilim harbored an instinctive mistrust of those not of their own clan's line. The animosity had only intensified through the ages, as the Watchers' descendants had fought for survival and for control of mankind. Heaven did not want them banding together.

The original Watcher leaders, Samyaza and Azazel, once as close as brothers, had fought bitterly for supremacy on earth. For millennia, their progeny had continued the feud. The battle was fierce and unending, with neither clan able to gain the upper hand for long. Many times throughout history, clan loyalty and unquestioning obedience to the clan chieftain had been the primary factor preventing Clan Samyaza's destruction. Oblivion awaited Cade and his clan now if Clan Samyaza could not face the current threat with a united front.

Though it nearly killed him to do so, Cade faced Artur and bowed. The gesture of fealty left a sour taste in his mouth, but Artur's acknowledging touch on his head was, thankfully, brief. The scent of the clan's collective relief took the edge off the humiliation.

The chieftain addressed the room. "Dusek has struck a knife into the heart of our clan. He has stolen our magic. He has won one battle. But make no mistake. He will not win the war. Clan Samyaza will wipe Vaclav Dusek and his sons from the face of the earth. We will consign Clan Azazel to Oblivion."

Cade had been a part of the clan for little more than a year. Before his transition he'd known nothing of his Watcher heritage; he'd spent the time immediately after his transition—immediately after Cybele had made it clear she did not return his love—learning what he was. He'd learned to master his blood cravings, control his Druid magic, and had sifted through five millennia of ancestral memory. He'd chosen his Watcher surname, as all Samyaza adepts did, from the pantheon of Latinized Celtic deities: Leucetius, god of lightning. He'd listened to tales of Watcher history. There were many things, though, Cade had yet to understand.

"You say Dusek has stolen Samyaza magic," he asked. "How is that possible?"

Artur and Brax exchanged glances, and a shadow flitted across Cybele's face. Gareth looked down at his hands. Unlike Cade, all of them had known what they were since birth.

It was Brax who answered. "There's only one way Dusek

could have done it. By making a slave. By anchoring a Samyaza dormant through transition and afterward retaining the power of mastery rather than setting the new adept free."

The talk of transition and crisis triggered flashes of unwanted memory in Cade's brain. Even though more than a year had passed, a hot flush spread up Cade's neck. Acid flooded his stomach. Slave. Yes, he had been that to Cybele. Still was, in some ways.

"Just imagine, Cade," Artur taunted softly, as if he'd heard Cade's thoughts. "It might have been you who were enslaved." The chieftain's gaze fell on the woman who had once been his bonded mate. "If Cybele had not been so honorable as to set you free."

Cybele stiffened. Cade's fingers curled into fists. Artur, bastard that he was, loved to torment his former mate with the choice she had made that night. Cybele had broken her vows to Artur in order to save the life of a dying kinsman, a stranger she'd stumbled upon completely by chance. In doing so, she'd earned the hatred of the man she loved. Cade was all too aware of how powerless he was to repay the debt he owed her.

Brax sent Artur a repressive glance. "We know of no female Samyaza dormants," he continued pointedly. "They're very rare. But Dusek must have located one. An unaware dormant, living among humans."

Cybele met Artur's gaze. "We can't allow Clan Azazel to hold one of our kin. We have to free her."

"A fine goal." Brax's cool voice cut in. "For our own sake as well as for our unknown brother's. But at the moment, the notion is completely unrealistic. With a Samyaza slave under his thumb, Dusek has use of our magic. He can reproduce our spells as well as neutralize them. The slave gives him a clear advantage."

"For now." The merciless expression in Artur's eyes went a long way toward chilling Cade's blood.

"What does that mean?"

"It means, Leucetius, that we will attack Dusek with magic he does not expect. Magic we do not currently possess."

Cybele paled. "You can't mean for Clan Samyaza to take slaves of our own."

"That's exactly what I mean, Cybele, my love."

She ignored the stain of sarcasm on Artur's endearment. "But . . . how? We'd need to find a Watcher dormant on the cusp of transition. That's all but impossible."

Artur strode to the sideboard and poured a whiskey. He took a long sip before speaking.

"Dusek found a Watcher dormant. And you, Cybele, found Cade."

"My finding Cade was pure chance. One in a million," Cybele said tightly. "You know that, Artur. It's not likely to happen again. Our Druid earth magic provides protection and illusion; we don't have the advantage of Dusek's fire alchemy for remote vision and discernment. Even if we did, we have no idea what spells he used to locate his victim."

Artur tilted his glass toward his brother. "All very true. Even so, Brax has been, shall we say, working his own brand of magic. With great success, I might add. An hour ago, he located a dormant Watcher in the early stage of transition. Better yet, it's an unaware Watcher, with no inkling what's to come. All we need to do, my dear Cybele, is be on hand when the crisis strikes."

The last drops of color drained from Cybele's face. A seething turmoil of scents slapped at Cade's nostrils: rage, hurt, bewilderment. Cybele was the clan's only surviving female. Every Watcher in the room knew what that meant.

"You bastard," she whispered. "You can forget it. I won't

anchor him. I won't become a slaver. You can't ask it of me. You wouldn't."

"You're right." Artur's eyes darkened. "I wouldn't ask. I would command."

Cybele flinched as if he'd struck her. "I won't obey. I won't whore for you, Artur."

The whiskey glass clinked on the sideboard. Artur paced forward, slowly, stopping only when the tips of Cybele's breasts brushed his chest. Cade's eyes narrowed as Cybele lifted her chin and—foolishly, Cade thought—held her ground.

Artur's long fingers encircled her slender neck. "You will obey me, Cybele, when my command is spoken. I will make certain of it."

He pressed the translucent skin just above her windpipe. The scent of her fear spiked.

If that had been the only odor Cade's nostrils plucked from the air, he would have leaped to Cybele's defense, and blast the consequences. But it wasn't. Hard on the heels of her panic came the rushing odor of her desire. So Cade stayed where he was. Cybele had made it clear over and over again: she did not welcome Cade's interference. Not where Artur was concerned.

After a moment, Artur gave a humorless laugh. Releasing Cybele, as if the tense interlude had never occurred, he strode back to his drink. "Clan Samyaza will counter Dusek's advantage," he said, "We will bring new magic under our control, quickly."

"And what of Clan Samyaza's honor?" Cybele cried. "Are we to toss our self-respect in the trash and become everything we despise? Everything Jonas Walker believes us to be? Taking slaves will taint every one of us. Issue all the threats you want, Artur, but I, for one, would rather go to Oblivion than anchor a slave." She rounded on Brax. "You stand with him on this? How could you?"

Brax shifted in his seat. "The way I see it, Cybele, we have two choices. Fight slime with slime, or roll over and show our throats. You might be willing to embrace Oblivion, but I'm not. I agree with Artur. Slave-making is our only option."

"And you've already found our victim."

"Yes," Brax said. "I have."

"How? You haven't cast a spell all day. You've been staring at that computer."

Brax drummed his fingers once on the table. "I've been hacking police reports on hellfiend activity."

"Why on earth . . . ?"

"Hellfiends sense the presence of Watchers and typically avoid them. They know they can't possess us. Quite the opposite, they're more likely to fall under our control or be slain outright. They know confronting Watchers will only bring trouble. Given that fact, it therefore follows that areas with a minimum of hellfiend crime will coincide with areas of Watcher activity. When these regions occur outside the territory of the known Watcher clans, it's possible the effect is caused by an unaware Watcher, one who's just entered the transitioning phase."

"One who's recently survived a near-death experience, you mean," Cybele said.

"Exactly." Brax tapped a few keys. "In the past, it's been difficult to track these patterns using only magic, but now, with computers and the Internet . . . All I have to do is cross-reference the crime-free areas with corresponding local hospital records of patients who've experienced a near-death trauma.

"Once I assembled a list of NDE survivors under thirty years of age, it was easy enough to search school and medical records and check for typical Watcher characteristics: prematurely dead parent, no full siblings, dysfunction in human society, tall stature, left-handedness. In effect, all the common traits compatible with Watcher genetics." He shrugged. "The methodology is tedious but simple enough. I didn't have to use magic at all."

"And you're sure you've found a transitioning dormant?" Cade asked.

Brax nodded. "Ninety-eight point two percent certain."

Cybele's face lost even more color, if that was possible. "And Artur intends to pimp me out to him. So I can bring him back as a slave for the clan."

"No," Artur said mildly.

"No? But you said—"

Artur chuckled. "As it happens, Cybele, your services—excellent as they are—won't be needed just yet."

Cybele flushed. "Then what—"

"Because the candidate is female."

She stared. "Brax has located a female? But Watcher females are so rare! One in five hundred."

Brax spread his hands. "Sometimes a half-percent chance comes through."

"Who's going after her?" Cybele demanded. "You, Artur?"

"No." Artur smiled. "I thought I'd give her to Cade."

The whole number of the angels, the Watchers, who descended from above, was two hundred. The first of their leaders was Samyaza; the last, Azazel.

The sons of Man had multiplied in those days, and daughters were born to them, elegant and beautiful. When the sons of Heaven beheld the daughters of men, they became enamored of them. They said to one another: Come let us choose wives among the children of men and have children with them.

Samyaza replied: I fear that I alone shall suffer for so grievous a crime. But all the Watchers answered Samyaza and said: We all swear, and bind ourselves by mutual execrations, that we will not change our intention.

So the Watchers took wives, teaching them sorcery, incantations, astronomy, and the dividing of roots. And the women conceived and brought forth the Nephilim, born of spirit and of flesh. The children of the Watchers became evil spirits upon earth, turning against men in order to devour them, to eat their flesh and to drink their blood.

—from the Book of Enoch

Chapter Three

Negev Desert, Israel

The new laborer was tall and broad and bare to the waist. A veritable Adonis. His back muscles rippled beneath an expanse of smooth skin. He was tanned, though he was not nearly so dark as the two Israeli men working with him.

He'd pressed his T-shirt into service as an impromptu bandanna, wrapping it around his head turban-style. A short black ponytail protruded from the faded green fabric. The ends of his hair curled at his nape.

Even from a distance, the sight made Maddie's skin tingle. An aura of danger seemed to cling to the man, reinforced, no doubt, by his extensive body art: a dark sleeve of Celtic knotwork covered his entire right arm. A nasty-looking dagger was inked on his chest. A third tat—a black and red snake—curled around one calf.

He worked the roped-off area to the north of the main dig site, about thirty feet away. Lifting a substantial stone, he hefted it into a wheelbarrow without apparent effort. He was left-handed, she realized, watching him maneuver a crowbar behind the next boulder. That was a trait only another lefty would notice. She experienced an odd feeling of familiarity.

Then pain stabbed behind her left eye, a light flashed, and all thoughts of the man fled. Panic bled ice water into her veins.

Oh, God, no.

She tore off her glasses. Roughly, desperately, she rubbed

her eyes. But the soft red glow remained, encircling the laborer like a halo.

A full minute passed before the light faded. Too long to pretend she hadn't seen it. Impossible to pretend it was a trick of the Israeli sun or her overactive imagination. Her head began to pound. She swallowed a bitter taste. Somehow, she managed to keep her breakfast from churning its way up her gullet.

So begins the end.

How long did she have? A couple months? Six? Certainly not more than a year. Oh, God. She'd been feeling so normal, so damn *healthy*. Brain surgery had almost killed her. Weeks of chemo to shrink the remaining cancer had left her weak. But once the poison had stopped dripping into her veins, she'd fought her way back tooth and nail. Her health had rebounded. Her hair had started to grow back. Her strength and sense of well-being had returned with amazing rapidity. She'd clung to every good day.

But she knew better than to hope. The reprieve wasn't permanent. All the doctors agreed, it was only a matter of time before the cancer returned. When that happened, she'd be back in the States, hooked up to machines and IV drips, mind fogged with drugs. Staring death in the face. Again.

But not yet. Not today, at least. And not tomorrow. She didn't intend to give in easily, even if she knew the battle was lost. She'd fight every step of the way. Grab every second she had left.

With a hand that barely trembled, she slid her glasses back onto her nose. The new laborer had hefted one final rock into his wheelbarrow. She blanked the future from her mind and watched him bend to grasp the handles and was struck anew by the sheer, savage beauty of his body.

At that precise moment, he turned his head and met her gaze. And lifted his brows.

Oxygen left her lungs in a rush. He knew she'd been

watching him. Good thing the desert was hot and her face already flushed. God. She'd been caught out like an adolescent girl ogling her latest crush.

His lips twitched. His eyes made a quick journey down her body and back up. Point made, he gave her his back, lifting the loaded wheelbarrow with stunning ease. Despite her embarrassment—he could hardly be impressed with what he'd seen—she didn't look away as he moved off.

"A nice hot one, eh?"

Maddie jumped. She hadn't realized her roommate, Hadara Stern, had come up behind her.

"And I am not, for once, speaking of the weather," the Israeli grad student added with a wink.

Maddie covered her embarrassment with a laugh. "Ari wouldn't like to hear that, I'm sure." Ari, another archeological assistant, had been angling for Hadara's attention.

Hadara smiled. "I am not blind. And neither, I think, are you. That new man, he is a work of art. What intelligent woman can resist a little artistic appreciation?"

The two women shared a completely feminine chuckle. Hadara touched Maddie's arm before moving off.

Maddie gave herself a mental shake and continued on the path to the water station, which had been her destination before the new laborer caught her eye. She wished Hadara had come along with her. Alone, she couldn't help brooding on her earlier visual disturbance.

Maybe, she thought, the red halo had been a product of dehydration. Not a signal the tumor had returned.

But she didn't really believe that. Self-deception had never been her strong suit. She couldn't deny the truth. This visual disturbance—her first since her surgery—meant the cancer inside her skull was reawakening. Unfurling its tentacles.

Her oncologist had used that exact word: *Tentacles*. Gliomas didn't grow in nice, round, easily extracted lumps. They crept like vines, unfurling insidious strands of death and despair. Her tumor lurked behind her left eye; one tendril encircled her optic nerve. Surgery and chemo had slowed the cancer's progress, but the ultimate outcome of her disease had never been in doubt. Visual disturbances. Pain. Blindness. Death. The utter waste of a life.

The clock was ticking. Today, it had sped up. Maddie was tempted to succumb to screaming panic. But she wouldn't. She couldn't. It wasn't in her nature to give in. She wasn't going to die today. And not tomorrow or the next day, either. At least three days more, then, to be lived. And more after that. Exactly how many, she didn't know. But she wasn't going to waste a minute.

She inhaled deeply. Her nerves settled enough to allow her canteen to fill without a drop running over. A good thing, since water was a precious commodity here in the Negev. There was no source at the dig site. Their supply was trucked in from Mitzpe Ramon and stored in tanks set in the shade of Mt. Ardon's north face.

The thrusting cliff wasn't a mountain in the true sense of the word. Mt. Ardon rose as a wedge-shaped outcropping of pale rock at the eastern edge of a desert crater known as Makhtesh Ramon. Some twenty-five miles long and up to six miles wide, the glacier-formed *makhtesh* was an impressive geological feature. The archeological site, at the base of Mt. Ardon, lay some fifteen hundred feet below the main level of the Negev desert. The canyon was stark and beautiful; hikers and jeep tourists crawled across it regularly, following a route once traversed by ancient caravans on the Spice Road. But long before the caravans, far more mysterious inhabitants had left their mark.

Here, legend claimed, angels once walked the earth.

* * *

Maddie didn't believe in angels. Not really. Not at all. She'd first learned of the Watchers, whose physical remains she was currently seeking in the dust of the Negev, through a public service ad placed by Demon Annihilators Mutual Network—a cult. The cult taught that the Watchers, a race of fallen angels mentioned in passing in the biblical book of Genesis, were the ancestors of a race of half-human, half-demon creatures known as Nephilim. According to DAMN, the Nephilim and their descendants had terrorized humanity throughout the ages. They were still at it, big-time, in the modern age.

DAMN's anti-demon exhortations were everywhere: TV, radio, Internet, billboards, buses—even on posters plastered on vacant buildings and telephone poles. The face of Father Jonas Walker, the Catholic priest who had founded DAMN, appeared on almost all of the propaganda. Almost indecently handsome, the priest claimed humanity was under attack by demons. Maddie thought Father Walker had drunk a bit too much communion wine.

But, hers was the minority opinion. Father Walker and DAMN enjoyed worldwide popularity and growing respect. Most people believed in demons these days. It was easy enough to find a person who claimed to have firsthand experience. Impossible to find someone who hadn't at least encountered a believer.

The most common demonic creature was the hellfiend. Pure demon, hellfiends lacked a corporeal form. They operated through humans, influencing weak minds with evil suggestion or controlling human behavior outright through possession of a victim's body and soul.

Hellfiends were vicious and brutal but lacked direction. According to DAMN, less numerous but far more dangerous were the half-breed Nephilim. These "archdemon overlords," clever and ruthless, stalked humans, killing them and drinking their blood. Capable of bending hellfiends to their will, the

Nephilim represented the greater threat. The ultimate goal of these creatures was nothing less than the enslavement and destruction of mankind. And in recent years, Walker claimed, the Nephilim had drawn very close to their goal. He pointed to the state of the world—wars, terrorism, increasing crime—as evidence.

Yes, there were thousands—millions, maybe—who had swallowed Father Walker's teachings whole. DAMN hotlines for reporting suspected Nephilim and hellfiend activity rang off the hook. Every criminal behind bars, it seemed, claimed demonic possession or influence as a defense.

Of course, the last thing the average demon-blaming wrongdoer on the street wanted to see was a unit of DAMN "field agents" coming at him. Operating in most major cities, the DAMNers were armed to the teeth with semiautomatic weaponry and holy water, and they tended to act first and ask questions later. Sporting military haircuts, camo gear, and flashy red berets, DAMNers were quick to mete out vigilante justice. Self-righteous urban citizens, as a rule, loved the group. Police, not so much. Criminals, not at all.

For a long while, deep into her university studies, Maddie had ignored the DAMN phenomenon, though she sometimes saw members of the student chapter prowling around campus. But then cancer had abruptly interrupted her life and halted her studies. And after her last round of chemo, suffering from insomnia, she'd become absorbed in an archeological documentary on late-night cable TV.

The film *Nephilim Origins: Fact or Fiction?* had clearly been inspired by the recent media obsession with Father Walker and DAMN. Maddie had watched as an Israeli archeologist, Dr. Simon Ben-Meir, spun the tale of the Watchers, a group of two hundred heavenly angels who, some five thousand years ago, became obsessed with earth and its fledgling human race. According to Genesis and the Book of Enoch, an apocryphal scripture, the Watchers were allowed to assume human bodies and live on earth provided they followed one important rule: they were forbidden to engage in carnal relations with the "daughters of men." Predictably, as with Eve in the garden, temptation proved irresistible. The Watchers lay with human women, who subsequently bore the angels' hybrid offspring. These unnatural angel/human creatures, known as Nephilim, possessed earthly bodies, heavenly powers, and unnaturally beastly appetites.

The archangels Raphael and Michael had delivered Heaven's wrath. A great flood—the same deluge Noah and his family survived—wiped out the fallen angels and most of their hybrid offspring as well. Only a handful of Nephilim escaped. But the curse of their fathers followed them. The human souls they had once possessed were replaced with finite demon essence. This meant that when the Nephilim outlived their time on earth, they had no souls to receive a heavenly judgment. They could not proceed as humans did to Heaven or Hell. Instead, their existence was snuffed completely.

Maddie shivered. Pure oblivion. It was a concept she'd been contemplating far too often lately, as she confronted her impending death.

Father Walker believed the descendants of the original Watchers, the Nephilim he claimed lived in the modern world, retained the magic of their ancestors. With no hope of life after death, modern Nephilim made the most of their limited span of existence by twisting the stolen power of Heaven to evil purpose. They commanded hellfiends. They enslaved humans, used them for foul purpose, and when they tired of them, decapitated them and drank their blood. In short, they exulted in all types of human misery.

The documentary archeologist, Dr. Simon Ben-Meir, felt differently. Not a DAMN believer, he maintained the Watcher legend as told by Jonas Walker contained a large dose of fantasy. The priest's zeal was so much misguided superstition. Ben-Meir's goal was instead to unearth remnants of the very human ancient chieftains who inspired the legend.

Father Walker immediately called Ben-Meir's explorations in the Negev misguided and dangerous. Nothing good, the priest asserted, could come from digging up ancient evil. According to Walker, the bones of the Watchers were best left buried.

Maddie had quickly dismissed the priest's religious mumbo jumbo. Still, the mystical overtones of the Watcher legend fascinated her as much as the archeological ramifications. For the first time in months, as she'd watched the TV documentary, she'd found her thoughts consumed by something other than cancer. She'd been pulled back to her studies.

In the days that followed, she'd read everything she could find on the Internet and in the library about the original Watcher angels and their half-breed offspring, the Nephilim. As luck would have it, the spring dig season in Israel was beginning. Within weeks she'd signed on as a volunteer archeologist on Dr. Simon Ben-Meir's expedition. Even now, she wasn't quite certain what she hoped to uncover here in the Negev. She only hoped she found it before she died.

* * *

Cade watched Madeline Durant bend to fill her canteen. The khaki fabric of her shorts molded against her round bottom. Blast it all to Oblivion. He was already hard, and all he'd done was look at her.

His arousal was nothing compared to his anger. He was rational enough, at least, to acknowledge the fact that the burning rage in his gut was not this unsuspecting woman's fault. The blame clearly fell on the bastard who'd ordered him to this forsaken chunk of arid earth. Artur. Bad enough the chieftain had commanded Cade to become a slave-maker. But sending him to the Negev, to walk the very dirt once trod by Samyaza and his cursed brethren? Cade half wished he'd let Artur kill him.

During the journey from England, he had wondered what would happen if Brax were wrong. A dormant Watcher was indistinguishable from a human. If a dormant came very close to death and survived, the experience triggered the transition to full adept power. It was only then that the dormant could be sensed by other Watchers who happened to be close enough. Brax, despite his confidence, could not be completely certain. The woman Cade pursued might be human. Even if she was a Watcher, she might not be a rival. She might belong to Clan Samyaza.

If she was kin, Cade would anchor her transition as an equal, as Cybele had done for him. There would be no shame in that. But also, no new magic for the clan. No advantage over Vaclav Dusek and Clan Azazel.

As much as Cade hated to admit it, Artur had chosen the only path to his people's survival. Clan Samyaza needed new magic. Without it, they were all bound for Oblivion. The instant Cade had come close enough to catch her scent, he knew his journey hadn't been in vain. Madeline Durant was a Watcher and a rival. He had only to feel his body's response to know that truth beyond a doubt.

A dizzying urge to conquer, to dominate, to enslave, threatened to send Cade hurtling toward her. He was aware of a deep, instinctive distrust of the woman and everything she represented—a product of the Watcher curse.

Cade felt that enmity with full force now, oddly coupled with an intense sexual attraction. He paused, forcing himself to hold motionless until the rush of emotion passed. When at last it had, it was only with great difficulty that he stooped to lift the loaded wheelbarrow and turned away.

Eventually, his anger ebbed. His arousal did not. Nor would it. A Watcher in transition exuded specialized pheromones designed to lure a Watcher adept of the opposite sex. The effect had evolved as a simple matter of biological survival. Without a full adept to act as anchor, a dormant could not survive transition. Cade, whose sense of smell was intimately entwined with his magic, was particularly vulnerable to Madeline Durant's unconscious enticement. Now that he'd scented her, there was no way he could turn away. Even if he wanted to abandon the chase, he couldn't. He was well and truly snared—by Artur's order as well as by the woman herself.

She would be his. There was no doubt. He only hoped he could restrain his sexual hunger long enough to gain her trust. Enslaving her would be infinitely easier if she trusted him.

It might not be too difficult. The biochemical attraction worked both ways. He saw that Madeline, upon emerging from the hut she shared with one of the other volunteers, had noticed him immediately. She'd halted as if rooted to the spot and watched him for several long moments. She'd flushed when he'd met her gaze. Ah, yes. Her body knew, even if her mind, ruled by the curse, mistrusted him. Her life depended on surrender to Cade.

He'd make his move soon. If he waited too long, her impending crisis—not to mention his own lust—would make matters difficult. Cade's mind shied away from drawing parallels to his transition. Even a year after the fact, the memory of his crisis was too humiliating, and too vivid, to examine with any semblance of detachment.

Like Madeline, Cade had been an unaware. He'd known nothing of his Watcher heritage. It had been a pure miracle Cybele had passed close enough to be snared by the pheromones his shuddering body had pumped into the frigid night air. The hours that followed had been . . . terrifying. Harrowing. And unexpectedly fulfilling. Cade had lived twenty-four years before Cybele had assumed control of his transition, but he could say with complete sincerity he hadn't truly been born before that night.

Madeline's experience, of course, would be different. Cade had been incredibly fortunate to be found by an adept of his own clan. If Cybele had been a rival, she would have left him to die, since Clan Samyaza did not take slaves. As it was, she had sensed a kinsman and stepped in to save him. In doing so, she had set him on a path to power he'd never dreamed possible.

Cade would anchor Madeline Durant as a rival. Her crisis wouldn't end with a transition to freedom; it would end in enslavement. Her magic would become Cade's. And through Cade, Artur's. Cade hated the prospect of the woman's subjugation, loathed the thought of himself in the role of slaver. His body, however, judging from the way it throbbed in anticipation, did not.

His quarry's scent, riding the thin desert air, drifted with unerring precision to his nostrils. He breathed deeply, saturating his lungs with her essence. His lust spiraled. The effort to bring it back under control made him light-headed. For a long moment, he could only grit his teeth and endure. His knuckles clenched until his hands went numb. Every nerve screamed, *Take her. Claim her. Here. Now.*

He dumped the load of stones before turning to track her with his eyes. She stood at the water tank, twisting the cap onto her canteen with shaking hands. Maddie Durant was not particularly beautiful, he decided, other than her dark, expressive eyes. She was tall, as all Watchers were. But thinner than she should be. Her form, which was probably naturally lean and small-busted, was now downright scrawny. She'd probably dropped a good bit of weight during her recent chemotherapy treatment. It was almost laughable, that she had believed—still believed—a human disease like cancer could kill her.

She sensed his scrutiny—he was sure that she did—and gave a nervous glance over her shoulder. He raised his brows in return. Her beautiful eyes widened.

Her hair was dark and curling. And far too short. When she was his, he'd order her to grow it long. He dragged the caress of his gaze slowly down her body, imagining a curtain of waves spilling over her naked skin.

She jerked around and scurried toward the lecture tent.

Yes, little rabbit, he thought. *Run. Run while you still can.*

Chapter Four

"The truth is here, beneath our feet."

Maddie tossed a month-old *People* magazine, abandoned by last week's crop of teen volunteers, onto a battered side table. Taking off her glasses, she rubbed the bridge of her nose. It hurt to look through the lenses. Almost as if they were too strong, absurd as that sounded. When did myopia ever improve? But she had to admit, tonight the world appeared sharper to her naked eyes, even though her vision should have been bleary from lack of sleep alone. It was close to midnight, and she'd been up since dawn.

After two months as an intern on Dr. Simon Ben-Meir's dig, Maddie was accustomed to these late-night sessions. As far as she could tell, the Israeli archeologist didn't know the meaning of the words *rest* and *relaxation*—not in any of the six languages he spoke. The man was tireless, obsessed with using every minute available until the dig was forced to close down for the hot summer months.

The team met late every evening in the largest hut on the site, where new artifacts were logged, cleaned, and tagged, to discuss the past day's excavations and to lay plans for the next morning. And while recent developments at the excavation had admittedly been exciting, at this particular moment Maddie wanted to be in bed and sound asleep.

She wasn't alone. Ari and Gil slumped in their seats, barely lucid. Maddie exchanged a wry glance with Hadara, who sighed and stifled a yawn.

Ben-Meir stood at the main worktable in the hut reserved

for lab work and artifact storage. Palms flat on the scarred wood, arms rigid, he stared down at a photograph of a relic known as the Pharos Tablet.

The actual Pharos Tablet was a smooth square of stone measuring approximately sixteen centimeters on a side. At present, it was ensconced in a Cairo museum. Dr. Ben-Meir's facsimile rendered the artifact at more than twice its actual size, as if enlarging the relic would encourage it to surrender its mysteries.

The piece had been unearthed two years earlier, at a construction site on the Isle of Pharos near Alexandria, Egypt. It was thought to have been part of the collection of the famous library of the Ptolemaic dynasty. Recovered in more than a dozen fragments, the Pharos Tablet had been painstakingly reassembled to form a surprisingly complete rectangle, missing only a few fragments around the edges.

Ancient markings covered the face of the stone. In the right lower corner, a hieroglyph denoting the Pharoah Teti of Egypt's Old Kingdom, dated the tablet to the twenty-third century BCE—the early Canaanite period, contemporary to the traditional date of the biblical flood. And to the Watchers.

Ben-Meir's finger lingered on a second glyph: a circle with a smaller circle inside. Egyptologists accepted the symbol as an early representation of the sun god Ra, whose cult was on the rise during Teti's reign. Ben-Meir, however, disagreed. He was certain the disc symbol denoted not the sun, but an eye, a symbol he insisted referred to the biblical angels known as Watchers. He believed the markings on the Pharos Tablet were not a narrative but a map. A map of Makhtesh Ramon, which Ben-Meir believed to be the ancient home of the Watchers.

Ben-Meir's assertions had unleashed a storm of scorn and ridicule in the academic world. Outside the universities, however, his theories met with more success, leading to the documentary Maddie had seen on cable. The *makhtesh* was today a harsh, dry landscape. During the Bronze Age, however, the canyon had been fed by two streams and sheltered from the heat of the upper desert. It would have been a lush, fruitful place, a rich stronghold for powerful ancient tribal chieftains.

The archeologist had chosen the precise location of his dig with the help of the Pharos Tablet. For months, the site had yielded little more than dust and the occasional pottery shard. Then, shortly after Maddie's arrival, came the discovery of a cache of bronze swords dating to the pre-Canaanite period, and an oblong stone that may have been an ancient smith's anvil. Very close by, the team had uncovered the remains of a well from the same period.

Dr. Ben-Meir had yet to make a formal announcement of the finds to the outside world. The last thing the expedition needed was a horde of DAMN zealots camping at his gate before he'd proven his theories on the Watchers to his scornful colleagues in the international archeological community.

The camp generators had been turned off for the night. An oil lamp, hanging from the rafters of the palm-thatched hut, spilled anemic yellow light onto Dr. Ben-Meir's thinning gray hair. The archeologist, on the far side of middle age, possessed a slight build and hunched shoulders. His complexion was unnaturally wan, especially considering he'd spent most of his career exposed to the hot Israeli sun. Ben-Meir worked round the clock, it seemed. He was rarely seen eating or drinking. Maddie thought a good meal could only do the man good, though she doubted many of his interns would rush to share a table with their boss in the mess tent. Not unless they wanted to come away from the meal with a long list of extra tasks to accomplish before sunset.

Ben-Meir pushed his black-framed glasses back up his nose. Pens, notebook, and a laptop lay to the right of the

Pharos Tablet photograph. A map of the excavation, inked on transparent Mylar, lay at the archeologist's left hand.

"The truth is here," Ben-Meir repeated. "I believe we are close, very close, to finding proof of the Watchers' existence."

He slid the transparent map of the dig atop the photograph of the Pharos Tablet, until certain features on the transparency covered markings on the tablet. The circle denoting the recently discovered well aligned neatly with an ancient glyph meaning "water."

"The Watchers lived in Makhtesh Ramon," Ben-Meir said. "I am certain of that. But my first calculations led us fifty meters too far to the south. Now, with the discovery of the settlement's well . . ."

He slid his finger to a series of square marks on the tablet, which seemed to suggest a cluster of habitations. "When we excavate the new area, I am confident we will uncover proof of the Watchers' existence."

The new area. Where the big, beautiful man with the Celtic tattoo had labored, hauling rocks away in preparation for archeologists' trowels and brushes.

"Here."

Ben-Meir's finger stabbed the merged graphics. Maddie saw the strike as a jagged strand of light. Bright lines, like shattered glass, exploded from the point of impact.

Pain pierced her skull. With a gasp, she pressed her fingers to her temple. A heavy weight descended on her shoulders. The sudden, invisible burden caused her to double over, head pressed to her knees.

She became aware of Ari kneeling beside her, his hand on her upper arm. "Maddie! What is it? Are you ill?"

Several moments passed before she felt it safe to answer. "I . . . It's nothing." She shoved herself upright and fought the dizziness. Five full beats of her heart passed before she'd gathered enough courage to look up. Dr. Ben-Meir stood frowning at her. Behind him, a soft, otherworldly glow bathed the photograph of the Pharos Tablet.

She bit her lip and choked back a sob. Ari's grip on her arm tightened. Hadara appeared behind him, her dark eyes troubled.

Maddie swallowed. "Really. I'm fine. I'm just . . . tired, I guess. And dehydrated, probably. That's all."

"You don't drink enough fluids," Hadara scolded. "I've told you that time and again. Gil, get her something."

Maddie's hand shook as she took the cup of guava juice that appeared before her. Obediently, she sipped it as her teammates huddled around her. The sickly sweet liquid stuck in her throat. She couldn't drink more than a few gulps.

"I feel much better now," she lied as she set the cup aside.

"You need sleep," Hadara announced, with a meaningful glance in Ben-Meir's direction.

"Ah, yes. Of course." The archeologist's expression was more annoyed than sympathetic. "Please. Seek your beds. I'll see you all back here at six a.m."

Hadara hustled Maddie off to their hut. But tired as Maddie was, sleep just would not come. She lay on her back on her cot, her mind racing along paths it didn't want to travel. Flashes of light, headaches . . . The tumor was growing. Soon the cancer would be too far advanced to ignore.

None of the team knew Maddie was living with a death sentence. They would have treated her differently if they'd known she was dying, and she had so desperately needed these weeks of normalcy. She had to leave before her condition became apparent. Next week, or the week after. She didn't intend to tell Hadara and the others the truth; she couldn't bear their pity. She'd make up some excuse to explain a sudden trip to the States and simply never come back.

Hadara's breath, deep and even, drifted from the other side

of the hut. Restlessness churned Maddie's limbs; she couldn't relax, couldn't get comfortable. The urge to get up and run as fast and as far as she could was almost overpowering. Only the realization that it would never be fast enough, or far enough, kept Maddie in her bed.

Finally—blessedly—sleep clouded her mind. Strangely, Maddie's last clear thought was of a broad, tattooed laborer.

* * *

She woke in blind panic, heart pounding, lungs sucking air. She lay supine, spine rigid, fingers clawing at the bedsheet. Try as she might to command her body, Maddie's elbows would not bend, her fists would not unclench, her knees would not lift. A dull force pressed down on her chest, forcing her to struggle for every breath.

For several sickening seconds, she stared blankly at her surroundings. Where the hell was she? The ceiling of sloping palm fronds, the whitewashed walls, the dark square of night outlined by the window frame . . . Hadara's soft snore rose and fell in peaceful rhythm.

She saw these things, felt them, heard them. But not as if she was present with them. She sensed them through a more immediate haze of water and flame, panic and terror. Torrents of hot rain stung her face. A tearing pain wrenched her gut.

She was drenched, lying on her side atop a makeshift raft, little more than boards hastily tied with rope. She was on her back, violent birth pains squeezing her enormously swollen belly. All around, a violent sea churned; bursts of flame leaped from oily patches on the surface of the water. A searing wind blew. Clouds of embers and ash burned her eyes, choked her lungs. Her robes were sodden. Too heavy. She wanted to strip them off. But she didn't have the strength.

It was pure hell. Or something very close.

The next contraction came too soon. Terror dragged her breath away. She was sure the baby was going to rip her in two.

The raging terror of the dream juxtaposed oddly with the calm interior of the hut. Like a double exposure on an old photograph. Like a waking nightmare.

The stormy vision faded slowly. Even when the terror-drenched floodwaters receded, unreality lingered. It was almost as if the hut was the dream and the lost nightmare reality.

Her heart pounded, hard and dull, inside her ribs. For a moment she thought she'd faint even before she came fully awake. She drew a slow breath, held it, exhaled. Again.

Five minutes passed, perhaps ten. She thought she felt almost normal. Cautiously, she took out the memory of the nightmare and turned it over in her mind. Thank God, it no longer felt real. Just a dream. It had been just a dream.

She rolled over onto her side. Her limbs ached, as if she'd really battled a burning sea and impending childbirth. Luckily, her thrashings hadn't disturbed her roommate. The silence was almost blatantly surreal. As if her head were wrapped in a lead blanket.

Then a soft noise intruded. A hiss. Propping herself on one elbow, she searched for the source of the sound. Slatted moonlight, shining through the hut's shutters, illuminated the dwelling's sparse furnishings. Table, chairs, desk.

Something moved on the floor near her backpack.

A flash of light accompanied the motion. Maddie went rigid. The next instant, to her great relief, the brief radiance vanished. But the movement continued. Sinuous. Stealthy. A thin, undulating shadow slithering across the floor.

A snake.

Sleep was impossible now. She couldn't close her eyes while a reptile slithered beneath her bed. She sat up fully, considering whether to wake Hadara. She decided against it. Hadara wasn't on the best terms with slithering creatures.

Maddie kept her gaze on the snake's last position as she slipped from under the covers. The plank floor was cool on her soles. It took only a moment to pad to the corner where a broom stood. A few tense minutes later, the snake ventured from its hiding place under a rack of books.

It took only seconds, moving quickly, to herd the unwanted visitor out the door. The *open* door, she noted with a frown. She darted a quick look around, but nothing seemed disturbed. Hadara must not have set the latch when they came in last night. Probably, she'd been too preoccupied with Maddie's near-fainting spell.

Reptile banished, adrenaline flowing, Maddie shot a glance at the bed. She doubted she'd sleep at all now. But she could hardly light a lantern. Nor could she sit in the dark, trying to keep her thoughts from turning even darker.

She dressed quickly, throwing on tomorrow's khaki shorts and a loose tee she'd draped on a chair. A brisk walk would do her good.

The cool night air was sharp with the sort of clarity known only to the desert. The black sky arched overhead; glittering stars dripped like crystal from a celestial chandelier. At the upper edge of the *makhtesh*'s surrounding cliffs, starlight vanished behind sheer rock. The canyon floor, where Maddie stood, was dark as a tomb.

Surrounded by such a stark, primitive landscape, she couldn't help but feel insignificant. It should have been frightening. Oddly, it wasn't. There was a perverse comfort to realizing how very unimportant her life was in the grand scheme of things. After she was dead and gone, the world would continue along its path without her. She was glad of that at least.

Leaving the cluster of huts, she picked her way along the

shadowed path that skirted the western edge of the dig site. Belatedly, she realized she hadn't thought to pick up her glasses. Though really, she could see clearly enough. Objects that should have been hazy were actually quite distinct.

The uneven trail meandered over a rocky rise a short distance from the excavations. She moved slowly, picking her way over rocks and crevices. Her thoughts turned grim. After months of reprieve, she'd experienced three visual disturbances, all within a few hours. Not good. She had to face it: the cancer was back.

Bitterness collected on her tongue. This time, there would be no surgery. No chemo. No reprieve. How long did she have? She knew there was no answer. She wouldn't look for one, then. The end would come when it came.

There was something surreal about facing your mortality. She'd had months of practice. Now, when she needed it most, the skill deserted her. She left the trail and struck out across the rocky desert.

Ironic, really, that she couldn't accept death, the experience that was the only constant of human existence. If only she could just . . . keep walking. Into darkness, into the black center of the *makhtesh*. If only she could stretch her arms upward and be absorbed into the night sky's perfect sparkle. Her soul would fly free without first having to endure the painful destruction of its body.

"A little late for a stroll, I'd say."

The rich male voice, reaching out from the darkness to shatter her bleak thoughts, arrested her forward motion. She spun about, searching for the speaker.

His low chuckle sent a tingle racing up her spine, to sparkle like champagne at her nape. His words had been light and lilting, spoken in an accent that placed the hint of a question after each word.

"Or, perhaps," he added, "it's a bit early, eh, *caraid*?"

She saw him then, standing about ten feet to her right. He leaned back against a boulder, long legs extended in her direction, elbows propped behind him on the stone's flat surface as if the rock were a table. She recognized him. She'd known it was him even before her eyes had found him. The new camp laborer. The one who'd caught her shamelessly ogling his half-naked body.

He looked just as good close up, limned with starlight. Dark hair hung loose to his shoulders, thick and black and slightly curling. His torso was broad and still bare. Soft faded jean shorts, unbelted, rode low on his hips. His right arm, tattooed with Celtic markings, looked much darker than his left. The other tattoo, a jeweled dagger, decorated his right breast.

"*Caraid?*" she said. "What's that?"

A flash of white teeth. "Little love. Darling, dearest, sweetheart . . ."

She took a step nearer, bemused. "I'm not your sweetheart."

"It'd be bloody tidy if you were."

She couldn't quite identify his accent. "Are you English?"

"Hardly." He straightened, arms dropping to his sides. "You know how to wound a man, don't you now?"

They stood only a few feet apart. Maddie was aware, suddenly, viscerally, of how very large he was. She was a tall woman, just a couple inches under six feet. He had to be six-four, at least. She had to tilt her head back to look into his eyes.

"Are you Scottish?"

"No." He stretched the syllable like taffy, giving it far more vowels than it possessed.

She tilted her head. "Australian?"

"I'm a Welshman."

She'd never met anyone from Wales. "You're a long way from home, Mr. Welshman."

He grinned. "Not as far as you are, *caraid*."

A small stretch of silence ensued, during which neither Maddie nor her companion moved. The perfect cue for discreet withdrawal.

Except that Maddie didn't want to withdraw. She couldn't bear to face that darkened hut.

"Why aren't you in bed?" she asked.

His brows rose, and his eyes roamed down her body. She flushed but didn't look away.

"I prefer the night." He opened his arms in an expansive gesture. "The quiet. The solitude. The freedom."

"Is that why you came to the Negev?"

"No," he said but didn't elaborate further. Instead, he held out one hand. "Come closer, *caraid*."

She wasn't sure why she obeyed. Why she wanted to get closer. The man disturbed her. Her reaction to him disturbed her even more. Her skin buzzed with sexual awareness. His extended hand caused a pulling sensation in her belly, as if he held the end of a silken thread and was slowly winding it around his fingers. He hadn't touched her. And yet she felt him. Intimately.

She took another step forward. Then another. He remained motionless. She halted within reach of his hand but didn't take it. After a moment, he let his arm drop to his side.

His scent teased her. Plain soap, mingled with dusty earth and clean masculine sweat. Insanely, she wanted to touch him. Taste him. Wanted him to touch and taste her.

This is crazy.

It was only with difficulty that she restrained herself from reaching for him. "I don't know your name," she said. "I'm Maddie. Maddie Durant."

"Cade Leucetius."

"Leucetius? That's an odd last name. Is it Welsh?"

"It's Celtic. Well, Latinized. Leucetius, god of lightning."

He seemed to hesitate. "It's not the name I was born with. I chose it when I . . . when I came of age."

She didn't know quite what to say to that. She settled for, "So what's a Welshman doing in the Negev?"

"Today? Moving stones."

"You interested in archeology?"

"Not particularly. Personally, I'd prefer the past to remain buried."

Like Jonas Walker? "That's not always possible."

"No," he agreed. "It's not."

He leaned back against the rock, resuming his earlier relaxed posture. A gesture of dismissal? Feeling awkward, Maddie started to turn away.

"Stay," he said. "Please."

That had to be a bad idea. This god of a man could hardly be interested in a scarecrow like her. But she really didn't want to face that dark hut.

"All right."

After a moment's hesitation she boosted herself up onto his flat-topped boulder. Just so he wouldn't think she was coming on to him, she made sure there was at least an arm's length between them. Turning her head, she saw his white teeth flash. Feeling awkward, she offered a tentative smile in return.

His eyes were light, she thought. Blue, maybe? It was too dark to tell for sure. Starlight dusted his profile. His cheekbones slanted sharply. His bold nose and strong jaw matched in angularity. It was a supremely masculine face, unexpectedly softened by lush eyelashes and the supple fullness of his lips. A dark, restless energy clung to him. Something . . . angry. She sensed it keenly, on a raw, personal level. The emotion was so strong, it was a wonder she didn't jump off the rock and run. Instead, insanely, she imagined herself soothing his rage. Inviting him into the refuge of her body.

She was insane. That was all there was to it. Imagining things that weren't there. The man wasn't angry. His expression—what she could see of it—was amused. His tone had been light and teasing. And he was, simply put, gorgeous.

Belatedly, she realized she was staring, like a teenager gawking at a rock star. What was she doing, letting her mind spin fantasies about this man? One look at Cade Leucetius was more than enough to tell her that even if she were beautiful and shapely, he was far too much man for a dying woman to handle.

She drew up her legs and wrapped her arms around them. She rested her chin on her knees and trained her eyes on the open desert. She sensed him out of the corner of her eye watching her.

"The DAMNers are right," he said at last. "The past that Ben-Meir works to unearth would be better off undisturbed. If the man truly understood what he's looking for, he'd pack up and leave tonight."

She turned her head and frowned. "That's absurd."

"Is it, *caraid*?"

"Yes."

"The Watchers were angels," he said. "Angels who stole the power of Heaven and used it in pursuit of their own selfish pleasures on earth. It's not inconceivable that remnants of their cursed magic remains under dirt they once trod."

She scoffed. "I can't believe you really believe in angels. The Watchers, if they did exist, were human men. Powerful men, most likely, but men just the same."

"You came halfway around the world looking for mere men? Dead men, at that?" His eyes mocked her. "Somehow, *cariad*, that doesn't seem worth your trouble."

A chill chased down her spine. No, she hadn't come to the Negev looking for long-dead men. But explaining exactly why she'd come here was difficult. Perhaps the best way to describe it was that she'd been . . . pulled.

She dropped her legs over the edge of the stone and slid to her feet. "It's none of your business why I came here."

He continued as if she hadn't spoken. "Have you ever wondered why, if Heaven is so wonderful, the Watchers left it in the first place? Why would they want to live on earth? Why would they trade eternal angelic bodies for mortal flesh and blood?"

"It's just a story," Maddie said.

"A very ancient one. According to the scribe Enoch, two hundred angels abandoned Heaven to take human bodies and live on earth. They were forbidden only one earthly delight: sex with the daughters of men." He laughed softly. "Doomed from the start, wouldn't you say?"

"Forbidden fruit is a common theme in ancient mythology. Adam and Eve faced a similar test."

"So we agree," Cade said. "The whole endeavor was a prescription for failure. Samyaza, the first among twenty-one leaders of the two hundred Watchers, was the first to fall. I don't imagine it took much to convince his one hundred ninety-nine brothers to join in the fun." He grinned. "Not with so many nubile young Canaanite women about."

"Probably not," Maddie admitted, amused.

"And yet, Samyaza's sins pale beside that of his brother and rival, Azazel. He was the last—and some would say the most powerful—of the Watchers' twenty-one leaders."

"You know, for someone who believes the past should remain buried, you're surprisingly well-versed in ancient legend," Maddie commented. Her eyes narrowed as a sudden thought occurred. "You're not one of those DAMNers, are you? Sent to sabotage Dr. Ben-Meir's work?"

His answering laugh was abrupt. "Hardly. I've merely been

browsing a copy of Enoch I found in the mess tent." His eyes glinted with sudden humor. "I can read, you know. Almost as well as I can haul rocks."

Maddie blushed. "I didn't think you couldn't."

"Azazel taught the art of war to men, and the art of seduction to women. Quite the sinner, eh? The bloke twisted Heaven's magic, transformed good to evil. In defiance of Heaven, he committed any number of perversions, corrupted any number of humans. Until the archangel Raphael defeated him."

"Enoch isn't literal history," Maddie protested. "It's a myth created by an ancient scribe. I hardly think the archangel Raphael actually swooped down from Heaven with a flaming sword to wipe out a band of rogue angels. Though I concede that the story might contain some small grains of historical truth. Dr. Ben-Meir believes a group of ancient human warlords called themselves the Watchers. Maybe the band came to a violent end—at the hands of their enemies, or fighting among themselves. Over the centuries, the story was embellished with angels, magic, fiery swords, and eternal curses. Makes for much better reading than everyday mundane violence, you have to admit."

Cade moved suddenly, abandoning his relaxed pose against the boulder. "If that's the case—if it's all so simple—why did you come here? Why waste your precious time?"

Her precious time. She felt sick, suddenly. But no, she reasoned, he couldn't know she was dying. It was just a figure of speech. But the spell was broken.

"I think I'd better go," she said.

"No." His tone was one of quiet command. "No, I think not. Not quite yet."

Stunned by his audacity, she opened her mouth to protest. Before she quite realized what had happened, he was standing close. Too close. His hands, warm and large, cupped the back of her skull. His lips were barely an inch from hers. He inhaled her startled breath and gave her a slow, wicked smile. Then he took her mouth in an aching kiss.

The ground under her feet seemed to fall away. She grabbed for him, her fingernails digging into his bare shoulders. A guttural sound vibrated in his throat. His hands tightened on either side of her head, holding her still for the invasion of his tongue in her mouth.

A burning finger of lust stroked down her body, touching her breasts, curling into her belly, contracting her womb. A hot wetness gathered on the insides of her thighs.

Her first coherent thought was that this could not be happening. This beautiful man could not possibly want her.

The second was that if it *was* happening, she didn't want it to stop. Instinctively she found herself returning the kiss. She opened her mouth and tangled her tongue with his. He tasted so good, she thought in a daze. Like freedom. Like life. *Why not have him?* she thought recklessly. She'd vowed not to waste a minute that was left to her. Why not let him . . .

Abruptly, he released her and stepped back. Cool desert air rushed between them. It felt like a slap in the face. She stared up at him, her lungs heaving. She was appallingly aware that her knees were on the verge of buckling. She reached backward; her trembling hands found the edge of the stone table.

For several moments, she fought to regain control over her breathing. All the while, his eyes, shadowed and inscrutable, did not leave her face.

At last she pushed free of the prop to stand on her own unsteady legs. The outline of Cade's body silhouetted a faint glow of dawn.

"I . . . I've got to get back."

He held out a hand. "Come to my tent."

She almost said yes. Every muscle, every nerve in her body

urged her to accept his offer. In fact, she'd already begun to lift her hand, to place it in his, when an aura of red light appeared about his head and shoulders.

Her lust evaporated, annihilated by a wave of debilitating fear. She spun away, clutching her midsection, gagging on a surge of bile. Oh God. It was back. Suffocating fear descended, paralyzing every other reality but the one she least wanted to face: death.

"Maddie—"

"No," she choked out. Tears blurred her vision. She held up a hand, as if to ward him off. "No. I can't. I . . . Please. Don't ask me."

"*Caraid*, wait—"

She didn't. She ran.

He didn't follow.

Chapter Five

"So where did that new laborer come from?" Maddie asked Hadara with studied calm the next morning over breakfast. They sat at an outdoor table set up under a shade canopy near the trailer that served as their kitchen. "You know, the hot one with all the tattoos?"

Hadara sipped her coffee and smiled. "The god, you mean?"

Maddie spread more jam on her bread. "Yes. He's not Israeli. In fact, he's Welsh. What's a guy like that doing hauling rocks in the Negev?"

The Israeli woman shrugged. "All I know is that he showed up a few days ago asking for work. I don't think Dr. Ben-Meir asked too many questions. He wants the new site cleared quickly, and that Welshman is strong as an ox." She grinned. "And . . . how do you say it? Eye candy?"

Maddie laughed.

Ari and Gil joined them. Hadara shifted over to make room. Maddie hid a smile. From the sour expression on Ari's face, he'd overheard Hadara's last comment.

"We will open the new area in a few days, I think," he said, pulling up a chair very close to Hadara's. "Then the laborers will be dismissed."

Hadara caught Maddie's eye and smiled. "Perhaps not," she said. "Dr. Ben-Meir may have other tasks for such strong men."

She sent a significant glance across the excavations,

seemingly oblivious to Ari's scowl, though mischief danced in her dark eyes.

Maddie followed Hadara's nod. Sure enough, Cade Leucetius was already at work, his dark head wrapped against the sun. Her body responded, tensing and softening in various places. She couldn't quite remember why she'd run from his unexpected proposition last night. So what if she was seeing weird lights? So what if she was scrawny and nothing great to look at? In a few months she'd be dead. If she could only stop thinking about the end, she might be able to enjoy all that strength and beauty. At least for a little time.

Why not? *Because he frightens me so badly.* She wasn't exactly sure why. She only knew that as strongly as Cade drew her, an instinctive fear tugged her in the opposite direction.

In a few days he'd likely be gone. The thought set her stomach churning. But why should it? He was nothing to her. As for his kiss— In the light of day, the whole episode had taken on the quality of a bizarre dream. The more she thought about it, the more she wondered if it had even happened. Maybe she'd been asleep in her bed the whole time.

Her gaze crept back to him. He had his back to her. An angry red scar angled above his left shoulder blade. A recent injury? It looked like a knife wound. She sucked in a breath. She knew nothing about Cade Leucetius. Nothing. Just what kind of man was he?

He inserted a crowbar beneath a stone and applied force. Muscles rippled. He shifted his grip and half turned, revealing the tattooed dagger on his chest. The jeweled hilt looked real enough to grasp.

Hadara laughed softly. "Still watching our friend, I see."

With some difficulty, Maddie tore her eyes away. Ari and Gil had moved on, leaving her alone with Hadara.

"It's kind of hard not to."

Her roommate inhaled a long drag of her cigarette and

exhaled a stream of smoke on a sigh. "So large! And what muscles he has."

Maddie stirred her cooling coffee and tried to look nonchalant. "If you like that kind of thing."

"If I like? If I like? What, I ask you, is not to like?"

The way I feel when he looks at me, as if I'm something he's about to consume.

Maddie forced a nonchalant laugh. She and Hadara carried their cups—and Ari's and Gil's, damn the lazy males—to the wash station. Hadara left to prepare for the day's excavations, but Maddie lingered by the trailer, her gaze once again drawn, quite against her conscious will, to Cade Leucetius.

He heaved another stone into the wheelbarrow. Her pulse raced. He straightened and looked toward her, as if he'd known all along that she was watching. Which, she realized, he probably had. Their eyes met. Hers, she was sure, showed her chagrin. His were laughing.

Mortified, Maddie spun around. She headed toward the parking lot where the volunteer bus, just arriving, churned up a cloud of fine white dust. It was Day One for this week's crop of American volunteers. The group, mostly teenagers, hailed from a synagogue on Long Island. Their parents had paid a steep program fee for the privilege of having their offspring work Dr. Ben-Meir's dig. Housed for two weeks at a hotel in the nearby village of Mitzpe Ramon, the kids would dig during the day and swim in the hotel pool each evening. Trips to local tourist sites had also been arranged.

This group consisted of a dozen teens and two adult chaperones: a young rabbi and his wife. Fourteen helpers-to-be divided among Maddie and the three grad students. Dr. Ben-Meir himself never claimed a volunteer group. He preferred to visit each team briefly, schmoozing the adults while laying the groundwork for future contributions of time and money.

Introductions were made. The morning was given over to

basic instruction on archeological methods and a lecture on the history of the Negev.

After lunch, Maddie led her group of three teenagers to their assigned area. As luck would have it, the section was on the eastern edge of the site, very close to where Cade was clearing the new quadrant. As she descended the ladder into the shoulder-deep pit, she caught a glimpse of the brawny Welshman in the act of vanquishing yet another boulder.

The rock didn't stand a chance. Maddie was very much afraid she didn't, either.

* * *

Another headache.

A throb sprang up behind Maddie's right eye, a small pain, one she wouldn't have even noticed before her diagnosis, and she tried to blame it on the glare of the desert sun. The brilliant rays spilled past the edge of the shade canopy, striking her in the eye whenever she snuck a glance at Cade.

He must have cleared twice as many rocks as the two Israeli laborers working with him. His bare torso gleamed with sweat. His midnight-sexy voice whispered in her memory. She knew he'd seen her staring. Every time she accidently caught his eye and hastily looked away she could feel his amusement. Still, she couldn't seem to stop her eyes from sliding back to him.

Didn't the man care about sunburn? Skin cancer? No one went shirtless under the desert sun, especially not a fair-skinned Welshman. But the relentless rays didn't seem to faze him. He worked steadily, hardly stopping for a breath or a drink.

The throbbing pressure in her temple increased. Her vision blurred. She took off her glasses, cleaned them on her shirt, and readjusted the sides.

With effort, she refocused her attention on her charges: three boys, ranging in age from thirteen to sixteen. Two of them—Josh and Jake—were brothers. Not twins, but alike enough to keep Maddie guessing. The third boy, Ben, was skinny and awkward.

Armed with trowels and stiff-bristled brushes, the three teens had spent the last few hours diligently scraping layers of dirt and gravel into shallow buckets. At regular intervals, they'd climbed out of the pit to sift the scrapings through a sieve. But Maddie could tell the drudge work was already getting old.

She sighed. It was only Day One. And they were lucky enough to be working in the pit that housed the dig's most exciting find, the rock-lined foundation of an early Canaanite well. Other relics had been unearthed in the pit as well: pottery shards, a charcoal pit, a bronze taper with a chiseled end, a small cache of bronze blades. Nearby, they had discovered an oblong stone Simon was sure was a primitive anvil. Ben-Meir theorized an ancient forge had once been located near the well. He was eager to discover more, to find some proof that the settlement had belonged to the Watchers.

Maddie glanced again in Cade's direction, then muttered a curse and looked away when she realized he and his loaded wheelbarrow were headed in her direction. The path to the rubble pile ran along the edge of Maddie's pit.

She held her breath as he passed, his knees level with her eyes. The snake tattoo winding his left calf was so lifelike, it looked as if it might slide down his leg and slither away. The creature reminded her of the snake she'd shooed out of the hut the night before. She made a mental note to be sure that tonight the door remained firmly closed and latched.

Cade dumped the wheelbarrow's contents. The axle creaked as he retraced his steps. His eyes caught hers as he passed. The subtle flare of his nostrils, and the challenging shift in his stance as he eyed her, caused Maddie's stomach to flip. The reaction was part sexual awareness, part fear. It wasn't a far reach at all to imagine Cade Leucetius as predator, herself as prey.

At the moment, however, Cade's only attack was his slow, wicked grin. A direct hit. Raw desire stabbed downward from her breasts to her womb. Her thighs contracted. Her knees actually wobbled. He tossed her a smug look.

Blue, she realized. His eyes were blue. The most vibrant blue Maddie had ever seen. An absolutely piercing color. Those eyes held her completely captive for five erratic beats of her heart.

Finally, he was past. She jerked her head around, cheeks burning. How humiliating, to have no control over her body's response to a man. How frightening. If she was ever alone with him again . . . Just the thought of it produced a confusing mixture of raw arousal and suffocating terror.

What, exactly, was she afraid of? She couldn't put a finger on it. And she was afraid to examine the feeling too deeply. She just knew that Cade Leucetius disturbed her on some instinctive level. At the same time, she was attracted to him like crazy. Oh, why couldn't the man just vanish?

He would, she reminded herself, in a few days. Or at most a week.

A lot could happen in a week.

The teens, plugged into their iPods, chattered loudly as they worked. Maddie bent her head and concentrated on scraping dirt into her bucket. It was nothing but dust and grit; the largest pebble was the size of a pea. She made a note in her field log and moved a few steps to the right, hoping for more fertile ground.

Her headache made it harder and harder to concentrate. The vise constricting her scalp tightened. The pain was impossible to ignore. She muttered a curse and tore off her glasses. Even before her diagnosis, they'd given her headaches.

Of course. That was the problem. Her glasses. Not the tumor. Please God, not the tumor.

She pressed her fingers to her temples. The throbbing eased. When she opened her eyes, she froze. The entire world had changed.

No. That wasn't right. The world was the same. It was her view of it that had changed. Everything before her—from her hand two inches in front of her face, to the distant rise of the canyon wall—appeared in aggressive, almost unreal detail. As if the world was a 3-D movie playing on a digital high-def screen. It was as if her vision had improved.

Cautiously, she replaced her glasses on her nose. The pain flashed back, stabbing behind her eye. Grimacing, she tore off the eyewear and crammed it into her shirt pocket.

A corner of the pit started to glow. Soft red light spilled from the depths of the ancient well. Maddie glanced toward the three teens working in the opposite corner of the pit. One had started singing loudly off-key to whatever music he was plugged into. The others, groaning, shouted for him to shut up. Even though one of the boys was facing the well, he gave no sign of having seen anything odd.

Maddie inched closer to the well. The team had removed the misshapen boulder that had been lodged in the opening, probably during some ancient earthquake. The rock lay now to one side, revealing a circular hole faced with hand-tooled stone. The dry bottom lay some twelve feet below the level of the excavation pit.

Red light covered the bare, packed earth. The more Maddie stared, trying to puzzle out what it might be, the more light-headed she became. It was as if the hovering radiance had seeped into her eyes and was now trying to lift up the top of her skull. The world faded in and out. The earthen walls and wooden shoring of the excavation pit turned translucent. The banter of the teens became muffled. The black shade canopy over her head somehow took on the aspect of a green, leafy bough.

Her toes were even with the edge of the well now. She peered down into a glistening sheen of water. *Water?* In a dry well? Panic twisted her innards. She stumbled and grabbed for the shoring crossbeam. She missed. And then she was falling, falling . . .

She flung out her arms—

"Ms. Durant?" A hand grasped her elbow. "Is something wrong?"

She looked up, dazed, to find herself crouching on the ground. The older of the identical brothers—Josh?—was frowning down at her. The two other boys crowded behind, their young faces troubled. All three bore traces of white light about their heads and shoulders.

She blinked and rubbed her eyes.

"Are you okay, Ms. Durant?" Josh asked.

She drew a deep breath. Thankfully, this time the strange auras around the boys disappeared. The excavation pit was as it had been. For one disoriented moment, all she could think was how oddly normal everything looked. Flat. Two-dimensional. Heartbreakingly dismal.

The well was dark.

"Ms. Durant?"

She inhaled and pushed to her feet, cheeks flooding with heat. She was the adult here.

Breaking contact with Josh's supporting hand, she forced a laugh and reached for her canteen. "Sorry. Got a little lightheaded all of a sudden. I haven't been drinking enough water." She lifted the canteen for emphasis. "Let that be a lesson to all of you. It's very easy to get dehydrated here in the desert and not even realize it until you're ready to fall over. You have to drink before you get thirsty. Everyone have their water bottles? Good. We'll all take a drink and get back to work."

The teenagers dutifully guzzled mouthfuls of water and returned to their scraping. Maddie gripped her own trowel and struggled to collect herself. Thankfully, the visual disturbances—the glowing and the weird 3-D movie effect—didn't return.

Unless her suddenly 20-20 vision qualified as a visual disturbance. Though her glasses remained in her pocket, she could see better than she ever had. Weird. Really weird.

She tipped her head back. Her eyes collided with Cade Leucetius's intense blue gaze. How long had he been standing there, not ten feet from the edge of the pit, looking down at her? Had he witnessed her dizzy spell? For some reason, the thought that he'd seen her so vulnerable scared her.

She frowned. Then, without waiting for his reaction, she turned her back. She assumed what she hoped was a casual demeanor and stepped over to supervise the teens.

"Find anything interesting?"

"Not a darn thing." Jake sighed, wiping his forehead with his sleeve. "Just dirt and more dirt. You know, Ms. Durant, I thought archeology would be fun. But this is really kind of boring."

"*Kind of* boring?" Ben groaned. "More like totally boring."

"Yeah," Josh said. "And just think, we've got two more weeks of this. I can't wait to get to the pool."

Maddie laughed. "You'll have time to swim tonight. Just remember, though, you can swim at home. You can't dig up five-thousand-year-old history in your backyard. This dig is something you'll remember the rest of your life."

Ben had the grace to look sheepish. "I guess it won't be so bad if we find something." The other boys muttered in agreement.

"Looks like you guys have about had it for your first day." She consulted her watch. "Tell you what. It's almost five. The bus'll be here at six. Want to pack it in early and get some sodas from the cooler?"

"Are you kidding?" A general stampede for the ladder ensued.

"Be sure to clean off your tools and stow them in the tool hut," Maddie called after them, amused. Despite her pep talk, she didn't begrudge the kids a bit of whining. Archeology was 99.9 percent brain-numbing boredom.

She scraped a damp curl off her forehead. She really should follow to make sure the boys' tools were cleaned and put away correctly. But when she turned to collect her own tools, she froze.

The light was back. It glowed—*pulsed*, actually—a brilliant, otherworldly red. And . . . it wanted her to approach.

An absurd thought but true. How or why she knew that, she couldn't say. But her obedience was immediate. Before she could even form her next thought, she found herself stepping toward it.

A blast of hot wind rushed her face. Pain stabbed behind her eyes. The pit, the shade canopy, the desert beyond—all bubbled like boiling water. Burning sand peppered her skin. Wood smoke, acrid and pungent, seared her nostrils, and reality transformed . . .

Azazel taught Man to make swords, knives, shields, and breastplates. He taught the fabrication of mirrors, the workmanship of bracelets and ornaments, the use of cosmetics, the beautifying of the eyebrows. He taught the use of stones of every valuable and select kind, and of all sorts of dyes, so that the world became altered.

Azazel has taught every type of iniquity upon earth. He has disclosed to the world all the secrets of the heavens. The whole earth has been corrupted through his works.

To Azazel, ascribe all sin.

—from the Book of Enoch

Chapter Six

She lingered by the well, watching.

He was the tallest, strongest, most handsome man of the tribe. Their chieftain. His power was vast. He had risen to rule over all his brothers. And she was his daughter—how proud she was! She filled her jar with sweet, cool water, dipped from a well that never went dry, even during the long summers when the rains stayed away and the rivers turned to dust. All the while she gazed at him from beneath down-swept lashes.

He worked a new blade. Sparks flew as he scraped the shining bronze along the face of the whetstone. Pausing in his labor, he lifted the sword and sighted its length. Something tightened in her chest when he pressed his bare thumb to the weapon's cutting edge.

He was her father. He was also a stranger.

He had never spoken a word to her. She had never sought his attention; she had never dared. As far back as she could remember, her mother, Zariel, had not been counted among his favored concubines. Her mother no longer went to him alone, only as attendant to younger, more beautiful women.

How bitterly she wished for her father's acknowledgment! If only she could claim just a fragment of the time he lavished on her half brothers. Her father took pains to teach each of his sons the arts of weapon-craft and war. Ezreth, the elder, was the favorite. To his first-born son he taught the secrets of magic, the secrets of Heaven. To his first-born daughter he taught nothing.

Tears stung her eyes. One dropped from her cheek into the clear water in her jug. With shaking hands, she raised the vessel to her head and stood. It was not fair. He was her father as well as Ezreth's. If she had been a man, she would have been Ezreth's equal! She shared their father's angelic nature. And his magic. Yes, that, too. She had always known it. The wings of Heaven beat inside her chest, but she did not know how to set them free.

She lifted her chin, steadying the heavy jug atop her head with one raised hand. Today, she vowed, her father would look into her eyes. Today he would see her.

Steadily she approached him, halting but a few steps away. She said nothing; the strange courage that gripped her did not extend quite so far as that. To speak first to her tribe's chieftain would be an unforgivable insult.

He was bent to the task of sharpening his sword. His power, a beautiful red swirl, surrounded his dark head and shoulders. He was aware of her presence, surely. But he did not look up. The urge to flee came upon her. She stayed.

She stayed but trembled. Her father exchanged his whetstone for an oiled rag. This he dragged over the new blade again and again. The bronze shone. It deflected a ray of sunlight into her eyes. She blinked against a tear. The blade might as well have plunged into her heart, so sharp was her yearning at that moment.

Look at me.

Her father put the sword aside and raised his eyes. She stared into those dark irises for what seemed like forever, far longer than the point in time when she should have dropped her gaze.

Silent, he studied her. And then he spoke.

"You are one of mine."

Joy blossomed. He knew her!

She trembled. "Yes, Father."

"What is your name, little one?"

"Lilith," she said.

His gaze swept her from head to toe. "Why have you come to me?"

She lowered the water jug from her head and placed it on the ground between them. "The sun is hot. You have labored long. I have brought you fresh water. Will you drink?"

He nodded. She found a cup among his tools. She dipped it into the water with shaking hands. He accepted the meager offering and raised it to his lips. She watched his throat move as he drank.

"My thanks, Lilith." A faint smile curved his lips when he had finished. "Daughter."

Daughter.

With that single word, he made her love him.

* * *

Daughter.

The word spun in Maddie's head. Slashed at her heart.

Daughter.

Her eyes flew open. At the same instant, the ground rolled under her feet. Her knees buckled. Her balance toppled. The ground rushed upward.

A low curse came from somewhere above and behind her. A heavy thud shook the ground. Arms—strong, masculine arms—caught her, enfolding her tightly from behind.

Bare skin touching bare skin. Electricity zinged at the connection. A giddy sensation of relief swirled through her veins like a drug. Safe. She was safe.

"Madeline."

His voice was low, urgent. Why? What was wrong? Wasn't she exactly where she was supposed to be? She pressed her spine into his warmth, her head resting against his chest. Again, she had the sensation she was falling. This time she didn't panic. He was here. He'd protect her.

"Maddie," she murmured, correcting him without opening her eyes.

"What?"

"It's Maddie. Not Madeline. I hate when people call me that."

"Maddie, then." Amusement softened his worried tone. He turned her body slightly in the circle of his embrace. She spread her hand on his chest and nestled her cheek beside it. His heart beat steadily under her ear. His ribs expanded as he drew breath.

Cade. She was with *Cade*.

He sat on the ground, his back supported by the wall of the pit. She was in his lap, his arms wrapped around her like a blanket. One of his big hands cupped her head, holding it against his chest. The other rubbed delicious circles on her back.

"Maddie," he murmured.

A surreal yearning floated down on her like stardust. His scent—earthy, virile, exciting—surrounded her. She felt something inside her give way.

"You smell good." She inhaled deeply and nuzzled his chest. "You feel good, too."

"Do I?" He chuckled. "That's tidy, then. You feel good, too."

The fog of the waking dream was fading. Lucidity was creeping up on her. Desperately, she held it at bay. In another few seconds, she knew, she was going to be horrified. But right now . . .

"I'm scared," she whispered, her lips touching his chest. "Terrified."

"Of what, *caraid*?"

Of you, she wanted to say.

"Of . . . of dying," she said instead.

It was a huge confession. In the year since her diagnosis, she'd never once voiced her fear. She'd been defiant. Optimistic. It wasn't in her nature to give up. Even when her last hope faded, she'd been practical. Everyone dies, she'd told herself. Her father and mother were both dead. It was inevitable. There was no point being afraid. No need to burden everyone around her with her angst.

I'm scared. What huge relief to say the words at last.

"I know, *caraid*." He smoothed the curls from her forehead. "I know you're frightened. But I'm here now. It'll be all right. Just rest a moment."

It'll be all right. The words tempted, like an apple that was ripe and shining on the surface but rotten underneath. She blinked back sudden tears of anger. How *dare* he mouth platitudes to her? How stupid of her to want so badly to believe him.

The anger wasn't rational; she knew that. Cade didn't know about her cancer or her death sentence. She couldn't stop the burst of resentment that sent her elbow hard into his midsection, though.

He grunted. She struggled to climb from his lap. He resisted her pitiful attempt at escape, his arms banding around her like steel.

"Let me go!"

She tried to get leverage, wriggling and shoving. Then she froze. His erection was pressed against her butt. Her body responded with a flood of moist, yielding desire.

She experienced a fresh surge of panic. Dear God, she had to get away! She renewed her struggle with a vengeance. She struck out, punching and kicking whatever part of his body she could reach. One solid arm encircled her midsection, trapping her arms while pressing her more firmly into his hard-on. His hand covered her mouth just as her chest heaved, drawing enough air to scream.

The restraint infuriated her. It was also maddeningly erotic. The more she struggled to free herself, the harder he got and the more her body softened to his restraint. The more she felt herself open to him. Damn the man! It was as if he'd cast some kind of spell over her.

She managed to free one hand to shove against his chest. Her butt wiggled. His erection jerked and throbbed under the pressure. His jaw went rigid; his nostrils flared. Air hissed through his teeth. A low growl rumbled in his throat. Their eyes locked.

Raw carnal knowledge arced between them. Maddie knew then—*knew*, without a doubt—that this powerful, aroused male was one heartbeat away from ripping off her shorts and plunging himself into her body. Worse, she was half a heartbeat from begging him to do it.

What the hell was happening?

"No," she gasped. "No. We can't do this. Not here. Not ever." The thought of surrendering to this man terrified her on some deep, primitive level. "Let me go."

"Maddie." His voice was hoarse. "You don't understand—"

"I don't care. I can't do this. I won't. Let me go. *Please.*"

A brief hesitation, then his arms fell away.

She scrambled to her feet. Or at least, she tried to. The disorientation left over from the waking dream hadn't completely disappeared. She stumbled.

Cade, already on his feet, caught her. "Careful, *caraid*."

She jerked away, steadying herself on the pit's shoring instead. Her canteen rested on a nearby ledge. She snatched it up as if it were a lifeline. She drank with shaking hands as Cade stood silent behind her.

Not turning, she forced herself to speak as if nothing disturbing had happened.

"Thanks for catching me. When I . . . I fainted. I don't know what happened. Heatstroke, maybe."

"No. Your skin is cold," he said.

And her hands felt like ice. "Dehydration, then. I haven't been drinking enough water."

"I doubt that had anything to do with it." His tone was grim. "It's this place. It's cursed."

She could almost believe it was true.

"Come on, then," he said. "You need to get out of this pit."

"That's . . . that's probably a good idea."

She was thankful he didn't try to touch her as she climbed the ladder, though he hovered close behind. Once she stepped away from the edge of the pit she felt much better. Until she made the mistake of looking down. The well was awash with red light.

Something's there. Something real. She wanted so badly to believe it, even though she knew there was nothing in the well but sand and stone. The source of the glow was not in the ground but in her brain. In the cancer growing behind her left eye.

Without a glance at Cade, she turned and fled.

* * *

Bloody hell. Cade had no experience with transition—other than his own, of course.

He'd begun his transformation after a knife fight had left him all but dead. Like Maddie, he'd been unaware. He'd thought himself fully human. He'd had no idea what was happening to him, what his body was preparing for. And then the first wave of his crisis broke.

He grimaced and blanked the memory from his mind. Even now, more than a year later, he avoided thoughts of that night. The emotions tangled up with it—a mélange of desperation, pain, and fear—were just too powerful. There had been pleasure, too, of course. Incredible, searing bliss. There had been the heat of Cybele's body. Her lush breasts, her hands, her mouth. The wet sound of his cock working inside her.

He'd fought his bonds like a madman. He'd been desperate to touch Cybele on his own terms, to bend her to his will. He'd been forced to surrender to hers. His wrists still bore the scars of his frenzy.

Every adept of Clan Samyaza had endured a similar transition. Each of the others, however, had grown up aware of what was to come with maturity. Each of the others had actually sought the brush with death that triggered his or her change.

Cade had believed he was human. Then he'd been flung from the precipice of death toward something far more terrifying. It would be the same for Maddie, and Cade wasn't at all confident of his ability to guide her through the experience.

He knew next to nothing about the role of anchor. Due to the imbalance in the ratio of males to females in Watcher society, few Watcher men were required to act as anchors. As far as Cade knew, of the surviving male members of Clan Samyaza, only Artur had ever performed the role. For Cybele.

Morgana—mature, wise, beautiful Morgana, slaughtered by DAMNers—had anchored Brax, Lucas, Niall, and even Artur himself. Cybele had anchored Cade. She'd been as inexperienced then as Cade was now.

She'd acted solely on instinct. Cade didn't fully trust his instincts. He wanted a plan. He wanted objectivity. He had neither.

When he thought of the coming days—when he imagined what Maddie would endure—pity warred with lust. His mind balked, even as his body hardened in anticipation. The Watcher pheromones her body was throwing in his direction made it impossible to think clearly. Impossible to set a course, to anticipate obstacles. There was really very little he could do to prepare Maddie for her crisis. He could hardly describe it to her. If she knew what was going to happen, she'd be paralyzed with terror.

She was well acquainted with fear, he imagined. She thought she was dying of cancer. Most likely she wondered, as all humans did, what the afterlife would be like. She had no idea that for her, as for all Nephilim, there was no life beyond this earthly one. After death came Oblivion.

Cade wondered what Maddie would choose if she were free to do so. Would she endure the crisis for the chance to live out a cursed Nephilim life? Or would she escape that fate by flinging herself into immediate, eternal nothingness? Which would *Cade* have chosen?

He thought she'd choose life. He sensed she was a fighter. She'd certainly battled her cancer like a warrior. But, it was a moot point. From the moment Cybele found him in that alley—shuddering, raving, half-mad—she'd taken control of his body and his life essence. She'd birthed his demon nature, as Cade would birth Maddie's.

But, not here. Not atop the very soil upon which Samyaza, Azazel, their brother Watchers, and so many of their first-generation Nephilim offspring had met their doom. Cade would not anchor Maddie in the very place where his defiant ancestors had forfeited their souls.

It troubled him more than he liked to admit that Maddie had collapsed in the pit this afternoon. Could her transition have caused the episode? An awakening dormant was subject to bursts of intense energy alternating with periods of intense fatigue. But somehow Cade didn't think Maddie's fainting spell was related to her impending crisis.

Her weakness had been caused by this land; he was sure of it. Incredibly, the stench of the Watchers' curse still clung to the desert rocks, even if five millennia had passed since the archangel Raphael delivered it. The odor festered in Cade's nostrils, a foul brown burning that coalesced in the back of his throat.

He needed to get away. He needed to get *Maddie* away. Quickly. Because if her crisis broke in this cursed place, only God himself would be able to save her.

God, Cade knew, wouldn't bother.

Chapter Seven

Lolo National Forest, Montana

He hadn't eaten in seventeen days.

The hawk's sharp cry preceded its earthward streak. A flurry of feathers and fur, a panicked squeal, a rustle of dry grass—then the kill was over, the raptor rising with its victim limp in its claws.

Lucas Herne watched the bird glide across the valley. He was that hawk. That killer.

The sudden disturbance over, the land around him calmed. Protective silence gave way to birdcalls, to movement in the grass, to the buzz of insects. Far from dulling his mind, his long fast had only sharpened his senses. Colors seemed brighter, sounds clearer. His dark blond hair, which he wore loose, lifted in the breeze, sending a tingle over his skin. His existence was alive with form and sensation; his world was vivid in a way it had never been. It was as if he were touching and seeing nature's soul rather than its substance. If only he could be certain what he sensed was real and not a fabrication of his mind.

He cocked his head, listening. He could hear the beat of his heart, the blood rushing in his veins. And with it all, the she-wolf's call. Closer than it had ever been.

His body tensed with anticipation. He'd been waiting for . . . how long? Hours? Days? A week? Impossible to tell; time had lost all meaning.

He'd been waiting his entire life, it seemed, but when the

animal finally appeared, he didn't even see its approach. He didn't recognize it until it stood before him. Her fur was a deep, dark cinnamon, shining with health and beauty. He reached out a hand and, trembling, touched one soft ear.

She shied away; he let his hand fall. A wash of shimmering light illuminated the beast. Reflexively, he shielded his eyes until the radiance passed. Upon lowering his arms, he beheld not a wolf but a woman.

She was past middle age, he could tell. Her eyes held wisdom if her red-brown skin remained unwrinkled and not a single strand of silver marred her arrow-straight black hair. When her lips parted, her speech was as strong and as delicate as the wind in the trees.

"You are a stranger to this place," she said. "Why have you come?"

"For guidance."

She frowned. "I guide only the living."

"I am alive."

She shook her head. "You breathe, Nephilim, but you are not truly alive. You are a demon."

"Yes. But I am a man as well."

"You have no soul," she replied. "And you are a killer."

"As is the hawk."

"The hawk kills for survival. You do not."

"I kill hellfiends."

"And the humans they inhabit."

Lucas shrugged. "Their souls are doomed anyway."

Her eyes seemed to look right through him. "Then perhaps you are fortunate you do not possess one."

"Am I?" Luc gave a harsh laugh. He growled, "Human hosts are doomed by their own weakness, their welcome of the evil creature that seeks to use their souls. We Nephilim are cursed by the sins of our fathers. Is this just?"

"Just? Is the killing of the mouse by the hawk 'just'? The

notion of justice is a human invention. It does not come from the Creator. Nature seeks harmony. That is not at all the same thing."

"Harmony also eludes the Nephilim."

The woman frowned. "That is true enough. What do you want of me?"

"A soul. Harmony with the Creator."

Her eyes, wolflike, seemed to widen. "I do not know if such a thing is possible. I do not know if the curse you bear can be reversed."

"Nature is closer to the Creator than any human being. I believe you can help me."

She tilted her head to one side. "It would be an interesting endeavor. But are you worthy of my aid?"

"I am willing to do whatever is necessary."

"Willing, yes. But able? That is the real question."

"I can but try."

She fell silent, her black eyes turning inward. "I sense your desire. It is pure. But you are burdened by hatred and pride. You lust after vengeance. You cannot achieve harmony while carrying these burdens. Can you put them aside?"

It was Luc's turn to look inward. He sensed a glib answer, or an eager one, would drive away the guardian spirit he'd struggled so hard to summon.

"I don't know," he said.

"Neither do I know if I can help you. But I will try."

He bowed his head. "That's all I ask."

* * *

"Cybele?"

Cybele turned from the bedroom window, glad for the interruption. She missed the countryside. Missed Glastonbury. She hated London. She despised the dirty streets, the fog, the crowds that wouldn't let her breathe. She especially loathed Artur's flat, with its dingy furnishings and endless clutter. How could he stand it?

"Gareth," she said. "Come in."

Had she been glad for the interruption? Forget that. One look into Gareth's wary eyes had her dreading the encounter. She wished she'd locked the door and shouted at him to stay away.

She closed her eyes briefly, wishing she could hide as easily. But there really was no avoiding this, was there? If she were honest with herself, she'd admit that she'd been expecting it.

He entered. For a moment she thought he might sit on the bed. He passed it by, in favor of making his stand in the center of the room.

His youthful face was flushed. The color clashed oddly with his cropped ginger hair and expressive, sky blue eyes. Whipcord-lean, he wore a black T-shirt and jeans with the knees ripped out. The scar on his left cheek, a reminder of the massacre, made him look older than his years. His forearms, dusted with pale hair, were surprisingly muscled. She'd never noticed that before.

He seemed to want her to speak first. She leaned against the window frame and said nothing. Finally, he ran a hand over his head and got to the point.

"You know why I've come."

"Do I?"

His cheeks flushed even redder. Her lips tightened. She wasn't going to make this easy on him. If he couldn't face this small embarrassment, how in hell did he think he could face the rest of it?

He drew breath. "I turned twenty last autumn. I'm old enough. I know it's the custom to wait longer, but with all that's happened . . . the clan needs every warrior. I have to act now. And you—"

"Even if I agree, it might not work. You could die."

"Cade didn't die."

Cade. Her closest friend since Artur had rejected her. She missed him terribly. Almost as much as she missed the man Artur had been before she'd laid eyes on Cade.

"That was different," she said. "Cade was an unaware dormant. He didn't go looking for his brush with death. It found him. If I'd come across him even an hour later, he would've been lost to Oblivion. I didn't want to anchor him. I did it because I had no choice."

"There's no choice now," Gareth said earnestly. "Vaclav Dusek has made sure of it. Cybele, I want to perform the death-seeking. I need to. You're the only one who can save me afterward."

"There'll be another possibility," she said. "When Cade returns."

"Blast it. A slave woman as anchor?" Gareth's expression twisted. "With Cade a part of it, too? As her master? I'd rather face Oblivion."

Cybele didn't doubt he meant it. The thought of a three-way transition with a slave turned her stomach, too.

Gareth came to stand before her at the window. He placed a hand on her forearm. "It has to be you, Cybele. You know it as well as I do. Will you do it?"

She tipped her head until the back of her skull tapped the window glass. She often forgot how tall Gareth was. How much raw energy poured off him. He might be young, a full four years younger than she, but he was of age. Undeniably a man. An unwilling pulse of interest kindled in her belly.

She exhaled. "Your death-seeking would be hell. For both of us. There's no guarantee you'll survive, even with my help."

It was a tricky thing, getting close enough to death to trigger transition without actually killing yourself in the process.

"I'll survive," Gareth said.

"I don't want you to even try! And anyway, this whole discussion is pointless. Artur would never allow you a death-seeking. Not with me as your anchor."

Was that pity that sprang into Gareth's eyes? Cybele felt suddenly ill. She closed her eyes against the rush of hurt she knew was coming.

"I already spoke with Artur," Gareth said, "before I came to you. In fact, that's why I'm here. He sent me to you."

* * *

He'd drank his fill of the water she had offered. He had called her Daughter. She had called him Father. He had not dismissed her.

Lilith stood, uncertain, as he turned back to his workbench. He lifted his new sword and ran one long finger down the edge of the blade. She could not look away.

He resumed his work, polishing the weapon. He drew a supple leather rag down the length of the blade, over and over, inspecting the shine after each pass. His touch was gentle, loving. How she yearned for just a fraction of that care!

How long she stood beside him, watching, her errand of water-drawing forgotten, she could not say. Her father was well aware of her continued presence. And yet, he did not command her out of his sight.

She would never grow tired of watching him. His Watcher aura was so strong. So beautiful. It framed his head and shoulders in pure crimson light. His hands were large and graceful. He stroked the cloth from the sword's hilt to its tip. The bronze gleamed as if lit from within.

Lilith found that if she stood very still, she could sense his celestial magic—powerful, glorious!—flowing into the earthly metal. When she blurred her vision, unfocused her mind, she could even see it. Feel it. A tingle of red. A sparkle on the blade. A sensation like a feather brushing her bare skin.

Her father raised his head. His dark eyes narrowed. She stared at him with wide eyes and open heart.

He put the cloth aside. Rising, he sheathed the polished sword in a newly made scabbard. He hung it on the rack with the others, then turned to face her. His gaze traveled the length of her body, from her headscarf to her sandals.

Spine straight, chin raised, she stood very still under his scrutiny. Excitement and fear beat inside her ribs with the wings of a trapped swallow.

"You wish to tell me, Daughter, of your magic."

Her throat closed. Her reply was nearly lost. "Yes."

He held out a hand. "Come."

* * *

This was crazy. For the second night in a row, Maddie found herself slipping out of the hut alone.

Hadara was asleep. A similar peacefulness eluded Maddie. She wanted to sit up and scream. How in the hell could she sleep with Cade's kiss playing over and over in her mind? All she could think of was him catching her as she fell, him cradling her in his arms. The lingering sensation of his erection—as huge as the rest of him—throbbed in the cleft of her buttocks. And so, for the second night running, she found herself alone under a star-studded desert sky.

This time she didn't wander away from the camp. Driven by an obsession she hardly understood, armed with flashlight, trowel, and bucket pilfered from the storage trailer, she headed to the dig.

Heart pounding, she climbed down the ladder into the pit where she'd fainted. Her torch cast an arching glow on the earthen walls. Strange ruby shadows lurched in the spaces between the shoring.

The red, pulsing light pouring from the ancient well

was utterly undeniable. Blinking didn't erase it. Neither did rubbing her eyes. She moved her head from side to side. The light didn't waver. It was definitely *there*. Not in her head.

The illumination was so strong, she switched off her flashlight and laid it on the ground. An eerie feeling of being separate from the mortal world overtook her. The earthen walls of the pit muted the sounds from the desert above. The only noise she could discern was a rhythmic, leaden thumping. Her heart.

She placed her palm over her chest, as if the gesture could calm the organ. It did not. She approached the well slowly. The light shone from the bottom, too far to jump. Not daring to stop and think about what she was about to do, she grabbed the ladder she'd just descended, dragged it over to the hole, and lowered it over the edge.

Bucket and tools looped over one arm, she eased herself over the ledge and down the ladder. Quickly she descended. And as she stepped off the bottom rung, she saw that a hazy red fog seeped up from between the grains of dust and grit under her feet.

Something was buried here. It had to be. Crouching, she began to trowel dirt into her bucket. Light filled the hole like a red puddle. She shoved away thoughts of blood and kept digging.

The excavated dirt was warmer than the earth that surrounded it. That was exceedingly odd, but Maddie didn't stop to consider. Sweat beaded on her forehead and dribbled between her breasts as she dug deeper.

The tip of her trowel glanced off a rock. Her hand slipped.

"Ow!"

She'd torn a fingernail on the edge of the digging blade. A drop of blood welled from the jagged rip. The broken chunk of nail hung from a sliver of cuticle. She brought her finger to her teeth and bit it off.

As she sucked at the wound, she scrutinized the hole about eight inches in diameter and probably twice as deep. Warm red light filled it, pulsing like a beating heart. A bead of blood formed on her ripped cuticle and trickled down the side of her finger. It dripped from her flesh into the hole.

"*My God.*" Was it her imagination, or had there been a flash of gold?

On her hands and knees, she bent low to peer into the hole. Something was there. A golden circle. The source of the light?

Heart pounding, she reached into the void.

Chapter Eight

The blighter throwing darts was host to a hellfiend.

His mates didn't know it, of course. A bearded man threw opposite the possessed man, unaware his friend's body was no longer his own. Two other blokes stood to one side, swilling ale and offering advice and jeers. To an untrained human eye, they were four working men spending a friendly evening at the pub.

Not a single DAMNer in sight to set things straight. Just Artur, his magic shielded behind a Druid glamour too complex for a hellfiend to comprehend.

Artur drained his whiskey. Poor human bastards. They'd be dead by dawn, the lot of them. Unless he interfered. Which would be messy.

But it might also be entertaining. Truth be told, he was tempted. A bit of action might keep his mind off . . . the other thing.

Under cover of the scarred tabletop, he eased out his modified Glock, which shot both mundane and magical projectiles. Annihilating a hellfiend was always a challenge. Sometimes, depending on how deeply the fiend's possession had taken hold, the human life was already doomed and the host died once the demon inside was gone. Other times, the host's soul was still alive and fighting its possession. In that case, if the demon could be driven out, the human life could be preserved.

Then there were times like these. When one had to put aside one's scruples in order to serve the greater good.

Artur slid his left index finger into place on the trigger. This was when the real fun began.

“So here you are.”

Every muscle in his body went rigid—along with something else between his legs. Bloody hell. He hadn’t seen her enter the pub, hadn’t so much as caught a whiff of her perfume. He peered into his empty glass. He must be rat-arsed indeed.

Quickly, with a glance at the hellfiend across the room, he expanded his glamour to include Cybele. She skirted the table and came into his vision, all lush breasts, round hips, and long, long legs. Her loose hair streamed down her back in a riot of unruly blonde curls. She might have been poured into that tee and those denims.

He stared broodingly at the glimpse of tattoo—a single rose on a thorned stem—peeping from the edge of her scooped neckline. His mood, already dark, blackened. The woman was a carnal invitation to the entire male gender. A glance about the pub showed any number of human males glancing her way, primed to accept.

He itched to kill every last one of the rotters, just for daring to look at her. It was a wonder his pint glass didn’t crack, his grip was so tight. Emotions seethed in his gut like a swarm of vipers.

When at last he looked up at her, his expression showed nothing but disdain. Her lips thinned. He willed her to turn and leave, which would keep things simple, he told himself. He liked things simple. Right.

She slipped into the empty seat across the table.

“Blast it, Artur. What are you doing in this dive?”

His cock twitched at the sound of her husky Texas drawl, and he raised an eyebrow. “I could ask the same of you. I’d have thought you’d be spending the night quietly at home, watching Gareth kill himself.”

Anger hissed through her teeth. "You bastard. Why did you put him up to this?"

She was so beautiful, he ached. "Why shouldn't I? So you won't have to deal with it?"

She flushed scarlet. "He's too young. He'll suffer. Horribly."

"Gareth's of age and perfectly capable. As an adept, he'll be a valuable asset to the clan. We need him."

"You could have put him off until we see what magic Cade brings back. There's no need for Gareth to risk a death-seeking so soon."

He regarded her steadily, not really hearing her words. His gaze was focused on the movement of her mouth. There was only one place he wanted those plump red lips, and it wasn't across a table, bitching at him.

"Are you listening to me?"

"It's Gareth's right to choose. It's your right to refuse." Under the table, the rough grip of the Glock was a comfort to his palm.

"Damn you, Artur. Just . . . damn you."

"A bit redundant, that, wouldn't you say? Come on, Cybele. Gareth's a fine male—but if he's not up to your standards, simply tell him no."

"It would serve you right if I told him yes."

Artur leaned back in his chair and forced a laugh. In truth, he wanted to punch something.

"If I refuse Gareth," Cybele continued through gritted teeth, "I challenge your approval and shame you before the clan. You'd be forced to kill me or lose the chieftaincy. If I anchor him, you've got an excuse to hate me even more than you already do. As usual, you've manipulated the situation to punish me. There's no honorable way I can escape your trap."

Artur tilted his glass and looked down into the dying froth. "Sometimes dishonor is the only choice."

She shoved to her feet. "Forget it, Artur. Forget I even came here to try to reason with you." Her loose hair swung forward as she rounded the chair. An emotion very near to panic squeezed Artur's chest as she turned and began to walk away.

"Cybele," he said. "Wait."

She stopped in her tracks, her hands fisted at her sides. Several seconds passed before she turned.

"I suppose you want my decision. Well, I—"

"No. Not that." Artur's eyes cut to the dart game. "Over there. Bloke in blue. Next up to throw. What do you make of him?"

Cybele's confused gaze followed his. An instant later, she sucked in a breath. "Possessed."

"Help me kill him," he said.

She huffed out a laugh. "As if you need my help! And anyway, that poor human host's eyes are still his natural color. Not a trace of demon red. What he needs is an exorcist, not a hole in his chest."

"And his three friends? What do they need? Look closely before you answer."

She turned back to the dart game, brows furrowed. He saw the exact moment the truth hit her. It amazed him, sometimes, how no one else seemed to see these things as clearly as he could.

"Shit," she said. "They're already marked. Three of them!" She bit her lip. "That fiend must be very ancient to have managed that."

Artur smiled. It was unusual to find a fiend old enough to mark two humans simultaneously, let alone four. This one would be a pleasure to annihilate.

"Exactly," he replied. "It would be impossible to destroy such an ancient without killing its host. Not when it's got three potential hosts ready and waiting."

He could shoot with magic only, preserving the human

host's life, but the fiend inside, with three backup host souls already marked, would have plenty of time to dive into one of them. And the mark on the first host couldn't be erased without the assistance of a trained exorcist. As long as the four humans remained alive and marked, the fiend could pop back and forth between them indefinitely.

"Have you got a weapon on you?" he asked.

"No," Cybele replied.

"I thought not. So. With only one weapon between the two of us, any fight we undertake that tried to preserve the host's life would be a messy proposition. Not at all healthy for bystanders, I'd say. And ultimately a failed effort." He paused. "But if I shot to kill the human . . ."

Cybele sighed. "The fiend would be trapped in the dying body long enough for you to annihilate it as well."

He grinned. "High marks for that conclusion. So . . . a decision. Kill one human? One who's probably on his way to Hell anyway? I've been watching him. Or should we allow an ancient hellfiend to go on its merry way, strewing the blood of innocents in its wake?"

Cybele's white teeth caught her plump bottom lip. Artur felt the bite straight down to his groin.

Finally, she shook her head. "Blast it, Artur. I hate this."

"You think I enjoy it?"

Her green eyes flashed. "Frankly? Yes."

His jaw clenched. "You didn't used to think the worst of me."

"You didn't used to try so hard to make me hate you. And why? Because I saved Cade's life."

He hissed. "You broke our bond, Cybele. I didn't."

"What I destroyed was your pride. I exchanged it for Cade's life. I thought it a fair trade at the time. I still do."

"You might have summoned Morgana. It was her duty, her right to act as anchor. Not yours."

"I didn't think there was time! Cade was already half-mad when I found him. I . . . I was sure he'd die."

"He wouldn't have. Not if you'd gone straight to Morgana."

"I didn't know that. I didn't think. I—" She shoved a hand through her hair and abruptly laughed. "Oh, no. I'm not doing this again. We've had this argument more times than I can bear. There's no apology I can make that will satisfy you."

"I don't remember you making any apology."

"And I won't." The heat of her anger had raised the color in her cheeks. "I'm not sorry. I did what I believed was necessary. I'd do it again in a heartbeat."

Everything she'd said was true. Artur, when beset by a rare objective moment, recognized himself as the villain of the piece. There was no way he could be absolutely certain Morgana would have reached Cade in time. Cybele hadn't wanted to betray him.

But, she had. And there was nothing he could do to change that fact. Cybele, his bonded mate, had fucked another Watcher. She might speak of apologies, but Watchers—*Nephilim*—were not known for their loving, forgiving natures.

Avoiding Cybele's eyes, Artur studied the possessed man. The dart game was over. The hellfiend and its host's mates had sat down at a table, fresh drinks in hand.

"Looks like their night's just getting started," he commented. Draping his arm over the back of his chair, he nodded to the seat opposite. After a brief hesitation, Cybele sat.

Artur signaled for a couple pints. The plump and pretty barmaid—Janey, he thought her name was—brought them quickly. She brushed Artur's arm with her breast as she set the glass before him.

"Thanks, love." He cupped her round arse and squeezed. She giggled and ran a lascivious hand along his shoulder.

"For you, Artur? Anytime."

The contemptuous flash in Cybele's eyes was supremely gratifying. "One of your human sluts?" she asked when the woman was gone.

He grinned. "Jealous?"

"Hardly. It's beneath you, is all. Crawling from pub to pub. Pickling your brain. Screwing whatever catches your eye."

"I have a duty to beget children for the clan," he said.

She snorted. "Give me a break. You didn't give human women a second look when we were bonded."

"Ah, so that's it, eh? You'd prefer I drag along after you, like Cade does."

"You're an ass, Artur. You know very well that Cade and I didn't continue our . . . physical relationship after his transition."

"He wanted to. Still does. Perhaps you should have him. Sex might improve your mood. Celibacy is hell for a Watcher."

A muscle jumped in her cheek. "I doubt you would know. When was the last time you went a night without?"

"Humans," he said dismissively.

"That's not the point! You're our chieftain. You're better than this."

But he wasn't better. Didn't she know that by now? The thought brought a wave of something perilously close to despair. Suddenly, he wanted nothing more than to have this war with her stop.

Closing his eyes, he passed a hand over his face. "I assure you, Cybele, I'm not better than this. In fact, I'm far worse. What do you want me to do? Change the past? Forget our broken bond?"

She stared at her untouched ale. "I . . . I don't know. I just want . . ."

Long seconds ticked by.

"What?" he prompted, hating himself.

She seemed to deflate. "Nothing. Nothing at all."

Her hand lay on the table. He wanted to cover it with his. He didn't.

She sighed. "I loved you, Artur. I truly did."

Loved. Past tense. He laughed without humor. "Now you hate me. As you should."

She closed her eyes. "Maybe you're right. Maybe I do hate you. Even so, I doubt I hate you half so much as you hate yourself."

True enough, he supposed. He was Nephilim, and a nasty bastard besides. Of course he hated himself.

He shrugged, letting his gaze wander toward the possessed man and his mates. All four were now on their feet. He watched them and his bloodlust simmered.

Artur rose. Extracting a bill from his pocket, he slipped it onto the table as the hellfiend herded its prey toward the door. Adrenaline bled into his veins. He slid the Glock into his belt. Bloody hell, but he needed a kill right now. Whacking hellfiends was like Nephilim crack. He ought to sign himself up as a sodding DAMN recruit.

"Go out ahead of them," he ordered Cybele. "Swing your ass. Draw them down the alley to the south. I'll close in from behind."

"Oh, all right. Why the hell not?"

Something in her tone had him catch her gaze. He was stunned to see her eyes reflecting his own anticipation, and she flashed him a grin.

"You know, I think I'm almost looking forward to this. I always thought, Artur, that killing hellfiends was what we did best together."

Bloody hell, how he missed her.

"Actually," he said softly, "it was second best."

* * *

"Ms. Durant? Is that you?"

Maddie froze with her left hand on the door latch, acutely aware of the object clutched in her right. She could just make out the figure of a man sitting at the worktable.

"Dr. Ben-Meir? Why . . . why are you sitting here in the dark?"

The archeologist produced a cigarette lighter, then stood to light the oil lamp hanging overhead. Anemic light spilled across his scattered papers. He bent his head to examine the battery-powered lantern on the worktable. He flipped a switch, then shook his head ruefully.

"Dead. It must have gone out after I fell asleep." He frowned. "What time is it?"

"I have no idea," Maddie said cautiously. "One, maybe?"

Her answer caused him to look up, as if he'd just realized the oddity of her presence in the work hut. "Ms. Durant. What brings you here at this hour?"

Maddie's instinct was to turn and flee. She fought it. She stepped into the hut and closed the door.

"I came here to do some research. I . . . I found something."

His eyes narrowed on her hand. "Indeed. Is that it?"

Her fingers clenched. *It's mine.*

"Yes," she said, backing away. She'd changed her mind. She couldn't trust Dr. Ben-Meir. She should have run as soon as she realized he was here.

No. She gave herself an abrupt mental shake. What the hell was she thinking? Of course she trusted the professor. She forced her hand to unclench.

The archeologist stepped toward her, brow furrowed. When he reached out, it was all Maddie could do to stop herself from slapping his hand away. She knew she was being irrational.

This was Dr. Ben-Meir's dig, and she'd unearthed a relic, most likely a very important relic. Of course he needed to see it.

She forced herself to place it in his hand and immediately wished she hadn't. Her chest contracted with anxiety as Ben-Meir examined the artifact.

The disc was the size of his palm. Maddie had rubbed off some of the dirt, revealing scorch marks and discoloration. In a few places, however, the gold still gleamed. But the metal was undeniably damaged, creased through the center of the disc as if it was struck by something sharp and heavy. The impact had severed the delicate strips of gold that held the gem in the center of the piece. The stone itself, which must have once been a full inch in diameter, was now a lopsided half circle. That crystalline fragment glowed a deep, rich red.

"Ms. Durant, this is magnificent." Ben-Meir tilted the relic into the light, examining the faint tracery pattern on the gold.

"Hammered embossing," he breathed. "So intricate." He bent his head. "An ornament for a breastplate, judging by the four holes at the perimeter. Maybe," he mused, "it took a blow in battle. And the etching! If I'm not mistaken . . ." He rubbed off a bit more of the dirt with the hem of his sleeve. "Yes. Just as I thought. The Seed of Life."

Maddie frowned. "What's that?"

"A very ancient design. See?" Reverently, his forefinger hovered over the etching. "One central circle, with six more circles arranged in symmetry around it. Each pair of edges overlap to form an even earlier symbol, this vaguely fishlike shape. It's known as the *vesica piscis*."

His tone assumed the quality of a man accustomed to lecture halls. "Early cultures considered the *vesica piscis* to be the place where the spheres of Heaven and earth meet—the place and time where life begins. It's thought the seven circles of the Seed of Life pattern, with each overlapping circle segment forming a magical *vesica piscis*, represent the seven days of creation. To the ancient world it was a powerful symbol indeed."

He tilted the piece, catching the light. Maddie counted the seven circles. Repeated at regular intervals around the central stone, the circles created what looked like a six-petal flower.

"How old do you think the relic is, Dr. Ben-Meir? Could it be from the time of the Watchers?"

"Certainly it could. The Seed of Life symbol was known in Assyria and Egypt at least three thousand years ago. The symbol was likely well-known in the early Canaanite period." His hand trembled as he touched the central stone. "This must have been very beautiful when it was whole. I wonder what caused the damage."

It did not escape Maddie's notice that Dr. Ben-Meir had not mentioned the pulsing red light. Of course not. He couldn't see it. He couldn't *feel* it, like she did. Because it wasn't there?

The archeologist's head came up, and his dark eyes fell on her. "Where did you find this, Ms. Durant?"

Maddie swallowed. "At . . . at the bottom of the Watchers' well."

"That well was empty."

"It was buried." She twisted her hands together to keep herself from snatching the ornament. She wanted it back. It seemed so . . . *wrong* in Dr. Ben-Meir's hands.

"And you dug it up this afternoon?" Incredulity crept into his voice, along with a touch of anger. "With those American teenagers? And you didn't report it to the team? You just . . . pocketed it?"

Maddie couldn't drag her eyes from the disc. "No! No, sir. I didn't have it this afternoon. I found it just now. Tonight."

Ben-Meir's dark brows met over the bridge of his nose. "You went to the dig in the middle of the night? Alone? Why would you do such a thing? You know the protocol. If you suspected something, you should have informed me." He stared down at the broken ornament. "A discovery of this magnitude . . . it should have been photographed in situ, before you even touched it."

"I know. I know I should have come to you first. I'm sorry."

A red light pulsed in the stone; the tarnished gold glowed white. Sparkles of light darted around and around the edges of the circles like tiny frolicking faeries. A red heart beat at the center of their dance.

Staring at the display made Maddie slightly dizzy. What caused the light? Some fusion of metal and crystal? Natural phosphorescence? Or was it simply a product of her disease?

Dr. Ben-Meir turned the disc over. At the same moment, Maddie became aware of a white light outlining his head and shoulders, the same sort of aura she'd seen surrounding the teens this afternoon. She rubbed her eyes.

Dr. Ben-Meir retrieved a brush from the tool cabinet. Gently, he dislodged some of the dirt encrusting the rear face of the disc. Maddie clenched and unclenched her fists. She didn't like him touching it. She should never have given it to him. She wanted to snatch it back. To cradle it between her breasts where it *belonged.*

"Perhaps this piece was created in the forge near the well," he was saying. "Perhaps it was even formed on the anvil we excavated. Often an ancient metalsmith left his mark on his pieces . . ." His hand stilled suddenly, and he sucked in his breath. "What have I found?" he breathed. "Dear God. Is it possible?"

What I *found,* Maddie wanted to shout. *It's mine. Only mine.*

"What is it?" she asked, moving closer.

Ben-Meir's hand was trembling. "Look. The eye of the Watchers. Right here, in the center. Just as it appears on the Pharos Tablet."

It was true. The symbol on the disc, a small circle within a larger disc, matched the marking on the Pharos Tablet.

"Let me see." She reached out. "Let me hold it."

He snatched the disc away. "Are you insane, Ms. Durant? This relic, this treasure, should not be touched. Not even by me." Crossing to a shelf, he located a square of chamois and spread the cloth on his palm. He placed the disc atop it. The red light flared, then commenced a slow pulse. Strands of white wove around it.

"Do you see the light?" Maddie asked suddenly. It couldn't be all in her mind. It just couldn't be.

"What are you talking about, Ms. Durant? What light?"

"Red light. And white." She stretched out a finger. A gossamer strand of crimson arced from the broken stone. It was shocking as it struck her skin. She drew a startled breath and rubbed her thumb against her tingling forefinger. "Did you see that?"

"See what?"

"That arc of electricity. It came from the stone."

"I saw nothing."

"Let me hold it," Maddie pleaded. "I'll show you."

"Ms. Durant. Clearly you're overtired." He folded the chamois around the piece. "Why don't you retire to your bed. I'll see to the relic." His fingers closed around the bundle.

He doesn't see anything, Maddie thought. But did he *feel* it? Did he feel what she did when she looked at the disc? When she touched it?

The thought brought panic. She couldn't leave, couldn't let him hide the disc away. If she did, she would never see it again. She'd been a fool to hand it over to him. She'd found it. It was *hers*. She had to get it back.

Rather than retreat to the door, she took a step forward. "What are you going to do with it?"

"Photograph it, of course. Measure it, and make a log entry. Then it's going into the safe. Tomorrow, early, you and I will go to the dig. You'll show me exactly the spot where it was found."

"You can't lock it away." Maddie's voice shook. "You can't hide it away in a vault or a museum. The relic's mine, Dr. Ben-Meir. I found it." She held out her hand. It was shaking. "I want it back."

Ben-Meir stared. "Ms. Durant. You're talking nonsense."

Her rational brain agreed. She had no right to the relic. The artifact represented the pinnacle of the archeologist's career. It was the means by which he would regain the respect of his peers.

No! It's mine. Mine. Mine, mine, mine.

Panic. Blinding, unreasoning panic. She didn't care how hard and long Ben-Meir had worked, or about the professional ridicule he'd faced. She couldn't let him have it. She lunged for his hand. She pried at his fingers, tore at the chamois cloth.

"Ms. Durant! Really!"

"Give it to me! Now!"

She dug her fingernails into his wrist, deep enough to draw blood. Ben-Meir grunted with surprise and pain. His hand spasmed; he swore. Maddie snatched the prize away. Relief crashed through her.

The archeologist stared down at the blood welling from the gouge on his arm, then up at her. "I cannot believe you did that. Ms. Durant, have you gone insane?"

The chamois fluttered to the floor. Maddie backed away, cupping the disc between her breasts. "I told you it was mine. Mine. I found it."

"Ms. Durant." He advanced slowly, palms raised, as if approaching a wild animal. A trickle of blood dripped down his arm. She stared at the dark red line, transfixed.

"Yes, you found it." The archeologist spoke softly, without threat. She wasn't fooled. His aura was pulsing, bright with anger. "You are the first person to touch the disc in thousands of years. I am sure it feels as though it should belong to you. But it does not. It is not mine, either," he added when she opened her mouth to protest. "This is public land. You know that. The relic belongs to my country. To its people. To all Jews, all over the world. It is our heritage."

She made no reply.

"Enough. Give it to me." His tone had turned brisk.

"No." She hugged the disc fiercely. Warmth seeped from the gold, from the stone, into her skin. "No. Never."

Ben-Meir continued talking, calmly, firmly, his slow steps herding her toward a corner of the hut. Her eyes darted to the door. She'd never make it past him to freedom.

"Ms. Durant!" He was angry now, very much so. "Have you heard a word I've said? Answer me!"

She stared at him blankly.

"I heard you were feeling ill yesterday. Dehydration can affect the brain. I understand that. So just give me the relic. Give it to me now, and I'll forget this episode ever happened."

He held out his hand. He was very close now. Too close. The disc's heat intensified. It burned her chest, her hands. The pain made her dizzy. Tingling sensations ran up Maddie's arms. She eased the disc from her skin.

He must have thought the gesture was one of surrender. His hand shot out; his fingers closed like bands of iron on her wrist.

"No!"

She tried to snatch her arm back. He dragged her closer. She struggled, to no avail. His free hand pried her fingers back, one by one, and wrenched the disc from her grasp.

Something tore inside Maddie's chest. She bent double, gasping. A black hole of despair gaped inside her rib cage. She'd failed. She'd . . .

"What the hell—?"

Her head jerked up. Ben-Meir stood motionless, staring down at the disc. The ancient gold tossed white sparks into the air. The red stone spat a beam of light directly into the center of the dancing pattern. That light splashed onto the archeologist's face, and Maddie had a fleeting impression of blood.

Could he see the phenomenon at last? He must. His hands were shaking.

Maddie could never quite remember exactly what happened next. She recalled a blinding flash, an exploding force. Her body flew backward, curiously light in the air. She heard no noise. Her ears felt clogged. Dr. Ben-Meir might have shouted, but she couldn't be sure. The back of her head smacked something hard. Everything went black.

* * *

Cade smelled crimson anger and sky blue astonishment. And fear. Murky, sour yellow, paralyzing fear.

The window of the work hut blazed bloodred. A wave of magic swept past, hot wind on the desert, lifting his hair, searing the breath in his lungs. What the bloody hell?

He abandoned stealth and ran. It had already been well after midnight when he separated Dr. Ben-Meir's jeep from the two other vehicles in the car park and pushed it noiselessly out of the camp. He'd left it about a mile up the road and jogged back to the camp on foot.

He didn't need the jeep, of course. He could have Maddie far away from here, and quickly, without it. But he'd thought she'd have an easier time of it if she didn't have to face the truth of what he was—what *she* was—so abruptly.

He approached the hut, now dark and silent like the others. None of the other archeologists' huts or laborers' tents seemed to have been disturbed by the hot surge of magic.

It couldn't be Maddie's magic. Not for days yet, until—*if*—she completed her transition.

He didn't pause to knock. Wrenching the door open, he plunged inside . . . and drew up short, stunned by the scene that greeted him. It wasn't anything he could have predicted.

Sulfur and ash assaulted his nostrils. Maddie crouched against one wall, clutching something to her chest. Her eyes were wide and unblinking, but—physically at least—she seemed unharmed. Cade couldn't say the same for Ben-Meir. The archeologist lay flat on his back, arms and legs flung wide, eyes open and staring. His neck was bent at an impossible angle.

Blast it! This was a complication he just didn't need. With a troubled glance at Maddie, he went down on one knee and pressed two fingers under Ben-Meir's jaw.

Dead.

Maddie didn't move a muscle. He doubted she was aware of anything in the room. Her expression remained blank even when he sank into a crouch before her and waved a hand in her face.

"Maddie?"

He took her hands and pulled them away from her chest. Surprisingly, she didn't resist. He stared down into her cupped palms at a primitive gold disc set with a fractured red stone. The piece was tarnished and dirty, as if it had recently come from the earth. The sulfurous scent of blood magic clung to it.

Hell. What was this? A Watcher amulet? Where had it come from?

"Maddie." Cade grabbed Maddie's upper arms and hauled her to her feet. Avoiding the ornament in her hands, he touched her chin, lifting it until their eyes met. "Maddie, *caraid*, can you hear me? Can you see me?"

He pressed his finger to her pulse and spoke a single jarring word. The magic caused a shudder to pass through her, and she blinked.

"Cade?"

His shoulders sagged on a flood of relief. She was still with him.

"What's . . . what's happened? I feel . . . I feel so strange."

"Don't fight it," he said. "Just breathe."

He pivoted her body as he spoke, intending to block her line of vision to Ben-Meir's body. But he didn't execute the maneuver quickly enough.

"Oh my God. Dr. Ben-Meir!" She strained against Cade's restraining arm. "We've got to call an ambulance."

"No use," Cade said. "There's nothing they'll be able to do. He's dead."

Maddie sucked in a sob and buried her face against his chest. "Dead? But . . . why? How?"

He held her close. "You don't remember, *caraid*?"

"No. No, I . . ." She jerked her head back, shoving against his chest. The amulet burned his skin. He hissed a curse and held her at arm's length.

"Was it you?" she demanded. "Did *you* do it? Did you kill him?"

"Me? I wasn't even here."

Her odor of panic spiked; she fought his control. "I don't believe you. Let me go."

"Not bloody likely. Come on. We're leaving."

"Yes." She sucked in a sob. "We've got to wake the others. Hadara, Ari—"

"No."

"What do you mean, no? Of course we do."

"They'll wake up soon enough on their own. In the meantime, I'm getting you out of here. And you're going to come with me quietly."

She stared. "You *did* kill him."

"I didn't. But that's neither here nor there." He grabbed her wrist and hauled her to the door.

"Let go of me!" She twisted and clawed at him one-handed; the other hand continued to clutch the golden disc to her chest. Cade wasn't sure she even realized she still held it.

Blast it all to Oblivion! What was that thing? Where had she found it? And how had a spell of Watcher blood magic, with its rotting, choking odor, come to be cast upon it?

"Murderer!"

She landed a hard, painful kick to his knee, and her sudden burst of strength caught him by surprise. He bent her arm—the one not holding the disc—behind her back. When she opened her mouth, he clamped his free hand over it.

Hauling her against his body, he hissed in her ear, "Don't even think about screaming. I didn't kill Ben-Meir."

No, the relic she clutched between her breasts had murdered the archeologist. He'd stake his life on it. What had stopped the blood magic from attacking Cade, he didn't know.

She bit his hand. Grunting, he pressed his other hand to her chest and spoke a single word. Her eyes went wide. A moment later her lids drooped and her body went limp. Cade removed his palm. Her chest expanded convulsively, and then she released a sigh. Her body slumped forward.

He caught her around the waist before she fell. The gold disc tumbled from her fingers and thunked onto the floor. Rolling across the uneven floorboards, it traced a wobbling path, jumping the edge of a small rug and landing on Ben-Meir's dead body. The smell of red, rotted blood intensified.

Cade stared uneasily at the disc, loath to touch it. But he could hardly leave lethal Watcher blood magic behind for anyone to find. Bracing Maddie's weight on one knee, he bent to retrieve the amulet.

The gold burned his fingers. He cursed, nearly dropping the thing. Snatching up a square of cloth he spied on the floor, he wrapped the amulet and shoved it into his pocket. It lay unnaturally warm against his thigh.

Which clan's magic did it contain? he wondered. Artur would know; he was uncanny at sensing the nuances of power. Cade wondered, too, what Artur would do with the relic. But these were questions to be answered later.

He strode to the window and looked out. The camp remained silent; the fatal disturbance had gone unremarked. With luck, Ben-Meir's body wouldn't be discovered until dawn. By then, Cade would have Maddie miles away. Hefting her limp body over his shoulder, he carried her off into the night.

Chapter Nine

He paused before his tent. "Lilith."

"Yes, Father?"

A smile touched his lips. "Remove your headscarf, Daughter. I would gaze upon your face."

Heat rushed to her cheeks, but she did as he commanded, unwinding the long cloth that provided protection from the desert sun and winds. Underneath, her long dark curls were unbound, and his dark eyes passed over her.

"Your magic," he said. "It shines." Then, softly, as if to himself: "Why have I never noticed?"

"I am female."

"Indeed." Reaching past her, he pulled back the tent flap. "Come."

Her heart pounded as she preceded him into the dwelling's antechamber. A bowl, a jug of water, oils, and perfume lay at hand. He sat on a low stool.

"Bathe my feet, Daughter. Then tend to your own."

It was a familiar ritual. Kneeling, she poured water into a bowl and added three drops of oil scented with jasmine. Kneeling before him, she removed his sandals.

His feet were beautiful, large and well shaped. She placed them in the water and gently sponged them. When they were clean, she blotted them with a dry length of cloth. He nodded his approval and rose.

She took his place on the stool as he stood waiting. Quickly she stripped off her sandals and made use of the same bowl. Then, when the water, dirty twice over, had been discarded, and the damp towel hung to dry, he lifted the flap leading to the tent's inner chamber.

"Come, Lilith."

* * *

Maddie woke with a jolt. And another. And another. It took a moment for her to realize she was no longer in her father's tent.

No. Not *her* father. The girl Lilith's father. A dream. It had only been a dream.

The world jolted again. She grabbed for something solid. Her hand connected with a dashboard.

She was in a car? A jeep. Dr. Ben-Meir's jeep, if she wasn't mistaken. The top was down. The vehicle was speeding through pitch-black desert with Cade Leucetius at the wheel. The headlights were off.

She grabbed for the safety strap. There was no moon, and the stars didn't begin to shed enough light. Were they even on a road? They couldn't be. The roads in Israel weren't this bad.

The front wheels hit a rock or a rut. The vehicle bounced and shuddered. Sand whipped over the windshield and into her face. Her eyes stung and her nostrils burned. She ducked her head behind the glass.

Night shielded the landscape. Beside her, she could only just make out the details of Cade's solid form. He wore a white shirt with short sleeves. He looked too large for the jeep. The steering wheel was a toy in his big hands.

A hot wave of lust glided through her, scouring her raw. An aching pulse leaped between her thighs. She muffled a groan. God, she wanted him so badly it burned. And he hadn't so much as glanced at her. What was she doing here, in Ben-

Meir's jeep, with Cade? She tried to remember, but the near past was a dense fog.

Her arousal spiraled; she tried not to squirm in her seat. And failed. She stared at his hands, imagining them on her breasts and between her legs. Lust stabbed her belly and twisted. This time, she did groan.

He glanced her way. "Awake. That's good. How do you feel?"

Horny as all hell.

"Like shit," she muttered.

The jeep slammed into another rut; she nearly broke her nose on the dash. Her stomach lurched up her throat. Bracing an arm, she made a belated grab for the seat belt.

"For God's sake! Slow down."

He laughed. "Sit back and relax."

"You're out of your mind." Fear washed through her. "What's going on? Where the hell are we going? And why . . . why am I even with you?"

He sent her a swift sidelong glance. "You don't remember?"

"Remember what?"

"What happened earlier tonight."

The jeep lurched. Her teeth cracked together. "N-nothing happened. I . . . I went to bed. And . . ." Bits and pieces of memory were coming back to her. "I had a dream . . ."

"Of course. You've had quite a few dreams lately, haven't you? Very vivid ones."

She gaped at him. "What do you know about my dreams?"

"I know they seem as real as your waking life."

That was the truth. It frightened her that somehow he knew. How? She hadn't told a soul.

His gaze remained facing forward. Though how he could possibly see what was ahead in the darkness she didn't know.

"And when you woke?" he asked. "After the dream? What then?"

She tried to remember. "I . . . couldn't sleep. I went to the dig. Yes, that's it. I went to the Watcher well. There was something I had to find—" Sudden panic nearly choked her. "Where is it? Where's the disc?"

"I have it."

She sat up, rigid. "Give it to me. Give it to me now."

He hesitated, then slid his hand into his pocket. Even in the stygian darkness, she caught a faint glimmer of red light as the cloth fell away.

She snatched the relic and hugged it to her chest. Warmth spread through her body. Her shoulders sagged, her breath sighing from her lungs. *Yes.*

Cade's expression was inscrutable. "You found that in the Watcher well?"

She hugged it tighter. She didn't want him looking at it. "Yes. Buried at the bottom."

"How did you know it was there?"

"I . . ." She broke off. "I don't know. Instinct?" If a mysterious red light qualified as instinct.

He snorted. "Something a little stronger than instinct, I'd say."

"What's that supposed to mean?"

He didn't answer. "After you found it, you took it back to Ben-Meir?"

"I took it to the work hut, yes. I wanted to clean it off. Dr. Ben-Meir was there. He'd fallen asleep. I woke him up . . ." She frowned. "That's the last thing I remember."

Cade was silent. The jeep lurched on.

"Where are we going?" she asked.

"You'll find out when we get there."

"This is Dr. Ben-Meir's jeep. Did he . . . did he lend it to you?"

"No," Cade said. "I stole it."

Fear bled through Maddie's veins. "Then . . . why am I with you? Are you . . . are you kidnapping me?"

"I'm taking you, yes. You can call it kidnapping if you like."

She sucked in a breath. He sounded so cool, so calm. Clearly, the man was insane. A psychopath. "Are you going to kill me?"

He made a sound of disgust. "If I wanted to do that, *caraid*, you'd be long dead."

"Rape me, then?"

He yanked the steering wheel hard to the right. The sudden movement threw Maddie to the left, and her shoulder collided with his. The contact was electric. The desire that had been building the past few days rushed at her with blinding force. Raw need clawed at her vitals. She clenched her fists, digging her nails into her palms. She would not grab him. Would not rip off his shirt and run her hands over his smooth, bare chest. She would not *beg*.

Somehow she managed to scuttle back to her side of the jeep. She clung to the passenger door, legs pressed tightly together, gasping.

He gave a low, humorless laugh. "I think we both know it won't be rape."

Won't be. An anticipatory tingle shot to her nerve endings and she sucked in a breath. "I . . . This isn't me. This isn't right. You've drugged me, haven't you? Slipped some aphrodisiac thing into my dinner or my canteen."

"Don't flatter yourself."

"You must have. It doesn't make sense, otherwise. How much I—"

"Want me?" he suggested.

Yes. Desperately.

She pressed her lips together and didn't open them until she was sure she could control what she said. "You can't do this. You can't just kidnap me! It's crazy. They'll find you. You'll be arrested."

He shot her a glance, then shifted his eyes back to the windshield. When he spoke, his voice held a new softness. "I'm sorry, *caraid*. Truly, I am. I wish there was some other path for your life to take. But there isn't. You should sleep now, while you still can. Later, you won't be able to."

"You're insane," she whispered, her fingers creeping to the door handle. He made no sense at all.

How he saw the movement in the darkness, she didn't know. "Thinking of jumping? Stupid idea. There's nowhere to run. I'd be on you in two seconds."

She swallowed. "Why are you doing this? Why would you want to? I'm nothing special."

He gave a short laugh. "I'd have to disagree, *caraid*. There aren't many like you."

"What is that supposed to mean?"

"You'll know soon enough. Right now, you need rest."

He said another word, one she didn't understand. It sounded heavy. Peaceful. She thought she'd heard it before. A warm wave swept over her and her eyelids drooped.

Drugged, she thought. *I've been drugged.* It was her last thought before sleep claimed her.

* * *

Sheepskin pelts covered the floor of her father's tent. Lilith's clean, bare toes curled into the unexpected luxury. Soft drapes hung on the walls. An oil lamp, suspended from the tent's arched frame, spilled soft light. Spices, smoldering in a brass brazier, spun sweet haze into the air.

Her father entered the tent behind her and dropped the skin over the entrance. Lilith stood awkwardly gazing about in awe. A low couch strewn with cushions occupied the center of the space. Before it stood a table scattered with precious items: A jeweled dagger crossed the rim of a hammered bronze cup. Gems of all colors and nuggets of silver and gold surrounded it. Engraved discs of metal and stone were strewn across the polished wood.

Lilith's eyes lit on a figurine in the shape of a naked woman. Pendulous breasts hung to a rounded belly. Beside that, a rendition of an erect male member, cast in bronze, stood boldly upright.

Lilith blushed at that last and hastily looked away.

"Leave us," her father said.

With a start, Lilith realized they were not alone. In a shadowed corner two women lay on a bed, arms and legs entwined. At her father's order, they disentangled their limbs and rose. Their life auras did not shine with the red of Watcher magic but with the white sparkle of human essence.

Lilith recognized the pair. They were human women, Ayalesh and Nivah, her father's favorite concubines. Their kohl-darkened eyelids exuded mystery. Men could not look away when their reddened lips pouted, but no man of the tribe would dare touch what belonged to their master. The entire Watcher settlement treated them like queens. Lilith herself bowed low whenever they passed. Before this moment, neither woman had given her a second look. Before this moment, Lilith had never seen them naked.

Though her cheeks flooded with heat, she could not draw her eyes from that smooth expanse of feminine skin, from those perfect, rounded breasts, from the rouged nipples, from the jewels nestled in the curling hair between their thighs.

The women were clearly not pleased to see Lilith in their domain. Nivah shot her a daggerlike glance as she reached for her silken tunic. Ayalesh's expression was more circumspect, but venom filled her eyes.

When they turned to their master, only smiles graced their painted faces. They bowed low.

"As you wish, Lord Azazel."

Azazel's eyes lingered on their departure. When they had gone, he turned to her. "Are you like them, Lilith? Have you known a man's touch?"

She blushed furiously. "No, Father! I have not. I am . . . I am pure."

"Ah," he said. "Good. You will remain so."

"Of course, Father! I would never shame you. It will be as you wish."

He gestured her to a seat on the couch. He took a place beside her, an arm's length or more away. Leaning forward, he lifted the chalice and dagger. He placed the blade on the table, the cup into Lilith's hands.

"You offered me water, Daughter. I offer you wine. Drink."

She took the cup and pressed her lips to the rim. The wine was bitter and very strong. Heat blossomed in her chest. Fire, licking her heart. Azazel leaned back against the cushions.

"Drink it all, child. Then we will talk."

She obeyed without question.

* * *

The wine, the tent, Lilith, Azazel—all of it vanished in a crackle of fire. Blue flames. Maddie jumped to her feet—she'd been kneeling—and backed away. She didn't get far. Her shoulders hit a wall. Her palms flattened against it.

She was still dreaming. She knew it, and yet she didn't quite believe. The strange fire was so real, so close. Heat licked her face, her breasts, her belly. Searching, tormenting. She looked down, and realized she was naked. Vulnerable. Trapped.

Then the fire vanished and rekindled in her womb. That flame taunted her breasts, her arms, her legs. It licked between her legs. She writhed and sobbed. She wanted to make it stop. She knew she couldn't. At least, not by herself . . .

She parted her legs, pressed them together. Oh, God. She was going mad.

* * *

She woke clawing at Cade's arm. Her skin was flushed and slick with sweat. The dream fire burned under her skin and smoldered between her thighs. A sob caught in her throat. She wanted. She *needed*.

With a strength that seemed to come from somewhere outside herself, she pried Cade's right hand from the steering wheel. The jeep gave a sickening lurch to the left, the right tires lifting off the ground.

"Blast it." He threw his weight to the right. The vehicle slammed back to the earth. "Hold up, love."

"I can't." She heard herself moan. The sound was more animal than human. She was burning up; the fire was inside her. She couldn't get away. "I . . . can't wait. Now, Cade. God. It has to be now."

His reply was surprisingly gentle. "I know, *caraid*. I know."

The jeep bounced to a halt. Cade barely had time to shift into park before Maddie pounced, sliding atop him, legs splayed wide. Wedged between the steering wheel and the hard bulge of his erection, she wanted their clothes gone. Now. She rubbed against him. Too damn many layers of cloth. The friction brought no real relief. She needed him closer. She needed more. She needed him inside her.

They were in such tight quarters she couldn't even fit her hands between their bodies to undo his jeans. She wriggled, trying to get into better position. From a point above her head, her rational brain looked down on the scene in horror.

Cade's hot hands molded the sides of her torso. Between

her legs, he was hard as a rock. His breath heaved almost as violently as hers.

He jerked his hips. His hard-on was a stabbing between her legs and she cursed their clothes. His palms cupped her shoulder, her face, her breasts. He plucked at her nipples through her T-shirt and she choked out a moan.

"Not . . . enough room."

"Wait."

He fumbled at the door; the latch clicked. His big body lurched backward. Maddie knew a moment of weightlessness as she tumbled after him. She landed atop him, her hands braced on his chest, her knees scraping desert sand.

Vertigo. Something was wrong with her head. The world was whirling, lurching. She couldn't get her bearings. The disorientation brought with it blinding panic. Her life was spinning out of control. How would she ever find her way back? Perhaps it would be better to give up. Give in to the roaring chaos.

Terror squeezed the air from her lungs. Consciousness faded. Red and black blotches filled her vision, but Cade's voice, steady and strong, at last cut through the madness.

"Maddie. Maddie. Come back to me, *caraid*."

"I can't—"

"You can. I'm here. Grab onto me."

The world rolled to the left. Something solid connected with her shoulders. It was the ground.

Cade was there above her. His silhouette blotted the stars. Red light clung to his head and shoulders, and when he moved, the illumination dissolved into a trail of crimson sparks. Need speared her womb. She arched her hips. She had to have him inside her. She grabbed fistfuls of his shirt.

"I need you."

"I know, Maddie. I know."

His voice was a cool, soothing balm to the heated insanity.

His hand moved between their bodies. His fingers brushed her belly, slipped between her legs. He touched her where she longed for him. Even through the fabric of her shorts, it felt delicious. She nearly sobbed with relief as the frightening madness began to recede.

"Easy, *caraid*. Easy. I'm here. I won't let it take you."

She believed him. She opened her legs wider, and he rubbed with strong, circular strokes. Pleasure blotted the chaos. "Oh, God. Yes."

His free hand roamed her body, stroking breasts, belly, thighs. The constriction of her waistband loosened; her shorts slipped over her hips. Cool fingers eased into her heated core. They burrowed into the burning center of her need. She hissed, arching, straining.

"Relax, *caraid*. Not so tense. That's it."

His crooning continued—cooling, reassuring, stark in contrast to the rolling fire he stoked between her thighs. His long, strong fingers parted her slick folds, slipped inside her body. His relentless thumb circled her taut bud. The fire leaped, blazed. Burned hotter than the sun. She exploded into bliss.

Again the universe spun. This time, though, she felt no fear, only a deep sense of safety. Of rightness. Cade's hands were on her body. The pleasure he'd wrought filled her mind. There was no room for madness.

Too soon, the climax ebbed. As the savage wildness drained away, she became aware of his cradling arms. She sat in his lap; he rocked her gently, like a child. His lips touched her hair.

"That's it. Let go now. It's over, I've got you."

Words tenderly spoken. But as the real world slowly intruded onto Maddie's dazed mind, the awareness of what she'd done—how she'd *begged* him—shoved its way to the front of her consciousness. Cade's comfort seemed suddenly shameful. With her sudden and insane sexual need sated, reality reared its ugly face.

Dear God. She'd gotten off with a virtual stranger! With a criminal who'd brazenly stolen a vehicle and kidnapped her. She wanted desperately to fling herself out of his arms, but once she did that she'd have to face the gloating satisfaction in his eyes. She wasn't ready to face that yet. Or him. She doubted she'd ever be.

God. What had happened? Had he slipped some kind of date-rape drug into her canteen? Or was this another trick of the tumor, scrambling the arousal center of her brain?

It was Cade who made the first move to separate. Easing her off his lap to the ground, he rose and paced a few steps away. Maddie was acutely aware that he was still fully dressed. For some reason, he hadn't penetrated her. Would it have been rape? she wondered. She'd been begging for it.

Face burning, she snatched up her shorts and underwear abandoned in a rumpled heap nearby. She dressed quickly under the moonless sky. When she was done, Cade rounded the jeep to the passenger's side and yanked open the door.

"Get in. We've got to get moving."

She hugged her torso. "Not until you tell me where to."

"You'd rather stay here?"

"Of course not." Here was nowhere but empty desert stretching for miles in every direction.

"At least tell me . . . what that was," she demanded. She hoped the darkness hid her crimson face. "What we just did, I mean. It sure as hell wasn't a natural attraction. Tell me the truth. You drugged me, didn't you?"

He sighed and rubbed the back of his neck. "No."

"You must have! I don't throw myself at men I barely know."

"Apparently you do."

She flushed crimson.

"There's a lot more about yourself you don't know, Maddie. I'm here to help you face it."

"By kidnapping me? By stealing Dr. Ben-Meir's—" She cut off with a strangled sound as an image flashed in her brain: Ben-Meir, sprawled on the ground, neck bent. Glassy eyes, open and staring. This time, she knew it was no dream.

"Oh. My. God." Hugging her waist, she bent double, gasping. "Oh my God. Dr. Ben-Meir."

Her knees folded, but Cade's strong arms interrupted the collapse. Scooping her up as if she weighed nothing, he deposited her on the passenger seat and locked the seat belt around her. Slamming the door, he strode to the driver's side and took his place behind the wheel. He didn't turn the key. Half-turned in his seat, he regarded her gravely.

"You remember."

A crashing wave of terror threatened to suck her under. "He's dead."

"Yes."

"How?" she asked.

"The man was on the floor when I arrived." Cade seemed to hesitate. "I suspect it had something to do with the amulet in your pocket."

"Amulet? The Watcher disc?" Her head ached with the effort of remembering. "I gave it to Dr. Ben-Meir. Then I wanted it back. He wouldn't give it to me. I tried to take it, and then . . ."

The scene reformed in her mind, red-tinged and hazy. "And then something exploded. I think . . . I think it was the stone fragment in the center. Oh, God. That's impossible!" She shoved her hand into her pocket and pulled the relic out. It lay warm and heavy in her palm. "The stone's right here. See? It's safe."

His expression didn't change. "That's an odd choice of word."

She traced the seven golden circles. Ancient dirt stained the angry crease that nearly split the disc in two.

The few unbroken prongs held the remaining fragment of stone too loosely. She bent the gold prongs, tightening them around the crimson gem. She peered at it intently. She could no longer discern any illumination. Had the light ever been real? Or had it been in her mind?

"This relic couldn't have had anything to do with Dr. Ben-Meir's death," she said shakily. "That's ludicrous."

Cade didn't answer. During the stretch of silence, more fragments of memory assembled. Maddie remembered anger. Her anger. And Ben-Meir's. Also, perhaps, anger from a third source. From the red stone itself? No. That really was insane.

The scene played over and over in her mind. A flash of light. The archeologist's head, whipping violently to one side. Her own body flying backward. Pain exploding in the back of her skull.

Cade was telling the truth, she realized. At least about not killing Dr. Ben-Meir. He hadn't been there when it happened. She remembered crouching on the floor, trying to work up the courage to approach the corpse. The door had swung open. Cade appeared. He stared at the body with a shock that couldn't have been feigned.

But if Cade hadn't killed Ben-Meir, who or what had? She and her boss had been arguing over the disc. She might have shoved him. Could she have pushed him hard enough to break his neck? Maybe. But there had been an explosion. She was sure of that, at least. What had caused it?

"Why did you come to the work hut?" she asked Cade. "At that particular time, I mean. Did you see the explosion? Did you hear it?"

"I heard nothing," he said. "I saw a flash through the window. A dark red light."

Hot tears stung Maddie's eyes, which she closed tight. It hadn't been the tumor. This was real. Cade had seen the red light, too. Cade had seen the red light.

Whatever relief she felt at his confirmation died when she opened her eyes and stared down at the disc. She murmured, "And . . . you think this amulet somehow caused the explosion? But how can that be? It's just a hammered sheet of gold with a red stone in the center. It's harmless."

"Not harmless," Cade said. "Not even close. That talisman was formed with Watcher blood magic. It's deadly."

Maddie's head jerked up. "Be serious."

"Oh, I am. I assure you."

"But . . . the Watchers weren't really magical. They weren't fallen angels. They were men. The legend is just that. A legend."

"Many legends hold truth."

"*Rational* truth, maybe," she insisted. "Not fantasy come to life."

"The Watchers are no fantasy, Maddie. They're real."

"Real fallen angels living on earth? Mating with human women? That's just ridiculous."

"That amulet isn't ridiculous. It's lethal. It killed Ben-Meir."

She stared at the thing. "If you really believe that, maybe we should get rid of it. Toss it into the desert."

"And risk someone else finding it? Not bloody likely."

"Destroy it, then." But even as she spoke, something deep inside her recoiled.

"Easier said than done."

She exhaled in relief as Cade shook his head. "But what if it . . . explodes again?" she asked.

"I suspect as long as I don't try to take it from you, the way Ben-Meir did, it won't."

"He didn't take it," she said. "I gave it to him."

"You said you tried to take it back," he reminded her. "That's when it exploded. And killed *him*."

"While he and I were struggling for it." She stared at Cade. "You think the argument somehow triggered that explosion?"

He shrugged. "I think it's a good possibility."

Chilled to the bone, Maddie shivered. How had her life turned into this bizarre nightmare? She frowned down at the piece, then, for want of any other option, slipped it back into her pocket. Its heat seeped into her thigh. Somehow she didn't feel any warmer.

"We've got to go back to the dig. Once the sun comes up, Hadara and the others are going to find the . . . the body. I need to be there. I need to tell them—"

"What? That a five-thousand-year-old golden amulet killed their dig leader? You really think they'll believe that?"

"I—"

He cut her off. "Or will they believe something much more probable? That you or I—or you *and* I—killed him."

She gaped. "You think they'd suspect us?"

"Think?" Cade laughed. "*Caraid*, I know they will. Ben-Meir is dead under suspicious circumstances. In another couple hours, police will be crawling all over the scene, if they're not already. They'll be wondering about the missing jeep. And the missing assistant and laborer."

His scenario was very likely, she realized. And it was highly unlikely the Israeli police would believe a foreigner's shaky explanations.

"Oh, God. What am I going to do?" She drew a pained breath.

"You're going to stay with me. No one will get near you as long as you're under my protection." He reached out and brushed a curl from her forehead. "Trust me, Maddie."

She wanted to laugh. Or cry. "You're kidding, right? Trust you? You kidnapped me, drugged me, made me crave sex—"

"No, Maddie. No drugs. That's not what's happening here.

It's . . . Blast it," he said under his breath. His hands flexed on the steering wheel.

She thought he was going to say more, but he seemed to think better of it. He turned the key but didn't put the vehicle in gear. At last he sighed.

"Look. I'm making a mess of this, I know. I should have figured out a way to explain a few things before the first wave hit."

"First wave? First wave of what?"

He shook his head. "Let me put it another way. Why did you come to Israel?"

"I saw Dr. Ben-Meir on TV. On a documentary about the Watchers."

"Where did you first meet the man in person?"

"I attended one of his lectures. He was in the States, raising money for the dig. I was fascinated."

"Of course you were."

She shook her head. "What's that supposed to mean? It's not surprising that I was interested. I was an archeology student. The legend is intriguing. And I wanted—" *To escape a death sentence.* "—to travel. To see something of the world."

"Before the cancer did you in, you mean."

She jerked her head around. "How the hell do you know about that?"

He shrugged.

Maddie's stomach lurched. "You've been stalking me, haven't you? Even before I came to the dig." That had to be the reason he'd approached her. Otherwise, he wouldn't have given her a second glance. But why? She couldn't fathom it. "You know about the cancer. You know I'm terminal. You knew it before you came to find me."

"You're the reason I came to Israel, yes."

If Maddie had been frightened of Cade before, now she was

terrified. "Why? What could you possibly want from a dying woman?"

"You only think you're dying. You're not."

His arrogance left her gasping with rage. "I *think* I'm dying? *Think?* God damn you to Hell, Cade Leucetius. I *am* dying. I've got inoperable brain cancer."

"No. You don't. You're perfectly healthy."

Her laugh was tinged with hysteria. "Healthy? I have a malignant glioma! I'll be underground in six months. Probably sooner. That's a fact. You can't tell me it's not."

"That's exactly what I'm telling you. Maddie, you may have had cancer a year ago. But not now. Your disease is gone."

Hot tears stung her eyes. How many times had she hoped, had she prayed, to hear those words? *Your cancer is gone.* But, spoken by a doctor. Not by a psychopath.

And yet, even knowing the words were utterly false, she couldn't suppress an irrational surge of hope. Hope that poured kerosene on the flames of her anger.

"Damn you, Cade Leucetius. Damn you. You think I need your lies? Your sick jokes? I don't. I know what's happening to me. I know what's ahead. Did you really think I would swallow your fairy tale?"

He gave a grim chuckle. "What you're facing, Maddie, is no fairy tale. But cancer isn't a part of it. Your glioma disintegrated not long after the brain surgery that nearly killed you."

"I had chemo after the surgery. That shrunk the tumor."

"No. It happened naturally."

She struck out. Her balled fists connected with the solid muscle of his shoulder. "You bastard. What the fuck do you know? Nothing. You're not a doctor. You're not anything. Damn you." She choked on a sob. "Damn you to Hell."

She pummeled his shoulder, his stomach, anywhere she could reach. He caught her wrists, first one and then the other.

He pressed them both to his chest and held them there until the fight went out of her.

"Calm down, *caraid*. I'm mucking this up, I know. But please. Try to listen. We don't have much time before the next wave hits."

"Fuck you, Cade Leucetius. Just . . . fuck you." Tears streamed down her cheeks. "I don't have to listen to this. I'm dying, damn you. *Dying*. Don't tell me I'm not. I gave up hope months ago. I can't . . . Not now, I . . ." Her words dissolved in a convulsive sob.

He released her wrists and grabbed her shoulders. His fingers bit into her skin as he gave her a swift shake. Her sobs stuck in her throat.

"Listen to me, Maddie. I'm not telling you what you aren't. I'm trying to tell you what you *are*. It's no coincidence Simon Ben-Meir's work drew you here to Israel, to that singularly cursed canyon. The man wasn't digging up some obscure legend. He was digging up the rotting carcass of your own past. A corpse that is very real. And uglier than anything you could imagine."

Fear coiled in her belly. "What . . . what are you talking about?"

"I'm talking about you, Maddie. I'm talking about your very existence, proof of your Watcher forefather's unforgivable sin. You're not dying of cancer. You're changing. From what you thought you were into what you've always been: the forbidden offspring of a fallen angel. A crossbred atrocity, cursed by God and man alike. A human with demon essence where your soul should be."

He dragged in a breath and said, "Maddie, you're Nephilim."

Chapter Ten

The trouble with killing hellfiends, Cybele thought, was that the deed left you feeling dirty and wondering if perhaps you weren't every bit as disgusting as your victim.

Oh, she didn't deny it was fun. Exhilarating, even. There was a sexual rush to the chase and the strike. The high lingered for hours after a kill, and the lust . . . The sexual hunger awakened by a kill was fierce. Even the sight of the poor dead human who had been the hellfiend's host didn't diminish that. Nor had the bumbling, panicked escape of the three marked humans.

No, it had taken Artur to kill her high. After the hit, he'd simply turned his back and walked away without a word. He'd left her standing alone at the mouth of the alley. She'd spent a full five minutes hurling curses at his back. Blast the man straight to Oblivion; the cold wall he'd erected around his heart just wouldn't crack. How she wanted to smash it, obliterate it, reduce it to rubble! Sometimes she felt that her heart would never be whole until she'd brought Artur Camulus to his knees. Until she heard him rage, cry, and howl. Until he could *feel* again.

She wondered if he ever would, or whether it would be better to follow his example herself. If you didn't feel, there could be no pain. No regrets. Just . . . nothing. A preview of Oblivion. Maybe Artur was already halfway there.

After dealing with the hellfiend, after Artur had abandoned her, she'd returned to the East End alone to find both Brax and Gareth had left Artur's flat. She had the place to herself. Now, hours later, she was still alone.

Restless, she prowled the bedroom, the living area, the kitchen, and wished the place was bigger. Sick of brooding about Artur, she brooded instead about Cade's mission in Israel. If all went as planned, he'd return with a slave. The role of slave master would change him in ways she didn't want to contemplate. Her own bond with him, born during his transition, would be weakened if not broken entirely. As Artur had surely intended, she realized now.

And, what about Lucas? Was her brother even alive? He'd left London for Texas six months ago. Three months had passed since he'd last checked in. Luc had always been a loner, but he'd never been out of touch for so long. It was hard not to imagine the worst. Especially since the Glastonbury massacre.

DAMNers were more zealous in the States than they were here in Europe. Had a DAMN demon annihilator blasted Luc to Oblivion? She broke her pacing and dropped onto the sagging couch. She was staring at the blank television, debating whether to turn it on, when the door to the flat opened and Artur stepped into the room. Their gazes locked. For several wild beats of Cybele's heart, time hung suspended. Then Artur advanced, his leather duster billowing behind him, like a movie image that had just been taken off pause.

He shrugged out of the coat, tossed it over a chair, and stood silently looking down at her. The expression in his eyes told her nothing.

"I thought you might be out with Brax and Gareth," she said at last.

"I wasn't."

"So I see."

He strode to the sideboard where he kept his liquor. "Well, then. The two of us can enjoy a cozy night at home." His sarcasm, as always, lit her fuse.

"You shouldn't have sent Cade to Israel," she said to his back, mostly because she knew it would piss him off.

He paused in the act of pouring his whiskey. "I don't remember asking your opinion."

"He's angry about the massacre, grieving for his son."

"Please. He hardly knew the child."

"That's what's so terrible. On top of that, now you've bruised his pride. It's not a good combination, Artur. He could turn violent."

Her warning described Artur's mental state more than Cade's; surely Artur realized it. He shot her a glance, something ugly flaring in his eyes, and Cybele braced herself. He'd walk out the door now. Or retaliate with a cutting remark and a reminder of his dominance.

He did neither. He set aside his full whiskey glass. Lowering his tall body into an armchair and slumping against the cushion, he passed a weary hand over his eyes. "What else was I to do, Bel?"

She stared in shock. He hadn't used the old nickname since . . .

"Cade was on the verge of challenging me," Artur continued. "Sure, he backed down in time, but if I let him stay here, eventually he would have spoken the words. He wants you for a mate."

"He knows that won't happen," Cybele said.

"Intellectually, maybe. In his gut, no. As long as he feels that way, he's in danger of challenging me. And you know if he does that, I have to kill him. And despite what you think of me, I really don't want to do that."

The honest exhaustion in his voice set her heart to pounding. Blast it. She knew how to deal with Artur's anger. She'd become an expert at deflecting his contempt. She had ready weapons against his sarcasm. But this? This glimpse of vulnerability? It was all she'd hoped for, but now, confronted with the reality of it, she found she didn't know what to do. What to say. She didn't even know if she liked it.

"Cade might still go for your throat when he returns," she said at last, shakily, as if in consolation.

Artur, one arm flung over his eyes, laughed.

"That wasn't supposed to be funny."

"No," he agreed, sobering. "I admit it's possible he'll try. Much less likely, though. He'll have anchored a dormant. And he'll be a slave master. His bond with you will be very much weakened."

He seemed on the verge of adding something. He shook his head instead, as if clearing the thought from his mind.

"Still," Cybele insisted. "You shouldn't have sent him to Israel. He's too new, too inexperienced."

Rising, Artur retrieved his glass and took a long sip. Pacing the threadbare carpet, he paused at the window. He set his hip against the sill and said, "You worry he'll hurt the dormant. He won't. Much as I dislike Cade, I know he would never harm an innocent."

"And if this unaware female isn't innocent? If her power turns out to be greater than his? He might not be able to enslave her. She might enslave him."

Artur leaned against the wall, cradling his glass in his hand. "An unaware in transition enslave a full adept? Impossible."

"Cade's only been adept for a year," Cybele pointed out. "He was unaware before that. Acting as anchor is a lot for him to handle. Maybe too much. You should have sent Brax. Or gone yourself."

Artur's black eyes turned mocking. "What? You wouldn't have minded? But no, of course not. You would have delivered me right into the female's arms." He sipped his whiskey. "And, perhaps, stayed to watch?"

She hated him then. Hated him every bit as much as she loved him. "Go to Hell, Artur."

He laughed. "Sorry, love. Our kind doesn't even rate that privilege."

He had a mocking answer for everything. When had the cynical light in his eyes turned permanent? She wanted to wipe it out. She wanted to hurt him as he hurt her every damn time they were together.

"Gareth wants to perform his death-seeking as soon as possible," she said.

The set of Artur's features didn't change, apart from a slight hardening around the eyes. "What method is he contemplating?" For all the emotion he betrayed, he might have been asking Gareth's dinner order.

"Blade."

"Good." He nodded once. "A courageous choice."

Cybele's own choice had been poison. "I still can't believe you put him up to this."

"He wants it. And the clan needs every adept it can muster."

"And you need to punish me."

The ugly expression was back in his eyes. He put aside his glass. With angry steps, he crossed to her chair and stood looking down at her. "Believe me, Cybele," he said, "if I wanted to punish you, I wouldn't use Gareth to do it."

His gaze raked her body so lewdly that she felt stripped of her clothes. She fought the urge to cover herself—or fling herself at his feet. Eyes raised to his stare, she let her anger and her contempt show.

"Just how *would* you do it?" she taunted.

His jaw tensed. "You've sworn fealty, Cybele, like all the others. You owe me your obedience."

Her lips curved into what she suspected was a ghastly smile. "And submission, Artur? Willing submission? Do I owe that, too?"

He reacted not at all to her dripping sarcasm, nor to her insolent smirk. Only to her words. He leaned over her, his right hand supporting his weight on the arm of the chair. It took conscious effort for her to not shrink back into the cushions. His left index finger touched the base of her throat. Slowly, he drew a line down, down, between her breasts and over her belly. He stopped a scant inch short of the throbbing pulse between her legs.

"You do owe me submission, Cybele. Willing or otherwise. I am your lord. Your master. For now, I allow you the illusion of freedom, but not forever. One day, I promise you, I will issue the command. And you will not refuse."

The words were meant to shock, and they did. But try as she might, Cybele could not deny the truth behind those words. She was Artur's. She always had been.

His finger hovered over her sex. Even through a thick layer of denim, his touch burned. Raw need, like boiling honey, poured through every cell in her body. Her nipples constricted and tingled, her belly spasmed. Moisture wet her thighs.

Primitive animal arousal. And yet, so much more. She was acutely aware of Artur's life essence. All that she was yearned in response.

She wanted desperately to grind her hips against his hand. To beg him to issue that command *now*. How he'd laugh at that!

Somehow, she found the strength to remain silent. But in her mind, she begged. *Kiss me. Oh, please, Artur, kiss me. Forget Cade. Forget the choices I made when I found him.*

He didn't. Didn't touch his lips to hers, didn't plunge his tongue into the welcoming depths of her mouth. His eyes grew cold. His hand withdrew; he stepped away. And she knew she'd lost him again. He'd withdrawn to a place as distant and unreachable as Heaven or Hell.

He flashed a nasty grin. "That should hold you, love. Until I want more."

A flush crept from her chest to her neck and face. The bastard. She hated him. For what he wouldn't give her, and for how the loss of what he'd once given so freely drove her to places she didn't want to go. Never before had she experienced the urge to wound. If only she could force a spark of heat into his icy black irises.

"I look forward to it." Her voice, at least, remained calm. "But tell me this, Artur. When I anchor Gareth, do you intend to watch?"

His expression chilled even more. "No."

"I don't believe you," she pushed. "I think you will. I think you won't be able to stay away. At the very least, you'll be outside the door, listening. Imagining every act, every touch, every wave of pain and pleasure . . ." She laughed. "It would feel like you and me. Together again. Except this time, with roles reversed."

Artur didn't move. He didn't reply. His eyes were a void. The sight chilled Cybele to the bone. It was like catching a glimpse of Oblivion.

He turned and left the room without a word. Cybele wondered what the hell she was doing.

* * *

Civilization was ugly. And dirty, too, Luc thought as his boots kicked up a cloud of dust, staining the legs of his jeans. He made his way across the unpaved parking lot toward a tired building, passing a couple rusty pickups and a Ford sedan on the way. The single window by the entrance cast tired fluorescence into the night. Above it, an illuminated sign stuttered. CROS _ROADS D _NER, it read.

The interior was cleaner, at least, though a scent of grease hung in the air. The dull linoleum floor showed no dirt past the mat at the entrance. A television mounted from the ceiling droned a late-night talk show. His gaze swept the room: two men—one old, one young—on stools at the counter. A pair of middle-aged women sitting in a booth near the entrance. Sisters, probably, from the looks of them. A lone waitress wiping down a table near the kitchen. All four heads swiveled in his direction. One of the men grunted a greeting, then returned to his meal.

Luc folded his large frame into a corner booth near the cigarette machine, back to the wall, aware of an acute discomfort. It had been three months since he'd entered any man-made structure. His instincts screamed for him to get out of the place. The sky belonged above his head, not stained yellow ceiling tiles.

He ignored the urge to flee and picked up the menu to study his choices. His stomach rebelled. In three weeks, he had eaten only what he'd foraged in the wild, and he knew he had to reintroduce civilized food carefully.

The waitress appeared by his table, order pad in hand. She was short and plump, pushing forty, he thought, her frizzy blonde hair laced with gray. But the lines of fatigue around her blue eyes smoothed and her gaze kindled with interest as she examined him.

"You're not from around here, are you?" she said. "Looking for a job at the mill?" Her tone approached hopeful.

"No," Luc said. "Just passing through."

"Figures." A sigh escaped her. "Well, hon, what'll you have?"

"Eggs," he said, putting aside the menu. "Over easy. Toast. And coffee. Black."

"Sausage?" He considered his queasy stomach and declined.

The volume on the TV kicked up a notch as the talk show yielded to commercials. Reflexively, Luc glanced over. A blindingly handsome priest had appeared on the screen. *"Demon Annihilators Mutual Network is an international nonprofit organization dedicated to the eradication of demonkind. I'm Reverend Jonas Walker . . .*"

Blast it all to Oblivion! Luc gritted his teeth as DAMN's public service announcement played out.

"Nephilim!" one of the sisters in the booth exclaimed with a shudder. "Just imagine. I've heard the cities are crawling with them. Thank the Lord we're safe here in the country."

"Don't go thinking we're clear of them out here," the young man commented from the counter. "I heard talk some of them Nephilim creatures holed up on a ranch south of Seeley Lake."

"No!" The second sister's eyes went round. "You don't say."

"Bah." The old man at the end of the counter, his face whiskered and weathered, gave a dismissive wave of his hand. "Nephilim. Hellfiends. What a load of bull. Just another excuse for criminals to get off. 'The Devil made me do it.' Ain't I heard that one before. Only liberals and gossiping fools believe that crap. So what if folks are keeping to themselves out on their own land? No crime in that."

The younger man protested. "Bud Harkin's land is up that way. He says he's had seven calves gone missing in the last six months. And he found a sheep carcass without a head."

"Wolves," the old man countered. "Damn vermin are everywhere now. Ain't no Nephilim. Ain't no hellfiends. Tell me, has anyone here seen a demon?"

"But . . . how would we know if we had?" one of the sisters protested. "According to Father Walker, Nephilim look like regular folks. And hellfiends . . . they work their evil *through* humans. By influence and possession. A person might do any nasty thing if a hellfiend's got control of him."

The waitress snorted. "If that's the case, then I reckon I've seen a few demons in my day."

The old man grinned. "Aw, them were just men, Annie, darlin'. Doin' what men always do."

Annie turned to Luc and winked. "What about you, hon? You believe in demons?"

"Not at all," Luc lied.

* * *

Cade cursed his lack of experience, cursed his lack of subtlety, cursed his lack of control. For good measure, he directed an extra-foul curse at the great Artur Camulus, because if anyone deserved to be cursed, Artur did. The next few days were going to be a nightmare.

Cade had lived through one crisis. His own. He wasn't sure he had the stomach to anchor someone else's. Especially not Maddie's. Blast it all to Oblivion. He liked her. More than liked her. She was a haunting combination of fragility and determination. He wanted more than anything to erase the ordeal to come. She didn't deserve what was going to happen to her. It was going to be shit, doing what had to be done. But it was for her own good, he reminded himself. For her survival. And for his clan's. He vowed that once it was over, once she was his slave, he'd treat her well. Protect her from Artur. If he could.

Outside, the desert sped past. They were on a proper road now, unpaved but relatively free of ruts. He switched on the jeep's headlights. He didn't need light to see in the dark, but if they passed another car, it would seem suspicious to have them off. And Maddie seemed to sleep more calmly with the headlights on. Her death grip on the safety strap had eased.

Ideally, he'd have gained her trust before her first wave hit. Trust would have made things easier. He hadn't trusted Cybele when she'd found him—far from it—and his transition had been all the harder. If Maddie trusted him now, she'd submit to his will without question. As it was, he feared she was going to fight him every step of the way.

At least their wild interlude in the sand had allowed him to strengthen the tenuous mental mastery he'd introduced with his kiss the night before. She didn't trust him, but it didn't matter. Her body, bent on survival, didn't care about trust. She wanted him. Badly. Soon she'd be begging for it, and he wouldn't hesitate. He had no more choice in the matter than she did.

The enormity of his responsibility—to Maddie, to the clan, to the memory of the small person who had been, too briefly, his son—weighed like a boulder strung around his neck. What if he lost her, too? He didn't want to think about that. But it could very well happen, no matter how hard he tried to stop it.

She didn't believe his talk of Watchers and Nephilim. Well, he would have to overcome that resistance. Fast. He had to offer her something solid to hold on to before insanity became her only refuge from the truth.

"You think I'm Nephilim? Yeah, right. I'm beginning to think you're one of those idiot DAMNers after all."

"If I were, I'd have killed you on sight. No, Maddie, I'm just the opposite. I'm Nephilim. Like you."

"The Nephilim are a myth." She spoke slowly and enunciated clearly, as if presenting the truth to a half-wit. "Angels never walked on earth. Never mated with human women. Never produced half-human, half-angel hybrid creatures. The whole idea is preposterous."

"It's not. You and I are the proof. We're the descendants of the few Nephilim who escaped the archangels' vengeance. Our forefathers fled to every corner of the earth. My own ancestor was Samyaza's eldest son."

"Samyaza, who, according to *The Book of Enoch*, was the original leader of the Watchers?"

"That's right." Cade glanced in his rearview mirror. A glow hovered on the eastern horizon. "But eventually the Watcher

Azazel displaced him. After the curse, Samyaza's Nephilim son fled to northern Europe, where he taught his father's stolen heavenly magic to his descendents. They became the Druid priests of the Celts."

"So now you're a Druid, too?" Maddie laughed. "You *can't* expect me to swallow that. Especially since you've left off the white robes."

He shrugged. "Believe what you want. You'll learn the truth soon enough. Your crisis will leave no room for doubt."

"You keep talking about a crisis," she snapped. "If you think that's going to scare me, forget it. I've got terminal brain cancer, remember? All the fear's been leached out of me."

A car approached, motoring in the opposite direction. Cade stepped on the gas and flew past it. "You're wrong about that. Believe me, Maddie, there's going to be plenty of room for fear when you confront your demon nature."

Time passed before she spoke again.

"You know, not that I'm even close to believing you, but that's one thing I don't understand about the Watcher legend. The Nephilim were the children of angels, yet Jonas Walker and his DAMNers call them demons. Archdemons, even. Why?"

She was asking questions. Cade chose to take that as a hopeful sign.

"Angels and demons are virtually identical," he said. "The only difference is whether their existence is blessed or cursed by Heaven. Lucifer was originally an angel. When he lost God's blessing, he became a demon. Satan, Lord of Hell. The Watchers followed a similar path. They rebelled against Heaven and refused to repent. As punishment, Raphael was sent to destroy them. The Watchers' half-human offspring were cursed and given the vile epithet *Nephilim*. The Nephilims' human souls changed to demon essence."

"And you think I'm one of them. A half-human descendant of one of the fallen angels. A Nephilim."

"We call ourselves Watchers, after our forefathers. We consider Nephilim to be an unbelievably foul term. The worst insult you can hurl."

"But you called yourself Nephilim," she pointed out.

"Yes," he said. "I did."

She was silent a moment, a vertical line etched between her eyebrows. "It hardly seems fair," she ventured after a moment, "for children to be cursed for their fathers' sin."

"Fairness doesn't enter into it," he replied. "We Nephilim are crossbred atrocities. Our very nature is tainted. And on some level, Maddie, you've known that all your life."

A hit. No Watcher—no *Nephilim*—not even an unaware, escaped the race's instinctual self-loathing. Maddie turned abruptly to look out the passenger window.

Cade eased up on the accelerator and the jeep lurched to a halt. Half turning, he draped one arm over the back of the seat. "We call ourselves Watchers. Angels. But we know what we are. Even our young know. We're demons."

Maddie didn't look at him. "I'm not sure I want to hear any more of this."

He wasn't willing to allow the retreat. "Watcher children—dormants, we call them—are indistinguishable from human children. If a dormant belongs to a clan, is aware, he learns his heritage from birth. He prepares twenty years or more for the crisis that awakens his full power. But aware dormants, children of Watcher adepts, are a minority. There are hundreds, perhaps thousands, of unawares scattered over the world. Like you, they grew up believing they were human. Most of them never learn any differently. They live out a human life and die young."

"How young?"

"Before age thirty, always. Usually earlier. Sometimes from accidents or violence, more often from disease. But thirty years is plenty of time to produce the next generation of unaware offspring. Like you and me. Just over a year ago, I was dormant and unaware. My mother was a prostitute. She birthed me when she was sixteen and died of cancer when I was twelve. I spent the following twelve years on the streets of Cardiff, Wales. Then Cyb—" He cut himself off and swallowed. "Then my clan found me." He paused. "Your father died young, I understand."

"Yes." She didn't express outrage at his intrusive knowledge of her family history. Not anymore. "Of cancer, when I was a baby. My mother died in a car accident when I was fourteen. She was thirty-seven." Her voice wavered, and for a moment, Cade thought she would succumb to tears. "I bounced around in foster care afterward."

"That must have been hard."

"It was. It was miserable. But I wasn't the rebellious type. I worked even harder at school once she was gone. She made me promise her that before she died. I told her I would go to college and live a good life for both of us. And that I wouldn't waste a minute, and I'd never give up. So I worked hard and landed a university scholarship. Then the cancer came."

"And you fought it just as hard," he said.

"But it didn't do any good."

"It's gone now," Cade said.

"So you say."

He shifted in his seat. "Since your mother lived into her thirties, it must have been your father who carried the Watcher gene. He died young and never came into his full power. And you got brain cancer. You might have followed the same pattern if you hadn't survived the operating table. You nearly died there."

Her eyes touched his and slid away. "You know about my NDE?"

"Of course. My clan never would have located you otherwise." Cade leaned forward, willing her to accept what he was saying.

"Your near-death experience triggered what we call transition. Once a Watcher enters that state, he or she becomes immune to human diseases. That's why your cancer's gone. Because you looked death in the face and survived."

She scoffed. "An interesting premise."

"It's the truth, Maddie. A truth I lived through."

"You had a near-death experience?"

"I had a knife in the ribs during a botched robbery. I was the thief. I didn't dare show my face at the local surgery, so I hid out in a scummy cellar. The wound festered, my fever shot sky-high . . . I threw off the infection. Barely. But that was only the beginning. The real nightmare began three months later."

She stared down at her clasped hands for a long time. When she spoke at last, it was to ask a question Cade hadn't anticipated.

"Your NDE. What was it like? Did you feel weightless? Did you float down a tunnel? Did you see that loving white light people always talk about?"

He snorted. "None of the above. I felt as though I was choking on pitch-black sludge."

She fixed her gaze on a distant point beyond the windshield. "I saw the tunnel. Just like in all the NDE testimonials. I even . . . I even saw the light and sensed the loving presence. But when I arrived at the end of the passage, the light went dark. It was like . . . it was like a door slammed in my face. There was no loving presence. No God. No dead relatives waiting to welcome me to the afterlife. Just . . . nothing."

Her voice caught. "You always hear about people coming out of an NDE with renewed faith. Not me. I came out convinced the atheists have it right. There's no Heaven. No Hell. This life on earth is all there is."

A tear rolled down her face. Cade caught it with his thumb. Threading his fingers through her hair, he turned her head and forced her to meet his gaze.

"There is a Heaven and a Hell. Both places are for humans, though. And for angels and hellfiends. Not for us. For Nephilim, for you and me, there's no final judgment, no afterlife, whether it's endless bliss or eternal torment. We live, we die. If our true nature remains dormant, we die young. If we're strong enough, lucky enough, to endure the crisis, that brings us into our full power. Afterward, if we can avoid getting killed by our enemies, we have a chance to live out a life span of one hundred twenty years. But in the grand scheme of the universe, any earthly interval is no more than a blink of the eye. That's the curse we carry, the punishment for our fathers' sin. Oblivion."

Maddie didn't answer. Neither did she throw off Cade's hand. He slid it to her shoulder and squeezed gently. She was trembling.

"Tell me the truth. Is this . . . is this some kind of mind game you're playing with me?"

"I wish it were," he said. "I wish I could tell you that you're a beloved child of God, and that when you die, your afterlife will go on forever. But it won't. This is no game. You're a Watcher, and your transition from dormant to adept has begun. The first wave of your crisis has already hit. There will be no stopping the next one."

She squeezed her eyes shut. "You're talking about . . . about . . . what happened back there when you stopped the jeep. How I begged for it."

Cade repressed a wave of sympathy. Maddie thought that short roll in the sand was embarrassing? She'd better toughen up. She had no idea how truly desperate things were going to get.

"I thought you'd drugged me," she murmured.

"No. Your hypothalamus is flooding your body with Watcher hormones. Your body's responding. You think last night was bad? It was nothing. Your sexual cravings are just beginning. Soon they'll consume you. When that happens, I'll be your only hope. A Nephilim can't become adept alone. He or she needs an anchor." His fingers tightened on her shoulder and she opened her eyes. "A sexual anchor, Maddie."

"So what you're saying is, if I weren't . . . a Nephilim, you wouldn't be here. You wouldn't have given me a second look."

He wasn't sure how to answer that. No, he would never have been sent to find her if she weren't a Nephilim. And if she'd been born aware, to become a full adept of a rival clan, their paths never would have crossed except in battle.

"That's what I thought," she said quietly when he didn't answer.

"You mean you don't think you're attractive," he said. "That's not true. Yes, I was sent to you, but if I had somehow encountered you elsewhere, I'm sure I would have been drawn to you." Despite the curse. How to explain? He didn't understand it himself. But it wasn't just the pheromones that had captured his attention when he first saw her.

"Please," she scoffed. "Save it."

"Maddie—"

"What if I don't want you?" she asked abruptly. "What if I want to handle this transition thing on my own?"

Cade held her gaze. "Does this mean you're beginning to believe me?"

There was a touch of hysteria in her laugh. "What I'm doing is hoping this is all just an elaborate pickup line. But, really, dinner and a movie is just fine. You don't have to resort to fallen angels and eternal curses, and you don't have to excuse as biological my sudden craving for the closest available hard-on." She turned away. "Tell me, Cade. What happens, exactly, if I reject your gallant offer to act as my sexual anchor?"

"You go insane," he said. "And then you die."

Chapter Eleven

He was lying. Conning her. He had to be. Have sex with me . . . or go crazy and die? Just what every girl wanted to hear from a hot guy. She tried not to notice how troubled his eyes were. How utterly sincere.

Probably, he *was* sincere. Crazy people tended to believe the nonsense they spouted, right? She clung to that thought. The sun was rising. The red orb hovered on the horizon for one eternal moment before continuing its ascent into a lightening sky.

Cade faced forward and put the jeep in gear.

"Where are we going?" Maddie asked. Again. This time he gave her an answer.

"London."

"And just how do you expect to get me out of Israel and into England? My passport is back at the dig."

They reached a crossroad. Cade turned left, heading southwest. "It won't be a problem. Now get some sleep."

"So I can dream of you molesting me? No thanks."

"You need the rest, Maddie, for what's coming. And you *will* sleep."

He spoke a few words in a lilting language she didn't understand. Welsh? Or something older? The syllables flowed like water. Oddly, it seemed almost as though he spoke the words inside her skull.

"Sleep," he said again.

She opened her mouth to protest, but the words never emerged. She slept.

* * *

"What the hell?"

At first Cade thought the figure in white, standing with arms spread in the center of the road, was a mirage or a lost desert hiker. Then recognition struck. "Blast it all to Oblivion!"

He gunned the accelerator. The jeep flew toward Gabriel at one hundred thirty-three kph. Cade hoped the archangel would take the hint.

No such luck. Fifty feet out, the brake engaged and the jeep began to decelerate. The vehicle rolled to a stop precisely five centimeters from Gabriel's motionless body. The angel's snow-white robes didn't even flutter. In fact, the halt was so gentle that Maddie, sleeping with her head slumped on her chest, didn't even stir.

The archangel inclined his head and extended his wings with a flourish. The fluttering tips were purely for show, Cade thought sourly. As was the rose-garden scent and the stentorian greeting.

"Hail, Cade Leucetius."

Cade slapped the dash. "Damn it, Gabe. Get out of my way."

Gabriel stepped off the road. Cade stomped on the gas. Nothing.

Blast it. He sighed as the angel approached. "Do me a favor. Dial down that robe. The glare is giving me a headache."

"What is it with you Nephilim? Honestly. Would it kill you to be civil?"

"You want civility, stay in Heaven. Why are you bothering me?"

"Certainly not for the pleasure of your company. Why else? I've a message to deliver."

"Deliver it, then," Cade said, "and get the bloody hell out of my way."

Gabriel sniffed. Sweeping his robe aside so as to avoid contact with the dusty jeep, he leaned forward and looked past Cade to Maddie. "So that's the slave." He sighed. "Poor girl. You know, this crack-brained plot of Artur's—enslaving unawares—is bound to fail. I don't care how well you anchor her. The ones who spend the first part of their lives believing themselves to be human are never quite sane after transition."

"I managed," Cade said evenly.

Gabriel showed a glint of white teeth. "Ah, but you were a street thug. Already a monster. This woman . . . she's an innocent. Or as innocent as a Nephilim can be, anyway. Mark my words. She is not going to thank you for forcing her to face what she is. She'll go mad. Then you'll have to kill her."

"Get the fuck out of here."

"Your proud chieftain will be angry when you lose her. He'll blame you, of course. Artur would never admit his orders were flawed. But don't despair," Gabriel soothed. "It won't matter anyway. Magic harvested from slaves is not going to win the war against Clan Azazel."

Cade tensed. "What will?"

Gabriel's laugh was a trill. "As if I'd tell you! Oh, no. It's far more amusing to watch the lot of you fumble about." Maddie stirred, sighing, and the angel's pale gaze moved over her. "I suggest you kill this one now, Leucetius. Quickly and painlessly. In the long run it will be a kindness."

"No one has ever accused me of being kind," Cade replied through gritted teeth. "Least of all you. You've held me up long enough. Deliver your sodding message and let me get on with my life."

"Ah, yes. You're anxious to surf Maddie's next wave, aren't you?" Gabriel waggled his white brows. "You know, maybe I'll tag along. Become the proverbial fly on the wall . . ."

Cade itched to punch the immaculate bastard. To rub his

perfect, lily-white presence in black, oily muck. "And beat your useless wanker while you watch?" he taunted.

A flash of pink showed on Gabriel's pallid cheeks. The angel's odor of celestial roses, Cade was satisfied to note, turned sour. "Perhaps I'll take a pass," the angel muttered.

"Lovely," Cade said. "Now. Your message?"

"It's from Raphael. A warning."

"Oh, that's tidy. Is the boss too busy to consort with Nephilim himself? Sent his lackey in his place, did he?"

Gabriel's wings stiffened. "Raphael is . . . preoccupied at the moment."

Cade narrowed his eyes. "With what?"

"I'm sure it's none of your business. Or mine. Now. About that message." The angel sent a significant glance toward Cade's sleeping passenger.

"Your message has to do with Maddie?"

"Not precisely. It's about the Watcher relic she's unearthed."

Cade fought annoyance that Raphael and Gabriel already knew about the artifact. Sodding archangels knew everything, it seemed.

"Raphael wants it destroyed," Gabriel said.

Cade's brows rose. "Is that so?"

"I trust you'll see to it."

"Tell you what," Cade countered. "Why don't I give it to you and let you get rid of it?"

Gabriel's white hair bristled. "Me? I wouldn't touch the horrid thing."

"Because it scares the shit out of you." Cade grinned. "Or it would, if you had any shit in you."

"Very funny. Look, Cade . . ." Gabriel's expression turned uncharacteristically sober. "Just do what you're told this time. It's vital that you obey."

"And if I don't?"

"Then Raphael will be forced to, as you say, consort with Nephilim. He'll destroy the amulet and you and your slave along with it."

Cade snorted. "Right, then. You've delivered your message. Now take one back to your boss."

The angel bridled. "Raphael is not my boss."

"Whatever. Just tell Mr. Badass Avenger that the Watcher amulet is none of his fucking business."

Gabriel hesitated, then nodded once. Rising into the air, he paused with his white slippers dangling an inch from Cade's nose.

"I'll relay your message, Cade Leucetius. But I'm warning you, Raphael is not going to be pleased."

"Raphael," Cade said, "can go to Hell."

* * *

New York City

At that very moment—if it had been possible—Raphael would have been angry. Very angry. But he was an archangel and not a human. Archangels didn't feel anger. Truth be told, they didn't feel much of anything. Joy, love, lust—those were human emotions. Raphael was created to praise. To obey. To punish the wicked.

Plenty of wickedness was presently at hand. Humans, it seemed, considered cigars and alcohol to be necessary accompaniments to gambling and a prelude—or postscript—to illicit sexual congress. A sticky tile floor grabbed at the soles of his shoes. The air in his nostrils was thick. Raphael wondered, idly, how the humans hunched over the bar and the gambling tables could draw the rancid stuff into their lungs. Even he could almost smell it.

He straightened his tie and adjusted his suit jacket. He felt very odd dressed in this human costume; he much preferred his celestial robes. Judging from the looks of the establishment's patrons, he'd overdressed. Not that he cared.

He peered through the haze. The room was small, the tables set close together. A narrow stair hugged one wall; laughing couples climbed up and down. Raphael searched for his quarry amid drunken men and shameless women. Nothing.

A man of uncertain race stood by the bar watching him. An angry scar slashed from the top of his bald head down his cheek and along the length of his jaw. Sporting a pinstriped suit, a bloodred shirt, and heavy gold chains about his neck, the creature might have been the devil himself. But no. He was only a pale human imitation.

Raphael watched with dispassionate interest as the man set aside his drink and strode in his direction.

"Game?" the bald man asked, nodding to an empty chair at one of the tables.

"No," Raphael replied. "I'm looking for someone."

The man flashed a grin. "I have all kinds. Thin, fat, big-titted, fat-assed, you name it. And they'll do anything." He paused, letting that sink in. "Any-fucking-thing. For the right price, of course."

If Raphael had been capable of human emotion, he'd have felt disgust. "I don't want a woman," he said. "I'm looking for a man."

The pimp didn't miss a beat. "I can do that, too. It'll cost you extra, though."

"I'm not interested in one of your . . . employees," Raphael said. "The man I'm looking for is a patron."

The pimp's eyes shuttered. "I don't give out customer information," he said. "Bad for business. Unless, of course, you're willing to pay. Everything's up for grabs at the right price."

Everything came down to money with humans. Money and sex. Raphael didn't understand it. But then, it wasn't his duty to understand.

"Well, what'll it be?" the devil-man asked. "Pay or play? One of the two, or get the hell out."

Raphael was saved the trouble of a response. Michael was, at that moment, staggering down the stairs, hand in hand with a prostitute. In his ripped denims and snug black shirt, Raphael had to admit, no one would guess that his brother was anything but human. His disheveled brown hair and tanned skin completed the illusion.

At the bottom stair, Michael backed the prostitute against the wall. She submitted to a sloppy, openmouthed kiss before wriggling out of his embrace and strutting away. Michael sagged against the wall where she'd been and passed a hand over his eyes.

When he removed it, Raphael was standing before him. "You are a disgrace to our kind."

Michael grinned. "And you've got a stick up your ass, brother." He shoved off the wall and wove unsteadily past.

Raphael herded him toward the door. Surprisingly, Michael made no protest. They stepped out into a light rain.

"The Almighty would not be pleased," Raphael said.

"I imagine not," Michael agreed, straightening. He had no trouble at all navigating a path around the piles of crates and litter. He wasn't drunk. That would have been impossible.

Raphael studied him. "I cannot understand your behavior."

"Is it necessary that you understand?"

It wasn't, of course. Angels didn't need to understand; they only needed to obey. Curiosity was a human emotion. And yet, Raphael felt moved to delve deeper.

"You had sex with that human woman."

"I did."

"Why?" Raphael asked. "You can't feel it. Or, not more than the merest shadow of it."

"No. But she felt it. I gave her an orgasm."

"She's a prostitute. It was an act. She probably felt less than you did."

"No," Michael said. "It was real."

But Michael's eyes flickered downward, and Raphael knew his brother was far from certain.

Michael halted and faced him. "Don't you ever wish you could know what humans know? Don't you ever wish you could feel what humans feel?"

"No. Never. Human lust is not ours. Righteousness is."

"Righteousness is a piss-poor substitute for sex."

"True. It's far more valuable. And it is our duty."

Michael resumed walking. "Maybe I'm sick of duty. Maybe I want something more."

"There is nothing more," Raphael said. "We archangels vowed to put our individuality aside after the fall of the Watchers. We rejected the right to inhabit the wholly human flesh the Watchers once possessed. You're chasing a dangerous illusion, Michael. In the end you'll return to your duty—there's nothing else for our kind. Why pretend that there is? Why pretend to be human?"

"Why do you care?"

Raphael eyed him. "I don't."

"Then why are you here?"

Raphael hesitated. "Something has . . . happened. I may need your help dealing with it."

Michael's brows rose. "And just what is this . . . something?"

"An archeologist in Israel has unearthed something very dangerous. Something I thought I destroyed five thousand years ago."

They'd reached the end of the alley. Raphael stepped into

the spill of a streetlight but his companion remained in the shadows. And yet, Raphael had no trouble seeing Michael's comprehension as it slowly lit his eyes.

"Azazel's amulet," his brother said. "The Seed of Life."

"Yes."

"You mean that thing is still . . . active?"

"Partially," Raphael admitted.

Michael's chin went back. "Partially. What does that mean, exactly?"

Raphael hesitated. "The amulet is damaged. The bloodstone was split in two, and half is lost, I know not where. I'm not fully sure what the damaged piece is capable of. I do know I don't want to find out."

"Where is it now?"

"In the possession of Cade Leucetius of Clan Samyaza. I sent Gabriel to order him to destroy it. The message was delivered, but Leucetius refused to obey."

"Not surprising. But why even bother sending a message to a Nephilim? You know what they're like. If you want the thing destroyed, you're going to have to take it from him and do the job yourself."

Raphael hesitated.

Michael's brows rose. "You don't want to," he said. "You're afraid of the thing. Oh, that's rich."

"No. Not afraid," Raphael said. "Fear is a human emotion."

Michael snorted. "And emotions just aren't your thing, are they? You're a hypocrite, Rafe, you know that?"

"I do my duty, as always. Emotions don't enter into it."

"If you say so. Well. All this is very interesting, but I hardly know what it has to do with me."

Raphael drew himself up to his full height. "The amulet must be recovered and destroyed. We can't afford to fail this time. With you at my side, Michael, our victory is much more likely."

"*Our* victory?" Michael's lips thinned. "I think you're overreaching a bit there." He paused. "This call to battle—is it a command from on high?"

Raphael shifted his shoulders. "No. I . . ." He cleared his throat. "If you must know, I haven't yet brought the matter to the Almighty's attention."

Michael threw back his head and laughed. "Keeping this little error mum, are you? No wonder! It would cast you in a most unflattering light before the throne." He shook his head. "And you claim to have no emotion. You do know pride is an emotion, don't you? And one of the seven deadly sins?"

Raphael almost felt something akin to irritation. "There's much more at stake than my pride," he said. Abruptly, he spread his wings. "Come."

Michael shook his head. "No. As long as it's only you doing the asking, I'll give myself the pleasure of declining."

Raphael stared. "You cannot! Don't you understand what's at risk? Nothing less than the survival of the entire human race! You can't possibly refuse me."

Michael took a step backward and slipped farther into the gloomy alley. "Oh, no? Just watch me."

Chapter Twelve

"Good morning, little sister."

"Ezreth."

Lilith's eyes flew to her half brother. Ezreth was not in the habit of seeking her out. She smiled at him uncertainly.

He stepped closer to the well as she emptied the last bucket of water into her jug. Crimson light limned his head and shoulders.

"A drink, sister, if you please."

Frowning, she lowered the bucket into the well one last time. Pulling it back up, she offered it to him. He took it without thanks. His throat worked as he drank. When he was done, he threw the vessel aside and wiped his mouth with the back of one hand. Droplets lingered on his beard.

"Drawing water for Father?" he asked.

An innocent enough question. She wasn't sure why the query left her so uneasy. She lifted her jug to her head and steadied its weight with one hand. "Yes."

"You've been often in Azazel's company of late."

"Yes," she said again.

Her gaze darted past him, to the field beyond where the ewes and lambs grazed on a flush of spring green. The shepherds were far to the north, near the wall of the canyon. The women of the village had gone to the stream with bundles of dirty robes. Father, she knew, was not in his forge, nor in his tent. She and Ezreth were very much alone.

"You are often with him. In the village. At his forge." Ezreth moved closer. His aura turned dark, the color of pooling blood. "In his tent."

Despite her unease at being alone with him, she couldn't suppress a rush of satisfaction. She recognized that ugly light in his eyes. He was envious. Of her. A heady thought.

"I am," she said. "Father is teaching me the ways of magic." She lifted her chin. "He says I am the most apt pupil he has ever had."

Ezreth's gaze raked an insolent path down her body. "I can well believe it."

She turned wary. "I must go now. Stand aside."

He moved still closer instead, his left hand descending to grip her shoulder. He squeezed, hard, his thumb finding the tender hollow at the base of her throat. He pressed there until she couldn't help but gag.

He smiled and eased the pressure fractionally. The heavy weight of the water jug on her head prevented her from jerking out of his grasp. His grip on her shoulder tightened; he shook her slightly.

Instinctively, she raised her free hand to stop the jug from falling. The motion caused her chest to rise. Fire kindled in Ezreth's eyes. "You have grown womanly, sister." He reached out and cupped her breast. "So soft."

Lilith stood rigid, fear constricting her ribs, her breakfast threatening to rise up her gorge. Ten years her senior, Ezreth was broad and hard with muscle. He was strong in war magic. If he wished, he could take her right here by the well. How could she fight him? Not with her own magic. So far, Father had taught her only gentle arts.

She summoned her most imperious tone. "Take your hand off me or I will tell Father of your disrespect."

"Ah yes." His tone was taunting, unrepentant. His hands on her shoulder and breast tightened painfully. "Speak to me of our father. Has he had you yet?"

"You are disgusting."

"Why? It is no secret that Father has only one use for a woman."

"I am his daughter!"

Ezreth laughed. "What difference should that make? You have two legs to spread, do you not, a woman's hot core between them? I do not know why such talk should shock you, sister. The tale is all over the village. All the tribe believes you are Azazel's newest whore."

Heat bled up her neck and into her face. She gripped the jug on her head as if it would keep her upright. "That is Ayalesh and Nivah spreading lies."

Ezreth licked his lips. "So you are virgin still?" The dark light returned to his eyes. "Perhaps," he said thickly, "I will remedy that."

His thumb pressed hard on her windpipe. When a painful gasp parted Lilith's lips, Ezreth's mouth clamped onto hers, his lips wet and thick, his beard abrasive. His hand roamed her breast, squeezing her nipple.

The carnal plunge and retreat of his tongue in her mouth gagged Lilith's cry of outrage. In shock, she submitted to the assault for several long, nauseating moments. Then she became aware that her arms were still raised and gripping the heavy jug on her head. With an abrupt motion, she dipped her chin and jerked her body back. The vessel tumbled from her head. Ezreth yelped as the heavy clay glanced off his skull. The jug landed with a crash on the ground. Water drained between the fragments to soak into the dry, hungry ground.

"You swine!" Lilith hissed, wrenching out of her brother's slackened grip. "Look what you forced me to do."

"Me?" Ezreth glared, rubbing his head. "This is your doing, not mine."

The depth of his arrogance enraged her. "Father will learn of this betrayal, brother. *He will banish you to the upper desert. Your sorry carcass will bake in the sun. The buzzards will pick your bones clean."*

He sneered. "I do not think so. You will not want Azazel to know of your shame. You will not want him to know of your whoring."

"I am no whore!"

"No?" He gave her an ugly smile. "You came alone to the well. You greeted a man. You offered him water."

"You are my brother! There is no shame in that."

"You also flaunted your body."

"I did not."

Ezreth's expression was one of smug amusement. "It makes no difference. You are no longer pure. No longer untouched. If you wish, I will go with you to Father and help you confess all. I will offer to restore your honor by taking you as my concubine."

"You have your own women already! You have sons and daughters. You don't need me."

"But perhaps I want you."

"I would rather die," she said fervently, "than be your whore."

"I will go to Father alone, then. I will tell him what you've done and ask him to forgive you."

Panic rose. "You would not."

"I would. And he will let me have you once he knows you are no longer innocent."

Tears welled in her eyes. "I hate you."

Ezreth laughed. "I do not hate you, sister."

"Do not do this," she begged. "Do not tell Father."

"Perhaps I will not. For a boon. What shall it be?" He seemed to consider. "Ah, yes. You will come to my bed freely. You will give me use of your body—I am sure one night will be enough—and I will keep your secret. Or I will go to Father and you will be mine for as long as I wish to keep you."

She stared at him, aghast. "You could not be so cruel."

He smiled. "I assure you I can. With pleasure."

And Lilith knew she was trapped.

* * *

The residue of Ezreth's kiss lingered on Maddie's lips as she struggled toward consciousness. She wiped her hand across her mouth, nauseated. The terror, the disgust, the shame . . . it had all been so very real. But it was only a dream. A dream about the Watcher Azazel.

Hardly surprising. She'd been immersed in the Watcher legend for months. It was only natural the theme should show up in her sleep. She only wished it weren't so vivid.

She sat up, becoming aware of her surroundings for the first time. She'd fallen asleep in the jeep; now she lay on a bed she didn't recognize, in a room she'd never seen. The light was dim, but from the strips of sunlight showing through the cracks in the wooden shutters the night was ended at last.

It seemed Cade had brought her to a hotel. An exceedingly cheap one. The mattress was uncomfortable. Too hard under her hips. Too soft at her shoulders. She had a vague memory of being lifted from the jeep. Of Cade's strong arms carrying her up a narrow stairway. She might have drunk something warm. Tea, maybe? She wasn't sure.

Crooked strips of yellow light spilled across the frayed bedspread. A sort of haze, lush and yearning, filled the air. It also filled Maddie's mind. She sensed a whisper of a voice inside her skull, like a long-ago lover's breath.

She frowned, straining to hear more of the murmured words, but they were unintelligible. A second presence, a disturbingly real ripple of *otherness* inside her head, blocked them. It made the first voice melt away, and she was left feeling confused and frightened. And warm. Too warm.

She inhaled a deep breath. It didn't help. Her chest hurt as it expanded. A furnace had ignited inside her ribs, setting fire to the underside of her skin. The flames spread to every part of her body. Unsettling warmth licked at her hands, her arms, her legs and feet, flashed inside her shoulders and belly. Tongues of flame taunted her breasts, teased between her legs.

The thin wool blanket was coarse and itchy. She kicked at it but only managed to tangle it more tightly around her legs. With a start, she realized she was naked. Naked and yearning. She moaned, flinging her arms wide. Her head tossed.

A figure rose from a chair in a shadowed corner. Maddie went still. She hadn't realized she wasn't alone.

Cade stepped into the dim light as she lay panting. Waiting. Wanting. Needing. He'd said she'd be reduced to begging. If he didn't touch her soon, she would prove him right.

He took a step forward. Another dark form rose behind him to take up a position beyond his right shoulder. Eyes riveted on the apparition, Maddie sucked in a breath. But her scream froze in her throat.

Cade halted, dark brows drawn together. Briefly, he glanced over his shoulder. Couldn't he see the thing? Feel it? The creature was all but breathing down his neck. She could see it more clearly now, and couldn't rip her eyes from the hideous rotting skin, the gaping, drooling mouth. Flames crackled in the creature's eyes. Long yellow teeth dripped blood.

A gnarled limb reached past Cade to grasp at the foot of the bed. Maddie screamed and scrambled backward, crawling up the headboard. She pressed her spine against the plaster wall. The thing surged, drool oozing from one corner of its mouth. And yet Cade did nothing.

"Cade. Help! Please—"

She tried to escape. She tried to dive off the side of the bed. She couldn't. She couldn't move. She could only wait as it came closer and closer . . .

And then Cade was there, kneeling over her with hands braced on either side of her head, his broad form blotting out the horror. "Maddie. *Caraid.* Look at me."

"I can't, I . . . it's there, behind you. I—"

"Nothing's there, love. See?"

He moved slightly, allowing her a view of the room. It was empty. The creature was gone. And Maddie knew, without a doubt, Cade's presence had banished it.

First you go insane . . .

Her body went limp as rags. She licked her cracked lips. Her throat hurt.

"Cade?"

"I'm here with you, *caraid*. There's nothing else."

"But . . . I saw it. I did. It was—"

"I know you saw it," he said gently. "I know. But it's gone now. I sent it away."

"Th-thank you." *For saving me. For believing me.*

Gratitude quickly transformed to yearning. Tears welled, too, as waves of lust drove at her body. She arched her spine against the hot tide. It left her gasping and sobbing, broken on a rocky shore.

"Ah, *caraid*. I hate seeing you so frightened."

The unexpected sympathy in Cade's voice, the profound understanding she sensed from him, made the tears flow harder. Cade's arm slipped beneath her shoulders. Seating himself on the bed, he settled her in his lap. The smooth rim of a cup pressed her lips.

"Drink."

Cool water flowed over her swollen tongue. She gulped until the cup was empty. But with one need fulfilled, she became all the more aware of the others. Her breasts felt swollen, the tips unbearably sensitive when the rough wool coverlet shifted across them. A soft moan escaped.

Cade set aside the empty cup. Maddie grabbed his hand and pressed it to her breast. Her nipple beaded against his cool skin. His arm tightened around her as he rubbed in a circular motion.

Nothing had ever felt so good. For a moment. The sensation faded too soon, leaving her bereft and yearning. She stared up into his face.

"Is this the crisis?" she whispered. "The one you warned me about?"

His blue eyes had never looked so grave. "It's part of it. But not the worst. Not yet."

His quiet words frightened her. She felt as though she'd been flung into a mad inferno. If this wasn't the worst . . .

"I . . . I need you." She couldn't stifle a moan or stop her body from writhing, her lips from begging. "So badly. Please. Make love to me."

It was as if he'd been only waiting for her invitation. He stood and shucked his clothes without speaking. She watched him from her position on the bed, her breath shortening with each moment. His body was beautiful, all sculpted muscle and sinew. The meager sunlight that stole in past the shutters painted his large form in soft gold. Only his right arm remained dark, rendered almost black by the twisting tattoos.

He untangled the blanket from her legs and dropped it onto the floor. He replaced it with his body, covering her from breasts to toes. His weight bore her down into the lumpy mattress. It was glorious.

His erection, hard and hot, nudged between her thighs. She throbbed for him there with a deep pulse that seemed to well from her inner depths. She tried to open her legs, tried to welcome him into her body, but his knees kept her thighs pinned. His elbows constrained her arms. His blue eyes looked down on her, shadowed with something that almost looked like regret. His lips—his beautiful, mobile lips—remained silent.

Her lust began to turn painful. "What . . . what are you waiting for?"

"Maddie."

Softly spoken in Cade's lilting accent, her name sounded lyrical, almost magical. *Maah-dae.* She flushed, wanting him so much. And not just to chase away the fear, not only to banish the terrifying insanity lurking just beyond his shoulders. She yearned for something deeper. Something . . . enduring. But that truly was madness.

"Do you trust me, Maddie?" His voice rumbled, the vibrations transferring from his chest to hers. "*Can* you trust me?"

"I . . . I don't know. But what does it matter? I need you. I'm begging you. Just like you said I would. Isn't . . . isn't that enough?"

"No. No, it's not."

Abruptly, he rolled onto his back, taking her with him. The room lurched, then settled again. She found herself sprawled atop his broad body, hands braced on his chest. Her legs were parted over his thighs. His erection prodded hotly at her belly.

His hands rested loosely on her hips. Slowly he lifted his arms and tucked them behind his head. Her eyes followed the flex of his muscles, then collided with his watchful gaze.

"You want me," he said. "Go on, then. Take me."

Maddie, perched atop him, felt as though more than just her body was exposed to his eye. "You mean you want me to . . . to be on top?"

His grin was unexpected. "Don't you know how?"

His smile seemed to stab her heart. The glimpse of the boy he must have once been devastated her. "Of . . . of course I do. It's just . . . this way is so . . ."

His brows rose. "So what, *caraid*?"

Intimate, she wanted to say. *Revealing*.

Threatening.

He wasn't holding her. She could have climbed off him. Could have grabbed the blanket or found her clothes. Could have retreated to the chair in the corner. She sensed he wouldn't follow. But the shadows beyond the bed pulsed with the echoes of her glimpse into madness, and that was far more terrifying than any sexual vulnerability.

She encircled his shaft with her fingers, testing his size. He was big. Bigger than any man she'd been with. Slowly she stroked him from head to base. He lay still, allowing the exploration. But Maddie sensed violence under his calm, and she realized that he *wanted*. Perhaps almost as badly as she did. The discovery bolstered her courage.

She bent forward, trapping his shaft between their bodies. Her lips found his. His mouth opened, welcoming her tongue's invasion. He smelled of desire and tasted like salvation. She delved deeply, drinking him in.

Her hands smoothed over his shoulders, his chest. She toyed with his flat male nipples. He was damp with sweat, his skin satin over iron muscle. The contrast fascinated her. She pressed her lips to the pulse at his throat. She ran her tongue along his collarbone, tasting salt.

Lower she slid, dragging her tongue over his chest and stomach. She opened her mouth over the head of his shaft and then, with a groan, took in as much of him as she could.

Her body's dew flowed, bathing her thighs and his. This felt right, she realized. Inevitable, even. Her previous embarrassment faded to dim memory.

She sensed Cade inside her mind. Yes, she now recognized the steady presence she'd felt earlier as *him*. His life essence, his will. The invasion had ceased to be strange. It felt almost natural. The whispering voice, that other presence she didn't understand, had been far more disturbing. But it had fallen silent. She hoped it was gone for good.

She allowed him to slide more deeply into her mouth. The tip of his shaft touched the back of her throat, and she relished his low moan of pleasure. His hands tangled in her hair, holding her head as his hips lifted—

And then he was pulling her up his body, covering her mouth with his, his tongue plunging deep. His hands molded her breasts, stroked down to her thighs. She lifted her head, palms braced on his shoulders, and gazed down at him. His nostrils flared. His blue eyes spoke volumes, silent but eloquent.

His hands slid to her hips. He lifted her, positioning himself at the entrance to her body. But it was Maddie who joined them, Maddie who lowered her body onto his rigid flesh.

She impaled herself slowly, sinking down by slow degrees as she softened and opened to his penetration. Her hands, still braced on his chest, shook. His skin was hot, slick with sweat. His eyes remained locked with hers. If the world had ended at that moment, she couldn't have looked away.

He stretched her. Conquered her. Her breathing went shallow; her inner muscles contracted. Cade's fingers bit into her hips. A grimace almost like pain touched his features, and he adjusted the angle of her body and yanked her down hard. She cried out against a blinding spike of pleasure. Too much. Too vivid. How could anyone endure such vibrant bliss? But it was only the beginning.

Cade moved beneath her, inside her, his grip anchoring her hips, his strength preventing her retreat. There was no choice for her; she gave herself up to his body. To the rolling waves of pleasure he unleashed on her senses. But soon, to her surprise, she found it wasn't enough. She wanted more.

Matching his rhythm, she strained to meet each thrust. He groaned and pulled her down, matching the length of her body to his. His tongue thrust into her mouth, pulsing, surging, mimicking the movement of their hips. She shuddered and gave herself over to pure sensation that was building deeper, wider, higher and higher . . .

He stiffened and went impossibly hard inside her. Finally, it *was* all too much. She broke and shattered into countless pieces. Cade caught her keening cry with his mouth. His big body shuddered beneath her as they traveled to a place of pure, mindless perfection.

* * *

"My God," Maddie said.

She lay beside him, her head pillowed on his chest. Cade was aware of her body, warm and quiescent beneath his arm. The scent of her contentment, the purple odor of fresh-plucked violets, drifted past like a misty spring rain. It felt good, holding her. Despite everything, despite the grief and pain of the past weeks, despite the certain pain and danger of the future, he felt almost . . . happy.

It was unexpected. As a rule he didn't invest much emotion in sex. At least, not since he'd been with Cybele. That encounter had trembled with all the turmoil of his newly discovered Watcher essence. It had been inevitable, he supposed, that he had fallen in love with her. But had it really been love? Up until a few days ago, he would have sworn that it was. Now, however, with Maddie in his arms, he wasn't so sure.

Since Cybele he'd only had human women. His son's mother had been only one of many after Cybele made it clear any physically intimate relationship they shared was ended with Cade's emergence into full adept power. His subsequent sexual activity, a string of one-night stands, had been only minimally satisfying. Human sex just could not compete with a Watcher coupling.

With Maddie, he'd experienced even more than the explosion of pleasure he remembered from his union with Cybele. He was aware of a deep sense of fulfillment, of absolute *rightness*, that he'd never before known. Maddie was as sated as he, her body limp in his arms. Through their strengthened psychic link, he knew the utter repose of her mind.

"I had no idea sex could be like that," she murmured, her lips tickling his chest. "It never has been before."

Cade sensed she'd begun realize their union was more

than physical. That he was inside her head. Did she suspect how he planned to use that connection? *No.* She wouldn't be lying relaxed in his arms if she realized he was plotting her enslavement.

His contentment turned sour. "Watcher sex is more . . . intense than human sex," he explained, his voice colder than he intended.

She lifted her head and looked at him. "That's really what I am, isn't it? A Watcher?" She swallowed. "A Nephilim."

He exhaled. "Yes."

She disentangled herself from his embrace and rolled onto her side, facing away. "It's hard to absorb. So I'm not fully human. I'm half . . . what? Angel or demon?"

"I told you before. There's no difference."

She sat up. "Except that one is blessed and the other is cursed."

"That's right." His lips twisted. "Despite great sex and miracle cancer cures, you might not consider Watcher life an improvement over a fully human one. Not that you have any choice."

She wrapped her arms around her raised knees. "I know I'm not a saint, but what have I ever done to deserve being cursed?"

"You were born."

"That's hardly fair," she protested.

"Is life fair?"

Her frown told him she didn't like his logic. Too bloody bad. Philosophy was crap; the sooner she faced reality, the better off she would be.

He sat up, pity and guilt warring with practicality. Should he reveal more? There was only so much reality a person could face in such a short time. Without going mad, at least. He dragged a hand down his face. Maddie was cast adrift in a sea that would shortly turn raging, with only him as her anchor. What a mess. She deserved a better guide. But who? Brax? *Artur?*

A cascade of rushing anger impacted like a fist to the solar plexus. The thought of Artur touching Maddie boiled Cade's blood. He'd see the bastard in Oblivion first. If Artur dared lay one finger on Maddie, Cade wouldn't hesitate to issue a challenge. He'd kill Artur or be killed before he'd stand by and let his chieftain steal what was his.

The sheer violence of his emotions left him shaken. He drew a deep breath and tried to regain a measure of calm. He was getting too close, allowing himself to feel too much, and too deeply. He couldn't afford to forget that Maddie was, by the very nature of her ancestral lineage, his rival. It would be foolhardy in the extreme to imagine any true trust, any true love, between them. Ultimately, they could have only one kind of relationship: master and slave.

Maddie, beside him, sat up and wrapped herself in the discarded blanket. Perhaps she sensed his mood through their psychic link, because her scent went from happy violets to something close to mud. His mind brushed her thoughts. He sensed embarrassment and fear and a touch of unsettled anger. They weren't bound so securely that he could hear the exact words of her thoughts, but it was enough.

She needed space, he realized, as much as he did. He stood and moved a few steps from the bed. "Your clothes are there on the floor." He nodded toward an untidy pile of fabric. "Why don't you dress in the bath?"

She sent him an uncertain look. "Thank you."

Dragging the blanket with her—as if he hadn't seen every inch of her body—she scooped up her shirt and khakis and disappeared into the bathroom. He grabbed his jeans and shoved his legs into them. He heard a toilet flush and water running. When she emerged, her face looked freshly scrubbed. She wandered to the chair where he'd sat earlier and sank down on the ripped vinyl cushion.

"You came looking for me here in Israel. You knew I was Nephilim."

"Yes."

"How?"

There was no reason not to tell her. "An adept of my clan—Brax Cocidus—identified you. It was a tricky bit of detective work. Unaware dormants are indistinguishable from humans. It's impossible to detect them until a near-death experience launches them into transition. When that happens, their bodies start to manufacture Watcher pheromones designed to attract an opposite-sex adept. The range is rather limited, though. Most often an adept isn't at hand and the newly awakened dormant doesn't survive."

He watched closely for a reaction but saw none so continued. "Brax figured a way around the problem of proximity. He cross-referenced near-death reports from hospitals with police records of hellfiend activity. You came up on the radar."

"How would hellfiend activity lead to me? I've never seen or even felt a hellfiend. I'm not even sure I believe they exist!"

"They exist," Cade assured her. "They're foul, evil beings, always looking for a way into a human mind. But if they sense the presence of a Watcher, they back off. They can't influence or possess us. Our life essence is too similar to theirs."

"DAMNers say the Nephilim are archdemons. That the hellfiends are under their command."

"Such control is possible," Cade admitted. "But difficult. Some Watcher clans try to use hellfiends as slaves, with varying degrees of success. My clan does not. We'd rather see them annihilated."

"You've killed hellfiends?" Maddie asked.

"A few," Cade admitted. "Druid magic can create strong

illusions. A Clan Samyaza adept can shield his Watcher nature very effectively. We can get close to hellfiends, though it's still tough to catch one. They're disgusting things, though; as a rule, we avoid them, unless we're after an outright kill. That's not the case for other Watcher clans, however. Some pursue hellfiends with the intent to enslave. Which is why the hellfiends tend to flee whenever they sense a Watcher. After your near-death experience, the hellfiends fled your territory. That was the red flag that alerted us to your Watcher nature. Also, you joined an archeological expedition searching for evidence of the Watchers. That was no coincidence."

Maddie frowned. "The moment I saw Dr. Ben-Meir on TV, I became obsessed. My dreams started even before I arrived in the Negev."

"Not dreams," he told her. "Memories."

She shook her head. "Hardly. I dream about the Watchers. The original ones who lived five thousand years ago."

"Your dreams are really ancestral memories of real events. All Watchers have them. They're encoded in our genes."

She blinked. "You mean what I see in my dreams is the memory of something that actually happened to my ancestors?"

"Exactly." Cade watched her. It was time to discover how useful Maddie would be to Clan Samyaza. "Tell me what you've dreamed."

A small vertical line appeared between her brows. "I dreamed I was at a well, drawing water. The same well we uncovered at the dig. There was an older man nearby polishing a sword."

Cade's pulse quickened. "Who?"

"My father." She flushed. "Or rather, the girl in the dream's father. A Watcher."

"Which one? Do you know?"

"Yes." Her fingers twisted in her lap. "It was Azazel."

Azazel.

Cade's fist clenched on a visceral rush of triumph. He could hardly believe his good fortune. Maddie's power came from the same root as Vaclav Dusek's. With her enslavement, Clan Samyaza would bring Dusek's power under their command. The field of battle would be level. The death of Cade's son, and all the others who had died in the massacre, could be avenged. For the first time, Cade began to believe Artur's desperate scheme would actually work.

Maddie's eyes were troubled. "According to the Book of Enoch, Azazel was the worst of the Watchers. He was utterly depraved. But in my dreams he doesn't seem like such a monster. He was kind to his daughter. She loved him."

Cade went down on his haunches in front of Maddie's chair. Taking her hands in his, he waited until she met his gaze. "There are two sides to every story," he said. "Enoch was a man of Yahweh. The Watchers defied God's law. Having done so, they remained unrepentant. Of course Enoch would describe them as depraved. In his eyes, the Watchers deserved the curse flung down upon their heads."

"So they weren't really evil at all?"

"I'm not saying that. Azazel was no innocent. Neither were his brother Watchers. Their descendants are far from blameless. Some have committed atrocities against humanity." He brought her hands to his lips and kissed her fingers one by one. "I won't lie to you, Maddie. We share an ugly legacy. But we do *share* it. I don't intend to let you face it alone. Remember that promise and cling to it when the darkness closes in." *Even after I betray you.*

She exhaled an unsteady breath. "Thank you."

He felt nothing but trust radiating from her mind. The trust he'd worked so hard to put there. Trust he didn't deserve.

Guilt sliced at his innards. He was a bastard, to use her this way, to lead her, blind and trusting, to bondage. He released her hands and stood. Pacing to the window, he opened one of the shutters. The narrow street, two levels below, was painted with the long shadows of early evening. A shabbily dressed man trudged past without looking up.

"What time is it?" Maddie surprised him by asking. Such a mundane question.

"There's a couple hours of daylight left." He turned back to her. "You should rest. Before tonight."

He phrased it as a suggestion but in reality it was a command; the urge to blurt out the truth to her was very strong. He had to put some space between them before that happened. With the strengthened link between their minds, it was easy to force her acquiescence without her even knowing he'd done so. She yawned almost immediately. A moment later, her eyelids drooped.

"I don't know why I'm so tired all the time," she groused.

"It's normal during transition." That wasn't completely false.

He guided her to the bed. Unprotesting, she stretched out on the mattress and said, "Maybe I will sleep, just a little. But"—she blinked rapidly, fighting the heavy droop of her eyelids—"what happens tonight?"

Cade didn't answer.

Chapter Thirteen

Lead was for the earth, bronze for war, silver for joy. But gold—pure, shining, perfect gold—was the essence of enlightenment, the divine spark from which all creation sprang. If one possessed gold, one possessed all. To truly possess gold, one must create it. To create, one must sacrifice.

Lead, bronze, silver, gold . . . *Lilith breathed the progression as she scraped metallic, orange-red dust from a silver tray. The powder, every grain, dropped into a rounded clay vessel. She lifted her eyes to Azazel's.*

"Go on, Daughter."

She nodded. The hilt of the knife felt slick in her left hand. She adjusted her grip and pressed the tip of the blade to her right palm; her white skin opened in a red slash. Curiously, she felt no pain. She opened her hand over the clay vessel. Blood dripped. Silently, she counted seven drops before pulling away.

"Now, replace the cover."

A silver moon shone down from a brilliant sky, illuminating her task. The vessel was completely round except for three supports that kept the sphere from tipping. A copper sheet lined the inside. Under the watchful gaze of her sire, Lilith joined the two pieces. She twisted the top once, until the ridges on its edges locked into place with the grooves on the crucible's base.

"Good," Azazel said.

Hands trembling, Lilith took up a beeswax candle and touched its wick to the flames in the forge. Tilting the taper above the crucible, she dripped wax over the top and along the seam of the two pieces she had joined. She filled the gaps carefully, not lifting her head until she was satisfied every crack had been sealed tight, and she let out a breath when Azazel once again nodded his approval.

"The crucible is the woman's womb," he said. "The flame is man's desire. Join the two, Daughter."

Lilith lifted the small vessel—it was surprisingly heavy—and placed it on the fire. The flames rose; the wax melted, sizzling as it struck the coals. Lilith stared into the conflagration, aware of an all-consuming tension. Was she worthy of her father's faith? Would she succeed?

Azazel did not speak until the clay turned black. Then he indicated for Lilith to take up a small bronze rake and drag the crucible from the fire. She did so. Long moments passed. The cooling clay whistled and groaned.

Lilith waited, not speaking, not daring to raise her eyes. She would rather die than meet her father's eyes and reveal her rising fear. At last Azazel dipped his chin. Lilith stepped forward. Bare hands trembling slightly, she cupped them around the heated vessel. The air left her lungs in a rush. The burned clay was cool!

Her lips parted in surprise; her father's deep chuckle sounded behind her. "Come now, Lilith. You did not think I would allow your tender flesh to come to harm, did you?"

Flushing, she looked up at him in wonder. "But . . . it emerged from the fire. How is it possible?"

"The greatest virtue is knowledge," he told her. "All things are possible to the one who comprehends the divine."

"I do not understand," she said.

"You will." His dark eyes flowed over her. "Open the vessel."

It was more difficult to open the crucible than it had been to seal it. Azazel handed her a bronze knife; she inserted the tip between the vessel's two halves. Steam hissed free in an almost human sigh, and diaphanous yellow mist seeped into the air. The two pieces of clay parted. Lilith gazed into the top half of the crucible.

"Oh!" The copper sheet had changed. It was now a mystical, translucent red. "How beautiful."

Azazel smiled. His crimson aura sparkled. "The color tells us your effort has succeeded. Well done, Daughter."

Her eyes flew to the base. The reddish dust she'd scraped into the vessel had transformed into a shining black residue. When Azazel handed her a curved bronze scraper, she used the tool to transfer the dark material from crucible to a small stone bowl.

"The prime substance," her father said. "The seed of creation. Utterly devoid of light. As was the universe before illumination by the divine spark."

Lilith cupped the bowl in her hands, tilting the black powder—the prime substance—so that it spilled back and forth. The material was so black it seemed to cause everything nearby to brighten.

Some might have called it ugly. Frightening, even. But truly, it was the most wondrous thing Lilith had ever seen.

"And I created it," she breathed.

"That is only the beginning, Daughter."

* * *

Maddie woke, disoriented, the dream image burning the inside of her skull. She sat up abruptly, shaking her head as if to dislodge it. The mental experience was so real, almost as if it were her own memory. According to Cade, her dreams were actually her ancestor's. Lilith. A few days ago she would have scoffed at the notion. Now she believed him. Against her better judgment, against all instinct, she was beginning to trust Cade Leucetius.

Where was he? Her eyes darted around the shabby room. Something squeezed inside her chest when she realized she was alone. She let out a long breath, fighting a quiver of panic. She should be glad for a bit of privacy. Just thinking of what had happened between her and Cade caused her body temperature to rise several notches. She could hardly believe what she'd done. What she'd let him do.

It had been the most incredible sex she'd ever had. No. Scratch that. To call what she and Cade had done "sex" was like calling a category-five hurricane a summer shower. She felt stretched more ways than she'd thought possible. She was sore between her legs, and the tops of her breasts stung from the scrape of Cade's stubble. A red mark graced her shoulder from his teeth and lips.

The lock on the door, she found, was broken. But though the knob turned freely, the door itself wouldn't budge. She set her shoulder against it and shoved. Nothing. Kicked it. Nothing. She pounded on it with her fists and called out. No answer.

The door had to be bolted from the outside. There was a bright light in the hallway, illuminating the door's edges. Frowning, she ran a hand down the crack beside the jamb. The light was an odd color, dark and silvery, and when she pulled her hand away, opalescent ribbons followed her fingertips. Strange.

A day ago, she would have blamed the visual disturbance on the tumor. Now she wasn't so sure. If Cade's assertions were true, her cancer was gone and she was in the midst of some kind of transformation from human to Nephilim. Could the light be . . . magic? Some kind of protection?

Not protection. Imprisonment. The words rose in her mind, almost independent of her thoughts, a whispered voice in her ear. A chill ran through her. It intensified when she spied a flash of movement near her toes.

A snake! She jumped back, heart racing, and the creature slithered to a position in front of the door. She backed toward the bathroom as it lifted its head. It hissed in her direction, forked tongue darting past twin fangs.

Thankfully, the reptile stayed in position by the door. Almost as if it were a guard. Maddie frowned, examining the animal more closely. Red and black markings decorated its body. The thing might have been a twin to the one she'd shooed out of her hut two nights ago. Or the two snakes might be one and the same.

On that disturbing thought, she slipped into the bathroom and shut the door, questions rising into her mind like so many bubbles in a bathtub. Where was Cade? Why had he left her? What was he doing? Did she even want him to return? She couldn't help thinking of the snake tattoo on his leg, the one that looked so much like the snake in her hut and also like the snake in front of the door. Coincidence? Hardly. What the hell was going on?

Trembling hands braced on the rim of the sink, she stared at her reflection in the cracked mirror. Her hair hung limply, too dirty to curl. Her face was pale, her eyes underscored with dark half-rings. Dried sweat clung to her skin. She hardly felt human.

Her eyes locked with the eyes in the mirror. According to Cade, she wasn't human. She was like him. Part angel. Or, if she preferred, part demon. Soulless. Cursed.

If Cade was to be trusted, she was on the edge of a crisis. A crisis that brought overpowering sexual cravings. It might kill her. After it drove her insane.

He's lying. He's using you. The whispering voice echoed inside her skull.

She scrubbed her hands over her ears. "He hasn't hurt me," she said out loud.

He forced himself on you.

"Forced? Ha! I was the one who climbed on top of him."

If you trust him, he'll destroy you.

"Shut up."

Turning to the shower stall, she cranked the faucet. It protested with a metallic squeal. The stream of water was thin and lukewarm. The soap was brown and coarse. She didn't care; she stripped off her clothes and stepped in. She scrubbed her hair and body until her skin was red and her fingers sore.

She dried off with the single scratchy, threadbare towel. Cautiously, she cracked the door and peered into the main room. The snake was still at the door, but it lay still, its head down. She ventured in, treading softly. The reptile didn't move.

Clothes bundled under one arm, she retreated to the opposite side of the room from the door, near the window. As she stepped into her shorts, she slipped her hand in the left pocket. Her fingers closed on the amulet. The breath in her lungs left in a weakening rush. The union felt like a homecoming. The relic was safe.

She took out the disc and cradled it in her palm. Despite the deep crease across the center and the damaged central stone, the piece truly was beautiful. The Seed of Life pattern sparkled white. The red gem glowed in a slice of shuttered sunlight.

Dr. Ben-Meir's corpse rose suddenly into her mind's eye. A hot flush spread over her skin and she started to sweat. Ben-Meir was dead. Because of the relic? Because of her? Could the explosion that killed the archeologist really have been magical? Had it come from this bit of metal and stone in her hand? The very idea was ludicrous.

And yet . . . she could feel the magic in the disc. Feel its response to her touch. She'd been angry when Dr. Ben-Meir had tried to pry it from her hand. Had she somehow activated a deadly force against him? Could she have stopped it? Was it *her* fault he was dead?

She wished suddenly that Cade had gotten rid of the disc. He should have flung it into the desert. But coming close upon the heels of that thought was the realization that she would have fought to stop him. She would have fought him even if he'd insisted on holding the relic for her. If he took the disc, if she fought him for it, would the relic respond? Would it kill Cade, too?

That's what Cade believed, she realized. That was why he'd handed her the relic with no protest. He knew she was connected to the disc. It was hers. *Hers.* That scared the crap out of her.

She looked at the door, at the snake acting as sentry. If the disc was magic, could she use it to get out? Unfortunately, she had no idea how and she wasn't really eager to try. She had nowhere to go, anyway. She shoved the amulet back into her pocket and took to pacing back and forth in front of the window, from wobbly chair to paint-chipped table.

"Damn you, Cade. Where are you?" How could he go off and leave her trapped like this, without a word of explanation? She didn't want to be alone. She needed him here to tell her what was going to happen next.

Suddenly, her heart missed a beat. Her skin began to tingle. Her head lightened, as if the top of her skull was lifting off. She looked down at her hands and saw a strange glow flow across her skin, a light that was somehow dark and bright at the same time, similar to the light coming from the crack in the door. Charcoal and pearl and indigo, it moved and sparkled on her palms. It reminded her of a rare black opal she'd once seen in a jeweler's window.

Tongues of blue flame sprang to life in her palm. She stared at the phenomenon, aghast. Holy hell. Fire burned in her hand and she didn't feel it.

Waves of panic hit in such quick succession she had to gasp to draw breath between them. What was happening? She shook her hands, rubbed them together. The fire persisted, racing along her fingers.

A moment later, the flames died as abruptly as they had sprung to life. Maddie was left trembling and close to tears. Was this part of the mysterious crisis Cade had spoken of? What other horrifying things were going to happen? What, exactly, was she expected to face? Cade had been long on dire warnings, short on detail. He'd locked her in this tiny box of a prison and left her at the mercy of her terrified imagination.

Damn him.

She resumed pacing, rubbing her arms against a sudden chill, though in reality the room was quite warm. Fear and anger escalated with every step she took. She wanted Cade. Needed him. Hated him. Or rather, she hated her growing dependency upon him. Hated him for the secrets he was keeping from her.

The son of Samyaza is not to be trusted.

"Shut up!"

The needling voice inside her head fell silent.

Trembling slightly, trying to ignore the colors chasing over her skin, Maddie stepped to the window. The same dark light encircling the door frame ringed the window frame as well. She wasn't surprised when the wooden shutters refused to budge.

She sneaked a look at the snake. The creature seemed unconcerned, so she slid the left shutter's vertical bar and was rewarded when the slats tilted. Twin metal cables fastened on either side of the window supported an overhang just below the sill. Across the narrow alley, a pattern of cracks spiderwebbed across peeling stucco. Shabby wooden shutters, much like the ones on this window, were flung open. She detected no signs of movement in the rooms beyond.

At street level, off to the right, a restaurant board chalked with Hebrew characters was propped beside an open doorway. She wondered if the place ever had any customers. The alley, dingy and litter-strewn, was deserted save for a scrawny yellow cat. She watched its tail disappear around a corner.

She was just turning away when a new movement caught her eye at the end of the stone-paved alley. Human this time. Not Cade—the man didn't have his height or his bulk. She adjusted the slant on the shutter slats and leaned forward to get a better look. The man walked in the shadows on her side of the street, head down. A whisper of red light trailed after him. Just before he passed out of view beneath the overhang, though, he glanced up. Maddie choked back a strangled cry.

Dr. Ben-Meir! He wasn't dead after all!

She clutched the sill, waiting for the archeologist to reappear on the other side of the overhang. Long seconds passed, in which she was sure her heart would beat its way right out of her chest. Had he entered the hotel? Did he know she was trapped here?

No. The man had only paused. Another moment brought his back into view as he made his way down the alley.

Maddie stared after him, noticing for the first time his hunched shoulders and slightly limping gait, and she turned away from the window in denial. It hadn't been Dr. Ben-Meir after all. Of course not. He was dead. She'd seen that with her own eyes. The man in the alley was just a passerby.

She resumed pacing and worrying. The shifting patterns of dark light on her skin hadn't abated; if anything, the colors had grown more pronounced. A glance in the bathroom mirror told her the phenomenon had spread to her face. Even her hair shone. A small lick of fire ignited on her index finger; she smothered it in her fist, unnerved by the fact that it didn't hurt in the least. Where the hell was Cade? She was ready to jump out of her skin.

Though it felt like hours had passed, probably no more than ten minutes later his broad form filled the door. The strange illumination on the door frame faded as he entered. The door shut quietly behind him.

The snake slithered over his boot and wrapped around his calf. As it melted into his skin, Maddie stared.

"Your tattoo? It's . . . alive?"

"In a way." He made no further explanation. His eyes ran over her. "So. It's begun."

She lifted her hand. Dark pearlescent colors chased across her skin. Abruptly, she dropped it. "Where have you been?"

He held up a paper bag, an offering. She took and opened it, was greeted by the aroma of roasted meat. She forgot about the snake, forgot the colors on her skin.

"Food," she breathed. "Thank you. I didn't even realize how famished I was until right this second."

"It's to be expected," he said. "Roasted lamb," he added as she rolled greasy paper off pita wrapping savory slices of the meat. "Eat quickly. We've got a lot of ground to cover before the third wave."

Hunger warred with apprehension. "But—"

"Questions later. Right now, eat."

She nodded and tore into the food with a need that bordered on irrational. The lamb was barely cooked, dripping red juices. The first bite sent a shudder of delight through her body.

The last rays of the sun disappeared from the window as she ate. The instant she finished, Cade's thumb hooked toward the door. Then he paused.

"Where's the relic?"

"In my pocket. But don't think you're going to take it."

He snorted. "Not to worry. I don't have a death wish."

So. She'd been right.

He grasped her elbow. "Come on."

"Wait!" She resisted. "You said you'd answer some questions."

"Later."

"No. Now."

She thought he'd refuse her demand, but after a brief hesitation he sighed and released her. "All right. But make it quick."

She rubbed her arm, her gaze momentarily trapped by the shifting colors on her skin. "What *is* this?" she asked, lifting her arm.

"The beginning of the end," he said. "Of your transition, I mean. The third wave of your crisis isn't far off."

"How long?"

"Hard to say, exactly. It varies. Between twenty-four and thirty hours, I'd guess."

"What happens then? You keep talking about a transition, but you've given me hardly any details. What am I transitioning to?"

His eyes shifted to one side. "Your full powers as a Watcher adept."

The fierce anticipation curling in her belly startled her. Her palms grew damp and she rubbed them on her shorts. "You've said as much. But what does that mean? What powers am I going to have once this is over?"

"I don't know what all your talents will be," Cade admitted. "Magic varies from clan to clan, from Watcher to Watcher. Though, there are traits and powers we all have in common. From birth we're all tall and left-handed. After transition, you'll gain strength and speed, and the ability to see in the dark. And you'll experience your . . ." Frowning, he fell silent.

A ripple of fear passed through her. "My what?"

"In each adept, one or more of the five human senses is enhanced. For example, I have a heightened sense of smell."

She sensed that wasn't what he'd been about to say but decided to let it pass. "I . . . see trails of light around people's heads and shoulders," she offered. "And once, in the pit, everything looked . . . like more than it was." She gave a short laugh. "If that makes any sense."

"It does. Your sight is enhanced."

She looked up. "I thought it was the tumor."

"The tumor is gone," he repeated.

She absorbed his certainty and realized she actually believed him. She wasn't going to die. She was going to live. As a being she didn't begin to understand.

"What other powers do Watchers have?"

"Power unique to each original Watcher is channeled to his descendants through shared ancestral memory. My clan is adept with the magic once practiced by Samyaza. Druid magic. Enchantments and illusions, mostly. We draw power from earth elements, from soil, roots, natural stones . . ."

Maddie stared at her hands. "A few minutes ago," she remarked slowly, "my palm caught fire. It . . . didn't hurt."

Cade didn't seem surprised. "Clan Azazel is adept with fire elements. They're masters of alchemy."

Her brows rose. "Alchemy? You mean like turning lead into gold?"

Cade's lips compressed. "For a start."

* * *

The waters of the Mediterranean shone darkly; the sparkling lights of the coastal towns were strung along the shore like diamonds in a necklace. The beauty was lost on Cade. The quicker he left the land of his cursed ancestors behind, the happier he would be. He and Maddie stood atop the rise of desert just beyond town. Their jeep, run dry of petrol, sat abandoned on the road at the base of the hill.

Maddie's second wave had forced him to delay longer than he would have liked. Thankfully, her sexual hunger was sated at the moment. But with each passing moment, the opalescent glow of her skin grew brighter. She balanced on the cusp of her transition. The pheromones pouring off her skin escalated Cade's arousal.

He wondered how much time they had. Not long, he was sure. The safest place for Maddie's transition was London, with Artur or Brax standing guard. He'd even sent a text to Brax telling him to expect their arrival. But the thought of involving Artur or his brother in Maddie's transition sickened

Cade. He didn't want either of them anywhere near her when the crisis broke.

His mind flashed forward, anticipating that moment. His body hardened against a backdrop of apprehension. Could he bring Maddie safely through? *Yes.* He couldn't afford to doubt his abilities now. He couldn't bear to think that he might fail, might have to watch her die. Or worse, might have to kill her.

Beside him, Maddie rubbed her bare arms against the chill of the desert night. "What are we doing here?"

His mind ran along the link stretching from his essence to hers. Since completing the sex act, their bond had strengthened. His sense of her emotions was strong. He could even hear into some of her thoughts, though the darkest corners of her mind were still closed to him. She was tethered to his will.

At some level, she knew it. Of course, she didn't yet know how strong those chains were. Soon he would show her.

"Are we . . . meeting someone out here? Another member of your clan?"

"No."

She slipped her hand into the pocket of her shorts. He knew she touched the Watcher amulet.

Her bond with the talisman was an unexpected complication. Cade was more than wary of the danger the piece represented. At the moment, its magic seemed dormant. But he couldn't count on it remaining so. Not with Ben-Meir's fate waving like a warning flag. Given Maddie's obsession with the piece, Cade was sure the amulet had been created by one of her ancestors. Perhaps even by Azazel himself. If so, the secret to its magic was buried in Maddie's ancestral memories.

The presence of the relic was sure to complicate Maddie's transition, too. It was vital that Cade establish absolute control of both Maddie and her magic. No matter how repulsive slave-making was to Cade, he recognized that his dominance of Maddie was required to give Clan Samyaza control of her magic. Cade didn't want to contemplate a scenario where Maddie came into her power freely. She might very well choose to stand with her kin. With Vaclav Dusek and his sons. Cade couldn't imagine a worse disaster. Free and aligned with Dusek, Maddie would be the final nail in Clan Samyaza's coffin.

Atop the hill, illumed by the night sky, he turned to face her. The colors on her skin were kaleidoscopic. Her eyes had begun to change as well, taking on a soft reddish tint. He was very glad she hadn't seen that in the cracked hotel mirror.

Though, really, what would it have mattered? It was time. Time for her to know what she was. Truly.

Apprehension festered in his gut like rotted meat. How would she react? She picked up on his unease; her mind released tendrils of curling fear. The acrid odor pinched Cade's nostrils. He could delay no longer.

"Maddie."

Though her eyes reflected fear, she met his gaze calmly. Something in the vicinity of his heart lurched.

"I'll take care of you, Maddie." His voice was low and fervent. "I give you my promise. I'll see you through this. I'm here to protect you, not to hurt you. Never that. Whatever happens, whatever you see, think, feel, no matter how frightened you are, just trust me. Will you?"

She stared at him a long while. He held his breath.

At last she nodded. "Yes."

She could not disguise her terror. His attempt at reassurance had only frightened her further. Why had he even attempted consolation? He knew it was impossible.

It was time. Capturing Maddie's glowing red eyes with his, he made sure she watched as he willed his human facade to fade away.

His own eyes heated and became demonic red like hers. Maddie's breath hissed out. Horror distorted her features, and her jaw worked reflexively. Her hand crept to her throat as darkness poured from Cade's being to sparkle on the surface of his skin, opalescent light, shifting charcoal with hints of pearl and indigo.

Maddie swallowed, wet her dry lips with her tongue. She looked down at her hands, her forearms. Then back at Cade. "Your skin . . . it's like mine."

"That's because we're the same, Maddie."

"My eyes. Are they—?"

"Yes. They're red like mine."

Choking revulsion rushed from her mind to his. Her scent turned turbulent, a churning river of mud and fear and denial.

"No," she whispered, staring at her hands. "No. Not this. This can't be happen—"

"There's more," he told her.

I'm sorry, he wanted to add. *I'm sorry I'm the one who must show you.*

The sound of ripping fabric told him he'd forgotten to strip off his shirt. Shredded cotton fell away as the muscles in his back contracted. The odor of hot sulfur tinged the air. Pain knifed through him. He gritted his teeth and braced for what came next. His demon essence, rising to the surface. Skin darkening, glowing. Dark wings, unfurling. A rush of blistering wind.

Maddie began to scream.

Chapter Fourteen

"Fire, Lilith, is creation's purifier. As is pain. Feel the fire, Daughter. Feel the pain. Pass through it to power. Open your heart and you will be rewarded. The pain will vanish into your magic."

Lilith closed her eyes and did her best to obey. It was hard. So very hard. When she'd first touched the fire, aided by her father's power, the sensation had been exhilarating. Now it was nothing but agony. That sensation, he had told her, was a sign of her lack of faith.

Aware of her father's harsh gaze upon her, she bit her lip to keep from crying out. She tasted blood on her tongue. Tears gathered in her eyes. Azazel's voice turned harsh.

"Life begins in pain and ends in pain. How will you master the secrets of life, Lilith, if you cannot master pain?"

The fire seared her skin. Tears leaked through her eyes; her breath came in spurts. But she did not flinch. No sound passed her lips. She was determined to prove her worth. She would show her father how much she loved him. She would learn what he wanted so much to teach her.

The agony multiplied. Tenfold. A hundredfold. Into infinity. Panic scraped sharp claws inside her chest. Her flesh would be charred; it would peel from her bones and crumble into ash. She would be crippled. Useless. Pitied. Lost in shame forever. A scream tore from her throat at last.

Her father's frown silenced her. She was better than this. True, she was a daughter of the earth, but she was also a daughter of Heaven. Heaven's magic lived inside her, was a part of her very being! That stunning knowledge vibrated in her bones, in her flesh, in her consciousness, and it demolished at last the barrier of her mind. The pain vanished.

Her eyes flew open. She looked down at her hands. Blue flame leaped from her palm, snapped the length of her fingers. Yet there was no heat. No pain. Her skin remained unmarred.

She met her father's gaze. She saw his pride, his immense satisfaction.

"You have gone beyond, Lilith. To a place few have the courage to enter."

He smiled and lifted the fire from her hands. Joy welled in her breast. She'd pleased him! For her, there could be no greater pleasure.

Azazel placed the fire in the forge and leaned forward to press his lips to her forehead. "Well done, Daughter."

* * *

The glittering monster, standing where Cade had been moments before, rose. Its charcoal wings swept forward. In another second it would catch Maddie, utterly and completely, in its embrace.

The screams piercing her ears were her own. She stumbled backward and fell, arms flailing. The impact with the sharp stony ground drove daggers of pain into her hands and buttocks, and she scrambled to her knees. She had to run. Had to escape. Somehow, her limbs wouldn't move.

"Maddie."

Cade's voice came from the monster's mouth. He sounded so normal. So human. And yet red eyes shone from a face of sparkling darkness. His torso and arms were shining, too. His fingernails had curved into claws. And his wings . . . She shuddered. They were dark and charcoal-feathered. The gleaming edges looked razor-sharp.

Dear God. Everything he'd told her was true. He was an archdemon. A Nephilim. And so was she. She screamed and screamed and screamed.

She couldn't move. Couldn't run. His presence was in her mind, overriding the commands her brain sent to her limbs. With dawning horror, she realized the bond enabled him to control her.

He stalked toward her slowly. Inexorably. All she could do was stare at the ground in front of her feet and tremble.

His wings settled around her, sheltering, imprisoning, but not touching. "Maddie," he said. "Look at me."

"No," she croaked. "No. I can't." Shudders racked her body. "Oh, God. I can't."

"I told you what I was. What you are."

"I . . . I didn't believe you. Not really. Or, maybe I did but I didn't really *know*—" Another tremor rippled through her. "Oh, God. Am I . . . am I going to look like you? Like this?"

"Yes," he said. "I'm sorry."

Maddie had thought she knew what fear was. She'd thought she was as scared as a person could be when her doctors told her, without a shred of doubt among them, that she was dying. She'd thought she'd known what despair was. She'd been wrong. What she'd felt then was only a shadow of the terror that consumed her now. She was a *monster*. A cursed atrocity. She squeezed her eyes shut. "Maybe . . . maybe I should just give up. Just die."

"You don't believe that." Cade's voice was too close to her ear. It almost sounded like it was inside her head. His breath rasped. "You're a fighter, Maddie. Brave."

"Brave enough to kill myself."

She'd been living under the specter of death for more than a year. Living with dread. Denying and preparing for the end. Fighting to make every second count. But for what? Death would come in the end. She was as ready as she would ever be. And accustomed to the idea by now. Surely it wouldn't be so difficult to take the plunge.

"But you won't," he said. "You'll do as I say. You've only just begun the third wave. There's much more to come. You won't run from it, Maddie. You *will* face it. With me."

Her panic was all consuming. "No. Go away. Please. Leave me alone. Maybe . . . Maybe I'd rather die than become what you are." But her voice lacked conviction. She wanted to live. At any price.

And Cade surely knew it. His arm snaked around her waist. "You'd rather fight. And you will."

She opened her eyes to find her face just inches from his chest. The shifting colors on his skin—dark shadows of crimson, indigo, jade, and amber—filled her with violent terror. Something inside her snapped. Fight? Yes, she'd fight! But, not the way he envisioned. Instead she assaulted him, clawing, punching, slapping. She tried to wrench her body out of his grasp.

He lifted her easily, imprisoning her against his torso as she kicked and scratched. She sank her teeth into his arm and was rewarded with his grunting curse. His stiff arousal prodded her stomach. His palm found her ass and squeezed. A wave of hot lust careened through her body. The will to resist drained from her mind and her limbs. As quickly as the battle lust came over her, it evaporated. She sagged against his unyielding hardness. She was sick of this roller coaster of emotion. She wanted nothing more than to steady herself in the safety of his strength. Even if his strength was that of a monster.

"Make no mistake, Maddie. You are mine."

The whispered words sounded inside her head as well as in her ear. She experienced a shudder of understanding. It was true. She was his. Utterly, completely.

He held her body. He spoke in her mind. He'd all but claimed control of her life essence. She suspected that last would come, very soon. There would be no escape. No death. No end to the nightmare. She was Nephilim. And if she wanted to survive her transition, she was going to have to do it with Cade as her anchor.

His arm shifted. His muscles banded like iron around her torso. "I'm sorry," he said again.

Dark-feathered limbs filled her vision. The desert dropped away with dizzying speed, and the steady beat of his wings matched the rush of her heart. They were airborne, gliding toward the black expanse of sea. Emotions churned, and Maddie struggled to put a name to them. Fear? Despair? Terror? Anticipation? Wonder? Awe?

All of these.

The sparkling lights on the shores of the Mediterranean merged with the night sky. Cade set a course over open water. As she felt his whisper in her mind, Maddie closed her eyes and let him take her.

* * *

A jagged line appeared on the horizon: rocky cliffs, rising from the sea, far away but sharp to Cade's enhanced vision.

The Mediterranean crossing had been uneventful. The weather had been calm, and Maddie remained quiet in his arms. The unfolding of his wings and the long flight had exacerbated the wound he'd taken during the massacre. His shoulder hadn't fully healed, he realized. The pain was worsening, throbbing with each sweep of his wing. But it didn't slow his progress. He made sure of that. He scanned the dark sea below. He'd passed a spattering of Greek islands and the larger bulk of Sicily advanced. He was close enough to see breakers pounding against the shore. Another few hours would see him across Europe and into England. With luck, they would make London in time.

The sudden slash of a flaming golden sword less than a meter from his face nearly caused him to drop Maddie. Raphael, all bright wings and righteousness, hovered before him. Bloody, bloody hell. Cade tucked his wings and dove, narrowly missing a second slash of the archangel's sword.

"Cade Leucetius," Raphael roared. "My brother brought you my command. You did not obey."

"No shit," Cade shouted up at him. Maddie stirred, groaning. Cursing under his breath, he tightened his grip around her waist. "I don't take orders from self-important prigs."

Except Artur, he amended.

The angel flared. "Take care, Nephilim. Defy me at your own peril. Oblivion awaits."

"And I suppose you think you'll be the one to send me there."

Cade maneuvered into a more defensible position, soaring up on Raphael's left side, angling to position his body between the angel and Maddie. Her muscles stiffened and her eyelids fluttered.

Raphael circled, yellow flames trailing his celestial blade. "It would be my greatest pleasure to fling you and your whore into the void."

Cade laughed. "In your dreams, Rafe."

Maddie clutched at him. "Cade? What's . . . what's going on? Who—?"

He couldn't risk taking his eyes from Raphael. "No one important, *caraid*. We'll be on our way in a moment."

Or so he hoped. But he wasn't a fool; an angry archangel was a formidable foe. Unburdened, he might make a good showing. With Maddie in his arms? How was he going to fight?

The angel's flaming sword slashed forward. Maddie

screamed. Cade lurched back, but not before a line of fire burst along his wing. Blast it all to Oblivion! Rafe had sliced the shoulder that had been injured in the massacre, reopening the badly healed wound. Cade gritted his teeth against the searing pain. He'd be damned twice over before he'd give Raphael the satisfaction of hearing him groan.

The archangel's expression turned smug; his teeth flashed. "You want to keep your precious damned life? And your whore? Maybe I'll let you. Once Azazel's amulet is destroyed."

"Fuck off," Cade growled.

He dove. The black waters of the Mediterranean hurtled toward him. Maddie whimpered, her arm hooked in a death grip around his neck. Raphael hurtled in their wake, golden hair streaming, his wings a bright smear against the starry sky.

Cade reversed position and soared upward. The maneuver did nothing; the archangel streaked after him. The heat of his fiery sword licked the soles of Cade's boots.

Because Maddie's safety was his first priority, Cade considered obeying the angel and destroying the Watcher disc. Almost immediately he rejected the plan. Bowing to an archangel went against his nature. If Raphael was so obsessed with the disc's destruction, he must be afraid of its power. That in itself was reason enough to hold on to it. Cade wasn't even sure he could safely wrest the relic from Maddie's possession, let alone destroy it. He wished he knew more about the nature of its power.

He spiraled higher, his right arm encircling Maddie's waist. She clung to him. The air grew frigid as they careened upward, Raphael on their heels. The wound on Cade's shoulder continued to burn. Higher . . . just a bit higher . . .

"Leucetius," Raphael roared. "You cannot win. Destroy the talisman. Or give it up to me."

Cade pressed his lips against Maddie's ear. "You like roller coasters?"

She wrapped her legs around his waist. "I hate them."

"That's a shame, *caraid*."

It was a gamble. He wasn't at all sure the move would work well enough to allow their escape, but it was all he had. Streaking upward, he swept his left palm over his right arm. The sleeve tattoo, a deftly interwoven web of Druid incantations, came away in his hand. It trailed behind him, heavy and sparkling.

Cade soared through a high cloud. Twisting, he swung the mass of magic in a half circle around his head. As Raphael burst through the mist behind him, Cade dropped the net. It fell neatly on the angel's shining head. Then Cade wrapped Maddie in his arms, tucked his chin, and dove.

The archangel's roars of rage chased him. As he hurtled seaward, Cade allowed himself a grim smile. He hadn't even guessed Raphael knew some of the words currently erupting from those pure, celestial lips.

The angel twisted and slashed as he plummeted. A few strands of Cade's net snapped, but on a whole the spell held. The harder Raphael fought, the tighter the snare contracted. Each sweep of the angel's wings worsened his situation. Feathers hopelessly tangled, Raphael tumbled downward. His curses cut off as he plunged into the black waters of the Mediterranean.

Cade drew up sharply, hovering a few feet about the surface. Elation shot through him. He'd done it!

"That's tidy, then," he said.

"You're insane," Maddie gasped. "Absolutely insane."

He grinned. "You noticed."

"Is he gone?" She peered over his arm.

"For now."

But, the battle had taken its toll. His left wing felt as though it was on fire.

Reluctantly, he faced the truth: there was no hope of reaching London tonight. He set a course for the rocky coastline.

* * *

They landed hard in a tangle of limbs and wings on unforgiving cobblestones. Cade had set them down—whether by chance or design, Maddie didn't know—in a trash-littered piazza at the heart of a dreary hill town. Every door in every heavy gray building was shut tight. Every window was dark. The first streaks of dawn stained the sky.

Every muscle in Maddie's body screamed. She picked herself up off the ground slowly, sure she'd left her stomach in the sky: there was nothing but a hollow feeling in her gut. She still couldn't quite wrap her mind around it all. Angels, demons. Cade was a cursed monster. *She* was a cursed monster. She wondered if heavenly creatures would be assaulting her on a regular basis from now on.

Cade caught her under one elbow. "Anything broken? Bruised?"

He sounded so . . . normal. She stared down at his hand, transfixed by the pearly gray opalescence of his skin. She swallowed hard.

"Look at me," he commanded.

She didn't want to, but somehow her wishes didn't enter into it, just as it had been in the desert right after he'd changed. She'd tried to run, but his will had superseded hers. If she concentrated, she could feel his presence in her mind. It felt . . . not unpleasant.

Who was she kidding? If she were being scrupulously honest, she would have to admit it felt . . . right. Better than right. Like the feeling you got when you knew the man you wanted was about to kiss you.

And if that man also happened to be an archdemon? One that wanted her, not for herself, but because of the magic she could bring to his clan?

His skin glowed with the darkest hues of the rainbow. She

looked at him. His gleaming red eyes gazed steadily back. And his face . . . His features hadn't changed. Neither had his body, if she discounted the missing tattoo on his arm and the massive silvery charcoal wings now folded against his back.

When she'd first seen them, the feathered edges of his wings had appeared sharp and forbidding. Now they looked wispy and soft.

Before she quite knew what she was doing, she'd reached out a hand. "Can I . . . can I touch you?"

His answering smile was tight. "Anywhere you want, *caraid*."

Hesitant, she put her hand on him. His wings felt as soft as they looked—like silk, but warm and alive. His eyes closed at her touch, and a tremor rippled through his big body.

He opened his eyes. His irises were blue now, intense and human. Once again she was hurtling downward through a starry sky, falling, falling, falling into a desire she knew she was helpless to control. And this time, it had nothing to do with her approaching crisis. Her body was her own; it wanted his. She wanted him. It wasn't love—she knew that. At least, not on his part. Maybe it was because they were two of a kind. Nephilim.

She stroked her hand down his wing. Her fingers hit a snag and sudden pain contorted his features.

She snatched her hand away. "You're hurt."

"Not badly."

Maddie wasn't so sure about that. Her eyes ran over the place she'd touched. The feathers were torn; the skin below had a ragged rip. She spied a trickle of red.

"You're bleeding!"

"It's nothing."

He tipped back his head and spread his arms wide. The rush of power took her by surprise; she hadn't expected to be able to see it so clearly. A wave of opalescence washed over his skin, touched his wings, and they folded and shrank. Magic. The sparkling color faded to pale flesh. He lowered his head, completely human again.

She exhaled. "Can you . . . can you change anytime you want?"

"Yes. It's my nature."

And mine. Maddie's brain supplied the unspoken words. She was . . . that.

"Does it hurt? To change, I mean?"

A grimace passed over his face. "A bit. But once you're fully in your natural form it feels good. And it's much easier to fight."

"That was an angel that attacked us, wasn't it?"

"The archangel Raphael. A self-important bastard."

Until yesterday she'd thought archangels, like Nephilim, were a myth. It was hard to wrap her mind around the fact Cade, in Nephilim form, had just done battle with one.

"Did you . . . kill him?"

"No," Cade said. "Not by a long shot. I'm not sure that's even possible."

She couldn't stop herself from slipping her hand into her pocket. "He wanted the relic."

"Yes."

"Maybe . . . maybe we should have given it to him."

Cade echoed the whispered voice in her mind. "No. I won't give it up. If Raphael wants it destroyed, it must be vastly powerful."

"Is that what you want? Power?"

"Yes."

"Over Raphael?"

"No." His eyes shifted away from her. "Over a rival Watcher. One who's sworn to wipe my clan from the face of the earth."

"Can he do it?"

He paced a few steps. "He's already begun. Less than two

weeks ago, DAMN annihilators attacked my clan with weapons pimped with Samyaza magic. Our clan wardings didn't so much as register their approach. We didn't even know they'd entered the compound until the first explosion."

"How horrible!"

"A Watcher named Vaclav Dusek engineered the attack. Dusek has sworn he will send Clan Samyaza to Oblivion. Somehow, he's gotten himself named to DAMN's international board of directors. Now he's in a position to use DAMN as his own personal army." Cade's expression was grim. "So far he's doing a fine job of it."

"There were . . . deaths?"

His voice was raw. "Yes. Only six of us remain."

"You and five others?"

Cade nodded. "Artur Camulus, our chieftain, and his half brother, Brax Cocidus. Another pair of siblings, Cybele Andraste and Lucas Herne. Luc wasn't in Glastonbury the night of the massacre. There's also Brax's cousin, Gareth, our only surviving dormant. Twelve others—Watchers and humans under clan protection—died in the attack. Some were children. One . . . one was only an infant."

The grief in his voice unnerved her. She'd begun to think of him as a monster, a Nephilim with red eyes and no soul. Now, before her eyes, he'd transformed into flesh and blood. Into a man grieving for his family. She wasn't sure she wanted him to be so vulnerable. To still be so . . . human.

"Did you lose someone you loved?" she asked. "A woman?" She tried to ignore a stab of jealousy.

"No," he said. "Not a woman. A child."

"Yours?"

"Yes. My son. An infant barely a month old."

"What was his name?"

"I . . . I don't know. His mother left him on my doorstep a few days before the attack. I'd only been with her once and hadn't seen her since. Didn't know I'd gotten her pregnant. She didn't leave a note with the boy. I don't know if she called him anything. I hadn't gotten around to giving him a name. I barely spent an hour with him before he was killed."

"Which must have made it even more difficult to lose him," she realized, hearing it in his voice.

He looked up. "It did. It does. And I don't think anyone else understands that. I'll never forgive myself for failing him. Never. But I can at least avenge his death and the deaths of the others. That's why I came for you, Maddie. The clan needs your magic. We hoped . . . we hope your power can help take down Dusek."

"I hope it can, too," she whispered.

The rasping voice in her skull returned: *A sad story indeed. It holds some truth, because he speaks with desperation. But only a fool would trust a desperate man. Are you a fool?*

She did her best to shake off her unwanted thought—if it truly was her thought and not the thought of someone or something else.

Cade turned and started walking, cutting a path across the piazza, skirting a row of parked cars. She hesitated, watching him go. Eventually, she trotted after him. What else could she do, bang on a door and ask for help? She was beginning to understand that no one could help her except Cade. And to understand that she wanted to help him in return. Maybe he would come to love her for it. The way she was beginning to love him?

Appalled at the turn her thoughts had taken, she pushed them aside, catching up with him as he entered a shadowed alley. "Do you know where we are?"

"Sicily."

They continued in silence until they reached the far edge of the village. By now, dawn owned the eastern sky. An open field lay before them, dotted with brown smudges that resolved into clusters of cattle as the sky brightened. To the right, the land halted abruptly before the sea.

Cade stopped and looked back at her. “Hurry,” he said. “There’s not much time.”

Chapter Fifteen

The cottage was clearly someone's vacation retreat: Two rooms enclosed with amber stucco walls, topped by a terra-cotta roof, looked out over the sea from a precarious perch. Crooked steps followed a steep path to a narrow beach.

The lock had been simple to break, even without magic. The furnishings were few and sturdy; an open larder was stocked with basic Sicilian necessities: bottled water, pasta, olive oil, anchovy paste. The few electrical items in the house were powered by an ancient generator. There was a full petrol can, but Cade didn't bother with it. Time was running short.

He led Maddie to a bed in the back room where she succumbed to exhaustion. She lay there in fitful sleep. She wouldn't remain unconscious for long, though. The third wave of her crisis was building. The scent of her body's growing arousal assaulted Cade with each inhaled breath. As he worked, he was acutely aware of her restless stirrings. Every few moments a soft moan reached his ears. The sound was like a hot tongue on his cock.

The day had dawned gray and windy, and a damp chill lingered in the cottage. He shoveled a load of coal into the kitchen stove and lit it with a match he'd found in a tin canister. The first element of protection was fire. He'd found some candles in a drawer. He lit five of them and set them in a circle on a broad oaken table.

Water was next. He emptied one of the bottles he'd found in the pantry into a shallow bowl. This he set in the center of the candles.

Earth? Five stones taken from the grounds around the cottage. He set them in the spaces between the candles.

Air. Slowly, he exhaled over the table. The spell of haven was almost complete. Just in time. The Celtic knot pattern had begun to redraw itself on Cade's skin. Raphael was sure to be in a rage over his failure to steal Azazel's amulet, and he had clearly thrown off the snare. He'd soon be on the hunt again.

Cade slipped the Watcher relic from his pocket, uncertain exactly what to do with it. There had been no explosion, no flash of light, nothing at all when he'd taken the artifact from Maddie. Of course, she'd been asleep at the time. Perhaps she needed to be awake to trigger the magic.

The metal's inner warmth disturbed him, as did the depth of power he sensed in the damaged stone. Blood magic. He didn't trust it. Or, more precisely, he didn't trust the Watcher who'd cast the spell. Was this piece truly a product of Azazel's hands? Of his celestial blood? Unexplored, unmastered, misunderstood, the magic of the amulet was a dangerous, unstable force. Conquered, the disc's magic could be the means to Clan Samyaza's victory over Dusek and his sons.

Cade didn't doubt for a moment that Artur, once he held Maddie's Clan Azazel magic, would master it. But what to do with the disc during Maddie's transition? He could imagine no truly secure place for it.

He ended up setting it in a corner of the main room, as far from the bedroom as possible. He muttered a word and the tattoo snake slid off his calf. Slithering across the floor, it took up a position as sentry. That would have to do.

A low, feminine moan gave way to a sob. Cade's glance cut to the open doorway where one corner of an iron footboard was visible. Maddie's thrashings had snagged a white sheet in the decorative ironwork, and Cade's belly clenched with equal parts lust and fear as the fabric pulled taut.

He stood at the table and gazed into the bowl of water.

Raising his left hand, he touched the hilt of the dagger tattooed on his right breast. The weapon became solid in his grasp. The edges of the jewels pressed into his palm. The blade's iron edge gleamed like night.

Without hesitation he pressed the tip into his right palm. His blood was dark crimson, almost black. He tilted his hand and let a drop fall on the water's surface, then onto each of the five stones he'd laid out. He whispered a spell of protection in the language of his Druid ancestors, those men and women long lost to Oblivion. Now they endured solely in the memories of Cade and his kin, their descendants.

As the last word fell from his lips, a dark sphere rose from the water. The sphere swelled, touching the rocks and the candle and continuing to expand until it passed through the walls of the cottage. Cade shuddered as power passed through his body and his mind. Maddie's cry came next, startled, fearful. In her oversensitized state, she would feel the blood magic as a sting on her being. Cade fought the urge to rush to her side. But, not yet. With no clan brother or sister to stand guard, it fell to Cade to set the boundaries of Maddie's protection.

It was difficult to concentrate weighed down by the burden of celestial judgment; Raphael's sword had left a residue of righteousness festering in Cade's wound. Only Maddie's fitful sobs, filled with increasing despair, enabled him to focus. He wondered what she saw in her nightmare.

Soon he'd know. Soon he'd know everything about her, every experience she'd lived, every secret she guarded in the depths of her heart. He'd uncover all the secrets of her Nephilim ancestors. Everything she knew, everything she was, would be his. If he didn't fail her. If he didn't lose her to madness and death. Her survival depended on his skill. It was an unwelcome sensation, this responsibility. Before now, the only person he'd been responsible for had been, briefly, his son. And there, he had failed.

Ultimately he would fail Maddie, too. It couldn't be otherwise; to set her free would mean risking the survival of his clan. Maddie might claim to support his cause, might even believe that she loved him. As he had loved Cybele, which ultimately had meant nothing. It was almost inevitable that an awakening dormant would form such a bond with his or her anchor.

No, what Cade had experienced with Cybele had not been the true love of bonded mates. Similarly, whatever Maddie felt for Cade was wrapped in lust and desperation, not freedom. How could he trust the constancy of any vow Maddie made during transition? She had no idea of the power that awaited her on the other side of her crisis. Once she claimed her magic and that of her ancestors, she would know who she was: Azazel's descendant. Dusek's kin. A natural enemy of Clan Samyaza. His enemy. Even if he saved her life—and he would fight to do that with every breath in his body—she'd emerge from the crisis enslaved. She would truly despise him then.

He shoved that thought into a dark corner of his mind and opened the door leading out of the cottage, then paced once around the building within the sphere of protection. Returning to the door, he entered and spoke the spell's final word. The windows went black. Only the five candles illuminated the gloom.

It made no difference to Cade. What he was about to do was best done in darkness.

* * *

The blue center of the flame danced. Instinct screamed for Lilith to avert her gaze. She did not. The light hurt; it seemed to bore a hole through each eye. Even from an arm's length she could feel the heat.

She knew the magic would not hurt her. How could it? The power was part of her.

"The flame is neither form nor thought," Azazel said. "It is beyond those earthly attributes. It is a thing of the sky, born of the lightning that strikes with the storm. It is the power of Heaven. But only those with the magic of Heaven in their being may know its secrets."

The magic of Heaven lived in Lilith's being. Sometimes it battered against her ribs trying to break free. The sheer power of it frightened her. But with her father at her side—guiding, coaxing—the menace faded into nothingness.

"Open your hands, Daughter."

She obeyed, and Azazel transferred the ball of fire into her possession. She felt its heat but no pain. The flames danced in her palm, shot spikes of light along her fingers. Power seeped through her skin to meld with her own magic. Her body grew heavy, as if her feet had sent roots into the soil. Something subtle stirred in her dark, private woman's place.

"It is so beautiful," she whispered.

"Beautiful," her father said, "and deadly. When called by one too weak to wield it, the magic will take its own course. Or it will be snatched by a more powerful adept. You must be master of the power you wield, Lilith. Always."

She spilled flame from one hand to the other and back again. "With your help, Father, I will learn."

His lips curved, and her heart sang at the sight. She had pleased him. It was all she lived for.

"You learn quickly, Lilith. I am pleased." His dark eyes raked over her. "Very pleased indeed."

At Azazel's direction, she placed the flame in the forge. There was no fuel for the fire to consume, but that did not matter. Its fuel was Lilith's magic. The fire remained steady.

The clay crucible lay open. In the base was the powder her father had called the prime substance. It was so dark it looked like a hole in the universe.

Lilith took the knife and held the tip to her right palm. Thin red lines crisscrossed the flesh there, badges of her courage, of her devotion. This time she hardly felt the bite of the blade as it opened a new gash.

Blood dripped into the bowl to mingle with the black powder. She capped the crucible swiftly and sealed it with wax, then set the orb on the blue fire. The flames burned in her heart as well as among the stones.

She knelt before the forge, watching, waiting, until Azazel nodded. Without hesitation she reached into the fire with her bare hands. Her flesh did not burn.

Azazel leaned close, his breath quickening. His crimson aura pulsed. "Open it, Lilith."

His hand came down on her head as she worked the blade. The clay parted at the joining. She lifted the upper half and laid it aside.

A gasp parted her lips. The prime substance was gone. In its place lay a crimson jewel, round and glittering, as large across as the first joint of her thumb. It had been born of her magic, and of her blood.

"It . . . it is beautiful."

Satisfaction laced her father's voice. "As are you, Lilith. You have done well. Indeed, you have exceeded my wildest expectations."

She glowed under the praise. The red stone glowed as well.

"What is it?" she whispered.

Azazel lifted the gem from its nest and placed it in her cupped hands. "What does it feel like?"

She closed her eyes, as he had taught her, and listened with an angel's understanding.

"Life," she said. "Life eternal."

"And so it will be," Azazel said.

* * *

Fire.

Fire in her hands. Fire on her skin. Under her skin. Burning her from the inside out. Licking the tips of her breasts, the swell of her belly, the entrance to her womb. Maddie's body was the crucible. Her nature was sealed inside. Magic was the fire, the transforming force.

She was hot. So hot. She couldn't bear it. She tore at her T-shirt. It was dirty, soaked with sweat. Plastered to her skin. She had to get rid of it.

The fabric ripped and fell away. Cool air struck her bare chest. It wasn't enough. The fire inside her ribs was too strong. It burned. It tortured.

The inferno between her legs was worse. It pulsed with ferocious rhythm. Her inner muscles contracted on nothing. She pressed her hand between her legs and moaned. She was so empty. She was on fire. For him.

For *whom*? She opened her eyes and looked wildly about. She couldn't remember.

Where was she? Jackknifing into a sitting position, she whipped her head around, taking in whitewashed walls and spare, heavy furniture. What was this place? This room? She didn't know it, didn't remember it. How had she gotten here?

Four walls, floor, ceiling: they all twisted and roiled. The bed and her stomach lurched. She grabbed at the white sheets. Light raced over the plaster walls, leaving trails of sparks. The stars zinged in her direction. She ducked.

Mocking laughter erupted from a gaping, ravenous maw. The horrific creature from the dingy Israeli hotel crouched at the foot of her bed. Its dripping tongue lapped at her toes. She scrambled backward and collided with the bars of an iron headboard; her fingers clung to the cold, curling metal.

The monster slithered across the mattress. It was coming to take her! Consume her. Destroy her. Suck her into madness. She couldn't surrender to it. *Wouldn't*. She flung herself from the bed.

Her knees hit the stone floor. Pain exploded and she cried out. But, *Stay calm*, a voice whispered. *Pain is an illusion. You will defeat it when the magic comes. And then you will use your power to escape the son of Samyaza.*

The words ricocheted inside her skull. Was it truth? Was Cade the monster?

No. Cade appeared in an open doorway. The instant she caught sight of him, the monster howled. Did it fear him? As she focused on him, the creature receded to the corner of the room.

Cade wanted her to come to him; she felt the command in her head. The urge to obey was overwhelming and she didn't even consider resisting. Nor did she want to.

I love him. The truth exploded with blinding clarity. She loved this man, this Nephilim demon who had shown her nothing but tenderness and understanding.

She scrambled off the bed and flung herself across the room. But the doorway, and Cade with it, kept moving. First to the left, then to the right. She couldn't reach him.

The monster mocked her failure, chortling with gleeful laughter. The voice whispered into her ear, *Fool! You do not love him. You cannot. He means you harm. You must flee.*

But Cade's voice was also present in her mind: *Maddie.* Caraid. *Come to me.*

Need throbbed between her legs and deeper. Inside her. She wanted Cade. She would do anything to reach him, and in the end it was his command—and her acceptance of his right to make it—that prevailed.

She lurched into his outstretched arms. The monster and its laughter drained away; even the whispering voice fell silent. She nearly sobbed with relief. Sliding down his body, she knelt at his feet. Her frantic fingers tore at the button on his jeans.

As she ripped open his zipper, he sprang hard and ready into her hands. She loved the feel of him. So firm, so smooth. She inhaled deeply; the heady scent of him spun her senses. She stroked him, pulling hot velvet skin over an iron-hard shaft. He let out a sound midway between a groan and a growl.

Fisting his hands in her hair, trapping her, he held her motionless, her lips just inches from the broad, smooth head of his shaft. The restraint was safety. Bliss. She craved his power, trusted in it. With Cade in control, the madness could not touch her. He was her anchor; only he could stop her fall into a yawning pit of insanity.

She opened her mouth and licked her lips. "Please."

A shudder passed through him. On a rough exhalation he hauled her to her feet. When he spoke, his voice was harsh while his words unexpectedly tender.

"Soon, *caraid*. Soon. I know what you need. I promise you, you'll have it soon."

"No," she begged. "Now."

He lifted her into his arms and strode back to the bed. The sensation of weightlessness was disorienting. She felt a surge of something that could only be magic that was inside her, under her skin, inside her ribs, buried in her deepest being. Beating its wings, demanding freedom. It *would* be free. She could feel it awakening. Expanding.

Too strong. Too fast. Too big. Her frail human body could never contain it!

Tingling needles pierced her skin everywhere, or so it felt. She stared at her arm crooked around Cade's neck. It glowed in dark rainbow colors. Her skin was translucent and sparkling.

"No!" Denial. Terror that struck her like a slap to the face. The love she'd felt just moments before ripped to shreds. This couldn't be happening. Not to her. It wasn't real. She couldn't be transforming into . . . what Cade was. She was human. Not a monster. Not *Nephilim*.

"No!" Trust forgotten, love forgotten, she tried to twist from Cade's arms. Tried to fling herself over the edge of the bed to the floor. His arms tightened around her as her struggles turned frenzied. This was his fault. He'd forced this on her. He'd seduced her, kidnapped her, drugged her, made her want him. He wanted to imprison a demon's nature in her human body. She couldn't let him do it.

Now you see the truth. Now you know what is at stake. Your freedom. Your life. Stop him. Get away. You have the power.

The rasping voice was back, whispering inside her skull. *Get away. You have the power.*

Did she? And if that was true, how could she use it? She was on the bed, all but helpless, Cade's weight pressing her down. And it felt good, so good, despite her fear, despite her panic, despite the warnings of the voice in her head. Waves of ravenous lust lifted her hips. She needed him. Needed him to fill her craving. She didn't want to escape him.

War raged on in her mind, her doubts battling her need. Whispers inside her head urged her to fight. Finally, the voice succeeded in drowning out Cade's gentle voice. Panic exploded.

"No!"

With a sudden burst of strength, she clawed at Cade's face, his arms, his chest. He responded with curses. She landed a blow to his ear and almost escaped. One leg was over the edge of the mattress; her foot touched the ground. Then his hand clamped on her upper arm and yanked her back.

Something cool encircled her wrist and tightened. With a cry she tried to break free, but the cord held, its knot sealing into a seamless cuff around her wrist. She stared, uncomprehending. This was no normal rope. Not something to be cut, or torn, or unknotted.

The cuff glowed with magic. She followed its trailing end to Cade's arm, where it disappeared into the pattern of his tattoo. The cord *was* his tattoo. But . . . he'd thrown a tattoo net at Raphael. It had disappeared with the angel under the sea

When and how had it returned? How could it be that he was unraveling the same tattoo, transforming ink into fetters?

His expression was grim. He tore the rope, leaving a length trailing from Maddie's arm. He yanked its free end toward a corner of the bed's iron headboard. He meant to tie her to it.

"No!" she screamed. "No!"

She couldn't let this happen. Bound, she'd never escape.

She threw herself at him, hissing and clawing. The rope wove tightly about the bed's decorative iron scrollwork, immobilizing her left arm. She punched out with her right fist, only to have that arm caught and secured by a second length of magical cord. She was now bound, naked from the waist up, arms spread.

The restraint increased her frenzy. Kicking, churning, cursing, she threw all her rising madness into the fight. The monster, emboldened, reappeared and approached from the shadows. Its terrible gaping jaw was laughing.

Cade stood out of reach at the foot of the bed. His expression was blank, his massive body immobile but powerful. He watched her struggle until her strength gave out and she collapsed onto the mattress, panting; only then did he move, grasping one ankle and securing it to the footboard. The second ankle was swiftly handled the same, almost before her mind had time to register what he'd done. She lay open and bound before him.

"No," she gasped. "Please. I don't want this. Untie me."

He didn't answer. His left hand came up to touch the tat on his right breast. The image of a jeweled dagger separated from his skin and became solid in his hand. She was trussed like an animal. The magical shackles couldn't be broken.

He turned the blade toward her, and she sucked in a breath. All this just to kill her? Was she to be trussed and offered as some kind of sacrifice?

He mounted the bed, leaning over her. She felt him in her

mind then. His presence pushed away the dark, gaping mouth of insanity. Even the whispering voice fell silent. Only the tide of her rising desire remained. And she knew the truth: she was his. He was her master, utterly and completely. It was useless to resist.

As his knife neared, she did nothing to stop it. But the blade did not touch her skin. It sliced instead through her shorts and underwear. Cade yanked the last shreds of fabric away, and she had no defense left. His gaze raked down her body.

It was as if he trailed a finger over her, awakening lust in every cell. When his scrutiny lingered on her breasts, her nipples peaked. When he gazed between her legs, a flood of slick lust poured from her body. His skin glowed, matching the colors chasing over her. His chest rose and fell heavily, but his eyes gave away nothing.

He left the bed and shoved his pants, already open at the waist, over his hips and to the floor. He stood before her, naked, aroused and magnificent. His eyes glowed red, his opalescent skin gleamed with dark menace. His shaft, rising from that nest of dark, curling hair, jutted toward her.

Her demon nature responded.

Chapter Sixteen

"He's gone, isn't he?"

Why she bothered to ask, Cybele didn't know. She always knew when Artur was near. The sensation was like effervescent glitter rushing through her veins—or tiny, painful shards of glass. With Artur, she never knew which extreme to expect.

This morning, when she woke, there was . . . nothing. Maybe this was what Oblivion felt like.

The scent of strong coffee had drawn her from bed to the kitchen. Brax, seated at the table, glanced at her over the screen of his laptop. Hearing Cybele's inquiry, he leaned back in his chair and reached for his mug.

"He left a few hours ago."

"Where?" she asked.

"Prague."

"Damn." The warmth drained from her face and ice-cold fingers clawed at her throat. Knees abruptly weak, she sat down hard in the empty chair across from Brax. "He's gone to confront Dusek."

Brax shook his head, but his eyes were troubled. "No. He wouldn't. Not even Artur is that reckless."

Cybele offered a withering glance. "You can't believe that."

"He's gathering information. That's all. Blast it, that *better* be all he's doing. He'll be back soon enough. After Gareth . . ." He trailed off into silence.

Cybele looked at her hands. After Gareth's *transition*, he'd begun to say. "Artur expects me to grant Gareth's petition," she said.

Brax stood and filled another mug from the coffeepot on the stove. "Artur knows what's best for the clan."

"What about what's best for me? What about what's best for *Artur*?"

He handed her the mug. Reflexively, she took a sip.

"Artur doesn't care what's best for himself," Brax said. "He does what's necessary. For all of us."

The coffee was very hot and very bitter. "If I anchor Gareth, it will be the end of Artur and me." *Not that there's much left.*

"If you don't, it could be the end of the clan," Brax said. "We need every adept we can muster. Artur knows that. You know it."

"He left the choice to me. He didn't order me to do this. He could have, but he didn't." She swallowed. Her throat burned, but she didn't think the coffee had anything to do with it. "That has to mean something. Maybe . . . maybe it's a test. Maybe he wants me to refuse. So we can start over."

"Cybele . . ." A grimace crossed Brax's handsome face. "I know you want to believe Artur will forget what happened between you and Cade, but—"

"No. He won't ever forget. I know that. But maybe . . . maybe he could get past it. Maybe he could forgive me."

"This is Artur we're talking about, remember? Forgive? He'd rather enter Oblivion."

"I hurt him," Cybele said.

Brax shook his head. "Artur, hurt? I'm not sure that's even possible. His heart—if he has one—is hard as a diamond. And just as cold."

Cybele stared at her hands. *Not true*, she wanted to shout. Except that, after this year, she was very much afraid it might be.

Brax returned his attention to his laptop. Silence ensued. Cybele sat, turning her empty mug round and round in her hands, wondering just how big a fool she was for hoping he was wrong. If only Luc were here. Luc, with his caustic wit and biting good humor, tempered—at least where his twin sister was concerned—by glimmers of honest compassion. Luc, who didn't even know yet about the massacre, or about Vaclav Dusek's challenge.

The simmering anxiety that accompanied Cybele's thoughts of her brother threatened to rise and pull her under. Where was he? Why hadn't he called? Full siblings were rare among Watchers—a Watcher female could bring only one pregnancy to term in a lifetime. She and Luc shared a unique bond; before they'd discovered their British kin and traveled to England, they'd rarely been parted. Three months was far too long for him to be out of touch.

Brax, eyes intent on his computer screen, gave a low whistle.

Cybele looked up. "What is it?"

"I've been doing a little investigating into the financial life of Demon Annihilators Mutual Network." Brax shook his head. "You'll never guess who's funding Dr. Simon Ben-Meir's quest to uncover the historical origins of the Watchers."

"DAMN? But . . . that's impossible. Jonas Walker has denounced Ben-Meir's expedition."

"True. And I don't doubt Walker's sincerity. But his business acumen? That's another story. I'm willing to bet the priest doesn't have full control of DAMN's finances. There's a clear trail from DAMN's New York bank to Ben-Meir's account in Tel-Aviv. Interestingly, the money's taken a brief detour through Prague."

Cybele stared, aghast. "Vaclav Dusek's diverting DAMN funds to Ben-Meir?"

"Looks that way. And it makes me wonder. Who's calling the shots on that dig in Israel? And why?"

Cybele shot to her feet. "What if Dusek visits the dig? Cade won't be able to compete with power like that. We have to warn him, Brax. Right now. We have to get Cade out!"

"Relax," Brax said. "As far as I can tell, Dusek hasn't been anywhere near the Negev in months. As for Cade, he's already left Israel."

"You've heard from him?"

Brax nodded. "He texted last night. He secured the dormant female and has left the Negev with her. Her crisis is approaching."

Cybele drew a steadying breath. "He's bringing her here for her transition?"

Brax shut his laptop with a click. "If he can make it in time."

* * *

Luc didn't have much to his name. Just a couple changes of clothes, a wide-brimmed hat, a cell phone and charger, a roll of cash, a gun enhanced for killing hellfiends, and a couple rounds of ammo. All were still safely stashed in a Missoula bus station locker when he went to retrieve them.

He put the hat on his head, grabbed the phone with one hand, and slung the pack containing the rest over his other shoulder. Standing in the station parking lot, he powered up the phone. The signal was weak, and three months out of use the battery was just this side of dead. Guilt, which he'd suppressed for three months now, had finally prodded him too insistently to ignore. Cybele was going to burn his ears when she finally heard from him. He felt a twinge of guilt over that. He had no idea what she would say when he explained to her what he'd been about roaming in the wilderness all this time. If he *could* explain it.

His text inbox was full; the symbol denoting unopened voice mail was flashing. The missed calls were largely from Cybele, with a few from Brax. One from Artur.

The phone went dead before he could retrieve any of it.

* * *

Lust and frenzy. Twin legacies of the damned. Cade would use both to his purpose.

The black pepper-spiced scent of Maddie's passion crackled like an unholy fire. The third wave of her crisis was peaking. She'd begged for him to take her, and he had no intention of denying her.

She'd despise him when it was done, when she realized he had no intention of relinquishing the role of master. But he wouldn't think of that now. He needed to concentrate on seeing her safely delivered into her Watcher power. Afterward, when she was securely enslaved, there would be time enough to face her hatred.

He stood motionless at the foot of the bed, letting her fevered entreaties wash over him. He didn't trouble himself to listen. Her passion had nothing to do with him, not really. She'd have begged any Watcher male with the same words. Cade remembered well enough how he'd pleaded with Cybele. And yet, the sweetness of Maddie's plea entranced him. He clung to the illusion that her passion was for him alone.

Exhausted, she fell back limp and panting, ceased her struggle against her bonds. Her scent softened into violets. She uttered a low moan.

He hardened unbearably. Reaching down, he stroked her foot. He started at the heel and drew his thumb along her instep, and her eyes opened in a flutter of inky black lashes. Their gazes clashed. His hand continued its path up her calf and lingered on the delicate flesh behind her knee. Her eyelids drooped. She drew a shuddering breath.

He watched her chest rise and fall. Her breasts swayed with the motion. Her nipples, dark and hard, resembled round, perfect pebbles. Between her legs, moisture glistened like dew. The musk of her surrender made his knees weak.

He removed his hand from her leg. Abruptly, her eyelids flew open and her gaze shot to a point behind his head. Raw fear flashed through her eyes.

"No—" she choked out. Hands fisted, she jerked against her bonds.

He wondered what, exactly, she saw. Something similar to the horrors he'd witnessed during his own crisis? Or were Maddie's private horrors entirely different?

Leaning forward, he closed his hand around her calf. "Maddie. Look at me."

She did not listen. "It's coming."

He rounded the bed and sat beside her right hip. The mattress depressed and her bound body shifted toward him. He laid his open palm on her belly.

"Look at me," he said again.

She dragged her eyes from whatever apparition it was that she watched. Her gaze met his and clung. She licked dry lips.

"Cade."

She remembered his name, at least.

"It . . . it wants me. It's coming. I can't stop it. I—"

He leaned close. "Don't try to stop it, Maddie."

"But—"

"I'm here. I'll protect you."

"You won't leave me?" she whispered. The desperate hope in her eyes wrapped around his heart and squeezed.

"I won't leave you. Ever. You're mine."

A shudder racked her body. "I want you. I need—"

He climbed fully onto the bed, sheltering her with his body.

He knelt between her spread legs, his hands braced on either side of her shoulders, and he looked down at her. "I know, *caraid*. I know."

He slid himself into her. It was so easy, so natural, that the joining almost took him unaware, though it had been entirely deliberate. They were one.

Holding himself deep inside her body, he slipped into her mind. And pitched headlong into screaming, clawing chaos.

* * *

Vaclav Dusek leaned back in his leather desk chair. Fingers steepled beneath his chin, he listened. A hoarse female voice, thick with worry, spilled from the telephone speaker.

"Two nights ago, Professor," the woman was saying in Israeli-accented English. "That is the last any of us saw Dr. Ben-Meir or Maddie Durant. We didn't realize they were gone until the following morning. Yesterday. Ari noticed Dr. Ben-Meir's jeep was missing. We thought perhaps he'd driven into Mitzpe Ramon for supplies. But Maddie and I share a hut. Why would she leave in the middle of the night without waking me?"

"Neither left a note?" Dusek asked.

"Not that we've found. There have not been any calls, either."

Dusek tapped his lips with his joined fingertips. "Have you notified the police?"

"No, sir. I thought . . . I thought I should speak with you first."

"A wise notion, Ms. Stern."

There was a brief pause. Then: "A temporary laborer went missing the same night. A British national."

Dusek frowned. "Does this man have a name?"

"Yes, sir. Cade. Cade Leucetius."

Dusek lurched forward in his seat. What was this? He spoke slowly and said, "I did not see that name on the latest roster."

"No, sir. He'd only just arrived. A few days before—"

"I should have been notified before Dr. Ben-Meir took him on."

"Yes, sir. I know that is what the contract states. But the man was not an archeologist. Just a laborer. He was to be here less than a week, clearing the east site. Dr. Ben-Meir did not think it necessary to bother you."

"Whose money is financing this dig, Ms. Stern?"

A sharp inhalation. "The largest share of it is yours, of course, Professor. Without your support we would have closed down months ago."

"You may close down yet, if Dr. Ben-Meir does not return to his post."

"I am sure he will return. That is . . . if he is able. This dig is his life. He wouldn't leave it. Not voluntarily."

"Is anything missing? Any artifact from the dig?"

"No, sir. Not as far as I can tell. Every item in the log is accounted for." The woman paused, and he heard her swallow. "There's just one odd thing . . ."

"What is it?"

"The ancient well we uncovered last month. Someone's been digging in it. But nothing was noted in any of the logs."

"I see."

Long moments passed before: "Professor Dusek? Are you still on the line?"

"I am." He stood. "Do not notify the police, Ms. Stern. Not yet. Carry on with your duties and await my arrival."

Chapter Seventeen

Prague, Czech Republic

Prague was a city of layers. At ground level lay the bustle of its streetscape. Next, the gray bulk of its residences and businesses. Higher still, medieval church spires reached skyward, and the great castle brooded atop its hill. A thick blanket of smog hovered above it all.

Artur was concerned with none of it. The strata he sought lay underfoot, in a twisting catacomb accessed from the cellars of Vaclav Dusek's gilded Baroque mansion. A lair on a level with the city's sewers, and just as filthy. All the gold in the universe couldn't disguise the evil that lurked within that sordid maze.

The doors of Dusek's palace—twin slabs of shining black teak—faced the Vltava River. Mist rose from the water, blurring the lines of a wide, cobble-paved bridge. The stone saints lining the span seemed to float atop the fog. Turning his back on the scene, Artur studied the portal of Dusek's mansion. He'd never before attempted access to Clan Azazel's stronghold. He didn't even know if it was possible, but at the moment he was in the mood for an impossible task. The more dangerous, the better. Anything to keep his mind from Cybele and the choice he'd flung at her feet.

The late afternoon sky was gray. Monochromatic. After brief reflection, Artur climbed the stairs to the palace doors. A gold knocker in the shape of a skull greeted him. He lifted it and let it fall. After several moments, muffled footsteps approached. The lock scraped.

The door opened a scant two inches. Artur met the stare of a young man—one of Vaclav Dusek's sons, certainly; his hooked nose and bright, malicious eyes proclaimed the relationship. As did the black collar around his neck and the gleaming white stone set in the smooth metal. At a guess, the lad had no more than seventeen years. A dormant.

"I've come to see Dusek," Artur said.

"The professor is from home," the youth replied in heavily accented English.

Artur considered the possible truth of this statement. He decided not to challenge it. "Who is in charge in his absence?"

"That would be Miklos." The dormant's eyes were disturbingly blank.

"I will speak with Miklos, then."

"Who may I say is calling?"

"Artur Camulus, chieftain of Clan Samyaza."

The youth's eyes went wide, but he didn't, as Artur half expected, slam the door. Instead, he opened it wider and stepped to one side. "As you wish. Come."

Artur followed his guide down a hallway bedecked with gilded plasterwork and hung with crystal chandeliers. It took very little effort to see the stains of Dusek's blood magic dripping down the walls or to taste the residue of black malice seeping up through the floorboards. The specter of the crimes committed in this place turned even Artur's stomach.

He was ushered into a small receiving room filled with delicate furnishings. Artur took up a spot in front of the porcelain mantelpiece and clasped his hand behind his back. Dusek's son withdrew, shutting the door behind him, and Artur wondered if the dormant had any sense of shame for who had spawned him. Or for what his sire had done to him

To be enslaved by one's own kin would be hell. To be enslaved by one's own father? Oblivion was preferable.

The door swung open. A second son entered. This one was a full adept, his dark eyes older and far shrewder. He wore a dark business suit, a red tie knotted in a precise Windsor. That neckwear didn't entirely hide the black collar and white stone.

"Miklos, I presume?" Artur said.

The Watcher inclined his head. "Artur Camulus. To what do I owe this unexpected pleasure?"

"I am here to speak with Vaclav Dusek."

"Indeed." Miklos clasped his hands behind his back. "I imagine you are anxious to discuss the missive recently delivered to your door. Unfortunately, I cannot help you. The professor is from home."

Artur strode across the Persian carpet, halting an arm's length from a dark Caravaggio. Sweeping aside the fall of his duster, he drew his Glock from its holster and trained the barrel on Miklos's chest. "I wonder," he said, "what the professor would say if I killed you."

Miklos shrugged. "It is no longer possible for you to do so. The point is moot."

Artur pulled the trigger. Nothing happened. His adversary smiled.

"Samyaza magic has its uses. A fine addition to our arsenal, I am sure you would agree."

Artur replaced the gun in its holster and braced himself for the counterattack that was surely coming. It did not. He frowned.

Miklos's smile grew. "I thank you for your visit. I am only sorry your trip has been made in vain. When the professor returns, I will be sure to tell him you called."

As if on cue, the dormant reentered the room.

"Ah, Petr. You will see our guest out, if you please."

There was not much Artur could do but retrace his steps

into the street. Oh, he might have fought, might have done some damage, perhaps even wounded one of Dusek's sons, but to what purpose? Clan Azazel's master was a ruthless bastard. The alchemist would hardly miss even the most favored of his slave sons.

He crossed the street to the stone rail fronting the river. Leaning against it, he stared broodingly back at Dusek's palace. After a time, his gaze dropped to the sewer grate in the street before the front doors. Coming to a realization, he straightened. Here was a possibility.

* * *

Trapped. Bound. Cade's arms were stretched and immobile, his ankles bound with rope. His body was naked. Exposed. Vulnerable. No protection.

Chaos. His sanity slipping away. Rage, fear, hatred, in his heart, in his mind. Madness like acid, dripping, pooling, eating away at his sanity. He dared not open his eyes; the thought of what he might see was far too terrifying. He couldn't think. Couldn't breathe.

A touch. Cool on his hot skin. She'd told him her name. Cybele. She'd come to save him. She was his anchor, his salvation— His love.

Cade's memory snapped like a rubber band stretched past its limit. Terror. Chaos. But not his terror. Not his chaos. Maddie's. Her mind boiled like a sea of horror. And this time Cade was the anchor, the dormant's only hope of surviving transition. If he didn't slam the lid on his own memories and fears, he'd lose her.

Her body was rigid beneath his, her face set with lines of terror. Her eyes were open and staring, but she wasn't looking at him. What she experienced was solely in her mind; he'd caught a glimpse of it. The sight had unnerved him so profoundly that it had thrown him into the memory of his own transition.

He couldn't afford this weakness. He wrestled his fear, transformed it into steely determination. His need to protect Maddie came first. His need to . . . to *cherish* her, as odd as that sentiment was, given the harshness of her situation. He was bound to her now, by Artur's order and by his own choice. He would not fail her. Neither insanity nor Oblivion would claim her. Not while he lived.

Neither of them had moved for long moments. His body was still buried deep inside hers. Levering himself up on shaky arms, his gaze intent on her face, he withdrew, but not so far as to leave her completely. Her muscles clenched, urging his return. He plunged back into her carnal invitation.

"Oh!" Her eyes snapped to his, wide and startled and suddenly, blessedly, in focus.

"Maddie." Cade watched her intently. "Do you know me?"

A tiny wrinkle appeared between her eyes. "You're . . . Cade."

"That's right. I'm here to take care of you. To help you fight."

A shudder passed through her. Her arms and legs jerked, pulling at her bonds.

"Then . . . why am I tied?" Her struggle quickened, and desperation spiked her voice. "I don't like it. I don't want it! Let me go, Cade—"

He cupped her face with one hand. "I'm sorry. It's for your own protection." And for his. "Frenzy comes with the crisis. These ropes will keep you safe."

"Safe? *Safe?* I saw what's coming after me. You can't keep me safe. You can't. No one could."

Her agitation returned full force, racking her body, driving strength into her limbs. If the ropes encircling her wrists and ankles hadn't been formed by magic, Cade was sure they would have snapped.

He cradled her head in his hands and locked their eyes. When he moved inside her, she shuddered and softened. But her expression was bleak.

"How can I fight it, Cade? How?"

He didn't answer, just concentrated on working his cock inside her body. In. Out. In. Out. Artur had sent him to Maddie for exactly this reason, but that didn't lessen the tenderness blossoming in Cade's heart. She was so strong, so brave. A natural warrior. Stronger by far than he had been, when he was in her place.

He feathered kisses over her forehead. A tear tracked down her cheek. "Hush now, *caraid*. Hush," Cade murmured against her lips. "You'll come through this. I promise."

Her hips lifted to match his growing rhythm. "You feel good. So good. But you can't possibly—"

"Shh. I can. If you let me in."

"I . . . don't understand."

Deliberately he let his presence expand in her mind. Her eyes widened, and the fear in them increased.

"The presence in my head. It *is* you. You've been there since . . . since we first . . ."

"Yes."

"I've felt you, but I wasn't sure . . ."

"Now you are. And now I need to go deeper. You need to let me in completely, Maddie, if I'm to help you. I need access to your deepest ancestral memories."

He might have used magic to compel her; he had certainly gained enough control over her will to do so. He resisted that path, however. The thought of thrusting into her innermost being by force sickened him. He desperately wanted her to want him there.

"Let me in," he said again.

She flushed. "I . . . I don't know if I can."

"You have to. I'm inside your body and inside your mind. I need to be part of your life essence."

Her head scrubbed the mattress. "No. I can't—"

"Please. Please trust me. The peak of your crisis isn't far off. I can't protect you unless you trust me. Unless you let me in."

Her eyes closed briefly, but her body remained stiff under his. He held himself deep and still inside her. Her inner muscles squeezed him like a tight, hot glove. He felt himself falling into a different kind of frenzy. One he knew he should fight but couldn't.

"I love you, Maddie." It was lunacy to say it.

Her eyes widened. "You don't. You couldn't."

"I do."

"Then . . . untie me. Please, Cade."

It had been hard enough to subdue her during the onset. He stared down at her and said, "That's not a good idea. When the peak hits—"

"Please." She jerked at her bonds. "Please. I hate this. I want to move. Oh, God, it's starting again. I can't stand it."

Cade stroked a damp curl from her forehead. "Then let me in. It can't hurt you if I'm with you."

"Untie me!" She jerked her arms. "I need to move! I need to fight! If you really love me, untie me."

He knew he should simply claim her ancestral memories, her magic and be done with it. She couldn't stop him. He was a fool ten times over to even consider granting her plea. If he freed her, how would he be able to subdue her during the first rush of her full power?

And yet, he hesitated. Blast it. If anything was madness, this was it.

He wasn't aware of consciously making the decision, only of speaking the words that had the knots sliding from her wrists and ankles. Those cords slithered back up his arm and blended into his skin.

The tension drained from Maddie's body. Her hands found their way to his wrists and stroked up his arms. That simple caress, freely given, was unbelievably erotic, and he gasped with the pure unspoiled shock of it.

Her hands slid over his shoulders as if measuring their width. Her eyes shone with tears. "Thank you. Oh, thank you."

He captured her gaze with his own. "Now keep your promise. Let me in."

She tugged his head down, matched his lips to hers. As the kiss deepened, he felt her surrender.

"I love you, Cade."

It was time. Ignoring the pangs of his conscience, he slipped more deeply into her mind, into her ancestral memory. Into the heart of Clan Azazel's power.

* * *

The memory was old. Very old.

The girl Lilith stood at an open forge, sheltered by a smoke-blackened canopy fashioned from animal skins. She tended a fire, moving blue flames with her bare hands. Cade moved closer in order to watch.

A clay crucible, black with soot, lay in the fire. The girl slid her hands under the vessel, and flames licked her flesh as she lifted it. Cade sensed the contact brought only a slight warmth and no pain. Even so, Lilith's lips compressed and tightness appeared at the corners of her eyes.

She used a bone-handled knife to pry the halves of the crucible apart. Inside, molten gold gleamed. She worked swiftly as the metal cooled, first wielding a brass hammer, then a small wooden mallet. Soon, seven perfect gold circles lay on the worktable.

Cade moved closer as Lilith overlapped two golden discs and joined them with the aid of a long-handled burin. She applied the chiseled end to the metal. Sparks flowed down her fingers to merge with the gold.

Cade's mind reached toward Lilith's magic, but the sparks were a shade of the long-dead past that he could not grasp. It was different, he knew, for Maddie. Lilith's mind and memories were part of her. Her ancestor's magic—Azazel's legacy—was a part of her, and when Cade became her master, he would own it, too.

Lilith worked quickly, uniting the third disc with the first two. The fourth followed. All the while, her magic flowed. The seven discs became one. The piece lay new and sparkling on the stone anvil.

The Seed of Life. The mystery of creation, bound in gold. Heaven's magic. All that was needed now was a spark of human essence. Cade understood this amulet was Lilith's gift to her father. How pleased Azazel would be! How happily would Lilith bask in his praise.

She produced the bloodstone—whole, round, and sparkling—from a fold in her robes and placed it in the exact center of the pattern. The gem, fashioned from Lilith's magic and blood, was to be the earthly anchor to the power of Heaven embedded in the amulet. Cade caught his breath at the audacity of the girl's intent. She meant nothing less than to bind eternal life to her creation. Lilith secured the gem, melding the ends of narrow golden strips to the disc with heat and magic.

The bloodstone secure, the girl turned the disc over. The rear side was smooth. Drawing a breath, she placed her finger upon the metal and shut her eyes. Blue flame burst from the point of contact, but she held the touch for several long seconds before lifting her finger.

Cade moved closer to peer at the mark she'd left: a small circle surrounded by a larger ring. It was the stylized eye of the Watchers.

Abruptly, Lilith lifted her head. Cade sensed a sudden waft of cool air. The girl frowned. Her eyes slowly returned from the realm of magic.

A burly figure approached her from behind. He laid a hand on her shoulder, and she jumped and spun about.

"Hello, sister."

"Ezreth." Lilith's eyes darted to a nearby tent, then to the fields beyond. Not another person in sight. "What are you doing here?"

"I think you know."

She backed up a step, her hip bumping the anvil. "No."

Ezreth advanced. His aura—angry, aggressive—flowed with him. Cade recognized the brutish force as war magic. Lilith's more delicate aura shrank before it.

His hand closed on her upper arm. "Remember our agreement. My silence in exchange for your body. It is time, Lilith, to made good on your promise."

She shut her eyes. "No. No, Ezreth. Please. Do not do this. Father—"

"You wish him to know how you have betrayed him?"

"You are the one who has betrayed him," Lilith whispered.

But Cade could sense the girl's doubt.

"Tell him, then. Tell him what we did here just days ago."

She shook her head. "No."

Ezreth smiled. "Then I will. The moment he returns from the upper desert."

"Please do not!"

Her brother's eyes darkened. "You know how to earn my silence."

She trembled. "Do not force this on me, Ezreth. I . . . I do not want you."

He struck her, backhand, across the face. Her head whipped to the side and she stumbled, grabbing at the anvil to prevent her fall. Her hand struck the gold disc and it tumbled to the dirt.

Ezreth tore off Lilith's head scarf. Fisting his hand in her hair, he thrust her to the ground. "Here," he said. "Now."

* * *

"No!" Dead weight compressed her chest. Maddie couldn't breathe. He was deep inside her and she couldn't bear the invasion. Hadn't she fought against it?

You did, the voice whispered. *But it was long ago. Now, you must fight again.*

"Maddie!"

The call was faint and far away. But its tone held the authority of command. Try as she might, she couldn't deny it.

She didn't want to answer. She wanted to listen to the whispering voice.

"You'll bloody well stay with me, damn you."

Cade. It was his voice hot in her ear. It was his weight holding her down, his presence inside her body. Not the hated presence of Ezreth.

A rush of pure relief softened her resistance. Cade had freed her arms and legs. He'd held her close when terror threatened. He surrounded her now. He felt safe. His solid body was her anchor to sanity.

Your anchor to slavery, the voice inside her skull rasped. *Do not let him bind you. Seize your freedom.*

Freedom? Freedom to be . . . what? A monster? A black-winged Nephilim? Yes, if that was the only life she could live, she would take it.

Cade was buried inside her. He flexed his hips, and sparks of pleasure scattered through her body. She couldn't stop her body's response. It felt good. Their union felt like life.

He released her wrists. "Hold on to me, Maddie. Don't let go. I'll see you through this. I swear it."

He moved inside her—long, slow strokes that seemed to never end. One melded into the next, deep and eternal. Fear and doubt receded. Pleasure built. Maddie curved her fingers into his shoulders and moaned.

But, the whisper returned inside her skull. *Follow him and you will become his slave. Is that what you want? Is that what you crave?* No. You long for freedom.

Was the voice right? Was it true? She couldn't think, not with what Cade was doing to her. She needed time. Time to think. Her body stiffened as she fought the pleasure pouring through her.

"No, *caraid*." Cade murmured soft Welsh words she didn't understand. "Don't push me away. Hold on to me. Trust me."

He continued talking, continued gentling her, pushing the whispering voice away until it fell sullenly silent, muffled by Cade's strength and tenderness. The tension drained from her body, and again, she surrendered.

His lovemaking was unhurried. He dipped his head and took her lips, and their tongues touched and teased. She loved the taste of him. Loved the increasing slickness of his sweat and the scent of his musk.

He released her wrists to sweep his hands over her body. Cupping her breast, he plumped the nipple to a point and took it into his mouth, pulling deeply with his lips and tongue. Scraping gently with his teeth. Tiny shots of lightning zinged through her body.

She could feel him, coaxing, demanding, taking. He wanted all of her; he wouldn't stop until he had it. The realization both thrilled and terrified her. He'd said he loved her. Could it be true? He'd untied her, as she'd asked. She ran her hands over his chest, his arms. Framed his face with her hands. He felt like heaven. How she wanted to trust him. She needed to trust him. To surrender. She wrapped her legs around his torso and tilted her hips as an offering to her master.

The voice returned with a vengeance. *Your master! For shame. You would throw away the freedom that's within your grasp? Give over your mind, your life essence to your enemy? Allow him this and you will never again taste freedom. You will be his slave unto death.*

A part of her brain almost believed the whispering voice. But despite the clamor in her mind. Despite the return of uncertainty and a growing panic, the pleasure Cade built climbed higher and higher, inexorably upward. It coiled her senses as it rose, until she was ready to snap under the pressure. She writhed beneath him, wanting to break, desperate to shatter. And still, he made her wait.

With every thrust, her bones and muscles stretched. He was everything to her: the stars, the moon, the sun. The universe. Then, subtly, the sensation changed. She became aware of another source of power, a power that beat inside her own breast. Magic streamed from the center of her being, from a reservoir of power she'd never known she possessed. She knew it fully now, for the first time, in wonder. Her magic awakened, expanding, stretching, growing. Soon—very soon—it would be too great for one frail human body to contain.

But, Maddie was not human. Her skin sparkled. Dark rainbow hues chased over her flesh. Her fingernails scored a path down Cade's chest and her eyes burned. Her shoulder blades itched. She was stretching, changing, transforming. From human to demon.

From freedom to slavery, the voice whispered.

No, she thought. *No.*

Chapter Eighteen

Cade sensed rather than saw the first sign of Maddie's transformation. Her body convulsed and his nostrils contracted sharply with the odor of her terror. Painful emotions unfurled inside his chest. When her sob of despair reached his ears, he felt as though his heart would rip in two.

He lay atop her body, his bare skin united with hers, his flesh hard inside her body. Energy gathered in the tension of her muscles. Soon now. Very soon, she would surrender to the inevitable. Or she would shatter and die.

It was an excruciatingly difficult task to release the illusion of humanity and embrace one's demon nature. Cade well remembered the agony. More times than he could count—both before and after his transition—he'd wished Cybele had let him die in that dirty alley.

He looked into Maddie's eyes. They were disturbingly blank. No, it would be more accurate to say her eyes were focused elsewhere. On her ancestral past? On her soulless nature? Neither was likely to be a pleasant sight.

Cade was horrified to realize his own eyes were burning with tears. He'd had a year to come to terms with what he was, but in all that time his anger at bearing an eternal curse earned by the sins of his ancestors hadn't diminished. Maddie would know the same despair. She would know the hopelessness of being counted among the unforgiven. But she would not give up, Cade knew. Just as certainly as he knew he would not allow her to face her new life alone. She was his. His to guide and protect for as long as he drew breath.

Her beautiful eyes misted. Her body jolted under his, her spine arching. The violence of the motion nearly threw him from the bed. Belatedly he grabbed for her wrists. Too late. Newborn claws opened hot red lines across his shoulder and chest. The gashes burned.

Blast it all to Oblivion. He never should have given in to her plea to cut her bonds. He'd shackled her for her own safety. And for his.

Spitting curses, he captured her flailing arms and pinned them over her head. She resisted, sputtering in outrage, and the force of her sudden strength surprised him, even though he'd expected it. He jerked his hips, reminding her she was still impaled on his cock. Her inner muscles contracted sharply, almost painfully.

"Maddie. Maddie! Can you hear me?"

Her sharply inhaled breath was a hiss. Her eyes opened, caught and held his. Her pupils glowed red as recognition slowly dawned.

"Cade." She swallowed thickly. "I feel . . . so strange."

Her skin was shimmering darkly now, sparkling in shades of pearl and crimson and indigo like the dawn emerging from a swath of night clouds. He felt his body changing to match hers. Panic flared in her eyes; shock ran through her body. She clutched at his shoulders, her nails biting his skin.

"What's . . . what's happening to me?"

He surged deeply inside her. "You're changing. Into Nephilim form."

"I . . . I'm not sure I want to."

"You can't stop it. Don't try."

Her skin shone with opalescent beauty. Their bodies slid slickly together. She clung to him, eyes open and staring, red power surging, magic unfurling. Her breath was shallow, her scent sharp. His nostrils flared. Her curls stuck to her forehead. Sweat dripped down the sides of her face.

He spoke into her mind. *Trust me, Maddie.*

He felt her stiffen. Confusion passed through her eyes. He lowered his head and clamped his lips around her nipple, and after a brief moment of resistance she seemed to relax. She lifted her hips and wrapped her legs around his waist. He cupped her buttocks. He stroked her mind with soothing thoughts.

But, wait. What was this? For a fleeting instant, he'd felt the flash of something *other* in her psyche. Something that wasn't Maddie and certainly not himself. A third presence.

A threat?

Out of the corner of his eye, he became aware of a deep crimson light pouring through the bedroom door from the room beyond. He turned his head and stared. The Watcher relic, reawakening? How? Why? And why *now*?

There was nothing he could do about it. Maddie needed every shred of his attention. The shock of her final transformation would strike in seconds. The first change to Nephilim form was the worst. If she could endure the next few minutes, she would survive. She would be his. His woman. His love. His slave.

He rolled onto his back, taking her with him, their bodies still joined. She sprawled with her hands braced on his chest. Grasping her hips, he pulled her sharply down, thrusting himself upward at the same time. She gasped at the deeper invasion and her inner muscles spasmed.

He called down the spell forms that would bind her, and spoke them into her mind. Power unfurled, and he felt a moment of triumph. He was moments from the goal Artur had set for him. Moments from claiming Maddie's magic as his own.

Her climax was almost upon her. He could feel the edge of bliss in her mind, feel it in the growing spasms of her body. He stared down at her, paralyzed with awe by the power of this moment in time. Impaled on his cock, legs splayed wide, spine arched and lips parted—she was so beautiful. Her skin was glowing, her arms stretched wide, ready to embrace her new world.

How he loved her.

It was the worst time to realize that truth. The worst time to realize that he didn't want her power, that he didn't want to take her freedom. He didn't want her as a possession, a reservoir of magic to be used at his will. Or, more accurately, at *Artur's* will.

He held himself still in her mind, caught in the knowledge of those unwanted possibilities—the power, the glory, the reality of Maddie's magic. And wondering what more they could be without the taint of slavery between them. If, as equals, they rejected the curse that branded them as enemies? Was that possible? With trust? With love?

If only he dared believe.

It was a risk. A great risk. Foolhardy in the extreme. Among Watchers, trust could only be given to kin. Rivals could only join as master and slave. At least, that was what Artur had taught him.

What if Artur were wrong?

No. He couldn't hesitate. He had to push forward, bind her utterly. Completely. But when he looked into her eyes, he realized there was, after all, a shred of humanity left in his being.

Curse or no curse, he couldn't do it. He couldn't make her his slave. Even at the loss of her magic for his clan, even for his lost son, even at the risk of stirring Artur into a killing rage.

"Maddie," he gasped. "I thought . . . I thought I could do this. I can't. I don't want to. Not like this."

She stared up at him. "I don't understand."

He held himself deep and motionless inside her. "I haven't told you everything. I . . . I was sent not only to find you, but to enslave you. For my clan. But now . . . I can't do it. I want you as a lover, Maddie. As an equal partner. But that can only happen if you're free. Free to choose me, too."

He wanted what he had never been able to have with Cybele, because Cybele had formed her bond with Artur long before Cade had known her. But Maddie . . . Maddie was free to love. As was Cade. Could they be free together?

Before he could change his mind, he drew a deep breath. The ritual words formed on his lips. "I give you your life. I give you your power. I give you your freedom."

* * *

"I feel . . . so strange," Maddie whispered. "What's . . . what's happening to me?"

Cade surged deep inside her. "You're changing. To Nephilim form."

She licked dry lips. "I . . . I'm not sure I want to."

"You can't stop it," Cade said. "Don't try."

Jumbled emotions battled inside Maddie's skull. Foremost was fear. Fear of transformation. Next was anger. Burning anger, rage at her helplessness. Rage at Cade, who'd forced her to face it. Then came shame and horror for the cursed creature that she was. But beneath it all was excitement and anticipation of her growing power.

Twin lines of agony burned down her back, scoring either side of her spine. The pain robbed her of breath. Every muscle in her body screamed. Her skin was hot and slick. Her ribs were expanding, poised to shatter.

Screeching fear overwhelmed every other emotion. She wanted to scream, but her voice was frozen. All she could manage was a whimper.

She clung to Cade. He was the only solid thing in a universe that had dissolved into chaos. Into turbulent fear and raging pain. He was deep inside her body, deep inside her mind. The sharp, rhythmic pleasure of his hard thrusting, retreating, returning home, was her only window to sanity.

Do not be seduced. The son of Samyaza is not your path to power. He is your path to doom.

The whisper was so close she imagined the moistness of breath licking at her ear, but when she turned her head, nothing. When she opened her eyes, there was only Cade. Above her. Surrounding her. Inside her body. Inside her head.

Cade spoke into her mind. *Trust me, Maddie.*

His voice was clear. Not like the other. But the whispering, rasping voice was inside her, too. It didn't cease speaking just because it shared her skull with Cade.

She stiffened, wary and confused, but Cade lowered his head and clamped his lips around her nipple. A hot spike of pleasure shot from her breast to her womb. He again plunged himself deep, stroking and building that pleasure. Her inner muscles contracted and for several blessed seconds the voice fell silent.

Her impending climax overloaded her senses; her hips rose, pleading for more. She wrapped her legs around Cade's waist. His hands were beneath her, cupping her buttocks. She clutched at him.

The world rolled. He'd reversed their positions! She sprawled with palms braced on his chest; his fingers dug into her hips and pulled her sharply downward. He thrust upward at the same instant. Pleasure. She was almost at the edge. So was he.

Demon fire lit his eyes. His skin shimmered. He was beautiful in this form, she realized with some wonder. Not a monster at all. It felt so strange to have him inside her body and her mind, so strange and yet so right. If she could, she would take him deeper. She'd become a part of him willingly. Because she loved him.

The voice returned, low and rough. *For love you are willing to be his whore? His slave?*

No, she protested. It isn't like that.

It is. He will be your master. He will bind you forever.

Dark panic welled inside her, toxic bubbles bursting in the sea of her well-being. Doubt polluted Cade's beauty, destroyed the wonder of his presence. Cade, a slave master? No. It couldn't be true. She wouldn't believe it.

Then you are a fool. You are not of his clan. You are his enemy. He is strong. Stronger than you, who have just begun to know your magic. He will own you, your body as well as your life essence.

No. He won't. He—

Low, mocking laughter. *Do you imagine he comes to you in love?*

Her heart caught. No. She hadn't thought that. Not at first. But then . . . Cade had told her that he loved her. Was it true? Or, as the voice insisted, was it a lie designed to gain her trust?

His face was set in harsh lines, his breathing as ragged as her own. His fingers acted as a vise on her hips as he kept them locked in powerful movement. Her position caused him to invade her body even more deeply than before, and it was a hot, sweet knife stabbing at her heart.

The transformation was almost upon her; she could feel its beginnings. Her shoulder blades burned. She couldn't stop this, as she couldn't stop her body from responding to Cade's. Nor could she eject his presence from her mind. He drove onward, forcing her into a climax she both yearned for and dreaded.

Listen. He is speaking the binding spell into your mind. Soon it will be too late.

She didn't want to hear that whispered accusation. But the words, like sandpaper on tender skin, forced her acknowledgment.

Listen. Hear the truth.

She listened and realized the voice was right. There were words in her head. Strange words, garbled words. Words she didn't recognize. Words unknown to her ancestors. Cade's words.

Look. See the truth.

She closed her eyes. With a rush of horror, she *knew*. Cade's spell drifted behind her eyelids as flowing ribbons of light, ribbons ready to twist into unbreakable shackles. Chains ready to bind her power.

You will be his slave, the whisperer spat into her mind. *Not his lover.*

No. No!

There wasn't much time. Skin and muscle on either side of her spine tore apart; pain forced a cry from her throat. Her power was gathering. Another few seconds and it would burst into the world, only to be bound by Cade's spell. A burning knife of betrayal cut deep. How could she have been such a fool? How could she have, even for a moment, believed in him?

How could she escape him now? His thrusts had deepened, strong and sure, urging her ever toward the snare he'd prepared, the place where her body, her life essence, her magic would exist solely to serve him.

He will own you. As Ezreth sought to shame Lilith, so he seeks to shame you. But you are strong. You can fight him.

Fight? But how? *How?*

The Seed. The Seed is the key. The amulet can protect you.

The Seed of Life. The relic had protected her from Dr. Ben-Meir. It could protect her from Cade. She understood that now. In her memory she'd begun to understand the magic Lilith had bound with the talisman. Azazel's daughter was Maddie's ancestor. So, perhaps she could call Lilith's power. Use it.

But the relic was far from her hands, not covering her heart where it was meant to be. Lilith's shining gold was five thousand years old, bent and blackened. The bloodstone was no longer whole. And Cade . . . Cade was master of Maddie's body and mind. She could never reach the disc. He would never allow it.

More pain ripped through her back. Her impending climax coiled just a bit tighter. Another heartbeat and it would break over her with tsunami force, another heartbeat and it would be too late to save herself. Panic froze her body, froze her mind. Even the voice of the whisperer faded. All she knew was Cade.

"Maddie."

He stilled suddenly, his gaze capturing hers. Doubt clouded those beautiful blue eyes. And then, incredibly, Cade lit the path to her escape—and to his own destruction.

"I thought . . . I thought I could do this. I can't. I don't want to. Not like this."

"I don't understand."

He held himself deep and still inside her. "I haven't told you everything. I . . . I was sent not only to find you, but to enslave you. For my clan. But now . . . I can't do it. I want you as a lover, Maddie. As an equal partner. But that can only happen if you're free. Free to choose me, too."

His tone broadened and deepened, as if he were reciting a passage from a holy book. "I give you your life. I give you your power. I give you your freedom."

The whispering voice returned in a hiss. *He lies. There can be no freedom. No equality. Among rival Nephilim, there is only master and slave. Which will you be?*

She could take no more; her climax burst upon her. She screamed as her human body split apart and sparks raced over her skin, down her arms. Blue flames erupted from her palms. An explosion shook the cottage. Red sparks showered her, and a hot wind swept through Maddie's body. Magic poured from her being. It unfurled in dark, sweeping wings of power.

A choice beckoned. She saw it clearly and made her decision. She seized the freedom Cade had so foolishly offered her.

You are wise, my daughter.

Chapter Nineteen

The sewer was dank and disgusting, but Artur had been in worse places.

He judged his position to be directly under the parlor he'd occupied a short time before. A narrow ledge ran alongside a channel of rainwater that churned in a course toward the river. Overhead, ancient pipes, joints none too tight, carried more odoriferous cargo. A drop of something foul splashed his shoulder. A rat ran across his foot. He took no notice of either. The stink of blood magic was stronger than any odor created by animal or human.

He inched his way along the ledge, senses alert and searching. Dusek would not want to limit his comings and goings to the streets above. There would be an entrance somewhere in this maze, he was sure.

He almost missed it. Shielded as it was by layer upon layer of magic, the portal was all but undetectable. In fact, he moved past without even recognizing the difference in the smooth stones and the joints between. But a few steps later, the hairs on his nape tingled as if someone were watching him from behind and he halted and turned. Eyes narrow, he picked out the line of a doorway gleaming through unmortared joints.

It took him several moments to find a way through the magical protections. As he worked, his uneasiness grew. Dusek had woven magic from no fewer than nine Watcher clans to create these wardings. Blast it to Oblivion. The Samyaza slave was not the only one Dusek had in his power. How many rival slaves had the alchemist collected?

The layer of Samyaza earth magic was last, and it was the most difficult to unravel. Artur was accustomed to commanding such power, not thwarting it. By the time the barrier fell, his leather coat stuck to his skin and sweat was dripping from his brow. A waft of chill air felt like a slap in the face.

He stepped into a very dark corridor. The space was much narrower than the sewer had been. The brick walls were close enough to touch on either side; a vaulted ceiling arched high overhead. A subtle red glow lit the far end of the passage. A haunting, echoing sob brushed his ears. A weeping woman? Grimly, Artur moved toward the sound.

The red light strengthened as he crept closer. There was no door at the end of the corridor, as he'd half expected. Only a sharp turn into a vibrant spill of light.

Artur kept his back tight to the wall as he eased around the corner. He stood at the top of a stairway. It descended in a steep slide of masonry into a miasma of blood magic. The force was very dense. Artur found he could not advance past the first tread of the stair, so he remained on the landing, a bitter taste staining the back of his throat. The magical aura of the place was deadening. His own magic felt far away, as if he were viewing it through the wrong end of a telescope.

Artur knew himself to be a hard, cruel man. There was no pretense to goodness in his demon nature. He'd done terrible things in his life, and he considered himself inured to the evil he perpetuated. Next to Vaclav Dusek he was an angel. In his arrogance, he hadn't fully appreciated the vastness of his enemy's power. He did now, and the knowledge sickened him. It was all he could do to summon enough power to peer through the gloom.

The room below him was perhaps thirty feet in diameter. In the center of the space a blue fire burned without any apparent fuel. A stone table like an altar rose beside the flames, and the slab bore dripping crimson stains. At the base, polished bones along with more complete remnants of a human body littered the floor.

Sobs drifted through the air like wraiths bound for Hell. The weeping came from prisoners—seven men and two women—secured at regular intervals around the perimeter of the chamber. Naked, bound by chains too short to allow them to stand upright, they cowered in the shadows, desperately trying, Artur thought, to avoid the notice of the three black-clad men in their midst.

The three wore black collars identical to the ones Artur had seen on the two sons of Dusek in the palace above. So, three more sons of Vaclav Dusek. How many more were there? How many offspring had the bastard spawned?

Artur knew the alchemist had somehow found a way to extend his life past the maximum one hundred twenty years allotted to a Watcher. Artur didn't know exactly how old Dusek was, but it was clear that he had been building his magic for centuries. Azazel's heir spawned sons, enslaved them, and somehow increased his lifespan by adding their life essences to his own. Now he collected slaves of rival clans as well.

The power he was harvesting from these unfortunate rival adepts must be nearly endless. For the first time Artur truly understood the confidence behind his enemy's arrogant challenge of Clan Samyaza. With his stolen magic, Dusek could wipe out his ancestral foes in one vicious swipe. Artur and his kin couldn't hope to stand against him.

The knowledge churned Artur's stomach like a rancid meal. It was obvious now that Artur and his kin were alive only because the alchemist had chosen to draw out the fight. He didn't want a quick victory; he apparently preferred to play with his victims, as a cat plays with an injured mouse before devouring it whole. But at any time Dusek might grow tired of the game and make his final move to consign Artur's heritage to Oblivion.

The sickening scene below illuminated Artur's impotence. He could do nothing for the wretched captives and yet he could not look away. Dusek's sons were slaves, too, but they seemed of a much higher order than the other captives. Or perhaps their present sport was due to their sire's absence.

One son tormented a chained male. The second applied a whip to the back of a female whom the third son approached. Her red hair was matted and dirty, her naked body covered with welts and bruises. Her chains forced her to kneel. Even so, she didn't cower. Arthur could well imagine the filth the bastard would soon demand of her. Her chin lifted nonetheless.

The magic of the room was a deadening pall that Artur couldn't pierce, though he tried. He couldn't so much as read the source of the individual prisoners' magic. Which captive was his kin? Was the Clan Samyaza slave here or suffering elsewhere in this hellish dungeon? Slow, impotent rage expanded in Artur's gut. It seared every cell of his body, scoured the corners of his cold heart. The organ was left raw and bleeding as fresh horrors unfolded before him.

There was nothing he could do. Nothing at all except wait for Dusek's next move.

* * *

"Here," Ezreth said. "Now."

He came down on top of Lilith, hurting her, pressing her into the ground. Trapping her with one broad leg thrown over both of hers, Ezreth shoved her robes up to her waist. His nostrils flared as he looked his fill. A sharp rock dug into Lilith's spine.

"Stop," she gasped. Her arms flailed but her fierce struggle moved him not at all.

"Fight me if you wish," he said. "I do not mind."

She watched with numb despair as he unbelted his robe and drew it aside. His shaft emerged, engorged and eager. She tried again to turn him away.

"If you do this foul thing, you will regret it. Father will—"

"He will give you to me." The crimson aura about his head and shoulders blazed. One implacable knee forced itself between her legs.

"No." Her fingers dug into the dirt on either side of her body. "He will not. He will . . ."

Her hand struck something warm. The amulet. The Seed of Life, centered by the bloodstone. She had all but forgotten it. In another heartbeat her brother would be inside her body; there was no time to think, no time to plan. Her fingers clenched on her only hope.

Dark sparks flew down her arm. The gold ignited in her hand. Blue flames burst from her skin, and she thrust the amulet between their bodies. Heat erupted. Light flashed.

Ezreth jerked back with a cry. "What—?"

The force of the explosion whipped Lilith's head backward. Her skull struck stone. Red lights danced in her vision and her recent meal surged up her gullet.

She struggled to rise. Grasping the stone wall encircling the well, she dragged herself to her feet. She had to get away before Ezreth realized she was hurt—

One desperate glance toward her brother stilled her flight. Ezreth would not pursue her, not ever again. He was dead.

* * *

Thinking was an effort. It was as if someone had thrown a dirty blanket over his brain.

Cade cracked an eye. He lay on the bed, on his stomach. The space beside him was empty. Cold. Sounds of movement drifted from the outer room, and his nostrils twitched at the aroma of coffee overlaid with the savory scent of freshly roasted meat. The last alarmed him.

He heaved himself to his feet. Every muscle protested. He stumbled to the door and found the kitchen littered with the remnants of a blood meal. A slab of charred flesh lay on the table, red juices flowing from a deep cut. The meat had been freshly slaughtered; the fragrance of life hadn't completely left it.

Maddie was in the room, though not at the table. She'd put off her Nephilim form and resumed a human guise. She stood by the counter, half turned away, sipping espresso from a white demitasse. She was nude from the waist up. A simple skirt in a delicately flowered pattern flowed over her long legs to mid-calf. She must have found the garment in a drawer.

She held the saucer in her right hand; her left rested against her thigh. The slope of her bare breast and the enticing peak of her nipple drew Cade's eye. It was a heartbreakingly beautiful pose.

And deceiving. No stain marred her skin, but the bloody mess on the table spoke for itself. Maddie had wasted no time in feeding her Nephilim cravings. In killing for blood.

He'd slept through the rampage. How could he have done such a thing? It was inexcusable. He should have been at her side, teaching her how to quell her blood craving. Cade thought of the cattle he'd seen dotting the fields on the slope behind the cottage and hoped like hell Maddie hadn't gone hunting for human prey. He dragged a hand through his hair and tried to remember the last moments before he'd lost consciousness. Unease snaked through his gut. Something didn't feel right. What the hell had happened?

The strong black scent of Maddie's espresso curled from her cup to his nostrils. The odor jarred him into action and he started across the room. Two steps later he halted, suddenly aware he was naked.

Maddie placed the cup and saucer on the counter and turned

to him, unsmiling. Her eyes glowed softly red. A second flash of crimson light, lower down, caught his eye. Maddie wore Lilith's amulet strung on a leather cord between her breasts.

Cade's eyes shot to the corner where he'd left the thing. His snake lay motionless, its tattoo body no more than lines of ink staining the tiled floor. His stomach turned. Cade strode toward her, cursing.

"Blast it, Maddie. What have you—?"

She held up a hand. "No, Cade. Stay where you are."

He jerked to a stop even before his conscious mind recognized her tone of absolute command. Once halted, his feet felt like stone blocks. He couldn't lift either heel or toe off the floor. Understanding rushed him like a suffocating storm.

Maddie's gaze raked over his nakedness. He wanted to retreat, to cover himself but wasn't able. He had no choice in his actions, he realized with dawning horror. He was compelled to perform whatever act Maddie commanded. *He* was the slave. She was his master.

"Put on some pants."

His body pivoted toward the bedroom. He grunted and threw all his strength into resistance. His effort was futile, as he knew it would be. His mind was not his own: *she* was there, present in every cell and synapse. Each command he attempted to give his body slipped like water between spread fingers. His will was no longer his own. He existed only to serve her.

His sense of betrayal was sharp. She'd done to him what he'd intended to do to her, because he'd pulled back at the last moment and offered her freedom. He'd given her that choice, and she had taken it. In his arrogance, he'd thought she wanted the same thing he did—love, as equals. Now he'd learned how wrong he'd been. His trust in her had been entirely misplaced.

He should have known a descendant of Azazel's line would spurn such a gift. Hadn't he sensed that Maddie's basic nature was that of a warrior? He should have anticipated this brutal turning of the tables. Instead, blinded by human emotion, blinded by *love*, he'd ignored the warning signs. From trust and love, he'd set her free. She, in turn, had seized the opportunity he'd handed her and used his faith to enslave him. His weakness had doomed his clan.

He snatched his jeans from the floor and jerked them on. There was only one thing he couldn't understand. How had Maddie managed to steal his spell? It shouldn't have been possible. Her magic was new and raw. It was incredible she'd even realized what he was doing. How could she have twisted his magic against him so quickly and easily? Cade hadn't even been aware that she'd done it. The answer had to lie with the cursed Watcher relic. The disc must have guided Maddie in claiming her power over him.

Cade's own arrogance was partly to blame for this predicament. He'd known the artifact was dangerous. Lethal. The archangels had wanted it destroyed. He'd seen the results of Maddie's disturbing link with the thing, and he'd known what she was: Azazel's own spawn. He hadn't wanted to believe she would betray him, so he'd given himself over to protecting her, loving her, and even, at the end, releasing her from the slavery Artur had ordained. A fool's mistake. His first loyalty should have been to his clan. He was a bloody idiot.

Maddie tilted her head. She looked into the space beyond him, a vertical line appearing between her eyebrows. It looked for all the world as if she were listening to something. But, to what? The disc strung around her neck? He watched her intently, trying to understand.

Her eyes refocused on his face. "Come."

"Where are we going?"

She strode toward the door. He followed—he had no choice. He thought she might not answer his question, but as she reached the door she spoke without turning. "To the beach."

"Why?"

"Enough questions."

Teeth gritted, Cade trailed her out into a very dark night. The protections he'd set around the cottage before her crisis were gone. Stars hung low and brilliant in the sky. Man-made lights were scattered like glowing pearls along the rocky curve of the shoreline. But the air was fetid. The odors of blood and death slapped him like an open palm across the face.

He spied the remnants of a mutilated calf carcass a few yards to his left. Intense relief caused his shoulders to sag. The kill was not human: Maddie hadn't yet crossed the line to total depravity. Though he wasn't sure what he could do now to prevent it. Was there a way to turn her from the path she'd chosen? He didn't know.

She halted mere steps from the edge of the cliff. Her eyes flashed red. Spreading her arms, she flung her head back. Her human body melted into her Nephilim form.

An unspoken command burned in his brain; she wanted him to do the same. Cade threw every ounce of his strength into resisting the compulsion to change. The effort left him sweating, breathless, and sapped of energy. And, in the end, defeated.

He changed. His human skin thickened into sparkling color. His hide felt as though it wrapped his bones and muscles too tightly. Everywhere he tingled.

He locked gazes with her. "Maddie. Don't do this."

Her chin lifted and she laughed. It was not a pleasant sound. "Don't do what? Don't force you, Cade? You hypocrite! This is just what you planned to do to me."

He swallowed thickly. "I planned to possess you, yes. I admit that. But not like this. Not in anger. Not in hatred."

"In *love*?" On her lips, the word sounded like the worst profanity.

"Yes," he said. "In love."

Silence followed. Then, "You make me sick."

Cade found himself facedown on the ground, lungs devoid of air, mouth full of dirt. The impact that had sent him sprawling reverberated through his bones. He heaved up onto his hands and knees, spitting dust and blood. Pain knifed his chest as he struggled to draw breath.

"Get up," she commanded.

He lurched to his feet. "Maddie! Please. Don't. This isn't you. It's that thing around your neck. Your ancestors created that disc with blood magic. Don't let yourself be snared by its evil. Resist it."

The briefest uncertainty flickered in her eyes. Recognizing it, he pressed the slim advantage.

"You said once that you trusted me. I know I didn't deserve it—not then. I intended to enslave you. But remember that when the moment came, I couldn't do it. I didn't want you like that, because I love you. I gave you your freedom because of that love. Please. Trust me enough now, love me enough, to do the same for me. Free me, and we'll destroy the disc together."

He thought he might have gotten through. For a long moment she remained silent. Then her head tilted and her eyes lost focus, as if she were hearing something else.

"Don't listen to it," he pleaded. "Don't."

Her gaze flicked back to him and her expression hardened. "You arrogant pig. You want my trust—my love—after all you've done? All you meant to do? Sorry, Cade. That's just not going to happen."

She showed him her back and unfurled her wings.

"Down the cliffs to the beach," she said. "Now."

Chapter Twenty

Maddie remembered so much now. She remembered all of it: centuries—no, *millennia*—of magical heritage. And the oldest memory held the most power. Ezreth's body, lying beside the Watcher well, his neck bent at the exact same angle Dr. Ben-Meir's had been. The Seed of Life—Lilith's creation, the repository of life-and-death powers—had killed both men. Maddie wasn't sorry.

She leaped over the edge of the cliff into nothingness, an act that just yesterday would have been unthinkable. Now, buoyed by her newborn magic, guided by the exultant, whispering voice in her head, she knew she could do anything. Even fly.

Human existence—how flat and gray it had been! Unbearable to contemplate. While trapped in her human form, Maddie had never suspected the glory that was her birthright. Now she knew.

A heady rush of power met the spread of her new wings. Her body was flush with the energy of the living blood she'd consumed during the first ravenous hours she'd spent in her Nephilim form. True, it had only been the blood of an animal, but it had been potent enough. At least for now. For now she knew wonder, power, glory. Exhilaration, strength, and freedom. Bliss.

Yes. Now you know. Now you are complete.

How could she have believed her small human existence was anything worth clinging to? How could she have not known that she was meant for so much more? For perfection!

The earth fell away. Each sweep of her dark feathered wings

lifted her higher and higher. The stars hung above her like twinkling diamonds, so close she almost believed she could pluck a handful to encircle her throat, adorn her wrist and fingers.

The earth, the sea, the sky—they offered a vividness her human self had never even guessed at. She'd caught glimpses with her Watcher sight in the past weeks: the auras, the blinding flash of clarity she'd experienced when digging with the American teens. She'd thought it was the tumor. She laughed now at the sheer absurdity of that fear.

She didn't glance back to see if Cade had followed; she knew he had. He had no choice. She'd locked him in the prison he'd meant for her. The hurt of that betrayal was a lump of acid stuck in her throat. He'd begged her to trust him. And—almost—she had. She'd even fallen a bit in love with him. Only to discover how he meant to use her faith and emotions against her.

But what had she expected? Love was human stupidity. Cade was an archdemon. Nephilim. As was she.

To a Nephilim, power was all. Power to wield over humans. Power to master Nephilim of rival blood. So simple. Maddie was a daughter of Azazel. More than a daughter—*much* more. Cade was a son of Samyaza. Her enemy.

Testing her wings, she flew out over the waves in a wide arc. The charcoal waters birthed white breakers, then, just as quickly, killed their foamy offspring. Maddie's demonic sight sliced easily through the night, searching out the peaks and valleys of the seascape below.

He is coming. Soon. Very soon.

Maddie didn't have to wonder at the meaning of the whispered words. She knew. Another fragment of Lilith's memory had fallen into place.

* * *

"Ezreth is dead," Lilith told her father. The back of her skull throbbed where it had struck the ground. "I killed him."

Flies were already gathering on the corpse, though the sun had hardly moved in the sky since his neck was broken. His aura was dark, but Lilith's mind had scarcely registered the fact her brother was truly dead until she'd looked up from his body to see her father striding toward her.

"I killed him," she said again. "I accept your punishment." She bowed her head and waited for Azazel's blow.

"I see," was all her father said. Then, "How did this come to pass?"

She didn't dare look up, though she wondered desperately what she would see in his eyes if she did. "I was here at the forge. I succeeded in transmuting the prime substance into gold. I formed the metal into the pattern you showed me, the Seed of Life. In the center I set the bloodstone we made."

Azazel's brows rose. "And where is this piece?"

"Here." She held the disc in her hand, thrust it out at him. He took and examined the amulet, his expression inscrutable.

"You have held nothing back," he said at last. His voice vibrated with emotion. "You have poured your entire essence into this gold, this gem. You have created with your innocence what I, in all my power, could not." His fingers tightened on the Seed. "Life. Life itself."

"It is a gift to you," she said simply, "who gave me life." She felt his eyes on her but couldn't bring herself to lift her head. "But . . . just as I completed the spells, Ezreth came. He ordered me to lie with him."

"Did you?"

"No!" She did look up then, imploring. "Never would I do such a thing! I . . . I remain pure, Father. As you commanded."

A small smile curved his lips. "And so I did." He gestured. "Continue, my daughter. Tell me all."

Haltingly, Lilith recounted her brother's approach and attack, and the explosion of magic that saved her. "My head struck the well. I . . . can't remember exactly what happened while I lay on the ground. But when I rose, Ezreth was dead."

Azazel's thumb stroked the jewel in the amulet. "Life," he murmured, almost to himself. "And death. Joined in metal and stone. Incredible."

Lilith flushed. "I . . . I am not sure I understand."

"Your creation is pure potentiality. And protection of that force. In short, immortality." His free hand descended to Lilith's shoulder. It felt heavy and warm. His eyes found hers. "Do you trust me, Lilith?"

"Of course, Father! With my life!"

"And you still wish to gift me with this work of your hands?"

"Yes, Father."

His lips touched her forehead. "Then come, my love. It is time."

She didn't know what time he referred to, but she loved and trusted him completely. She went without hesitation, her hand in his.

He guided her to the entrance of his dwelling. In the anteroom, she bathed his feet and hers as she had done that first day. His dark eyes remained upon her all the while. Whenever she chanced to glance up, the fleeting contact of their gazes tightened her chest.

Inside the tent's main chamber, Azazel placed the Seed of Life on the low table before the couch. He drew Lilith to stand before him. Then, slowly, almost reverently, he touched her bare head, her temple.

His touch felt good. Wonderful. It did strange things to Lilith's body. She felt alert and languid all at once. His fingers explored the tilt of her cheekbones, the line of her jaw. He spread the long fall of her hair about her shoulders. His thumbs stroked the sensitive skin below her ears. The pads of his fingers massaged the back of her skull.

His eyes did not move from her face. "You are a beautiful woman, Lilith."

Her heart thumped wildly. "I . . . thank you, Father."

"A beautiful woman indeed."

He bent his head and gifted her with another kiss. This one he placed not on her forehead but full on her lips. She stiffened slightly as his mouth urged hers to open. This was not the kiss of a father to a daughter!

Lilith's emotions, already raw, spun in confusion. For several long moments she knew nothing but shock. She felt as though she had drifted outside herself. Shame crept like a sickness into her chest. Azazel deepened the kiss. This was wrong! An abomination before Heaven. But somehow, even the knowledge of the perversion in which she was participating did not quite stop the liquid slide of pleasure that sluiced from her breasts to the hidden place between her legs.

She struggled to understand. This was Azazel. Her father. She loved him; she trusted him absolutely. He had laid her deepest emotions bare. He knew how much she loved him. And he loved her. He must! But not, it seemed, only as a daughter. He wanted her as a mate as well.

It was not in her heart to deny him anything. Even this. Tentatively, fearfully, her hands slid up his arms to grasp his shoulders; softly, they slipped around his neck. His kiss was gentle, coaxing, as if he knew just what she needed. Of course he did—he loved her! And he was wise. If he wanted this, it must be right.

His big hand wandered down her back. His palms molded her buttocks. He pulled her into his body, and his man's desire was hard and long. It pressed against her belly. His voice was rough when he said, "Do you give me your body, Lilith? To do with as I will?"

A tremor ran through her. One last doubt, urging her to turn away, sounded like a bell in her mind. But then he touched her again, so softly, so lovingly, and something inside her broke.

"Yes," she said.

"And your mind? Will you also entrust that to me?"

"If . . . if you wish it."

He left her. She felt bereft. But he returned swiftly, the disc in his hand. He pressed the gold to the bare skin just below the base of her throat and warmth seeped into her chest.

"Will you give me your magic also, Lilith? To use as I see fit?"

She hesitated but a heartbeat before surrendering. "All that I am is yours."

The whispered answer increased Azazel's smile. "The magic of the Seed, Lilith—your magic—is stronger than death. With it, together, we will live forever."

The magic of the talisman flowed over her. Lilith's body softened, then tensed when a knife appeared in Azazel's hand; with a deft motion he slashed his right palm. A trickle of crimson oozed free. He placed his palm over the amulet, pressing it into Lilith's skin, sealing their union with his blood.

*It was as if lightning had struck. Lilith jerked; her body sizzled with sensation. A cry burst from her lips. Dark waves of magic filled her being, entranced her mind. But she remained aware—*acutely *aware—of what was happening.*

Azazel untied the braided cord at his waist, stripped off his robes. This is wrong, *she thought one last time. Wrong, but inevitable. She had come from his body. Now she would take him into hers. The circle would be complete, and they would live forever.*

Together.

* * *

They would live forever. Together. Maddie's feet touched down silently on cold sand. The beach was narrow and strewn with rocks. The sea churned and eddied. Cade, still in flight, circled above Maddie's head. Testing his leash, perhaps? With a thought, she jerked him down.

He landed beside her, panting and angry. She was aware of his body, was acutely aware of his aura, burning an angry crimson. It crackled, and sizzling sparks burst across his skin.

He took up an unwilling position at her left elbow. She didn't turn her head to look at him but kept her gaze riveted on the horizon. *He* was coming.

A small shadow appeared upon the dark water. Maddie's

heart leaped. In the breathless moments that followed, the blur resolved into solid form: a small boat slicing through the waves. It cast no light on its landward journey; it generated no sound. And yet it passed, deftly and surely, through treacherous water and around deadly rocks to finally reach shore.

A man stood at the bow. When the boat halted, he stepped easily out. His feet seemed to skim the surface of the water as he walked the short distance to the hard-packed sand. His face and form were familiar. The red glow of his eyes was new, as was the dark crimson aura about his head and shoulders. Maddie thought her joy might burst out of her skin.

Cade rasped a sharp inhalation. "Impossible," he muttered. "That is not Simon Ben-Meir. Ben-Meir is dead."

"Yes," Maddie heard herself say. "He is."

The man who approached had only borrowed Ben-Meir's body. The cadaver, now bathed with its crimson aura, pulsed with a life that could not die.

She'd seen him, Maddie realized now, below the window of the hotel where Cade had briefly imprisoned her. At the time, she hadn't understood. Now she did.

Cade's angry hiss seared her ear. "This is evil, Maddie. Pure evil. You must know that."

She shrugged, never once taking her eyes from the man who approached. "Good and evil. Life and death. Angel and demon. There's really no difference. You told me that yourself, Cade."

"You twist my words. Not all power is subjective. Some powers are evil."

"And some," she replied, "cannot be denied."

He was almost upon her. The awareness of his presence was wonderful and unbearable. He had returned to her.

No. Not to her. To Lilith.

But . . . Lilith was gone. Dead. Maddie frowned. How could

that be? Lilith had created the Seed of Life. Azazel had vowed she would live with him forever.

The moment of Lilith's death hovered at the edges of Maddie's memory. When she reached for it, it receded. But, did it really matter? In a very real way, Lilith was still alive in Maddie.

"Is eternity worth your honor? Is it worth your self-respect?" Cade's cold rage deepened the twinge of unease in Maddie's gut.

"Quiet," she hissed, and he fell silent.

The newcomer halted on the sand, close enough to touch her, though he did not. She looked up into his eyes. The red glow of his irises went on forever. They were like flames inside her skull, licking at her thoughts, gently erasing her doubts. Cade was her enemy; she had defeated him. Of course he would try to turn her from her destiny.

He reached out and clasped her hands. His touch was warm. Somehow, she hadn't expected that. He wore a dead man's body; she'd expected him to carry a chill.

"I greet you, Daughter. With pride." His eyes fell to the Seed of Life nestled between her bare breasts. "You have pleased me well. Again."

A flush stole into Maddie's cheeks. "Father," she said. "I thank you."

"He is not," Cade hissed, "your *father*. He is Azazel."

But he was wrong. Azazel was her father—the father she'd never known. He brought with him worlds of possibility when just a short time ago she was convinced her life was at an end. She couldn't turn away from that.

The ancient Watcher regarded Cade through Simon Ben-Meir's eyes. "You, slave. You are a son of Samyaza."

Cade did not flinch. "I am."

"I once told my foolish brother that my children would

conquer his." Azazel's gaze swept Cade from head to toe. "I am pleased to know I spoke the truth. On your knees, slave."

The command washed through Maddie on its way to Cade. She didn't resist. Her father's will was her own.

Cade tried to rebel. Foolish man. She watched dispassionately as his face contorted and colored with effort. As his big body strained against the compulsion to throw himself onto the muddy sand. It was a battle he couldn't win. Didn't he realize that?

His crimson aura became a deep, dismal brown. He dropped to his hands and knees, barely able to hold up his head. Even his wings bowed, the tips kissing the sand.

"Very good."

Azazel advanced and swung a leg over Cade's back. He settled his borrowed human body atop his enemy's back as he might settle into a horse's saddle. With one hand, he gripped Cade's hair and pulled back his head almost to the point of snapping his neck.

Cade's teeth bared in a snarl. His body shook with fury even as he obeyed Maddie's command to spread his wings. Azazel just smiled and gestured to Maddie with his free hand.

"Come."

"Where are we going?" she asked.

His aura glowed darkly. "Where you lead," he said.

"I don't understand."

"You will. When you look inside and remember."

The words were cryptic, but she accepted them without question. Nodding, she unfurled her wings and, with a graceful leap, took to the air.

* * *

Vaclav Dusek surveyed the deserted hut. The untouched order of Dr. Simon Ben-Meir's workroom was deceiving, h thought. A distinct residue of blood magic lingered in the air. Blood magic and death.

He turned to his guide. "You say you found nothing to indicate where Ben-Meir and the woman might have gone?"

The woman twisted her hands together. "Nothing, Professor. Only an overturned chair here in the workroom. But Dr. Ben-Meir's computer, it is still here, as you can see. None of his clothes or belongings seem to be missing. Maddie's purse and passport are on the shelf in our hut, just as they have been for weeks. I do not understand it. Surely if there had been some kind of attack or struggle, the rest of us would have heard it."

She drew an unsteady breath and continued. "The jeep is missing—we noticed that when we rose in the morning. Ari and I thought Maddie and Dr. Ben-Meir might have driven to town for supplies. Though, it was odd that they would leave without telling someone. Then Gil noticed his Vespa was missing and the new laborer was also nowhere to be found. And the earth at the bottom of the Watcher well had been disturbed."

Dusek laid a hand on the back of a chair. "This one?"

The woman blinked. "What?"

"Was this the chair you found overturned?"

"Oh. Yes. Yes, it was."

He ran his hand over the wood. An image sprang into his brain of a man and a woman facing each other. Arguing.

Ben-Meir's assistant stumbled on in her heavily accented English. Hadara Stern was a particularly annoying human, Dusek decided. In a rare fit of charity he stifled the urge to kill her. A public death would not serve his purpose.

"It has been two days." The woman wrung her hands so hard it was a wonder her fingers didn't twist completely off. "I think, Professor, we really must call the police. I delayed until your arrival, as you asked, but now—"

"Of course." Dusek waved a hand. "Two days with no word

is certainly troubling. And the missing British laborer besides. By all means, notify the authorities."

"Do you think . . . ?" The woman's throat bulged with a thick swallow. Most unpleasant. Dusek imagined her naked and bloody, begging for her miserable human life. It was a mildly amusing thought. Perhaps . . .

"Do you think the laborer abducted them?"

"It is possible," Dusek said. "Or perhaps this Cade Leucetius stole something of value and Dr. Ben-Meir and his companion gave pursuit."

Relief flooded Hadara Stern's face. "I had not thought of that. It is very possible, is it not?"

"No doubt the police will have more theories. Please. Go and make the call. I will look about a bit more."

On the verge of tears, the assistant bit her lip and hurried away—a good thing for her, because Dusek had been perilously close to snuffing her life, consequences be damned. He lifted his hand from the back of the chair and rubbed the palm with his opposite thumb. Interesting. Just that small contact had caused his muscles to clench.

He closed his eyes briefly, reviewing his vision of Ben-Meir and Ms. Durant. The two had stood just so. The woman had stood between the table and the door; Ben-Meir had been positioned on a small, handwoven square of carpeting. There had been something in the archeologist's hand. An artifact, gold but dirty. No doubt it was whatever had emerged from the hastily dug hole at the bottom of the Watcher well.

Dusek drew a steady breath, steeling himself for the coming ordeal. His hand was steady when, crouching, he placed it palm down on the rug.

It was as if someone inserted a hot poker into his left eye. The pain was so intense that he couldn't suppress a sharp hiss of inhaled air. It was a struggle to look past the turmoil to the scene beyond. But he did. A body was lying on the ground, neck bent sharply: Ben-Meir, dead. The woman crouched nearby.

Dusek sucked in a breath; for an instant he felt as though he'd been struck in the chest. The missing assistant was Nephilim. Watcher magic glowed wild and red about her head. He sensed the unformed nature of her power; she was unaware but in transition.

The magic emanating from her presence was that of Azazel. Madeline Durant was a descendent of Azazel. She was Dusek's own kin.

He uttered a curse. Clan Samyaza did not possess the power of remote vision and discernment. How had Artur Camulus learned of this dormant's existence? Surely he had, if he'd sent one of his own to retrieve her. Enslaved to Clan Samyaza, the woman could prove a formidable challenge to Dusek's plans. Artur Camulus was changing the game.

A slow smile cracked Dusek's features. A challenge? He'd almost begun to think life had none left to offer.

He narrowed his concentration on the relic in the dormant's hands. The piece was bent and scorched, the central stone damaged, but the mesmerizing pattern of circles was clear to Dusek's questing mind. The Seed of Life. Lilith's slice of immortality, the weapon that had killed Dusek's ancestor Ezreth. The Seed of Life was the goal of Dusek's long existence. He had diverted DAMN funds into Ben-Meir's coffers in the hope the archeologist would unearth information relevant to this very amulet. It seemed the archeologist had far exceeded expectations.

The Seed's design contained the secrets of Heaven's creative power transmuted into earthly form. Dusek had often traced the pattern while creating alchemical potions and gems, but it was the elusive magic of the demonic bloodstone, the carrier of the true spark of immortality, that had over the centuries become the obsession of all Clan Azazel alchemists. The quest had even passed into human lore, where the bloodstone had assumed a deceptively innocent name: the Philosopher's Stone. For centuries Dusek's ancestors—the sons of Ezreth—had tried to create a duplicate of the stone. For centuries, they had failed.

By whatever name the gem was known, its magic was vast. And deadly. It had sent Dusek's ancestor Ezreth into Oblivion. The final moments of Ezreth's death lurked as a shadow in Dusek's ancestral memory. The first son of Azazel had been murdered by his Nephilim half sister, Lilith.

Dusek imagined the Seed in his hands. He imagined the power. The glory. And then he remembered the talisman was gone.

His scowl returned as the scene from the near past continued to unfold: The door to the hut opened, admitting Cade Leucetius. Dusek's fingers clenched. The Nephilim woman, caught in her trance, stared. She and Leucetius exchanged words. Dusek could not hear what was said, but whatever it was caused the woman to turn violent. She struck out; the Seed of Life flew from her hand. The relic hit the floor and traced an erratic, rolling line across the ground. The edge of a small rug sent the disc lurching into the air . . .

It landed atop Ben-Meir's body, and something *alive* passed from metal to flesh. Simply the echo of that magic caused Dusek's mouth to gape.

Leucetius, apelike fool that he was, had been consumed with settling the woman's outburst; he had not even been aware of the transfer. Having rendered the woman senseless, he approached the corpse and pocketed the amulet. Leaving the archeologist's body where it lay, he hoisted her into his arms and fled. Leucetius did not see the corpse's ribs expand, nor its eyes flutter open.

Dusek straightened. He had seen enough. The game had indeed changed.

* * *

Maddie took to the air. Azazel, carried on Cade's broad back, glided beside her. But which direction to take? She looked uncertainly in Azazel's direction. *Look inside and remember*, he'd said. The answer lay, then, in her ancestral memory. In the memory of one ancestor in particular . . .

* * *

Chartres, France
AD 1200

The architect known only as Scarlet, descendant of an unholy union of Watcher father and Nephilim daughter motioned his litter forward, into the shadow of the rising cathedral.

A lifetime he had devoted to the re-creation of Lilith's power. Her tools had been fire and gold; his were stone, mortar, and glass. Guided by his own magic and his ancestor's memory, he worked combinations of form, color, and light. Such ethereal elements would, he believed, reveal the path to immortality. He was prepared to sacrifice everything—fortune, renown, wealth—if only he could discover a way to cheat Oblivion. So many years he'd labored. Yet, the time was a pitiful span, a mere heartbeat in the scheme of the universe. And he had yet to uncover the secret. But his goal was close. He sensed it. Perhaps in this time, in this place, with this masterpiece, he would gain the ultimate prize.

Sacred geometry, he was convinced, held the key. He'd seen Lilith's amulet, the Seed of Life, in his dreams; he'd used his own magic to expand the vision. He'd added twelve circles to her seven, creating a pattern of nineteen overlapping rings. Into that design he'd introduced a magical, winding path. Now, at last, he would add his birthright: Lilith's bloodstone.

He had spent years exploring the mysteries of the damaged gem. Lilith's blood and magic lived in the stone. As did Azazel's will. The merged power hung suspended in the crimson shard, but the stone was incomplete. Flawed. This Scarlet knew.

And yet he'd carried it on his person since his father delivered it into his hand with his dying breath. Scarlet did not expect to pass the gem to his own daughter, however. There would be no need. Not if he succeeded in his quest. Not if he and his progeny achieved immortality.

His litter threaded its way through the piles of stone and mounds of sand and lime surrounding the building site. Masons and apprentices scurried like mice to clear a path. The lead litter-bearer cried the approach of the master builder.

Scarlet's chair did not halt until it reached the cathedral's great western towers. Parting the curtains, he alighted. The asymmetrical spires were the only portions of the old church left standing after the devastating fire of six years earlier. Scarlet might have had the towers pulled down, but their charred facades reminded him strongly of his own damaged birthright. He thought it fitting that they remain as sentinels guarding his new creation. He envisioned a great circular window in shades of deep red and blue spanning the space between them. But that glory would require some years yet to achieve. He smiled. If all went according to plan, he would have an eternity in which to perfect his magnum opus.

Tucking a scroll under his arm, Scarlet strode through the scaffolding that separated the towers, the peak of his hat brushing a cross timber as he passed beneath. The cathedral nave extended before him, as yet unroofed. The perimeter walls and the bases of the columns were not yet risen to shoulder height. But to Scarlet's eye, the graceful proportions of the design and the magical properties of the space were already evident. There was but one element to complete it.

Dusty lime misted the air and clung to the embroidered hem of his robe, but Scarlet took no notice. The mason directing the day's work hurried up. Upon a plank supported by two large blocks, the man unrolled the scroll Scarlet proffered. He had inked his masterpiece—the sacred labyrinth, a maze of tiles—in dark lines upon the parchment.

"You will re-create this pattern," Scarlet told the mason, "exactly as I have drawn it—in stone, here in the nave. I will show you the exact location for the pattern center."

The mason, his grizzled head bent, studied the plan. "One path, then, sir? Beginning at the outer edge, twisting into the center, then out again?"

"That is correct." Scarlet slipped a finger into the silken purse belted at his waist where he'd secured the bloodstone. It was warm to his touch.

The mason traced the drawn line with his finger. Back and forth, winding and twisting. "Ah," he said. "I understand."

Scarlet very much doubted that he did. But the mason's understanding, or lack of it, was immaterial. A man did not need to understand his destiny in order to fulfill it.

* * *

Maddie pulled her mind from Scarlet's memory, awash in a combination of sadness and triumph. The master builder of Chartres Cathedral had not succeeded in his quest. He had died, as had each of his descendants in turn. But not because his vision had been in error. It had not. His cathedral did indeed re-create the magical framework of Lilith's amulet. It was the fragment of bloodstone he'd possessed that had been inadequate. The damaged stone had not been able to bring the spark of life to Scarlet's creation.

But now . . .

Anticipation kindling within, Maddie flew steadily north.

The Lord said to Raphael: Bind Azazel hand and foot; cast him into darkness. All shall be afraid, and the Watchers be terrified. Great fear and trembling shall seize them. The earth shall be immersed in a deluge, and they shall be destroyed.

Destroy the children of fornication, the offspring of the Watchers. Incite them one against the other; let them perish by mutual slaughter. Upon the death of the Nephilim, wheresoever their spirits depart from their bodies, let their flesh be without judgment.

Thus shall they perish.

—from the Book of Enoch

Chapter Twenty-one

Two spires flanked the cathedral doors: one soaring toward Heaven, the other shorter, constrained by the earth. No light passed through the great window positioned between them. The masterpiece of stone and glass floated like a delicate black flower in the night.

Scant hours before heavy pewter clouds would yield to dawn, the city lay heavy and still. The church square was deserted. Compelled by the fist in his hair and the press of knees on his flanks, Cade dove earthward. He landed on all fours before the cathedral's main door. His wounded shoulder protested the hours of flight. It felt as though someone were sawing through bone with a hot, jagged knife. Cade gritted his teeth against the pain. He'd be damned if he let his agony show.

Azazel dismounted. Relieved of his loathsome burden, Cade started to straighten, only to bow down again when Azazel pressed a hand to the back of his skull. Ben-Meir's dead skin oozed the scent of rotting fruit. The stolen body quivered with anticipation. Of what, Cade couldn't begin to guess.

Maddie, landing gently at her ancestor's side, turned toward him. But Azazel did not take his eyes from the cathedral doors.

"Chartres," the Watcher whispered.

The name meant nothing to Cade. At the corner of his vision, he saw Maddie's wings fold gracefully over her back. Her Nephilim form morphed into a human outline; her peasant skirt swayed about her slender legs, coming to rest with a sigh. Her command touched Cade's mind. His body obeyed. He shed his own demon form.

Azazel stretched out Simon Ben-Meir's dead hand. Maddie took it without hesitation.

"Journey's end, Daughter. And a new beginning."

Their communion turned Cade's stomach. His hands fisted uselessly at his sides. Was this small defiance the only protest he was capable of? He tried to produce more.

He's using you, he told Maddie silently. *Can't you see that?*

Maddie's gaze darted to Cade and hardened. Pain exploded in his head; burning agony seared his lungs. Gasping, he bent double. But the punishment was well worth the knowledge he'd gained. His psychic connection with Maddie held. She'd heard him in her mind. If he could only get her to listen to him, perhaps he would not be completely powerless.

Azazel strode to the cathedral doors. Rows of somber saints stared down at him, but none of the stone figures moved to smite him, fallen angel and trespasser that he was.

The doors were, of course, locked at this hour. It proved no great impediment. At Azazel's nod, Maddie placed her palm on the ancient lock. Smoke seeped from between her fingers; iron dripped down the scarred wood. The doors creaked inward.

Cade wondered at Azazel's purpose in entering the cathedral. As a rule, Watchers avoided churches. Even as a boy, even before Cade knew what he was, he'd harbored an instinctive distrust of consecrated places. He didn't want to enter this one now.

But he did. The space loomed black and cavernous. The door swung closed behind them.

The high altar was very far away. The long nave was flanked by walls of pointed arches and fluted columns. Scant light filtered through the high window arcades. The night leached the color of the glass, leaving only deadened gray.

Rows of folding chairs were laid out directly before them.

A wave of Maddie's hand sent them careening right and left to slam against pillars and gallery walls. The clatter, strangely, died without reverberation.

Tense anticipation continued to radiate from Azazel's stolen body. The emotion was so powerful it almost overpowered the stench of Ben-Meir's corpse.

Cade moved to place his bulk between Maddie and her ancestor. The Watcher did not seem to notice. Azazel was all energy, all will and intent. Cade wondered how long the decaying human body could contain him. And then he realized the truth. It wouldn't. It couldn't.

Azazel pointed to the swath of pavement Maddie had cleared. "Advance to the center of the pattern, my love. Follow the path."

Cade's eyes traced the design on the floor of the nave: a path of light-colored paving stones defined by narrow, darker bands. The course arced around a central point, turning back on itself many times in its circuitous journey to the center. He sensed its power. A magical pattern, created by Watcher magic.

Without hesitation, Maddie approached the labyrinth entrance. As she set foot on the pavers, she lifted a hand to touch the Watcher disc between her breasts. The bloodstone glowed, painting her face an eerie red.

She advanced along the stone path. With each step, Cade's dread unfolded.

Maddie. Don't.

A slight jerk of her head told him she'd heard. He braced himself for a corresponding onslaught of retribution. None came. Encouraged, he pressed on.

Maddie. Turn back, cariad.

A hesitation. Then, *Why should I?*

Because you don't know what will happen when you reach the center.

Something wonderful.

No. Something evil. Something you don't want to be a part of.

Her anger slapped at him. *I'll be the judge of that.*

Punishment struck as he was forming his reply. His body froze. A great weight descended on his chest. He couldn't breathe. He started to lose consciousness, his vision blotting red. He concentrated all his energy on dragging air into his lungs.

At last the weight receded. Maddie seemed to have decided he'd endured enough.

Azazel moved to the start of the path but did not enter the pattern. Instead, he tracked Maddie's progress with glowing red eyes. Cade thought the Watcher had changed since he'd first appeared on the beach in Sicily. His shoulders drooped. The odor of decay was stronger. Ben-Meir's dead body was reaching its limit. Was Maddie to be its replacement?

The thought was sickening. And yet, Cade could do nothing. All thoughts he directed now at Maddie's mind struck a blank wall. Could he do nothing but watch her walk to her doom and hiss in frustration?

Back and forth, round and round she walked. At last she stepped onto the stone rosette in the center of the pattern.

The gem at her breast flared and blue flame sprang up at her feet. Not a consuming flame—there was no smoke, no odor of combustion. Cade wondered if Maddie could feel the blaze licking at her limbs.

If she did, pain didn't register on her face. Slowly, reverently, she lifted the cord holding the Watcher relic over her head. The disc swung free. She cradled the amulet in her palms, lifted it to her lips. Azazel's red, hungry eyes devoured the spectacle.

A ribbon of white brilliance appeared, flowing from the talisman. The Seed, seeking a path to life. The light retraced the path Maddie had just traversed, twisting and bending back upon itself in a slow journey to the pattern's starting point. Azazel, eyes alight, stretched out his hands to receive the magic.

Maddie stood transfixed at the center of the pattern. Blue flames licked her legs, and Cade abruptly realized the block she had erected between their minds had weakened. Had she reached the limit of her newborn magic?

Azazel, absorbed by the weaving progress of the ribbon of light, seemed to have forgotten his presence entirely. Though Cade's limbs were sluggish, they were once again under his command. He eased forward, throwing his thoughts ahead.

Maddie. Maddie! Can you hear me?

Did she hear him? If so, she gave no sign. She stood as still as a corpse, the white ribbon unwinding from the disc in her hands. Every second brought it closer to Azazel's grasp.

Maddie. He's using you.

A flicker in his mind. *No. You're wrong. He's not.*

He is. You won't survive this. Can't you see? He's done with Ben-Meir's body. Dead flesh won't sustain his essence much longer. He needs your body as a replacement.

Silence. Wavering doubt fueled by a shadow hidden deep in Maddie's mind, a memory that was there fleetingly and then gone.

No. He would never do that. He loves me.

Cade crept forward to the very edge of the pattern. The ribbon of white magic separated them many times. What would happen if he tried to cross it?

He needs you, he said. *It's not the same thing. He's using you. Do you think you've* chosen *to obey him? You haven't. You're his slave. As much as I'm yours.*

No. It isn't like that. It isn't.

Her protests rang angry and strong in his head. But they

weren't, he thought, fully confident. He'd awakened her doubt. He felt a snatch of memory flit through her mind, and Maddie's head jerked around. Her eyes collided with Cade's. Then he was falling, falling into bitter memory.

* * *

It would not stop raining.

The babe in Lilith's womb was restless, turning and kicking as if in the throes of a bad dream. But that was fanciful. The child had absorbed Lilith's own unease, born of the gloom of these endless nights of rain. The torrent beat down on the tent roof without pause. It was enough to drive one mad.

The canyon valley was sodden. If the deluge didn't stop soon, the tribe would be forced to move to the upper desert. Lilith hoped her babe would be content to remain inside her womb during the difficult journey, but as her stomach muscles clenched, relaxed, and clenched again, she very much feared the child would not wait.

Dripping water found gaps in the tent seams and defects in the oiled hide Azazel had thrown atop the roof the day before. He'd left at dawn, without word as to his destination, though Lilith had begged him to stay. She went into the anteroom and looked out through the flap. The valley was gray, the river swollen and dirty. Of Azazel's return, there was no sign.

Lilith's mother Zariel occupied a corner of the tent Lilith now shared with her father and lover; Azazel had ordered his former concubine to attend her as she neared her time. Neither woman wanted the other. Lilith's swollen belly reminded Zariel of her own time in Azazel's bed. Zariel's presence brought unwanted imaginings of the same subject to Lilith.

Reluctant to return to the main room, Lilith remained at the tent's entrance, supporting her belly with one hand as she scanned the valley with her eyes. The fields were empty of cattle and goats, the herdsmen having moved the flocks to the higher ground at the base of the leeward cliffs. Azazel's forge was wet and cold, the area around the well deserted. Silence covered the village. Not a single man or woman ventured out.

Another contraction, tighter and longer than the ones before. Lilith wrapped her arms around her belly, but dread curled and squeezed like a snake choking her womb. She reentered the main chamber of the tent and addressed Zariel.

"The babe is coming."

The hours that followed were a blur of pain. Great crashing waves of agony broke over Lilith, each higher than the last. She gulped for air as each swell receded, her terror of the next constricting her breath. Knives of fire slashed at her stomach. She was sure, in her sweat and terror, that Azazel's child would rip her in two.

Zariel built up the fire and closed the flap against the driving rain. Smoke gathered under the ceiling, and Lilith's lungs burned with each inhalation. Her skin itched from the heat. She tore at her clothes.

"Off. Off!"

Zariel helped her remove the sweaty robe. But when she would have lifted the Seed of Life from around Lilith's neck, Lilith clutched at the cord.

"I want Azazel." She had stopped calling him Father some time ago.

"I cannot bring your . . . your lover to you," Zariel said. "He goes where he will, as always. You, girl, must turn your mind to the babe."

The babe. Her son. Her brother. Her heart constricted with shame. The agony of birthing was punishment, she knew, for the grievous sin she had committed. The knife of agony that had pierced her gut was bent now on slicing her open. She screamed and screamed until her lungs spasmed.

When she paused to draw breath, Zariel shoved a bundle of rags into her mouth. "Bite this. And do not exhaust yourself. You will need all your strength later if this cursed child is to live."

Lilith sank her teeth into the rags. Later? How much later? She could not endure much more.

The winds howled. Pain pounded her in relentless tides. How long her ordeal continued, she could not have said; she knew only great crashing waves of agony followed by shorter periods of exhausted respite.

Sometime during her suffering, the tent flap lifted. A masculine voice addressed Zariel, and with an effort Lilith turned her head toward it. He was here!

"Azazel—" Her plea was muffled by the rag in her mouth.

He strode to her bedside and clasped her hand. She wanted to speak, to seek his reassurance, but the wave of pain was cresting again, and it was all she could do to keep from sobbing. She was at the limit of her strength. And yet, Zariel's terse answers to Azazel's queries told her the babe was not nearly ready to be born.

Perhaps he would never be. Perhaps she would die birthing him, and he would die with her. But, no. That wasn't right. She laid her palm on her chest, covering the amulet. Eternal life was hers. Hers and Azazel's. She had bought it with her blood. He had promised her they would live together, forever.

The relentless pain continued. As Lilith labored on into the night, it seemed the earth itself had joined her cause. The ground shuddered in measured cadence. The howling wind answered.

Azazel left her side to find repose on the couch while she worked to birth his child. The knife in Lilith's gut twisted round and round and round again. Would it never be done? Would she never be free of torment? Anger and fear threw her into a frenzy. She kicked at Zariel's restraining hands, spat the rag from her mouth and screamed.

Perhaps her fury reached the heavens, for at the precise moment Lilith collapsed, a great rumbling shook the tent. A gust of wind howled. The oiled hides over her head ripped in two, rain pounded down upon her, and tingling power seared the air. A bolt of lightning exploded in her bed, barely missing her body.

The force of the strike flung her to the ground as thunder crashed. Searing pain knifed her left arm. Gasping, she clutched at her shoulder, only to cry out when the contact brought worse agony. The sweet-sick odor of burned flesh assaulted her nostrils.

She snatched her hand away. Charred bits of skin clung to her fingers, and Azazel was on his feet, shaking his fist at the sky. "You will not win!" he shouted.

Lilith did not understand. Flames leaped from the bed coverings, hissing and smoking under the pelting rain. Zariel cowered, and Azazel shouted curses to the storm. Lilith's pain-riddled mind could process none of it. The next contraction was upon her. She hunched over her belly and emitted an animal moan.

The ruined tent was suddenly bathed in brilliant light. Lilith rolled to her side, gasping. Far above, framed by blackened clouds, floated an ethereal figure clothed in blinding light, its unfurled wings the color of pure gold. Yellow flame spat from its gleaming sword; the weapon showered sparks upon the earth.

Panicked screams burst from the village. The men were out in the open, shouting. The wails of the women and the sobs of the children formed a desperate kind of music.

The holy angel spoke, and his voice boomed like thunder. "Abominations! Defilers of earth! Perversions of nature!"

"Raphael!" Azazel roared. His fist shook. "You will not vanquish me! My power is too great! You cannot defeat it. You cannot destroy me!"

Raphael streaked from the sky. His feet touched the ground not three strides from where Lilith lay, miserable and panting, and the archangel flourished his flaming sword. "You destroy yourself, Watcher, with your unspeakable desecrations. You have polluted the daughters of men, brought forth unnatural offspring. You have lain with your own daughter. You have forced her to labor with your twisted son. By these sins and more you have wrought your own death."

Azazel's white teeth gleamed. "You fool." He threw back his head and laughed. "Death means nothing to me."

The pangs of childbirth, which had been almost suspended by the shock of the lightning strike and the descent of the angel, chose that moment to reassert their power. Lilith bent double, cradling her tightening stomach and gritting her teeth against the pain. Even so, her desperate wail would not be silenced.

She gasped for her mother but received no answer. When the pain receded, she dared open her eyes. Zariel was fleeing, scrambling over the fallen tent supports, stumbling toward the village. She was absorbed in a huddle of frightened women.

Raphael lifted his sword. "Now," he told Azazel, "I dispatch you and your whore daughter to Oblivion."

No, *Lilith wanted to cry. She tensed for the blow.* No!

She was suddenly on her feet, crying aloud with pain and surprise; Azazel's iron grip banded her upper arm. Midway through a convulsion, she bent forward, moaning, but heedless of her pain he hauled her upright. His forearm pressed the tops of her breasts as his arm encircled her neck from behind, and she sagged against him as the contraction drained away.

The amulet burned her skin. Azazel covered it with his palm. "I will never see Oblivion," he snarled. "The Seed of Life will not allow it."

"We shall see," Raphael replied.

The angel lifted his sword and pointed the tip at Lilith's chest. His merciless gray eyes sliced through her agony.

"No. No." She spread her hands on her belly, felt the muscles contract in preparation of the next wave. Twisting desperately, she tried to free herself from Azazel's grip. "No. Please! Our child. My child. Do not hurt him. He has done nothing."

"He was conceived," Raphael said. "That is sin enough."

"Let me go," she sobbed. "Let me go."

Raphael's sword did not waver. "There will be no mercy. No forgiveness. Not for the Watchers, and not for their unholy spawn, the Nephilim."

Azazel's arm tightened. "The Seed cannot be destroyed. It is my eternal protection."

"It is your doom."

The next wave of Lilith's pain gathered into an unbearable pressure. The babe could not be long in coming, she realized.

"Not my child," she gasped again. "Not my son. Do not hurt him. He is innocent."

Something akin to emotion flickered in Raphael's eyes, but it was quickly suppressed. "The Watchers have sealed their doom. Their misbegotten spawn must be destroyed."

"But the babe—"

"Is doomed as well. Prepare, then, to die."

She had no time to react. With a fiery slash, Raphael's sword blazed. Azazel shoved her into the blow. The impact reverberated in her bones. But she did not die. The Seed of Life had, incredibly, deflected the killing blow. The avenger's blade had struck the amulet.

Raphael, his face twisted with righteous rage, surged forward. Lilith staggered backward, choking. She tried to turn, tried to run. Azazel gripped her from behind. His right arm held her in front of his chest, a shield against the angel's fury. With his left hand her father hurled blue fire.

Raphael parried. "You use this woman and her child for your protection rather than come to their defense?"

"She is my daughter," Azazel snarled. "Her magic is mine to claim. Her life is mine to use. What better way for her to die than in my defense?"

Lilith could not believe what she'd heard. Even the cold gaze of the avenger softened to pity as his gaze flicked over her swollen belly. It could not be! He could not betray her thus! She'd given body and life to this man—her father, her lover. He had promised her immortality in return. Now he would steal her magic, sacrifice her life, and that of their child, to save his own miserable existence. What a fool she had been!

"No!" she screamed. Rage and a rushing sense of shame poured through her. "No! This is not my battle! I will not protect you! I will not die for you! My son *will not die for you!"*

"Silence, woman!"

The agony of his betrayal was worse than anything she had ever experienced—even worse than the pain racking her body. And it was all for the amulet, the gift she had created with such love. She hated the thing now. It burned her skin. She tore it from her neck. Whipping the broken leather thong in a circle above her head, she released it. The Seed of Life flew into the sky, arcing through the rain in a flash of gold and crimson.

"No!"

Azazel launched himself after the prize. As he leaped into the sky, Lilith watched in shock. Her father's body was changing. Dark colors chased over his skin and great wings unfurled from his back. A long, narrow tail erupted, snapping like a snake behind him.

She stared. By all Heaven and Hell, what was he? What, in all his evil, had he become?

With a sweep of bright wings, Raphael leaped into pursuit. Lilith cowered in a puddle of cold water. Her stomach began to tighten once again, and she braced herself for the pain. She felt as if she'd been laboring forever. Would the agony never stop? Would her child never be born?

As she rolled to her knees, a glint of red in the mud caught her eye. Reaching out, she grasped it. The shard of crimson was a fragment of bloodstone severed from the Seed of Life; Raphael's blow had split the stone in two.

The contraction was fierce. When it had peaked, Lilith hauled herself upright on shaking legs. Reaching for a sodden sheet, she wrapped it around her nakedness as the rain pounded down ever harder. The wind whipped with a force she'd never before witnessed, and the earth beneath her feet trembled. The world was surely ending.

She stumbled over sodden hides and tent poles. Whether the world was ending or not, she had to find help—a woman to ease her child into life, however short that life might prove to be. Gasping, lurching, she made slow progress to the village, where a cluster of men and women huddled together amid sodden, ruined tents. They all watched the sky. Lilith followed their frightened gazes to two figures that battled far above. One was shining and pure, the other sparkling and dark. Golden flame clashed against crimson.

Wind howled through the canyon. Another tremor shook the ground. Lilith reached out in pain, and she gasped with relief when a woman gathered her into her arms. All the while, the brutal contest raged in the sky above.

Azazel pressed the offensive, shooting red flame with his left hand. Raphael evaded. When Azazel roared his fury and renewed his attack, showers of gold and crimson exploded. For a span of time, it seemed as though the Watcher would prevail, but Raphael did not relent.

With a roar that shook the air, the angel circled his sword above his head and brought it down upon Azazel's right hand. The impact lit up the sky. A golden streak flew from Azazel's fingers as the Seed of Life hurtled earthward. Through a haze of pain, Lilith watched the amulet vanish into the well near Azazel's forge. A hissing cloud of steam poured forth.

A cry of outrage shook the skies. Lilith lifted her eyes. Her father, furious, struggled against dazzling ropes. Raphael, triumphant, lifted his sword and held his struggling prisoner aloft for all to see.

"See your master, bound and enslaved. He sought to cheat death. He longed for immortality; I grant his wish. He will exist for all eternity—in a realm of darkness and evil far below the earth. As for you, Nephilim, spawn of the fallen ones, know this: your souls are forfeit. Your time on earth is all you possess; no Heaven, no Hell, awaits you after death. Only the despair of Oblivion. As for the land you have defiled, floodwaters will cleanse it of your filth. When the tide recedes, it shall be as if you had never existed."

The angel streaked from sight bearing Azazel with him. In the next instant, an ominous rumble sounded.

At first Lilith could make no sense of the high churning wall that spanned the width of the canyon and rushed toward her tribe. With abrupt horror, she realized it was the floodwater of which Raphael had spoken. Angry, black, deadly, white foam flying from its crest like spittle.

I am dead, *she realized.* My child is dead. We are all dead.

Shouts rang out. Someone grabbed her arm. The villagers scurried like rats; streaming in all directions, they made for the paths leading to higher ground. But the merciless wave was faster than any man. Lilith barely had time to cry out before the waters crashed over her head and swept her away.

* * *

Pain woke her. She was soaked through, cold and miserable, lying on her side atop a makeshift raft. Screams and sobs sounded all around her. Tossed on the tempest, men and women wailed as they clung to whatever bit of flotsam they could grasp. Lilith's craft was little more than a few boards hastily tied together. She lay on her back and gripped her belly.

"Push," a woman commanded.

The child was coming. At last! But to what purpose? Its birth was hopeless. Violent sea churned to the horizon in every direction. Bursts of sulfurous flame leaped from oily patches on the water's surface, and a searing wind blew. Clouds of embers and ash burned her eyes, choked her lungs. Was this Hell? No, Raphael had forbidden her kind entry to even that cursed realm. Life, then. But for how much longer?

The sheet around her body was sodden. Too heavy. She wanted to strip it off but couldn't. It was bound tightly over her arms. Someone was holding her from behind.

"Push!"

She was too weak to disobey. Clenching her fists under the sheet, she pushed—and gasped when something sharp bit into her palm. It was hot. Burning.

The bloodstone fragment. The legacy of her ruined magic. She remembered now; she'd found it in the mud.

"Push!"

Driven by the unknown woman's fierce urging, Lilith gathered the last of her strength. Gripping the stone for courage, she gave a mighty push, one that threatened to explode her skull. The infant slipped from her body in a torrent of blood. Lilith's life gushed out as well. Her last thought was that she was not wholly lost to Oblivion; there was the bloodstone. Damaged, yes, but still powerful. And not completely evil, surely. It had been created in innocence and offered in love. Before those gifts had been defiled.

Perhaps the stone would protect her son from the flood. And perhaps, if he survived the ordeal, the magic his mother had offered in love and innocence might redeem, at least in part, the shame of his existence.

Chapter Twenty-two

Maddie emerged from her ancestral memory sweaty and panting. Shame was slimy on her skin and in her lungs. Defiling. Suffocating.

She stared at her hands, at the amulet Lilith had created. Blood magic flowed from it, channeling the power of life toward Simon Ben-Meir's dead body. Azazel had used his daughter's magic and her body—and her love—to defy Heaven. And then he had betrayed her.

Gradually, Maddie became aware of Cade. He was at her side in the center of the tile maze, tangled in burning ribbons of magic. He clenched his jaw against the pain as he gripped her shoulders. She could no longer hear him in her mind. When her last memory had fallen into place, the thread of connection between them snapped.

"Maddie!"

He shook her. Her chin bounced forward and back as she stared at him. She didn't understand what he wanted.

"Drop the disc."

He spoke slowly, urgently. Clearly, he was telling her something important. But he might as well have been speaking a foreign language. His words made no sense to her at all. She tried to concentrate on the movement of his lips. Maybe that would help.

"Drop the disc *now*, Maddie. Before Azazel touches the other end of that ribbon." He grasped her wrists and held her hands up to her eyes. "Drop it! Do you understand me? Drop it!"

The disc glittered in her hands. The broken bloodstone gleamed. Drop it? Could she do that? She doubted it. Her numb fingers wouldn't open.

"I . . . I can't," she gasped.

"You can. Maddie. Look at me."

She raised her chin and stared into his blue, blue eyes. The expression she saw there caused her heart to contract.

"I love you," he said steadily. "I love your determination and your stubbornness. I love the way you refuse to give up, even in the face of overwhelming odds. You're a warrior, Maddie. A beautiful warrior. And you're mine, in love. I refuse to let Azazel own you in slavery. I would rather face Oblivion. If you won't drop the disc, I'll take it from you by force. You know what will happen if I do that."

Yes, she knew. The relic would kill him. The thought of Cade sprawled dead on the ground set her trembling.

Her gaze darted to Dr. Ben-Meir. No. Not Ben-Meir. Azazel. The ribbon of light was almost within his reach. His eyes shone as his fingers reached out—

"No." Maddie's hand opened. The disc tumbled from her grip. Metal struck stone with a hollow sound.

Azazel's exultant shout rang out. The end of the ribbon of light was already in his grasp.

"No," Maddie whispered. "No." She stood rooted to the spot as Azazel advanced through the path of the labyrinth, wrapping the white ribbon around his wrist as he came.

Cade shoved her behind him. The strands that had tangled around his legs as he'd plunged across the pattern slid from his limbs, leaving raw, burning strips. The white ribbon disappeared harmlessly into Azazel's dead flesh.

"You won't take her," Cade snarled. "I'll kill you first."

Azazel sneered. "Do you think I would stoop so low as to inhabit a female body? Even my own daughter's?"

"Maddie is not your daughter."

But Lilith had been. And Lilith was Maddie's ancestor; her memories lived on inside her many-times great-granddaughter. In that instant, the horror of Maddie's origins hit her full force. Her relationship might be hundreds of generations removed, but in the end it came down to the same thing: her very existence had sprung from the loins of this creature standing before her; she was the product of his sins, his incest, his evil. How could she bear to live, knowing that?

"Ben-Meir's body is decaying." Cade's angry voice sounded very far away, though he stood right beside her. "Soon it will be no use to you."

"Soon I will not need it." Azazel lifted the final length of ribbon. The Seed of Life dangled from the end, and the Watcher's hands closed upon it.

The ground gave way. Maddie lurched backward, into Cade's chest. A crack appeared in the stone rosette where her feet had been an instant before.

"What the—?" Cade said. He dragged her back a few steps as the crack expanded.

Amber smoke seeped from crumbling masonry. A flash of light, red as blood, illuminated Azazel's face. A sulfurous odor rose. Gaze intent, the Watcher knelt and gazed into the widening hole.

Maddie knew what Azazel searched for, what he would find here: the stone hidden by her ancestor. Searching for the key to eternal life, the master builder known as Scarlet had steeped this monument with Watcher magic and alchemic power. He had buried his birthright, the fragment of Lilith's bloodstone, under the stone in the center of the labyrinth. And there it had remained after his death.

Azazel stood. In his hand the small stone gleamed with bright crimson light. Gaze intent, he fitted the missing fragment together with its other half.

Light exploded. Maddie ducked behind Cade's arm as

Azazel's exultant shout echoed off the cathedral's vaulted ceiling. A high-pitched wail filled her head. Gasping, she pressed her hands over her ears.

The ground began to shake. With a rolling lurch, the pavement beneath her feet crumbled. Maddie cried out, scrambling to avoid the disintegrating stone. Cade jerked her back to solid footing, nearly wrenching her arm from its socket. His muttered curses battered her ear. She clung to him.

She could hardly see through the thick screen of sulfur rising from the deep. The chasm widened, splitting the pattern of the labyrinth. One end of the fissure raced toward the altar, the other toward the cathedral entrance. Yellow dust and putrid smoke poured from the crack.

The screaming wind outside the cathedral reached fever pitch. Thunder shook the walls. And as the rumbling explosion of sound faded, the wail of an emergency siren arose.

Maddie clutched at Cade's arm. "What's happening?"

"I don't know. And I don't want to be around to find out. Let's get out of here."

He hauled her across the nave. The labyrinth crumbled completely to dust as the fissure expanded, dividing the nave in two. At one end of the church, the altar cracked down the center, the fissure continuing on to shoot up the wall behind. The apse windows exploded, spewing showers of colored glass.

At the rear of the church, the vestibule doors, massive wood slabs that had stood for centuries, splintered. The lintel above groaned under the stress. Rain spat through cracks in the crumbling masonry overhead, and rubble poured from the vaulting. Maddie threw her arms over her head. How long before the whole roof came down?

Azazel stood in the center of the destruction, at the edge of the widening pit. He stared into the smoking depths of the chasm, one hand extended in anticipation.

"What's he waiting for?" Maddie gasped.

"Something's rising," Cade answered.

She looked in horror and saw it was true. A beastly figure clothed in dark opalescence climbed from the depths. Its head and limbs were vaguely human, but a long tail curled, snakelike, around its body. Great black wings unfolded from its back, assisting its rise.

A cold hand of dread squeezed Maddie's heart. She knew this creature. She'd seen it in her nightmares.

"Azazel," she breathed. "As he was."

Cade's grip on her arm tightened painfully. "Come on. We've got to get out of here!"

But neither of them seemed capable of flight. To Maddie, it seemed as if the world had passed into the strange slow motion of nightmares. Her feet would not lift from the ground. Even her breathing seemed suspended.

The creature gained the cathedral floor. Its tail, supple and pointed, uncoiled.

The thing had no aura, though its eyes glowed and its limbs moved. Maddie turned this odd paradox over in her mind. If the monster had no life force, could it be truly alive?

Ben-Meir's dead body stepped forward to embrace the monster. At the instant of contact, the glow surrounding the archeologist's corpse evaporated. A heartbeat later, red light bathed the winged horror.

"Oh, no." Maddie's fingernails dug into Cade's arm. "No. Not this."

* * *

Simon Ben-Meir's body crumpled. The newly risen demon spread its wings over the corpse. Staring, Cade felt his stomach turn. This was no common hellfiend.

"I thought it would be your body he possessed, Maddie. Not another Nephilim's."

Maddie stood rooted to the spot, eyes trained on the monster. "That's . . . Oh, God. That's not a Nephilim. That's Azazel's own body. The demon he turned into during his battle with Raphael. It must have been waiting, all these years, to be reunited with its life essence."

Bloody hell. Cade eyed the creature warily. It was stretching its limbs, as if relearning to use them. If a newly resurrected Azazel had returned to the world, the human race was in grave peril.

So far, Azazel in his new form had taken no notice of them. Cade thought he'd like to keep it that way. He began to ease away, slowly, pulling Maddie with him. To his relief she didn't resist. But neither did she seem fully aware of what he was doing.

"Azazel and Raphael fought," she whispered. "I saw the battle in Lilith's memory. The Seed of Life was Azazel's defense. A blow from Raphael's sword split the bloodstone in two. Azazel couldn't stand against the avenger then, but he wasn't completely defeated. Raphael must have imprisoned only his body. Azazel bound his life essence to the amulet."

Cade guided her around a pile of rubble. "And the disc ended up at the bottom of the Watcher well."

"Yes. The other half of the bloodstone remained with Lilith. It passed to the man who built this cathedral. Lilith's descendant." She swallowed. "My ancestor."

"A Nephilim of Clan Azazel," Cade said.

"Yes. He was known by the name Scarlet. He was a master builder and alchemist."

The burning red eyes of the newly risen demon swept the cathedral. Cade went motionless, his arm around Maddie, and willed the creature's scrutiny to pass them by.

It didn't. That horrible red gaze fell directly upon them. But only for an instant. Almost without pause, Azazel turned his attention to Ben-Meir's corpse.

Maddie's breath hitched as her demonic ancestor lifted the archeologist's body from the ground and bit off its head. With a sickening crack, strong jaws cracked the skull, and the creature chewed and swallowed. Then, upending the headless corpse, it fastened its lips around the severed neck. The beast's throat worked as it suckled.

"Oh, God." Maddie bent double. "I'm going to be sick."

Cade held her as she retched. The black stench of evil burned his nostrils; he was on the verge of losing the contents of his own stomach.

Azazel looked up from his feast. Blood dribbled from bulbous lips and his head executed a slow swivel. Cade shoved Maddie behind him.

The red gaze lit upon them, and a clawed hand beckoned. "Daughter. Lover. Come to me."

Cade knew Maddie wanted to obey. At least, her body did. It yearned toward the monster even as she clutched at Cade and sobbed. He wrapped his arms around her and put every ounce of his strength into helping her resist the summons.

Azazel's eyes burned. "Lilith. Long ago I promised that you would live forever. Now, at last, you will. Come."

Maddie strained in Cade's arms. "Let me go to him."

His arms tightened. "Like hell I will."

"You can't hold me for long. Don't you realize that? Azazel's here. He's alive. He wants me. There's nothing you can do. The only choice you have is whether you're going to get yourself killed trying to stop the inevitable. So just . . . let me go. Get out. Let me fight Azazel on my own."

"The hell I will. You think I'd do that? Leave you here with that stinking creature? Forget it. We fight together. Always."

"He'll tear you apart!"

"Then we'll die. Together."

"You'll die. Not me. *Me*, he wants to keep alive."

Cade's voice roughened. "That sort of existence would be worse than death. I'd kill you before I let him take you."

Azazel hissed. An angry crash of thunder shook the walls, and wind whipped through the wounds in the masonry. The siren was louder now. Cade heard men shouting. Humans must be gathering beyond the cathedral doors.

He looked down at her and watched the knowledge of the truth he'd spoken come into her eyes. Their time was running out. "I'm sorry, Maddie."

"No," she said. "Don't be. It's me who's sorry. For what I did to you during my transition. If I'd trusted you—"

He cut her off. "That wasn't you doing those things, Maddie. That was him."

She closed her eyes and nodded. "If you have to do it, Cade, if you have to kill me . . . Just make it quick. And as painless as possible."

Her trust awed him. He opened his mouth to reply, but his words were cut off when, with a subtle down-sweep of wings, Azazel landed before them. Claws scraped rubble as he landed. The scent of arrogant pride flowed from his pores. Cade's nostrils flared, but he met Azazel's red stare unflinchingly. There was no retreat. There would be no surrender, either.

He brushed the hilt of the dagger tattooed on his chest and touched cold metal. Pulling the weapon free, he imagined how much he'd enjoy plunging it into Azazel's heart.

The chance of that was slim. The dark shining shield of Azazel's power encased his demonic body and Cade's power was a child's toy in comparison. The best outcome he could hope for in the coming battle was his own death—and Maddie's.

Red eyes flicked over Maddie's body. Azazel's long tail swept out in an arc, brushing softly up against her leg. "My love. My daughter. We are together again."

She shuddered. "Cade. Do it. Do it now."

Cade clenched his weapon but could not bring himself to use it.

Azazel extended a hand. "Come, Lilith."

"I'm not Lilith."

"You were." His claw clutched at her arm. "You are. You will be, forevermore."

"No . . ."

Cade struck. He aimed his first blow at Azazel's chest, but the blade bounced harmlessly off. The Watcher laughed. Cade slashed at Azazel's back, his arm, his thigh. His blade made no contact, and the angel-turned-demon hoisted Maddie in his arms.

"Cade! Don't let him—"

With a vicious curse, Cade swung one last time. This time, his target was Maddie. The blade flashed as it descended, the point trained on her heart. Something in his own heart wrenched as the dark metal connected—

And shattered.

Black iron exploded everywhere. Shards of metal spewed into the air and sparks flashed. Cade stared stupidly at the untouched swath of Maddie's skin, then at the stumpy hilt he held clutched in his fist. He'd failed. Thank Heaven, Hell, and earth, he'd failed.

Azazel lifted Maddie's struggling body higher in his arms. He pressed his thickened lips to hers. As she sputtered and gagged, he drew back and gazed down at his descendant with an almost tender smile.

"Let her go," Cade snarled. "You disgust her."

Azazel's head swiveled. "Son of Samyaza, spare me your righteousness. You would have used her as your slave. Now I have her safe."

"You want her as your own slave."

"No. Lilith is no slave. She is my lover."

"Maddie isn't Lilith. She's not the daughter you turned into your whore. She's not your victim. And she never will be. I'll see to that."

"Silence!"

A flick of Azazel's wrist flung Cade into the air. His body slammed against a wall, then flopped to the ground. He tried to rise; he found he couldn't move.

Azazel lowered Maddie to the ground. She stood rigid at his side as he considered Cade. "The only question is whether to keep you or kill you."

Rain pelted through the shattered window above Cade's head. Wind roared, sirens wailed. A slow, rhythmic pounding began on the cathedral's shattered entrance. Stupid humans. They should be running for their lives.

Azazel took no notice. His eyes swept Cade. "It would be amusing to keep you. Your magic is strong enough to be useful. And your blood"—he licked his lips—"would be most welcome. But you dared touch my daughter. You defiled her body and sought to enslave her. No doubt it would distress her to have you near. No, it would be impossible to keep you. You must die."

"You'll slaughter me as I lie defenseless rather than face me in battle?" Cade spat out a laugh. His only hope lay in stirring Azazel's pride. It was not in any Watcher's nature to back down when facing a challenge from a rival of lesser power. "Five thousand years of bondage must have shriveled your cock."

Azazel's eyes blazed. The next instant, Cade found himself on his feet. He flexed his arms and tested his mind. Both were clear and unencumbered. A wave of elation rushed through him.

"As you wish, son of Samyaza," Azazel snarled. "We will fight. To your death."

A strangled sound emerged from Maddie's throat. "No!"

"Silence, woman!" Azazel roared. "You will not interfere."

He flung Maddie to the ground. A dark half-sphere of magic sprang up around her. She jumped to her feet and pounded the wall to no avail. Her mouth was open and screaming, but no sound emerged. Even her voice was trapped inside Azazel's dark protection.

Cade sprang into action before Azazel had fully turned to the battle; he flung the hilt of his ruined dagger at the demon's head. Azazel, surprised, staggered back. His tail whipped forward and fixed his balance.

Crimson fire exploded the floor under Cade's feet. He jumped back and brushed his palm down his arm, sweeping the Celtic knot tattoo into his hand. The twisted strands gleamed with Druid magic.

Growling, Azazel beat his wings. His body lifted. Cade melted into Nephilim form and rose with him.

Cade dodged as red fire spat from Azazel's fingers. Masonry exploded behind him. Shifting his wings, he dived low, watching for the best moment to throw his snare. He didn't fool himself that he could defeat Azazel, but this net had driven an archangel into the sea. If Cade could immobilize his enemy long enough to snatch up Maddie and escape—

Azazel hurtled through the air. Cade rolled, flinging the net behind him, and his aim was true. The snare struck its mark. Instantly, the magical strands wrapped around Azazel's limbs and tangled his wings.

Cade wasn't quick enough, however, to avoid retribution. His enemy angled his plummeting body, and Cade and the creature collided. The monster's weight slammed him into the ground, and he heard and felt a sickening crack. Pain electrified his left wing, and Cade cried out, gasping. His shoulder blade felt as though it had been ripped from its supporting muscles.

He stumbled to his feet and lurched toward where Maddie stood trapped, palms flat on the dark sphere of Azazel's magic.

He had to reach her, had to get her away somehow before their foe broke free.

Pain bludgeoned him to his knees. Roaring, Azazel rose almost to the cathedral ceiling. Dark lights flashed on the arching stone, and the Druid magic binding his wings exploded. The last of Cade's hope drained away. He'd failed. In moments he'd be dead.

"Maddie." He stumbled toward the sphere of protection and imprisonment, yelling her name, though he wasn't at all sure she could hear him. He placed his hands upon the surface, over hers. The magic that separated them burned his palms. "I'm sorry," he said.

The last shreds of Cade's tattoo net fluttered to the ground. Azazel hovered above, black wings beating the air. A searing wind rushed through the cathedral and flames ignited everywhere.

Cade turned to face his enemy. His last thought was of Maddie, who would live on as Azazel's slave. It was a final moment tainted with bitter shame.

Power gathered in Azazel's demonic claw. Laughing, he took aim.

"*No!*"

A blue streak blazed past Cade. Maddie's fire bolt struck Azazel in the chest, driving him back. Cade spun. Maddie was on her feet, flames spurting from her palm. Azazel's protection had shattered, and it lay in dark shards at her feet. Cade's warrior lover surged in attack. Cade's chest tightened; her fury filled him with awe. After what he'd planned to do to her, here she was, battling in his defense.

"Get away!" the beast roared.

"You will not kill him," she shouted. Blue fire blazed.

"You will not interfere!" Azazel roared in reply.

"I will!" Maddie yelled. She sprinted to Cade's side. "We stand together."

An indigo fire bolt erupted from her hands. It met a matching torrent of Azazel's power, and the two streams of energy collided and exploded. Maddie careened backward, while Azazel, dark and angry, rose.

The ancient demon let out a hideous screech. "Enough! You wish to die with your Samyaza lover? So be it. No longer will I call you Daughter." A ball of red flame appeared between his clawed hands. Snarling, Azazel raised it above his head.

Cade grabbed Maddie around the waist. "I love you," he said again, and he braced himself for the killing blow.

It never came. An impact caused the building to tremble. The remaining remnants of the cathedral doors exploded inward. Azazel was caught in a tornadic roar; his body slammed up and into the ceiling. His fireball went wide, crashing into a supporting column of the church. The stonework began to crumble.

The entire cathedral shook. The fissure that had previously stalled above the front portal streaked suddenly skyward. The great rose window shattered completely; colored glass spewed down like hail. Cade crouched over Maddie, shielding her.

And then, amid the chaos and destruction, a celestial chime sounded and a glorious golden light filled the gap where the window had been. Cade, looking up, raised his arm against the brilliance—and saw a winged celestial warrior brandishing a fiery sword. Raphael.

Holy shit.

Never in all his life had Cade been so happy to see an angel.

Chapter Twenty-three

"You!"

Raphael's booming voice reverberated through the cavernous space. "You, Watcher. Azazel. You dare to escape your bondage?"

Azazel hovered just below the vaulted ceiling. Blood dripped from gashes the exploded window had scored across his chest. He brandished the Seed of Life and snarled, "I dare that and more, coward."

"Come on," Cade said under his breath to Maddie. "We're not sticking around for this fight. That way."

They scrabbled across the ruined floor. Cade winced as his injured wing snagged on a pile of shattered masonry.

Raphael gave no notice to the fleeing Nephilim. He flew toward his adversary, his golden wings vibrant. "Your magic is flawed, Azazel. Do you imagine your evil will stand against my righteousness? It will not."

Azazel took up a position before the high altar. "It has. And it will again."

"Long ago," Raphael raged. "I was a fool. I showed you mercy. I let you live."

Laughter rang through the cavernous space. "Let me live? You? What farce. You had no choice! You could not kill me. The Seed of Life is mine. I am immortal."

Raphael's fiery sword rose above his head. "Immortal life will mean nothing once I return you to your prison. This time, you will not escape."

"I invite you to try, angel. You will fail."

Blue fire crackled in Azazel's hands. A burning plume arced through the air, but Raphael caught it on the flat of his sword. The magic dissipated in a shower of sparks.

Snarling, Azazel flew at his adversary. Raphael moved with equal swiftness, and fire and sword clashed. The air sizzled with both holy righteousness and unholy fury.

The great cathedral shook. A chunk of masonry plummeted from overhead. Cade yanked Maddie into the shelter of a massive column, and the falling stone exploded in the space they'd just occupied. A fragment struck his injured shoulder, and pain rang in his ears. He fought the blackness at the edges of his vision.

"Cade! Oh, God, are you all right?"

"I'm fine." But it was a lie if he'd ever told one. An entire quadrant of his body was on fire. His stomach was heaving, and the fight to maintain consciousness was a losing proposition.

"We've got to . . . get out," he gasped. "Whoever wins this fight . . . will be coming after us."

Maddie bit her lip and nodded. They moved farther into the shelter of the side gallery before she asked, "Which way?" All paths were blocked by rubble.

"Not out the front. There'll be a crowd."

"That window, then."

A ruined opening gaped above. Rain blew through, falling in sparkling drops on shattered bits of colored glass. The stone sill was several feet above their heads.

Shifting to Nephilim form, Maddie spread her wings and leaped easily over the destruction and through the breach. Cade, trailing his broken wing, followed more slowly. Heaving himself over the damaged wall, he dropped some twenty feet down on the other side.

He landed painfully. Several moments passed during which he could do nothing but gasp and battle for consciousness.

The shock of the cold rain, despite the partial shelter of a wide buttress, was all that kept him from passing out.

A fire bolt splintered the stone above their heads and Maddie gripped his arm. "One more hit like that and this wall's coming down."

Cade lifted his head. The twisted remnants of a wrought-iron fence separated them from a narrow street. Humans ran in either direction, shouting. Luckily, no one looked in their direction.

"Change," he choked out.

"What?"

"We have to change back. The locals aren't . . . aren't going to be friendly if they see us like this."

She'd forgotten they were in Nephilim form; the expression in her eyes told him so. "You're right, of course." She reached out and touched his broken wing. "*Can* you change? I mean, when you're injured like this?"

"Yes."

With a long exhale, he let his demon body seep away. Maddie did the same. In human form, his arm hung limply from a shattered shoulder blade.

Maddie circled behind him. "Oh, Cade. It looks like someone took a pickax to your back."

"It'll heal," he said shortly. Though he wasn't so sure it would. His back felt as though it had been flayed with an iron-tipped whip. He might not even remain conscious long enough to see Maddie to safety. The world at the edges of his vision was starting to disintegrate.

He leaned heavily on Maddie's shoulder as they stumbled in an uneven path through the ruined fence onto the narrow street. Turning left, they headed through the pouring rain toward a swatch of green parkland tucked behind the apse of the cathedral. But if they'd thought to avoid crowds, they soon discovered that impossible. A frightened mass of humanity huddled under the trees.

Maddie and Cade joined them. Sobs mingled with shouts, curses with prayers. Not one of the humans offered help to the wounded man who stumbled into their midst, or even seemed to notice his partially naked companion. Every eye was fixed on the shattered bank of windows that had once defined a great church.

A crashing explosion shook the ground. A nearby woman wailed. Blue and white—a firestorm of color—exploded through the roof of the cathedral and shot into the sky. The force of that blast threw Cade to the ground. Maddie landed heavily atop him. He fought to stay conscious as debris rained all around. Humans cowered or fled screaming.

Cade hunched over Maddie, shielding her from the worst of the fallout, taking the blows on his already mangled back. He gasped in pain as Raphael and Azazel spun into the clouds. Cade braced himself for their descent, but angel and demon, locked in combat, just streaked across the sky and disappeared.

Chapter Twenty-four

The ringtone trilled, sharp and tinny. Lucas pressed his now fully charged phone to his ear and steeled himself for the sound of his sister's voice.

"Luc? Is that you?"

"Hello, Cybele."

A beat of stunned silence. Then, "Luc! Thank the stars! You're alive. Are you all right?"

"Yes, I'm fine, Cyb."

"Where . . . where are you? Where the hell have you been all this time?"

"Montana."

It was an answer she clearly didn't expect.

"Montana," she repeated, as though it were a foreign word. "Why? What's in Montana?"

Hope, he wanted to say. He settled for: "I had some business there."

"Business that made it impossible to pick up a phone?" she demanded.

"Yes, actually."

"What could that have been?"

He hesitated. "I'd rather not say."

"Artur won't accept that for an answer."

Luc was very well aware that was true. "You will, though. For now, anyway," he added wryly.

Her voice carried a faint tone of amusement. "If that's all you'll give me. But . . . Luc . . . We need you here." She paused, all humor gone now. He could almost see her biting her lower lip and fighting tears. His gut clenched.

"*I* need you here, Luc. Please tell me you'll come to London."

"You're in London?" he asked, surprised. "Not Glastonbury?"

"No." Her tone was strained. "Not Glastonbury. Luc, there's been . . . Something's happened. Something terrible. We tried to reach you, but . . ."

The quavering catch to his sister's voice made his blood run cold. "Cybele. What is it?"

"Oh, Luc . . ."

As she relayed the tale of the massacre, Luc's blood ran cold and colder until ice seemed to fill his limbs. While he'd been self-absorbed in the wilds of Montana, pondering redemption, communicating with spirits he had no right to summon, his clan had been fighting the opening battle in a deadly war.

A war that, despite Luc's newfound hope, was also his own.

* * *

Cade was dying.

Maddie didn't want to admit it, but she knew it was true. Huddled in a toolshed tucked in the back corner of a neat vegetable garden, she fought the urge to break down and cry. How could it have come to this? It seemed impossible that she and Cade had survived distrust, dark magic, kidnapping, her transition and his enslavement, and various battles with a vengeful archangel and a resurrected Watcher demon only to face Oblivion in a muddy shack amid hoes, rakes, and watering cans.

"Cade?"

He lay on his stomach, his head cradled in her lap. His breathing was very shallow. She stroked his hair and forced herself to inspect the gaping wound in his back. It turned her stomach.

"Can you hear me?"

His eyes opened a fraction. "I can, *caraid.* Not . . . dead yet."

Her heart clenched. "You're not going to die."

The sound he made might have been a laugh. "I am. And I . . . I don't think I'll be much longer about it."

"No."

"Promise me . . ."

"No," she said again. "I won't listen. There's nothing to promise, because you won't be leaving me—"

"*Promise me.*" He lifted his head, the effort making him grimace. He was so pale. Deathly white. His aura was no more than the barest sparkle.

"Of course," she said quickly. "Anything. Just . . . just rest. Don't tire yourself."

"My warrior queen," he said, mouth quirking. "Beautiful and passionate to the bitter end." He tried to smile, then winced and compressed his lips. "After I'm . . . after this is over, go to London." He spoke a street name and flat number that meant nothing to her. "Ask for Cybele. Tell her . . ." His breath caught and his body went rigid. Several seconds passed before the spasm was spent. "Tell Cybele everything. Tell her I . . . I loved you. Tell her I want you to take my place in the clan. She'll think it won't work. She'll think the clan can't accept you. Tell her they must. For me. She'll smooth the way with Artur. She's the only one who can." He reached out a hand and she gripped it.

She pressed her lips to his ear. "Of course I'll go," she murmured. "If you want me to."

"Good." He closed his eyes. His grip on her hand slackened.

"No!" Tears stung her eyes. "No. Don't leave me." She shifted, bending over him, searching frantically for evidence of breath. Was it done, then? Over? She couldn't believe it.

She *wouldn't.* She hadn't survived this far, through her transition and her encounter with Azazel, only to let Cade slip away now. She had one last, desperate hope. She dreaded putting the power to the test; the very thought was awful. It was impossible to predict what the consequences would be. But the alternative was losing Cade, and she refused to admit defeat until he was dead and cold.

Slipping her hand into the pocket of her skirt, she drew out the Seed of Life. The relic, restored to its original perfection, had been in Azazel's possession when he'd clashed with Raphael in the cathedral. The battle had burst through the roof, raining fire and rubble down into the park where she and Cade had taken refuge. Cade, despite his wounds, had protected her. He'd gathered her into his arms and shielded her with his damaged body. But not before a flash of fire had shot through the sky and landed almost in her hand.

Mere chance, that Lilith's amulet had fallen so close? Or had the relic actually found her?

Her human mind would once have scoffed at the suggestion of such a thing. Her newly acquired Watcher perception accepted the truth of it without a qualm. Maddie had only to recall her dreams—her ancestral memories—to know what was possible. White light sparkled across the gold, and a red glow suffused the bloodstone. The metal was scorched and bent where Raphael's sword had struck so long ago, but the bloodstone, for the first time in five millennia, was whole. Lilith's power pulsed within. Did Maddie dare claim it?

The talisman had brought pain and death to Lilith. She had created it with love for her father, but Azazel had used it for his own selfish purpose. The nature of the amulet was by no means clearly on the side of good or evil. Even so, Maddie had only begun to understand its power. She was not at all sure she could control it. But to save Cade, Maddie would dare anything.

She traced the seven circles with her finger. The Seed of Life. The talisman could create life or destroy it. Which would it do for Cade? There was only one way to find out.

She wasn't sure exactly how to begin. With a hesitant hand, she laid the relic atop Cade's gaping wound. He was so far gone into unconsciousness that he didn't flinch. Nothing happened, either.

Reaching out, she covered the sparkling disc with her palm. The metal was cool. Inhaling a centering breath, she closed her eyes and entered a world of darkness. For several long heartbeats, the only sensation she experienced was that of Cade's life essence fading toward Oblivion. Soon he'd be beyond reach.

Panic spurred her after him. She moved through a developing and shadowy landscape until she came up against a gap in the terrain. Something like a wide river. Except, the channel ran not with water but death and despair. She looked past the turbulence, to a figure standing on the opposite bank.

Cade.

There was no bridge. She called out to him, but he made no reply. Her heart contracted. Was she too late? Was he gone?

He turned away.

No!

She threw herself forward and plunged into a void of bitter hopelessness. Light and sound fled. Emotion like oil clogged her lungs. Despair clawed at her feet and legs.

Frantic to free herself, she reversed course. Instantly the restraints released her and the water turned clear. She understood then that she had only to turn back to make her escape. Alone. It would be so easy. Far easier than struggling onward. She was not even sure she could reach Cade without casting herself into Oblivion with him. But she had to try. Cade had risked his life for her. He could have escaped the cathedral without her, but he'd stayed to see her safe. At this moment, he could have been in London with his clan, while she lived as Azazel's slave. Instead, he was here with her, dying because of her. She owed him her freedom. Selfishly, she didn't want it without him by her side.

She swam on through despair and panic. She fought off the clutching claws. At last her feet struck something solid. A shore? She couldn't see to be certain.

She tested the ground, stepping forward cautiously. It held. But her surroundings were still pitch-black. Was she dead? Was this Oblivion? No. There would be no consciousness in Oblivion.

"Cade?"

Her call was weak. She inhaled deeply, intending a louder cry, but something foul clogged her lungs. Her breath ended in a painful spell of coughing.

A hand touched her arm. "Maddie."

"Cade!" She tried to throw herself into his embrace, but he held her at arm's length.

"What are you doing here?"

He sounded angry. She strained her vision, trying to see him. His life aura was a mere handful of dying sparks. She could make out nothing more distinct than a faint outline.

"I came for you," she said.

"This is no place for you. You have to go back. It's not your time."

"It's not yours, either!"

"It is."

"I won't accept that. You're standing here with me, aren't you?" Wherever here was. "You haven't been lost to Oblivion. You can still turn back."

"There's too little of me left. I'll be completely gone soon enough."

"No. I won't believe it. There's a way. There must be. I have Lilith's magic. I have the Seed of Life. I've faced the certainty of death, Cade, as a human. I'm not going to let you face Oblivion now. No matter what I have to do to save you from it, I'll do it."

A pause. Then, wearily, "Even that won't be enough. And in the end, what does it matter? Every warrior dies eventually. In the end, Oblivion takes all of us." Breath hissed from his lungs. "Just go, Maddie. Leave me to my fate."

"Go where? To your clan? They'll never accept me. To my own tribe? To Dusek? He murdered your people! His ancestor tried to rape mine! I'll never go to him. I couldn't. But how can I live on my own? I'd come to hate myself and what I am because you won't be there to show me how to make it better. I don't want to make it better. Not without you. I want you. I *love* you."

"Ah, Maddie. *Caraid.* You are so bloody stubborn. I love . . . I love that about you."

The word sighed from his lips, the last breath of his life. He was giving up.

"No!"

She made a desperate grab for him, body and mind and life essence, and landed in a violent maelstrom. Eternal forces threatened to tip her asunder. But she wasn't alone in the storm; Cade was there, still alive, still with her. It was all she wanted.

You shouldn't be here. This is my *death. My end. Not yours. Let me have that, at least.*

It doesn't have to be your end, Cade! It can be a new beginning. For both of us. Together.

A new beginning, not for each of them alone, but for both as one. Was it possible?

Lilith had created the Seed of Life in love, hoping to bind her existence to Azazel's for all time. She had created it out of pure love for her father. Azazel had twisted Lilith's love into something sordid and evil. He had seduced and corrupted his daughter, and used her love and her magic to cheat death.

But those crimes did not negate the essential nature of Lilith's magic. What had prevented the magic from doing good was the hatred Lilith had clung to after her betrayal. Forgiveness, Maddie now realized, was the true source of immortality. Forgiveness, which the Nephilim had been denied. Forgiveness, which Cade had denied to himself.

She called on all the love for Cade that was in her heart. "Your son and the others who died wouldn't want you to follow them into Oblivion," she whispered. "Not when you can celebrate their lives by living. They forgive you, Cade. I forgive you. For everything. Now, forgive yourself and come back to me. Back to life." She blinked back tears. "We'll face it together. Always."

She reached out a hand. The tip of her finger glowed, and by instinct she traced seven circles. Pure white sparks hung suspended in darkness. In the center she placed her love.

Cade placed himself beside her.

* * *

The garden shed was dark, muddy, and uncomfortable. Rain hammered the roof; cold drops of water found their way through the rusted metal. Maddie was half-naked, cold, and dirty.

Cade lay on his stomach, his head in her lap, too weak to move. But the gaping wound on his back was now nothing more than a fading welt on unbroken, healthy skin. His breath was steady.

His eyes were open and locked with hers. The crimson glow of his life aura was strong.

"We're alive," he said.

"And together," she whispered.

They shared a smile.

Never again shall I send a deluge upon the earth.

—from the Book of Enoch

Chapter Twenty-five

The furious lightning almost looked like fireworks, except that it wasn't July yet, and the display was taking place over the middle of the Atlantic Ocean. Brandon Schumaker, pilot of Atlantic Air Flight 1323, midnight departure from JFK to Heathrow, called the phenomenon to the attention of his co-pilot.

"What do you think, Greg? UFO?"

Schumaker was a science-fiction buff from way back, but Greg Marshall, sipping his coffee with a contemplative air, had a different take. "Hellfiends, more like. The things are freaking everywhere these days." He glanced at the navigation console. "We should alter our course. Keep out of their way. Just in case."

Schumaker couldn't believe it. "You're kidding me, right? You can't really believe all that crap on the Internet about a demon invasion."

"As if an alien invasion is any more likely," Marshall retorted.

Schumaker snorted. "You went to one of those demon annihilator rallies during our layover, didn't you? What happened? A little brainwashing?"

"Demon Annihilators Mutual Network isn't a cult. It's a respected international organization. And yes, I'm a member. I joined, during that telethon they had."

Gold and crimson exploded in the clouds to the right of the aircraft.

"Damn," Schumaker said. "Whatever it is, hellfiend or alien, it's real."

"About a mile off," Marshall remarked, sitting up, "and closing in."

Schumaker digested that fact, then, frowning, keyed a southern directional change into flight management. A few moments later the lightning disappeared behind the aircraft as the autopilot executed the turn. Ten minutes after that, everything appeared normal. Marshall returned to his coffee, Schumaker to his airline paperwork.

Without warning, the aircraft shuddered.

"What the—?"

The instruments went wild. The plane pitched, acting for all the world as if a giant hand had punched its underside. Coffee splattered the windshield like dirty rain, and Schumaker's flight case and paperwork went flying.

"Holy shit!" he cried.

Screams rang out from the cabin. Schumaker made a desperate grab for the control column, too late. By the time he got his hands on it, the craft had flipped more than ninety degrees and they were just about on their back. There was no way to maneuver out of this.

Schumaker's stomach went into freefall. His body slammed against the restraint belt. The craft rolled to starboard; then, with a sickening lurch, it plummeted toward the sea. At a speed well in excess of four hundred knots, impact was seconds away. They were dead. Carrie's face flashed through his brain. She'd have the baby without him. Was it a son or a daughter? Schumaker wished now they'd let the doctor tell them.

The plane lurched again and entered a slow, controlled rotation. What the hell? It felt as if the craft was righting itself. Impossible.

"What just happened?" Marshall croaked from across the cockpit.

Schumaker had no idea. But they were still alive, and they were flying upright. Muffled screams from the cabin penetrated the cockpit door. Better than dead silence, anyway. Shaking off his nausea, he scanned the gauges. The autopilot was correcting its course. Altitude was low but climbing. All the rest—heading, speed, attitude—was as it should be.

"Cabin pressure normal." Marshall's calm voice showcased his military training. "Tachometer reading steady. Hydraulics online. What the *fuck* do you think that was?"

"I have no idea," Schumaker muttered. "But there's bound to be injuries in the back. We've got to put down ASAP. What's closer? JFK or Glasgow?"

"Keflavik, Iceland, actually. About a half hour north."

"Do it."

"Aye-aye."

Schumaker leaned forward, peering through the glass. He could have sworn he saw a figure bathed in golden light hovering above the cloud cover off the starboard wing. If he were drunk, he'd have called the apparition an angel. But he blinked and it was gone.

"Damn." He rubbed his eyes. "Must be seeing things."

"All instruments normal," Marshall reported. "If you didn't look so shook up, Brandon, and if my coffee wasn't all over the cockpit, I'd swear the last thirty seconds was nothing but a nightmare."

"A nightmare," Schumaker said. "Followed by a goddamned miracle."

* * *

Raphael circled above the churning surface of the North Atlantic. All was calm as the taillights of the airliner receded.

Of Azazel, there was no sign. The Watcher had escaped to parts unknown. All because Raphael had carelessly allowed their battle to drift too close to a passing jet. Azazel had seen his chance to make mischief and hadn't hesitated. Raphael had only just managed to right the craft and avoid disaster.

The angel uttered a few decidedly unangelic words. For the second time in as many nights Watcher scum had scored a victory at his expense. First Cade Leucetius. Now this.

Anger burned in his breast. The sensation disturbed him. It had been so long since he'd felt anything like it. Perhaps Michael was right. Perhaps emotion did still exist for angels.

Long ago Raphael had destroyed Lilith's amulet and cast Azazel into eternal captivity—or so he had thought. In reality, he'd failed. The bloodstone had been split but the power lived on. Now, he was failing again. The amulet remained beyond his grasp, the bloodstone was whole and Azazel was free. God only knew what havoc was about to be unleashed upon an unsuspecting humanity.

Actually, Raphael hoped the Almighty hadn't yet turned his omniscient mind to the situation. He prayed he could act quickly enough to keep his mistake under wraps until he had a chance to fix it. He knew he could. But perhaps, he was forced to admit, not on his own. Should he call for help? Clearly Gabriel was useless; he was a messenger, and circumstances called for a warrior. It would have to be Michael. But Michael had already refused and it would not be easy to persuade him to change his mind. Unless Raphael could entice him in some way.

Pondering the boon he would have to grant, he set a course for land.

Chapter Twenty-six

Cade might have called ahead. He might have tried to explain, tried to pave the way for what the clan would surely see as a betrayal. He didn't. He and Maddie simply opened the door and walked into Artur's London flat unexpected and unannounced.

Cybele, Brax, and Gareth were present, strung along the sofa cushions watching a BBC report on the stunning destruction of Chartres Cathedral. Artur was nowhere in sight. Of course. When was Artur Camulus ever where he was expected to be? Cade didn't know whether to be irritated or relieved.

". . . Eight point two on the Richter scale, in an area not known for severe seismic activity," a sober blonde female on the telly was saying to the man seated beside her. "A sudden, devastating storm, and bright lights streaking over western France to disappear over the Atlantic. Honestly, George, it's hard not to lend credence to Reverend Jonas Walker's claim that the destruction of Chartres Cathedral, one of the greatest medieval Christian monuments of Europe, was due not to natural causes, but was, in fact, a premeditated terrorist act perpetrated by the hybrid human-demon creatures known as Nephilim."

George's head bobbed. "Yes, Cynthia, there are many, many people who believe the spin on the disaster put out by the European headquarters of Demon Annihilators Mutual Network. The unidentified headless body pulled from the rubble this morning certainly supports the theory that Nephilim terrorists are involved. DAMN supporters have taken to the streets in major cities all over the world. Why, here in London alone—"

"Cade!" Cybele spotted him first. Television forgotten, she hurled herself across the room and into his arms. "You're back!"

He embraced her tightly, briefly, in an entirely brotherly hug, and realized that was how he loved her now—as a brother. "Of course. You weren't about to get rid of me that easily."

Brax had also risen, though he hadn't come forward. He looked past Cade to where Maddie stood on the threshold. "You did it," he said. "You brought back the slave."

"No," Cade said quickly. "Not a slave. Maddie comes to us as a free adept."

"A free adept!" Brax exploded. His palm slapped the tattoo on his wrist and a deadly dagger appeared in his hand. The pepper scent of wrath assaulted Cade's nostrils.

"What the hell are you up to, Cade?" he demanded. "You had your orders. Artur told you to bring back a slave. Not a rival."

"I can explain."

"I don't want explanations!"

"Nevertheless, you'll hear them." Cade paused. "But first . . . Where's Artur?"

"Not here," Brax grunted, weapon still at the ready. "In his absence, I'm in charge." He eyed Maddie. "What clan is she?"

Cade shifted more fully in front of Maddie and braced himself. "Clan Azazel."

Cybele sucked in a breath.

Brax swore. "And you've brought her into our midst? As a free adept? Are you insane? If you couldn't enslave her, you were supposed to kill her. Stand aside while I do the job for you."

Maddie, silent until now, bristled. Blue sparks gathered on her fingertips. "I'd like to see you try."

Cade sent her a quelling look. Blast it all to Oblivion. This sort of Watcher posturing was just what Cade didn't need. All he needed was a formal challenge spoken and someone would end up dead.

He turned to Brax with raised palms. "Calm down. This is not what you think. Maddie is no threat to Clan Samyaza."

"No threat? Impossible."

Cade sent a beseeching look toward Cybele. Gareth had come to stand at her side. "Help me out here, please."

"Brax, wait a—" Cybele began.

Brax's knife point didn't waver. "This woman is our enemy, Cybele."

"And Cade is our kin! We owe it to him to hear him out."

"Thank you," Cade told her.

For a long moment, no one moved. Then, grimacing, Brax lowered his blade a fraction. He didn't, however, let it fade into a tattoo.

"All right," he said. "Cade, start talking. But this woman is Dusek's kin. I can't imagine what you're going to say that will change my mind about killing her."

Cade took Maddie's arm and drew her forward. "This is Maddie Durant."

"I know who she is," Brax said irritably. "I found her, remember?"

Cade nodded. "For that, I'll be forever in your debt. Maddie may be Dusek's kin—*distant* kin—but she has good reason to hate him. Her ancestor, Azazel's daughter, killed her brother, Dusek's forefather, after he tried to rape her. Maddie rejects her connection with Dusek. She's willing to freely pledge her loyalty—and her magic—to Clan Samyaza."

Brax frowned. "Even if she hates Dusek, why should she wish to align herself with us? She's not of our blood."

Cade held Brax's gaze. "I'll begin with the end. Maddie offered her life to save mine. She did it freely, and at great risk to herself. She's the reason I'm standing here now." He drew a breath. "The reason she's here with me is because we're bonded mates."

Cybele's brows shot up. Brax stared.

Gareth found his voice first. "But that's . . . impossible. Isn't it? Rivals can only be slaves. Not bond mates. Because of the curse."

"That was what you were taught, Gareth," Cade said. "What all Watchers have been taught for millennia. But Maddie and I are proof there's something wrong with that belief. We've mated as true equals. I'm not sure, but I think we were able to do it because our love and trust transcends the curse. And as my free mate, Maddie offers her power—Clan Azazel power—to our cause. It's power we desperately need to survive."

"How can we be sure this isn't a trick?" Brax said. "A ploy to move freely in our midst?"

"It's not," Cade said flatly.

Maddie stepped forward. "I'm ready to pledge my life to your clan. To use my magic in support of your cause, and against Dusek. If I break my vow, you are welcome to kill me."

"But Artur—" Brax began.

Cybele cut in. "Oh, stuff it, Brax. The great and powerful Artur Camulus isn't here, is he? And, as you pointed out, he's left you leader in his absence. So lead already."

"Maddie and I await your decision," Cade said.

Brax scowled. "It's not that simple. Blast it, Cade. Your mate? She offers her magic? If you'd done your job correctly, her magic would be ours already."

"I chose not to enslave Maddie. I couldn't. I love her."

"Love." Brax snorted. "Brilliant. When Artur learns of it, he's going to explode."

"Forget about Artur," Cybele said. "Make your decision."

"Seems you're trying to make it for me," Brax said. Stepping around Cade, he addressed Maddie directly. "You can't deny that you share Dusek's blood, however estranged your ancestors were. Why should I believe you want to help your natural rivals? How do I know you aren't plotting to betray us all?"

"Because I love Cade," Maddie said. "You'll realize soon enough how true that is. You heard him. I could have let him die. I didn't. I saved his life. Because he *is* my life. His family is my family now. I know what Dusek did to your clan. I know he's vowed to send the rest of you, including Cade, to Oblivion. Believe me, I want to stop that from happening as much as you do."

She offered an upturned palm. "I pledge my fealty to Clan Samyaza. For now and for the rest of my life. Please, Brax. Will you accept me? For Cade's sake if not for mine?"

Brax glanced at Cybele, who stared back at him steadily. Then he sighed and lowered his blade. His right hand passed over his left, and the stiletto melted back onto his wrist. "I may be in charge in Artur's absence, but this situation is beyond my authority. Your pledge will have to wait for Artur's return. But, all right. Until my brother shows up, you can stay."

The tension drained from Cade's shoulders. "Thank you. I know this request puts you in a difficult position. I appreciate your good faith."

"I only hope I don't regret it when Artur walks in that door," Brax said. "The last thing we need is a divided clan."

"That's the last thing Artur wants, too," Cybele told him. She smiled at Cade, and he saw relief in her eyes, and gratitude. Maddie's presence lifted a burden of guilt from her shoulders, he realized.

"I'm so glad you've found a bond mate," she said. Turning to Maddie, she offered her left hand, palm up. "Welcome, sister."

Maddie placed her left hand, palm down, atop Cybele's offer

of peace, and she uttered the reply Cade had taught her. "You honor me, sister."

Tentatively, Gareth also offered the ritual Druid greeting. Brax, still frowning, did not.

Cade didn't press the point. "Where is Artur, anyway?" he asked.

Cybele and Brax exchanged glances. It was Cybele who answered. "Prague."

Cade's brows rose. "He's gone to confront Dusek?"

"To gather information," Brax clarified. "At least, I hope that's all the blasted fool is doing."

The group fell silent, and the television became audible. They turned as one to the screen. An aerial pan of Chartres Cathedral showed the great monument cleaved in two as if by a giant ax. An announcer was quoting estimated damages in excess of five hundred billion pounds. But they all knew no amount of money could re-create what had been destroyed.

"They're blaming the disaster on Nephilim, of course," Brax said.

"That's not far off the mark," Cade said.

Brax turned. "You two know something about this?"

"We were there," Maddie told him.

"Blast it all to Oblivion," Brax muttered. "I'm not going to like what you're about to tell me, am I?"

"No," Cade said. "Definitely not."

Chapter Twenty-seven

There was wailing and gnashing of teeth. There were prayers begging mercy and promising repentance. There were also police, engineers, and reporters intent on their roles in the unfolding drama. And there was a swarming mob of demon annihilators, garbed in red and desert camo, shouting their outrage.

"Death to the Nephilim! Annihilation to demonkind!"

Behind it all rose the ruined shell of a once-great cathedral.

No one noticed the black-cloaked figure as it passed through the lines of demonstrators and supplicants, nor as it skirted the piled rubble and passed through the shattered portals of the condemned building. Vaclav Dusek touched the edge of the pit, and stared into the events of the near past.

Ah, he thought as the vision faded. *The game continues.*

Perhaps life was worth living after all.

* * *

"Cade's done *what*?"

Artur couldn't believe his ears. Brax had rung just as Artur had arrived at the rubble pile that had once been Chartres Cathedral. He stared at the destruction, cell pressed to his ear, and listened with growing amazement as his half brother filled him in on recent happenings.

"And now," Artur said when Brax had finished, "this Clan

Azazel female—Cade's bloody bond mate, no less—wants to pledge her loyalty to me and Clan Samyaza?"

"That about wraps it up."

Artur could not remember a time he'd ever been so stunned. "Blast it. I should kill Leucetius for abandoning my orders so spectacularly."

"You'd be well within your rights to do just that," Brax agreed. "But I'm telling you, Cybele would go ballistic if you did. She and Maddie are already thick as thieves, and Gareth is taken by her as well. Execute Cade and enslave Maddie, and we're going to have a full-out rebellion on our hands. And that's the last thing we need right now."

"True enough," Artur conceded. He had to admit, this unexpected turn of events—especially the bit about the ancient Clan Azazel relic—could translate into myriad possibilities. His mind raced down a thousand potential paths, when just the day before he'd been banging his head against a dead end.

He could almost applaud Cade's creativity in finding a way around the orders he'd received. In private, of course. Artur certainly didn't need the whole bloody clan thinking they could go off half-cocked any chance they got. He'd have to devise some suitable penalty for the disobedience, or his authority would be shot to hell.

"Tell Cade I'm on my way to London," he told Brax. "I'll deal with him and his bond mate tomorrow." Let the pair stew tonight.

"Done," Brax said. "But there is one other thing."

"What?" Artur demanded, his temper fraying.

"Good news this time. Lucas called in. He's alive and well."

"About bloody time. Where's he been hiding?"

"Montana, apparently. Wouldn't say why. He's on his way to London now, though."

Artur considered. "No. Call him and tell him his plans have changed. He's to go to New York."

"New York?"

"Yes. Once he's there he's to load his gun, weave the tightest magic-shielding glamour he can devise, and head for DAMN headquarters."

A brief moment of silence followed. Then, "May I ask why?"

"He's to apply for a position as a demon annihilator. And while he's on the job, he's to figure out who at DAMN is receiving Vaclav Dusek's anti-Nephilim weaponry." Artur's mouth twisted. "Once he finds the bastard, he's to kill him."

* * *

Maddie lay nestled with her head on Cade's shoulder in a real double bed with clean sheets and a thick quilt. It was Artur's bed. As it was the only one in the flat that wasn't spoken for, Brax had allowed them to use it. Knowing whose bed it was, and knowing its owner would show up the next day, Maddie couldn't quite get comfortable.

She was drowsy. She wanted to sleep, but couldn't. "Cybele is very beautiful," she said.

She felt Cade smile against her hair. "Yes, she is. Jealous?"

"Maybe a little," she teased.

He laughed softly. "Don't be. She'll never be anything more than a sister to me. While you . . ." He kissed her, long and slow and deep. "You're my heart."

"She's welcomed me far more warmly than I expected," Maddie said. "I can tell she's very glad you're happy. But she doesn't seem to be."

"She's not likely to be, as long as Artur continues to be a bastard."

"Maybe he'll come around."

Cade snorted. "Not bloody likely."

Maddie sighed. "Gareth has been wonderful as well. Is he really serious about the death-seeking?" Cade had filled her in on the ritual, which struck her as barbaric. She shuddered. "I hate the thought of him facing such danger."

"It's part of being a Watcher," Cade replied. "If he chooses to proceed, he'll come through it." But the doubt in his voice betrayed his worry.

"And Brax—" She drew a circle on his chest. "He's polite, but . . . I'm not sure he trusts me yet."

"Don't worry about that," Cade said. "It's just his way to be cautious. He'll warm up once he gets to know you."

"And Artur? Will he accept me?"

"Well, the phone didn't burn up in Brax's hand when he told Artur about you," Cade joked. A moment later, he sobered. "He's not about to strike you dead, at least. But he's plotting something, I'm sure. Something to do with you and the Seed of Life."

"That's hardly surprising," Maddie said. "I just don't know if I'm going to be able to live up to his expectations. I haven't been able to sense any power in the amulet since I used it to bring you back from the brink of Oblivion. And the bloodstone has been dark. Not a single spark. I'm not sure if I'm ever going to be able to get another drop of magic out of it."

"Time will tell. But even if the Seed doesn't reawaken, the clan's not about to pin all its hope on Lilith's talisman. Artur always has something up his sleeve. And now Luc's on his way to New York, to ferret out Dusek's contact at DAMN headquarters. And through you, we have access to Clan Azazel magic. There's every reason to hope."

"Yes," she said. "But what about Azazel? Do you think Raphael recaptured him? If he didn't—"

He rolled over, coming on top of her, and cutting her off with another kiss. "Maddie. I don't know what the future holds. None of us do. But, try to put it out of your mind. Let tomorrow take care of itself. Tonight, let's concentrate on here and now. On us. On what we have together."

He was right. It did no good to miss out on the present while worrying about a future she couldn't control. She concentrated on smoothing her hands up his arm, reveling in the rough texture of his skin and the rock-hard muscle beneath.

She smiled. "All right, then. Here we are, alone, naked, and lying in a comfortable bed. Just how do you propose we occupy our time? Watch TV? Surf the Internet? Read a book?"

Cade chuckled. "Trust me, *caraid*. I have a much better idea."

JOY NASH loves to write her dreams—and sometimes, her nightmares! She pens award-winning tales of love and adventure with a paranormal twist. When not reading or writing, Joy's hobbies include brain-numbing movie binges, staring into space, and wishing her house was clean. You can often find her watching YouTube videos with her kids. Visit Joy on the Web at www.joynash.com for excerpts, contests and more!

CPSIA information can be obtained at www.ICGtesting.com
Printed in the USA
239412LV00002B/2/P

9 781428 511224